Yarrun and I exchanged glances at the door of the infirmary. We hadn't said a word since we left to get the weapons. Now he smiled . . . a hideous sight. I nodded and palmed the *ENTER* plate.

Inside, the air smelled of disinfectant. Dr. Veresian had drawn Harque and Prope into his office, and was talking to them in a low voice. The admiral sat in an examination chair, drumming his fingers on the armrests.

Prope turned at the sound of our entrance and saw the stunners. "Is there some problem, Explorers?"

"In a manner of speaking," I said. "We're unhappy with this mission."

"That's understandable," she replied. "It's an open secret that Explorers have been lost on Melaquin. But the order came directly from the High Council."

"It seems foolish to throw away our lives for no reason." I raised the stunner. "What would you do in our position?"

EXPENDABLE

JAMES
ALAN GARDNER

AVON · EOS

AVON BOOKS
A division of
The Hearst Corporation
1350 Avenue of the Americas
New York, New York 10019

Copyright © 1997 by James Alan Gardner
Published by arrangement with the author
Visit our website at http://www.AvonBooks.com/Eos
Library of Congress Catalog Card Number: 96-95497
ISBN: 0-380-79439-X

First Avon Books Printing: July 1997

AVON EOS TRADEMARK REG. U.S. PAT. OFF. AND IN OTHER COUNTRIES, MARCA
REGISTRADA, HECHO EN U.S.A.

Printed in the U.S.A.

WCD 10 9 8 7 6 5 4

To my parents
(except the naughty words)

Thanks to the writing group who helped correct my first mistakes: Linda Carson, John McMullen, and Dave Till. Thanks to Rob Sawyer who helped correct my next mistakes, and to Jennifer Brehl who picked up the ones after that. If there are any slipups left, it's obviously my fault for hiding them too well.

Finally, a big hello and thank you to my fellow writers in FASS '77. Somewhere in our script meetings, the phrase "Expendable Crew Member" was spoken for the first time. It rattled around in my head for almost twenty years, and look what finally came out.

Part I
NIGHT

Flashback

"My name is Festina Ramos, and I take great pride in my personal appearance."
(Again.)
"My name is Festina Ramos, and I take great pride in my personal appearance."
(Again.)
"My name is Festina Ramos, and I take great pride in my personal appearance."
(Again. . . .)

My Appearance

My name is Festina Ramos and once upon a time, no one in the Technocracy took greater pride in her personal appearance.

I showered, shampooed, depilated, and deodorized every morning without fail. Nothing stood in the way of my morning ritual: not the fuzz of a hangover, nor the arms of a beckoning bed-partner. My discipline was absolute.

I exercised more than forty hours a week, and always complete workouts: martial arts, running, gymnastics, tai

1

chi ... even mountaineering when the opportunity presented itself.

My body fat ranked at the lowest percentile considered healthy. People said they envied my figure. For all I know, they might have been telling the truth.

I chose my civilian clothes with the care of an entertainer dressing for the chips. Even when I was in uniform, fellow officers said that black fatigues suited me.

Their very words: "Festina, that outfit suits you." They did not say, "Festina, you look good."

My name is Festina Ramos and even before I was given that name, I was given a lurid port-wine birthmark covering the right half of my face from cheekbone to chin. Years of operant conditioning gave me great pride in my disfigurement.

The Doctors

Each doctor began by saying my condition could be corrected. How would they cure me? Let me count the ways. They would cure me with electrolysis, with lasers, with cryogenics, with plastic planing, with "sophisticated bioactive agents conscientiously applied in a program of restoration therapy." Some even set a date when I would be booked in for treatment.

Then the appointments were canceled. Sometimes the doctor apologized in person. Sometimes the doctor invented excuses. Sometimes it was just a note from a secretary.

Here is the reason my birthmark endured with purple defiance in the face of twenty-fifth century medicine:

It had military value.

My Calling in Life

My calling in life was to land on hostile planets.
I made first contacts with alien cultures.

I went anyplace the Admiralty didn't know what the hell to expect.

Officially, I belonged to the Explorer Corps. Unofficially, we Explorers called ourselves ECMs—short for Expendable Crew Members.

Why

Listen. Here is what all ECMs knew.

Violent death is rare in the Technocracy. We have no wars. The crime level is low, and few incidents involve lethal weapons. When accidents happen, victims can almost always be saved by sophisticated local medical centers.

But.

There are no medical centers on unexplored planets. Death may come with savage abruptness or the stealthy creep of alien disease. In a society where people expect to ease comfortably out of this world at a ripe old age, the thought of anyone being killed in the prime of life is deeply disturbing. If it happens to someone you know, the effect is devastating.

Unless . . . the person who dies is different. Not like everyone else.

Two centuries ago, the Admiralty High Council secretly acknowledged that some deaths hurt Fleet morale more than others. If the victim was popular, well-liked, and above all, *physically attractive*, fellow crewmates took the death hard. Performance ratings dropped by as much as thirty percent. Friends of the deceased required lengthy psychological counseling. Those who had ordered the fatal mission sometimes felt a permanently impairing guilt.

But if the victim was not so popular, not so well-liked, and above all, ugly . . . well, bad things happen, but we all have to carry on.

No one knows exactly when the High Council solidified this fact of human behavior into definite policy. In time, however, the Explorer Corps evolved from a group of healthy, bright-eyed volunteers into . . . something less photogenic.

Potential recruits were flagged at birth. The flawed. The ugly. The strange. If a child's physical problems were truly disabling, or if the child didn't have the intelligence or strength of will to make a good Explorer, the full power of modern medicine would be unleashed to correct every impediment to normality. But if the child combined ability and expendability in a single package—if the child was smart and fit enough to handle the demands of Exploration, but different enough to be less *real* than a normal person . . .

. . . there was an Explorer's black uniform in that child's future.

My Class

As I record this, I have in front of me a picture of my class at the Academy. In the first row are the ones with problems the camera does not reveal: Thomas, the stammerer; Ferragamo, the man whose voice did not change at puberty; my roommate, Ullis Naar, who usually blinked convulsively every two seconds but managed to keep her eyes open for this photo; Ghent, loudly flatulent . . . yes, what a joke, who could take Ghent seriously? Not his crewmates when Ghent was flayed alive by savages during a first contact. A few days of superficial mourning, and then his shipmates forgot him.

The system worked.

Back to the photo. One row of visually acceptable Explorers, and behind them the rest of us: pop-eyed, three-fingered, obese, deformed. No one in the back rows smiled for this picture. Most tried to hide behind the heads of those in front.

What unthinking Director of Protocol demanded that we pose for such a photo? I'd always been told (in smug, self-congratulatory tones) that our society had progressed beyond the days of the freak show.

The majority of my graduating class could have been cured by modern medicine. We all knew it. Which of us hadn't jacked into a medical library and pored through the texts describing our conditions? Which of us didn't know the names of at least five techniques to make us into more-normal human beings? Yet those remedies did not exist for us. The Admiralty had a vested interest in keeping us repugnant. As long as we stayed as we were, no one lost sleep over sending us on dangerous missions.

Admirals need their sleep in order to make enlightened judgments.

My Duties

My most time-consuming duty was to review reports from other Explorers. The latest files were transmitted to our shipboard computer every day and stored on bubble till I went over them. Most of the time, the reports were simply copies of the running commentaries all Explorers gave when landing on an unfamiliar planet.

(Upon graduation, Explorers were fitted with permanent throat transceivers that transmitted continuously on planet-down missions. The transceivers were quite visible if you looked closely; but no one worried about a lump on the neck ruining an Explorer's appearance.)

Some of the transcripts I listened to ended abruptly. We called those transcripts "Oh Shits" because the Explorers often said, "Oh shit," just before their throat mikes went dead. You always wondered what they saw just before they stopped transmitting. You seldom found out.

"Oh Shit" reports weren't marked in any special way. Whenever I audited the log of someone I knew from the Academy, I wondered if it would end in "Oh Shit." An absent voice spoke in the quiet of my quarters and I never knew if the next word would be the last. Sometimes I listened to blank silence for half an hour, not wanting to believe that the report had ended.

The Admiralty never listed Explorers as dead. We were simply *Lost* . . . like old shoes that might turn up in spring housecleaning. In private, Explorers used a different expression: we talked about our friends Going Oh Shit.

My Lifestyle

I kept my distance from others on board our ship. I expect they were glad of it. I know I was.

There was once a time when I would eat in the public cafeteria to prove I wasn't afraid. As I carried my tray into the dining room, conversation would dwindle while the crew waited to see which table I chose. Some days I sat by myself. Other days I was invited to eat at this table or that. Now and then I purposefully joined the group that seemed most likely to lose their appetites looking at me; but I grew out of that after a few months in the service.

It took longer to see through those who welcomed me. Some were obvious, of course, like the ones with religious leanings. For obscure reasons, bright-smiling proselytizers with God in their hearts were drawn to me like beetles to carrion. They may have considered me desperate for acceptance of any kind—an easy convert. Perhaps too, those eager believers thought that associating with a pariah would purify their souls . . . like flagellation. Whatever the reason, I spent many mealtimes listening to guarantees of spiritual fulfillment, if only I would come out to regular Fellowship meetings.

Different crew members chose to strike up conversations for the purpose of seduction. After all, a woman like me had to be an easy sexual conquest; desperate and lonely, I would roll over like a dog at the first sign of attention.

And with the lights out, they wouldn't see my face, would they?

I took a number of those calculating seducers to my bed

anyway, just for the hell of it—I felt like I was tricking them, exploiting them. In time, however, I wondered who was fooling whom. Ultimately, I decided that celibacy was simpler.

Some people cultivated my friendship in the belief I could help with their careers—as Explorer First Class, I ranked second only to the captain and was sometimes thought to be important. In fact, my rank was merely a ploy to hide the reality of my situation. I would never get a position of command on a starship; I knew nothing about ship operation. My only expertise lay in personal survival.

Was I ever invited to eat with anyone who had no ulterior motive? I can't say.

Did I ever eat with someone who was interested in *me* . . . not my soul, not my body, not the things I might do for them, but for me? No. Never. Not one of them knew me.

After a few months of trying to mingle with the regular crew, I switched to eating alone in my quarters. Rank hath its privileges.

My Quarters

I spent much of the day in my quarters. I had little reason to go elsewhere. I was comfortable there.

My cabin had no traditional decorations. When I was assigned to this ship, the quartermaster offered me a number of standard wall-hangings "to brighten the place up," but I refused. I also refused to take any of his glass figurines that could be attached with magnets to any flat surface. Half the figurines were abstracts that meant nothing to me; the other half were little better than kittens, mice, and children with large eyes.

My quarters had a practical desk, a practical cartography table, three relatively practical chairs, and a fairly impractical bed. It was a double-sized bed with many active features, called The Luxuriator. I requisitioned it in a moment of folly, thinking if I found the right man or woman, a good bed might give me confidence.

Might make me feel prepared.

Might make me feel I had something to contribute.

No, I can't find the right words. It humiliates me to think about it.

My Collection

My quarters contained no ornamentation, but hidden in a closed metal locker was my collection. Most Explorers had collections. We were paid well, and had few vices that could absorb our salaries.

I collected eggs. Many people found that amusing: Festina Ramos collected eggs. They pictured a cabin filled with white hens' eggs, racks of them, bins of them, heaped hodgepodge wherever I had space. Not one of them ever saw my collection. They laughed behind my back about something I would never show them.

In my early days on the ship, I talked about my collection one day at the lunch table. I forget how the subject came up. I was just so glad to find myself in a conversation that wasn't shop-talk, I ignored my usual caution.

Of course the others laughed . . . and wanting them to understand, I tried to explain how beautiful some eggs can be. Every color of the rainbow, pale blues and soft oranges and golden yellows. All sizes, all shapes. Some with shells as fragile as tissue paper, some so hard you can squeeze with all your might and not harm them. Insect eggs, small and black like pepper. Amphibian eggs, chains of jellied eyes suspended in water. Eggs from extraterrestrial life-forms, unique as snowflakes, perfumed, cylindrical, clear as glass, red-hot to the touch. . . .

The other crew members didn't understand. Most of them didn't try. One or two put on intelligent expressions and said, "That's interesting." They were the ones who most made me feel like a fool.

After that, I never discussed my collection in public. I didn't try to describe it, because I knew I couldn't. I refused to show it to the crew because I would only be infuriated by their politely unappreciative attention. Why should I watch them feign interest?

Eggs are self-contained worlds, perfect and internally sufficient. On every planet that supports life, there are eggs. Whatever alien paths life may take, there are always eggs somewhere along the trail. My fellow Explorers found this time and time again.

If I heard an Explorer's report state that eggs had been found on this or that planet, I transmitted a personal request asking for a specimen. I almost always got what I wanted—Explorers help each other.

When I received an egg, I spent several days deciding how to display it. Some I mounted on wooden stands; some I set in china dishes; some I swathed in cotton.

Receiving a new egg was cause for celebration. I took it out of its packing case and cradled it in my hands, cherishing its fragility or its toughness or its warmth. Sometimes I could hold an egg for a full hour, dreaming I was in touch with the mother who laid the egg or the child who called it home.

But all the eggs in my collection were sterile. They never hatched. Some were never fertilized. The others had been irradiated by the Admiralty to kill whatever was inside them—transport of alien organisms is dangerous.

On nights when I couldn't sleep, I sat amidst them and listened to their silence.

The Call

It was on a night like that, a silent night, that I sat in my quarters, staring at a list of reports I ought to study. It was late at night, as time was reckoned on the ship. I took great pride in working late hours. Admittedly, time is an arbitrary convention in space; but I still enjoyed knowing I was awake while the rest of the ship slept.

The message buzzer hummed softly in the quiet of my cabin. I turned a dial on my desktop. "Ramos here."

The face of Lieutenant Harque, the captain's aide, sprang to life on the screen. Harque had an easy smile and curly good looks, a boy-next-door handsomeness that let him win over people without having a speck of true charm in his self-important body. "The captain would like to see you, Explorer."

"Yes?"

"In the conference room. As soon as possible."

"Does she want me to bring Yarrun?"

"I've already contacted Yarrun. Harque out." The picture went blank.

Typical. I had come to expect that sort of thing from Harque. If I confronted him about it, he would claim he was saving me trouble by calling my subordinate for me. I slid back my chair and sighed as I headed for the door.

The light over my desk turned off behind me. It did that automatically. The quick return to darkness always made me think the lamp was eager to see me go.

My Subordinate

Yarrun was waiting for me outside the door. His eyes were bleary—he must have been asleep when Harque buzzed him. Yarrun preferred an early bedtime. To compensate, he got up hours before anyone else was awake. He said he enjoyed the quiet of the ship in the early morning.

I don't know what he did with the time he had to himself. Perhaps he just tended his own collection—he collected dyed silk.

Explorer Second Class Yarrun Derigha was officially my subordinate because he graduated from the Academy three years after I did. Unofficially, we were equal partners. We worked as a team, the only two Expendable Crew Members among eighty-seven Vacuum crew members too valuable to be wasted.

Yarrun was missing the left side of his face. To be precise, the left half of his jaw never formed and the right hadn't grown since he was six. The result looked like half a head, with the skin stretched taut from his left cheekbone to his partial right jaw.

There was nothing else wrong with Yarrun. His brain was intact. His Intelligence Profile ranked higher than ninety-nine percent of the population. He had some trouble eating solids, but the Admiralty graciously accommodated that—the cafeteria stocked a large supply of nutritious fluids.

When he talked, his enunciation was unfailingly precise. Since it cost him a great deal of effort, he preferred not to speak if he could help it.

I had known Yarrun six years, first in the Academy, then on the ship. We had saved each other's lives so often we no longer kept count. We could talk to each other about anything, and we could be quiet together without feeling uncomfortable. I was as close to Yarrun as I have ever wanted to be with anyone.

And yet.

There were still times when the sight of his face made my skin crawl.

In the Halls (Part 1)

The halls were deserted at that hour. The ship only needed a twenty-person running crew at night, and the on-duty crew members usually stayed close to their posts. I loved to walk the empty corridors when the lights had been dimmed and every door was closed. Neither Yarrun nor I spoke. The soft clopping of our footsteps echoed lightly in the stillness of the sleeping ship.

Our ship was called the *Jacaranda*, named after a family of flowering trees native to Old Earth. The previous captain had actually owned a jacaranda tree and kept it in his quarters. When it was in bloom, he would pin a blossom to his lapel every morning. The deep blue of the flower went well with khaki.

When our current captain took command, she said, "Get that damned thing out of my room. It's shedding." The tree was moved to the cafeteria, where it got in everyone's way and frequently dropped petals onto plates of food.

A few months later, the tree suddenly died. Someone probably poisoned it. The crew held a party to celebrate the tree being reduced to proto-nute, and even I attended. It was the first time I tasted Divian champagne.

Now the only jacarandas on ship were stylized ones stenciled on walls and doors. The colors of these trees indicated the authorization needed to enter a given area. I was allowed into areas marked with red jacarandas and black. I was not permitted to enter rooms marked with orange, blue, green, yellow, purple, pink, or brown.

Red areas were public ones like the cafeteria. Black areas were reserved for Explorers and their equipment. The Admiralty denied that black had any special significance.

Our Captain

The jacaranda on the door of the conference room was red. The door opened as it heard our footsteps approach. Yarrun let me enter first—in public, we made a point of observing rank protocol.

Captain Prope stood at the room's Star Window, apparently lost in thought. She stared out on the star-filled blackness like the captain of a clipper ship inhaling sea air from the foredeck: spine straight as iron, hands on hips, head tilted back slightly so her chestnut-red hair hung free of her shoulders. If she had been facing us, we would have likely seen her nostrils flared to the wind.

No doubt she had assumed this heroic pose several minutes ago, and had been waiting impatiently for us to walk in. For some reason, she desperately wanted to impress us.

The door closed behind us with a hiss. Prope took this as her cue to turn and notice us. "Oh, come in, sit down, yes." She laughed lightly, a frothy little laugh guaranteed by Outward Fleet Psych-techs to make subordinates feel like equals. Prope was an ardent student of the Mechanics of Charisma.

"Sorry," she said. "My mind was somewhere else." She turned back for one more wistful peek at the night. "I can never get over how beautiful the stars are."

I did not point out that the view was a color-enhanced computer simulation. A real window would have jeopardized the integrity of the ship's hull.

The News

We sat in our usual chairs (me on the captain's right, Yarrun on her left), and rolled up to the conference table.

"Would either of you like coffee?" the captain asked. We shook our heads in unison. "You're sure? Some fruit juice maybe? No? Well, I hope you don't mind if I have a little something. I always enjoy a midnight snack."

She smiled in our general direction, but her eyes were too low to meet ours. Like most people, she could not look at our faces for any length of time. She talked to our chests or our hair or our ears . . . never to our faces, except for a quick glance now and then to confirm her squeamishness.

For some reason, she thought Yarrun and I didn't notice.

We watched as she poured herself coffee. In public, she drank it black. When she thought no one was watching, she used double loads of cream and sugar.

For a few moments, she stirred her coffee, even though there was nothing in it. I couldn't tell if this was reflex or affectation. Finally she said, "I suppose you're wondering what this is all about."

She paused, so we nodded.

"Twenty minutes ago," Prope continued, "I received a coded message from the *Golden Cedar*. You know the ship?"

"Admiral Chee's flagship," I replied. Everyone in the Fleet knew the ship. Half the children in the Technocracy had heard of it. Learning the names of the admirals and their flagships was a Common Curriculum memory exercise for seven-year-olds.

"In three hours, the *Golden Cedar* will pass within ten thousand kilometers of us." Prope was watching us out of the corner of her eye, so I knew she was about to drop a surprise in our laps. "At that time, Admiral Chee will secretly transfer aboard the *Jacaranda*. *Very* secretly—we three and Harque will be the only ones to know he's here. You two will see to the admiral's comfort." She looked at us with narrowed eyes, as if she doubted we could handle the job. "Any problems?"

"We'll take care of him." I kept my voice expressionless, despite the insult. I had been capably dealing with visiting dignitaries for six full years on the *Jacaranda*—it was one of my standing duties. As high-ranking officers with no shipboard responsibility, Explorers were ideal for babysitting VIPs. VIPs were either aliens who didn't care what we looked like or self-centered diplomats who didn't notice.

"Fine." Prope obviously felt she ought to say something more, but couldn't think of anything. She remembered her coffee and took a deep grateful swallow. Judging by the resulting expression on her face, the coffee was too hot.

Yarrun asked, "Do you know why the admiral is coming?"

"He'll tell us when he arrives. All I know is that it's not an inspection." She gave another standardized laugh, but this time it was strained with nervousness. "My orders say that if I give the slightest hint I'm waiting for inspection— if I sharpen up discipline, hold drills, even swab the decks—I'll be put on report."

She drummed her fingers on the table. None of us said anything for a count of ten.

"It certainly sounds like an inspection," I finally said. Prope nodded. "Damned right."

My First Admiral

Back in my cabin, I debated staying awake for three more hours (in which case I would be tired when the admiral arrived) or going to sleep for a while (in which case I would be groggy). I decided to lie on my Luxuriator bed and see what happened.

Staring at the asbestos white of my ceiling, I thought about the first admiral I had met, Admiral Seele. She was not the first admiral I had seen in person—more than a dozen admirals attended graduation exercises for my class at the Academy. The Admiralty always made a show of being interested in Explorers. The school administrators even said the admirals would be available afterwards to shake hands and make small talk.

I don't know if any of the class took advantage of the opportunity. I didn't.

Admiral Seele arrived on the *Jacaranda* in my first year with the ship. No one could say why she had come. She inspected the engine room, but made no comments or suggestions. She spent an hour alone with every officer, but reportedly spoke only of trivialities and glanced frequently at her watch. She passed one entire day secluded in her cabin, supposedly examining our ship's log on the computer . . . but when I walked by her door late in the afternoon, I heard her singing a bawdy song I recognized from Academy days. I hurried on, though I had intended to knock.

The admiral spent most of her time with me. It made me uncomfortable, even as I told myself I had nothing to fear. Mostly, we talked about the Academy and my missions. I had made only two Landings at the time, neither one eventful, but she seemed interested. Her questions showed she knew what was important to an Explorer . . . unlike most Vacuum-oriented officers, who had no idea what to pay attention to when they had solid ground under their feet. I guessed that part of being an admiral was knowing more than the rest of the pack.

On the last night of her stay, she asked how well I got on with the crew. Were they cooperative? I said I had no complaints. Did I have many friends? No. Any lovers? No. Was I lonely? No, I filled my time. Did I never want to reach out to another human being? No, I was fine.

She started to cry then. She tried to take hold of my hand, but I drew back quickly. She said I mustn't close myself to the world; I would be miserable if I didn't let other people into my life.

I walked out of the room without waiting to be dismissed.

The next morning, Admiral Seele left us at Starbase Iris. As she left, she saluted the captain and first officer, but shook my hand. She looked like she wanted to kiss me. Perhaps she couldn't decide where: on my lips, on my good cheek, or on my bad one.

I concluded then that my first admiral was a maladjusted woman who yearned for me. The Academy had taught us about people who are drawn to Explorers by our ugliness. The attraction has something to do with self-hatred.

Self-Care

The message buzzer hummed and I found I had been sleeping. My neck was stiff and my clothing rumpled. I rolled gracelessly to my feet and thudded over to the desk. "Ramos here."

Harque's face appeared on the screen. Wearing his dress gold uniform, he looked annoyingly fresh and knew it. "Admiral Chee is arriving."

"Thank you. I'm on my way."

"If I were you, I'd do something with my hair first."
The screen went blank too quickly for me to reply. Clever
retorts seldom come easily to me. I stomped angrily to the
bathroom and fumbled a while with a comb. Stupid people
flustered me so effortlessly. I wished I had a quick mind.

Years of conditioning would not let me leave my room
until my part was straight. That irked me too. What fastid-
ious programmer forced this obsession on me?

To smooth my feathers, I thought of childish ways to get
even with Harque. Some scandalous story about him passed
to the admiral? No, I was too smart to lie to an admiral,
and too ill-informed to know any dirt that was really true.
Some night Harque would pull down the sheets of his bed
and find a smashed egg there. The Sevro lizards of Malabar
IV laid eggs whose yolks were more corrosive than industrial acids.

Wearing a smile and taking great pride in my personal
appearance, I stepped confidently out my door.

Part II
MISSION

Worm, Sperm

WORM: The colloquial name for the envelope of spacetime distortion that surrounds each starship, allowing the ship to circumvent relativistic and inertial effects that would otherwise make space travel impracticable.

—Excerpt from *Practice and Procedures of Space Travel: An Overview for Explorers*, textbook published by the Admiralty

Only the Admiralty would have the nerve to claim that the colloquial name for our envelope was "the Worm." To everyone else (except in the presence of admirals), it was "the Sperm."

REASON 1: When a ship was at rest, the region of interface between its envelope and normal space glowed milky white due to spontaneous creation of particles in the envelope's ergosphere. The glow shifted to the blue end of the spectrum when the ship moved forward and to the red when the ship reversed, but the color we saw most, the color at anchor, was that suggestive semen white.

REASON 2: The envelope bulged like the head of a sper-matozoon where it surrounded the ship itself, then tapered off into a thin tail that stretched some 15,000 kilometers to our stern. In flight, random fluctuations of magnetic fields in space made the tail whip wildly like the tail of a swim-ming sperm.

REASON 3: Given time, a ship's crew will attach sexual innuendo to anything. It makes their jobs more exciting.

Waiting in the Transport Room

When I reached the Transport Room, Lieutenant Harque was grimacing at the tracking holo and gingerly twisting dials. Captain Prope leaned over his shoulder and blocked his light. Each time the lieutenant ducked to one side to see more clearly, the captain moved with him like a shadow. I'd seen the routine many times before, and Harque had never asked the captain to step back.

Vile little toady.

In the rare moments that he had a clear view of the holo, Harque was manipulating our aft electromagnets in order to wag the tail of our Sperm. Somewhere far behind us, the *Golden Cedar* was doing the same thing, with the goal of snagging one tail on the other and forcing the two to fuse into a single continuous tube. It was a ticklish business at the best of times, and worse with a captain breathing down your neck. The best operators in the Fleet sometimes spent more than twenty minutes at the job. Harque was not one of the best operators in the Fleet.

Yarrun sat against the far wall of the room, well out of everyone's way. He looked more alert now; either he had managed to get some sleep or had forced himself awake with a cold shower, caffeine, something. From the depths of his closet, he had rummaged up his dress blacks, as wrinkled as raisins. Every stitch of clothing Yarrun owned was rumpled and worn; he came from a splinter culture on

Novolith with a religious stricture against vanity in one's attire.

Thanks to Explorer programming, Yarrun was just as obsessive in keeping his clothes mussed as I was in keeping my hair parted straight.

I inflated a chair and sat down beside him. "Are they close?" I asked in a low voice.

He shrugged. "Since I arrived, the captain has shouted, 'You almost had it!' three times."

"Has she called him a fool yet?"

"No."

"Then they aren't close."

Yarrun and I had spent a lot of time waiting in that room. We knew each bleep, chirp, and fribble the machinery could make. We knew each bleep, chirp, and fribble a tail-operator could make. After a while, the noises blended into a harmonious whole.

"You almost had it that time, Harque! Can't you be more careful?"

"Sorry, captain."

The observation deck where we sat was a U-shaped mezzanine around the actual transport bay, twelve meters below and separated from us by thick pink-tinted plastic. The walls around us sported rainbow-striped jacaranda trees; this was the first area most visitors saw when they came on board, and Prope was desperate to make a jaunty impression.

The control console occupied the base of the mezzanine U. Opposite it, down in the bay, was the Aft Entry Mouth, a circular aperture leading out of the ship and into the Sperm-tail. At present, the Mouth was closed with an irising mechanism that bulged slightly outward under the air pressure of the ship. When the iris opened, anything in the transport bay weighing less than twenty tonnes would be propelled out the Mouth and spat through the tail like phlegm.

It wasn't an elegant way to travel—Admirals usually ar-

rived in trim little shuttles, as did delicate cargo ship-
ments—but receiving such deliveries meant dropping our
Sperm field, then waiting twelve hours while the forward
Sperm generator rebuilt the envelope. It only took a second
to reestablish the field itself . . . but aligning the tail to surround the ship rather than drift off on its own demanded
extensive calibration efforts that always left the crew in a
foul mood. Either the High Council of Admirals had decided not to put the Vac-hands through that strain, or
Chee's business with the *Jacaranda* was too urgent for any
delay.

I was glad it was Chee being transported, not me.
Though I had squirted through the tail more than a hundred
times, I never enjoyed it. Some Explorers did. Yarrun said
it felt like a ride at an amusement center: your feet swooped
out from under you, your brain dimmed to black, the space
distorting forces in the tail twisted you through a few hy-
perdimensions, and then you slid out the other end like
sound emerging from a trumpet. Dozens of people had done
it without even wearing an impact suit (despite safety regs).
The death rate was lower than any other form of transport
used in the Outward Fleet.

And yet. . . .

When I stood down there in my suit, waiting for the blue
light that said the tail had been secured, I sometimes prayed
something would save me from that five second ride.
"Sorry, Festina, all a big mistake, you don't have to go
today."

I was a child who never believed in fairies, but still told
herself fairy tales.

Then the light went on, and I would look around one
last time, at the rainbow jacarandas, at Yarrun counting the
seconds until our ejaculation, and at the iris that waited,
eyelike, ready to open.

I always faced that iris full on. No tail-operator ever saw
me flinch. Only Yarrun knew that I closed my eyes.

The Arrival

"Got it!" Harque cried with relief.

"About time," the captain growled. She twisted a knob on the console and spoke into a filament microphone. "*Golden Cedar*, this is *Jacaranda*. We have established connection."

There was a pause of several seconds as our computer coded the captain's voice for transmission, squirted it to the *Golden Cedar* 20,000 klicks away, received an answer, and decoded it into sound. "Connection acknowledged. Prepare to receive."

As Yarrun and I moved to the observation window, the iris blinked open with the speed of a bubble popping. The plastic in front of us, thick as it was, jerked slightly as the air on the other side exploded into the tail, and one of the windows boomed like a drum. Harque and Prope ignored the sound, so Yarrun and I did too.

"Mouth open and ready to receive," Prope said into the mike. She said it with a straight face.

Pause. "Acknowledged. Stand by."

Harque stifled a yawn as Prope looked at her watch. She pursed her lips in annoyance, then suddenly drew up into her most heroic stance, a calm smile taking possession of her face. "Let's look alive, people," she intoned, her voice half an octave lower than when she was kibitzing over Harque's shoulder.

Beyond the open Mouth, the milk white Sperm smeared itself over the black of space. Shimmering distortions rippled through the tail's surface like heat waves. At the heart of the aperture, like a fly floating on cream, lay the black gap through which the admiral would arrive.

A light flashed orange on the console and soft beeping filled the room. Harque murmured, "Five seconds."

The gap in the center of the hole suddenly expanded like a throat, vomiting out a figure in an impact suit that shone a burnished gold. The suit shot half the length of the room before landing chest first on the floor and skidding to a stop.

Harque leapt back to the console and spun some dials. The iris blinked shut soundlessly. "Pressurizing now," Harque said in a loud voice that clearly wanted someone to pay attention. But the captain was too busy posing: hands on her hips, and feet spread wider than I, for one, would find natural.

The figure on the floor rolled onto his back and went into a convulsion. His legs shook with quick little kicks and his hands clapped together again and again. "Oh shit, he's hurt," Prope said, breaking her stance and pressing her nose against the window. "Harque, buzz the infirmary and tell them to get their asses here on the double. Fast and quiet—the rest of the crew isn't supposed to know about this." She closed her eyes and whispered, "Don't die on my ship!"

As air rushed into the transport bay, the sound of metal clapping on metal became audible over the speakers monitoring the area. Ringing above the clapping was a tinny cry. At first it sounded like screeching, but then it solidified into something like "Wheeeeeee!"

I looked at Yarrun. He looked back, eyebrows slightly raised.

Down in the transport bay, the admiral scrambled to his feet and tossed off the helmet of his impact suit. He turned to the four of us standing at the window and shouted, "See? Like Jonah and the whale." He pointed to himself. "I'm Jonah." He pointed to the Mouth. "That's the whale. A *sperm* whale. Jonah comes out of the whale. See?" He hugged himself with a clang of metal gloves against the suit's chestplate.

Prope stared blankly at the wild old man. Harque, at her side, whispered, "Should I cancel the call for the medical team?"

"Not on your life," she answered.

My Second Admiral

Harque turned a dial and the observation deck began to descend, lowering itself to match levels with the transport bay. As we sank, doors within doors were revealed in the plastic separating us from the bay: a large door that could be opened to receive huge, heavy equipment; a medium door, just the lower half of the largest one, but still big enough to let robot cargo-haulers pass through; and a baby door, set into the medium one, just right for humans.

Prope was obviously reluctant to open any of those doors until the medical team arrived. With her heroic stance abandoned, she shifted her weight back and forth from one foot to the other, probably wondering how to preserve her dignity while dealing with a madman. On the other side of the door, Admiral Chee had begun clinking the metal of his pressure suit with his finger, idly checking which surfaces made which tones. He may have been trying to tink out a song, but I didn't recognize the tune.

Yarrun cleared his throat. "Captain . . . hadn't we better let him in?"

"How do we know it's safe?" she asked. "He might have a disease."

Yarrun glanced at me, then turned back to Prope. "Captain, the admiral's behavior may be peculiar by the standards of mainstream Technocracy culture, but we could be mistaken in applying those standards to him. If the admiral comes from a Fringe World, his apparent childishness may simply be cultural idiosyncrasy."

"Trust an Explorer to talk about cultural idiosyncrasy," the captain muttered. *And trust a Fleet captain to ignore it*, I thought to myself. Officers of the Vacuum Corps invariably came from the great homogenized paunch of the Technocracy, with no representation from the more eclectic Fringes. But the captain admitted, "I suppose we have to let him in sooner or later. Go ahead, Harque: open the door."

The human-sized door slid into the floor with a hydraulic

hiss. Harque snapped the admiral an ostentatious salute. Prope did the same a guilty second later, and Yarrun and I fluttered our hands somewhere near our foreheads. Chee blinked at all of us for a moment, then waved his hand dismissively. "Piss on saluting. I'm here incognito. I don't have to salute if I don't want."

"Of course not, sir," Yarrun said, smoothly changing his salute to a hand extended for shaking. "Welcome to the *Jacaranda*. I hope the ride over was pleasant?"

"The only fun I've had in thirty years. Can I do it again?"

"I'm afraid not, sir," I said after a glance at the tracking holo that glowed above the control console. "The *Golden Cedar* has already broken the tail-link, and it's heading out of range."

"I can call them back. I'm an admiral."

Captain Prope looked down the hall, apparently praying for the med team to arrive. In the meantime, I reminded Chee, "You're here incognito, sir. If you were to begin transmitting orders. . . ."

"Oh." His face fell. "This secrecy stuff was a piss-poor decision on my part. Or was it my decision? I forget. Let me read my papers."

He reached into the front pouch of his impact suit and pulled out four sealed packets. One of them had my name on it, but he shoved that one and another back into the pouch. He took one of the remaining packets himself and handed the other to Prope. While he fiddled with his packet's lock mechanism, Prope pressed a thumb to her own packet's registry plate and flicked the top open. She withdrew a slim viewpad and retired to a corner to read.

The admiral finally got his own package open and pulled out a sheet of paper . . . paper made from trees. I supposed that admirals were too exalted to receive orders by viewpad like the rest of us.

Chee shouted, "Aha!" as he looked at the paper sheet. "I didn't decide this. Orders direct from the Admiralty High Council. Can I countermand those?"

Yarrun and I busied ourselves examining the deck at our feet. Harque swallowed hard and answered, "No sir, you can't."

"Oh well," Chee shrugged. "Maybe some other time." He folded his orders into a paper airplane and threw it wobbling across the room.

Yarrun whispered to me, "I have a nasty suspicion. Ever been to Melaquin?"

"What do you mean?" I whispered back.

Before he could answer, Prope shut her viewpad with a crisp click. She had a far too satisfied smile on her face. "We're going to Melaquin," she said.

Under my breath I muttered, "Oh shit." But Yarrun only nodded to himself.

Melaquin—The Official Story

Melaquin (AOR No. 72061721)
Third planet in the Uffree system.
Orbital survey data: CLASSIFIED.
Explorational data: CLASSIFIED.
Historical data: CLASSIFIED.
Official status: INAPPLICABLE.

—Excerpt from the *Admiralty Object Registration Catalogue*, distributed by the Admiralty to all sciento-military personnel

Melaquin—The Unofficial Story (Part 1)

I first heard of Melaquin from a dying prostitute on the Fringe World He'Barr. She had taken a knife under the ribs in an alley fight and happened to collapse against the door of my dormitory room while wandering in a daze. I watched her bleed to death on my bed over the course of an hour and a half.

"Guess I'm on my way to Melaquin," she had said. I wasn't sure I heard her correctly—she was slipping in and out of coherency with no discernible transition between lucid speech and babble—so I asked her to repeat her words. "I'm on my way to Melaquin," she said. "That's the planet of no return. You know?"

I shook my head.

"Hell of an Explorer you are," she wheezed. "It was an Explorer who told me. They send you there when they want you gone forever and never coming back home to the blue blue sky pulling black curtains over the little baby boy. He saw me watching and smiled, a great big smile with all his teeth out, like black black curtains . . ."

While she rambled, I keyed up the registration catalogue and requested details on Melaquin. There was no information to be had.

In time, the woman fell silent with her eyes closed; I wondered if she had finally died. I got up to check her pulse, but she heard me coming toward the bed and shrank away. "You sure you didn't call the cops?"

"The who?"

"The police. The Civilian Protection Office."

"You asked me not to call them."

"I know. That doesn't answer my question."

"I didn't call them."

"Good." She coughed, and a trickle of blood dribbled from the corner of her mouth. She licked her lips as if she couldn't identify the taste. "I'm an Opter."

"I guessed."

"I'm opting to die."

"Yes."

She looked at me with a sly smile. Her eyes kept losing focus. "You don't understand this, do you?"

"I've read about Opters," I said. "Your religion claims that any attempt to prevent death is an affront to your god's will."

"You don't understand." She let her head flop back onto the plastic sheet I had put over the pillow. Her breath slid softly in and out, gradually slowing.

For a while, I watched her stare blindly at the ceiling. Those blind eyes gave her face an ecstatic radiance that annoyed me. Radiance always did.

"Can't you close your eyes?" I asked.

"Why?"

"I don't like the way you look."

"You don't want to have to close them for me," she said with scorn. But she did close her eyes. After a while she said in a quavery voice, "It doesn't hurt, you know."

"Of course not. I gave you 20 cc's of picollin."

She didn't hear me. "It doesn't hurt because God is kind to those who come when She calls. It doesn't matter what you've done, if you say yes, She'll just sing you to sleep. La, la-lah, la, la-lah . . ."

The tune she sang in a broken whisper was a lullaby my own mother sang to me, years ago on my home planet of Agua—a lullaby sung over the thunderstorms that rattled our environment dome each night.

> Day is done
> Night is nigh
> Farewell the sun
> Sleep deep, don't cry.

I couldn't bear to look at her as she sang her own lullaby. Her face was purple with bruises from the fight that had gotten her stabbed. I took out my textbooks and read survival manuals till dawn, long after the singing had stopped.

Melaquin—The Unofficial Story (Part 2)

Phylar Tobit was once an Explorer. He was an Explorer by virtue of being born with a flipperlike left arm that ended in a half-hand where the elbow should have been. The three fingers on the hand looked like tiny boneless sausages.

Tobit lost his malformed arm on a planet whose name was a number and whose dominant lifeform resembled a blotchy cluster of rocks. One of those rocks bit off Tobit's arm before he even knew the rocks could move . . . bit clean through his tightsuit, flesh, and bone in the blink of an eye.

The creature died with the first swallow halfway down its throat. Human meat was virulently poisonous to the beast. Statistics show that human flesh is toxic to eighty-seven percent of alien lifeforms who try eating it. Explorers take some comfort from this, like dying bees who know their stings have found a target.

But Tobit didn't die. His partner stopped the bleeding in time—Explorers are taught every possible emergency surgical procedure. Phylar Tobit returned to a medical base and recovered.

The new Tobit presented the Admiralty with a problem. He was no longer a repulsive flippered thing; he was merely a man who was missing an arm. Further, the arm could be replaced by a myoelectric one—not quite as good as a true arm, but a thousand times more effective than the one he had lost. Perhaps someone in the Admiralty contemplated giving Tobit a prosthetic duplicate of his flipper instead of a real arm . . . but that would have outraged the entire Explorer Corps, maybe even the regular Vacuum service. Anyway, an off-the-rack arm doesn't cost as much as a custom-built one, and the Fleet likes to be frugal.

The Admiralty had to accept that Phylar Tobit now looked too much like a real person to serve as an active Explorer. So Tobit and his new plastic arm were assigned teaching duty at the Academy.

He did not get along with his students, and we did not get along with him. This was normal. Our teachers were all former Explorers who had won safe desk jobs, by accident or by gutless sucking up. They were the dregs of the Corps, and we students knew it. The teachers hated us in turn because of the guilt they felt, blithely preparing us for short lives as planet fodder. Perhaps this was planned by the Admiralty, to show us how small-spirited Explorers could become.

What set Tobit apart from the rest was his drinking. The other teachers, still blessed with the repugnance that originally marked them as Explorers, stood under threat of transfer to active duty if they failed to toe the line. Tobit had nothing to fear but absolute discharge, and no Explorer feared that. While he put in his time, he soaked up the oldest drug in the world and was seldom sober.

Every morning he would stumble to class, surrounded by an alcoholic cloud we could smell at the back of the room. Every evening he would sit alone in the Academy lounge, his artificial hand wrapped around a whisky glass with THE BLIND PIG inscribed on it in gold letters. Eventually he would pass out and slide off his chair to the floor. We students would draw lots to see who would have to carry him to his quarters.

One such night, I happened to pull the short straw with another cadet named Laminir Jelca. I had a crush on Jelca at the time. He was a senior and I a freshman; I suppose that's all that was necessary. He had some kind of genetic scalp condition that left his skull bald and covered with lesions, but in low light, if you half-closed your eyes, the scabby patches almost looked like hair.

Jelca and I slung Tobit's arms around our shoulders and dragged him up two flights of stairs to the instructor dormitories. The man smelled of sweat and saliva and scotch. I happened to have the artificial arm around my neck and was afraid it might come off. It would make me look foolish in Jelca's eyes; I could picture myself staring slack-jawed at the detached arm, blood rushing to my cheeks (my cheek), so I carried the load as gingerly as I could and fretted Jelca would think I was making him take all the weight.

When we reached Tobit's door, we had to spit-wash some dirt off his hand before the security plate would recognize his palm-print.

Tobit's futon was unrolled just inside the door. Jelca was all for throwing the man on it (face down so he wouldn't drown in his vomit), then leaving immediately. Like a love-sick schoolgirl, I preferred to bask in Jelca's company as long as possible, so I persuaded him we should at least take Tobit's boots off and arrange the body comfortably.

It had been many days since Tobit had changed his socks. The musty smell of overwear rose up from them and our noses wrinkled as we untied his bootlaces. The smell was painful to us; I couldn't understand how Tobit could bear it. As an Explorer, he must have been programmed for obsessive grooming like the rest of us, but somehow he had sloughed it off.

As soon as we finished with the shoes, Jelca and I were desperate to wash our hands. Tobit's washroom was down a short hall, past the open door of a study whose floor was covered with fallen books, scattered botanical samples, and a whisky-soaked dress uniform: more defiance of Explorer conditioning. The mess turned my stomach, but also intrigued me. In his way, Tobit had freed himself from the rigidity of Fleet service.

Jelca and I washed our hands together, using a bar of white soap veined with dark cracks. We were talking about something—I forget what, the mess around us I suppose—and I was secretly wondering what a senior would do if a freshman kissed him, when Tobit's voice snapped our heads toward the doorway.

"Good evening." The words were slurred and he leaned heavily against the doorframe for support, but he appeared to believe he was charming. "I am about to piss. If the sight of a man pissing offends you, I suggest you avert your eyes."

"We'll go," Jelca said, shaking water off his hands.

"You will not go," Tobit replied. "I will." And he did, in the toilet beside us, while Jelca and I looked away at the filthy bathtub.

"I suppose you're wondering why you're here," he said as he zipped up. "You're here to celebrate my birthday."

"Actually, we were just helping you—" I started, but he ignored me.

"Today, I am forty years old . . . as they measure years on Rigel IV. Yesterday I was thirty-eight years old as they measure years on Barnard's Planet, and the day before I was fifty-six years old as they measure years on Greening. This is the greatest gift of humanity's drive to populate the galaxy. With the aid of the registration catalogue, you can celebrate a birthday every day of your life. Come with me."

He lurched out of the bathroom and disappeared down the hall. Jelca and I exchanged looks, then followed him into the study.

We found him with his forehead pressed against the screen of his computer terminal, as he painstakingly typed on the keyboard with one finger. "This is my birthday program," he mumbled into the terminal. "It's searching the databases to find where my birthday will be tomorrow. In case you haven't noticed, it's almost midnight, and I like to start celebrating right on the dot."

"If it's that late," said Jelca, "we really should be going."

"And leave me alone on my birthday? Heartless bastard. Don't worry, I'll pass out soon and you can sneak away. Steal something when you go—I'll never remember your faces. I have some good stuff here. Medal of Valor somewhere." He swept his hand through the clutter on his desk, knocking a stylus to the floor. "Well, the medal's not here now, but I got it out the other day, just to check. After a while, I forget whether things really happened. In case you hadn't noticed, I drink."

The terminal beeped out the first bars of "Happy Birthday" and Tobit roared in triumph. "Yes! It's going to be my birthday again tomorrow. See, on the screen? Come on, come on, look at it." He tapped the words on the glass and read, "HAPPY BIRTHDAY, PHYLAR, YOU OLD SOT. TODAY YOU ARE 41 YEARS OLD AS YEARS ARE MEASURED ON . . . Hot shit, I'm forty-one on Melaquin! How about that?"

He looked at us proudly, as if he'd done a trick. Jelca

frowned. "I'm not familiar with Melaquin, sir."

"Not familiar with Melaquin? Not familiar with Melaquin! And you call yourself an Explorer! Melaquin is the big one, cadet, the haughty naughty virgin. Discovered fifty years ago and she still has her cherry." We stared at him blankly. "Jesus Christ!" he bellowed, "she's unexplored!"

"You mean they've never sent Explorers there?"

"Dozens. Every one went Oh Shit within two hours. Or missing, anyway. Permanently out of communication, which is as good as Oh Shit in my book."

"What's so dangerous on Melaquin?"

"That's the question, isn't it? No one has a clue."

"If so many Explorers die," Jelca said, "why do they keep sending new parties there? The High Council can't be so criminally irresponsible. . . ."

"You don't know the council," Tobit replied. "Besides, Melaquin looks perfect for colonization: ocean, forest, grassland . . . more like Earth than Earth these days. It's fertile, it's temperate, the atmosphere's breathable. . . . Everything's lovely, except some mysterious something that's lethal. Could be microbes, could be plants or animals, could be sentients for all we know. Wouldn't that be a kick?"

"But surely," I said, "a significant culture of sentients would be detectable from orbit. Towns, irrigation canals, campfires. . . ."

"Don't lecture me on exploring, cadet—I teach that crap," Tobit snapped. "Melaquin breaks the rules, all right? Melaquin breaks all the rules."

He fell silent as if he had spoken a truth deserving long contemplation. When he began to snore a minute later, Jelca and I tiptoed out.

Melaquin—Yarrun's Story

"I had a friend in the Academy," Yarrun said. Several minutes had passed, the medical team had persuaded the admiral to undergo a physical, and Yarrun and I slouched against a bulkhead outside the infirmary. The time was 04:50 and the entire ship seemed deserted.

Yarrun kept his voice low. His face muscles hurt if he went too long without sleep, and he was ashamed when his diction degenerated. "My friend's name was Plebon. Did you know him? He would have been a freshman when you were a senior."

I shook my head.

"His face was like mine. Mirror images, we called ourselves, though he was African and I South Slav. We couldn't help but be close."

"Of course."

"When we graduated, he was assigned to the *Tamarack*, a frigate doing search and rescue in the Dipper Group. Only one Landing in his first year."

"Easy service."

"His letters said it was boring . . . but I think he was grateful. In the middle of his second year, the *Tamarack* secretly took aboard one Admiral O'Hara—over 140 years old and no longer helped by YouthBoost. Plebon said the man had begun a mental decline."

"A suspiciously familiar situation," I commented.

"Plebon and his partner were ordered to take the admiral to Melaquin. They'd heard of the planet's deadly reputation so they pulled some strings to demand a Mission Justification Statement."

"And?"

"The Council claimed that a Landing led by someone with an admiral's experience would have a better chance of success than a normal Explorer party."

I gaped at him, speechless. An admiral couldn't possibly contribute to a Landing. Outward Fleet policy manuals claimed that admirals could rise from any branch of the service—but admirals weren't deformed, were they? I was sure they were all pampered vac-captains like Prope, without the tiniest particle of planet-down experience. A freshman ECM cadet would know more by first midterms than an admiral learned in a lifetime.

Yarrun continued. "A few hours before the Landing on Melaquin, Plebon sent me a message telling me the whole story. He was afraid he wouldn't come back."

"Did he?"

"The party went no-comm in less than ten minutes."

"That's what 'expendable' means."

It was a phrase we Expendable Crew Members used among ourselves: *That's what "expendable" means.* It was better than "I'm sorry to hear that" or "I understand your loss." Those were things people said to distance themselves. And no Explorer was distant enough.

Melaquin—A Theory

"So," I said, "your friend was sent to Melaquin with an admiral who was going senile. And here we are, with the same kind of mission. You think the Admiralty might be using Melaquin to get rid of embarrassments?"

Yarrun shrugged. "When YouthBoost fails, mental decline can be rapid. Some admirals may become children overnight . . . and as children, they may refuse to resign voluntarily."

"They could be discharged with a competency hearing."

"The press always has a field day over competency hearings," Yarrun replied. "So do lawyers. It's unhealthy for Fleet morale."

"So to avoid bad publicity, the High Council assigns unwanted admirals to suicide missions? And who cares if they kill a few Explorers at the same time?"

Yarrun gave another shrug and a sigh. "That's what 'expendable' means."

Part III
PLANS

Planning (Part 1)

After a long while, Yarrun asked, "How do you want to try the Landing?"

I had been pondering the same question—self-pity could only hold my interest so long, and then training took over. "Phylar Tobit claimed Melaquin was more like Earth than Earth," I said. "If he was right, we won't need extreme heat or cold equipment."

"Suppose there's some natural phenomenon that produces bursts of extreme heat or cold."

I shook my head. "It's possible . . . but the drop-ship would be watching from orbit, and anything like that would be picked up by sensors."

"Of course. But would they tell us?"

"What?"

Yarrun didn't look at me. "Even if the High Council knows what is deadly about Melaquin, would they tell us? They don't want a successful mission. They want the admiral to die."

"Oh shit."

"Precisely."

A Possible Out

Harque and Prope came through a hatch halfway down the hall, saw us, nodded, and dropped their eyes. The captain asked my chest, "Is Admiral Chee still with the doctor?"

"Yes."

"Isn't that a long time for a simple examination?"

"No doubt Dr. Veresian wants to be thorough," Yarrun answered. "One doesn't like to misdiagnose an admiral. And this particular admiral is unlikely to be a cooperative patient."

"True." Prope looked at her watch. "It would still be nice to get some sleep."

Harque produced a smarmy expression and an unctuous voice. "Perhaps, captain, you could ask the doctor to hurry things along. The examination is just a formality, after all. Isn't it?"

He smiled more at us than at Prope, to see if we understood what he meant. We understood indeed. At least Prope had the decency to be uncomfortable that this was all a sham. She muttered, "I'll speak to the doctor," and entered the infirmary with Harque on her heels.

"Before the Landing, I'd like to kick Harque's teeth out," I said. "What could they do about it?"

Yarrun closed his eyes a moment, searching through the vast fund of regulations stored in his brain. "Maximum penalty for striking a subordinate officer is six months imprisonment, plus demotion."

"Hmmm." I tapped my fingers on the bulkhead behind me. "That's a lot better than landing on Melaquin."

Yarrun's eyes narrowed in thought, then he shook his head. "It's a secondary offense—punishment can be deferred if the offender has duties of overriding importance."

"Like accompanying an admiral to his execution."

"Mmm."

I considered the possibilities a little longer. "Of course, punishment can't be deferred for a primary offense."

"No. . . ."

"Primary offenses: treason, mutiny, desertion, homicide, possession of a deadly weapon on an interstellar vessel . . . anything else?"

"Assaulting a superior officer."

I contemplated the options. "Pity. I'd have to attack Prope instead of Harque. *You* could do Harque, though. A knee in the testicles would be appropriate, don't you think?"

"Dislocating his shoulder would be better—I'd like the crew to admire my restraint."

"Black both his eyes," I suggested, "and the crew will pay you a bounty."

"Where would I spend it? Melaquin?"

The joking died. We were ourselves again, in the night-lit corridor of a silent ship.

Still . . . I was appalled at the thought of dying stupidly.

"What's the penalty for a primary offense?" I asked quietly, though I knew the answer.

"Banishment," Yarrun replied. "There's no other penalty possible."

"The nearest exile world would be Mootikki, right?"

"It's the only one in this sector."

"Mootikki. . . . ninety percent ocean, and semi-sentient water spiders that eat anything with a pulse?"

Yarrun nodded. "That's Mootikki."

Pause.

"A cakewalk," I said. "Wouldn't faze the greenest cadet."

"We've seen worse," Yarrun agreed.

A long silence trickled by. My palms were sweat-moist behind me as I leaned them against the wall.

Yarrun finally spoke softly. "Are we going to do it, Festina?"

"The High Council is sending us to a planet that has killed who-knows-how-many teams already. They are providing us with no information, not even a standard AOR summary. They've put us under the command of a man who is clearly unstable, possibly senile, and certainly ignorant of the principles of exploration. To all appearances, they are dispatching us to die just to rid themselves of an embarrassment. What's a few bruises compared to that?''

Yarrun, in a whisper: "We'll need witnesses."

I pointed to the door in front of us. "If we go for Prope and Harque while they're in the infirmary, Dr. Veresian and the admiral will see everything."

Another long silence. At last, Yarrun said, "We'll just shoot them with stunners, won't we?''

"Of course," I replied. "We don't really want to hurt anyone, do we?''

Weapons

Stunners were Landing weapons, intended to stop alien animals without killing them. They fired an invisible cone of hypersonic white noise, intended to disrupt electroneural activity for two and a half seconds. Sometimes, the shock stopped whatever was trying to eat you; sometimes, it didn't. On a human, a single stunner blast caused about six hours of unconsciousness followed by a vicious bitch of a headache, but it did no true physical damage.

Every Explorer longed for a more powerful weapon now and then; but the matter was out of our hands. The League of Peoples utterly forbade lethal weapons of any kind on board starships, and as far as anyone knew, the ban had never been broken. No one could say how the League did it . . . although there were rumors that the races known to humans were merely the tip of the League iceberg, that there were far more advanced and mysterious creatures who simply hadn't bothered to contact us. It was suggested that these creatures watched us invisibly, maybe even living amongst us without being seen: gaseous things or sentient patterns of radio waves, monitoring our actions or even our thoughts.

Certainly, the League seemed to pick up intentions

clearly enough. After all, you can kill a person with almost anything, from laser drills to a plain old brick; but the League permitted such things to pass freely through their quarantine, because they weren't intended as weapons. On the other hand, if you had murderous thoughts about strangling someone with your shoelace. . . . Well, if you had murderous thoughts at all, you'd never leave your home planet ever. Somehow, the League simply *knew*.

Always.

It was disturbing when you thought about it—like magic. Any sufficiently advanced technology, et cetera.

Our Assault

When I took my stunner from the locker in the Explorer equipment room, the butt felt oddly cold and metallic. I had seldom touched the pistol with my bare hand—on a Landing, we wore tightsuits covering our whole bodies. Even on a planet with good atmosphere and temperate climate, there were a thousand reasons to remain sealed off from the environment. I couldn't remember the last time I had touched a stunner ungloved.

Yarrun and I exchanged glances at the door of the infirmary. We hadn't said a word since we left to get the weapons. Now he smiled . . . a hideous sight. I nodded and palmed the ENTER plate.

Inside, the air smelled of disinfectant. Dr. Veresian had drawn Harque and Prope into his office, and was talking to them in a low voice. The admiral sat without pants in an examination chair, drumming his fingers on the arm-rests.

Prope turned at the sound of our entrance and saw the stunners. "Is there some problem, Explorers?"

"In a manner of speaking," I said. "We're unhappy with this mission."

"That's understandable," she replied. "It's an open secret that Explorers have been Lost on Melaquin. But the order came directly from the High Council."

"It seems foolish to throw away our lives for no reason." I raised the stunner. "What would you do in our position?"

Prope calmly lifted a hand. The ghost of a smile played about her lips; maybe all her life she had been waiting for a chance to show how relaxed she could be at gunpoint. She turned to Harque as if there were no weapon trained on her. "Lieutenant, what's the punishment for a primary offense?"

Harque quoted the regulation with a smirk. "The offender shall be set down on an approved exile world with no less than three days food and water rations, two changes of suitable clothing, and a knife whose blade does not exceed twenty centimeters in length."

"And what is the nearest exile world, lieutenant?"

"I imagine it would be Mootikki."

"But suppose I were shot by a stunner and was unconscious for a few hours. Another hour to convene a court martial, perhaps two hours to go through the formalities. . . . Where would we be then, lieutenant?"

"Not far off Melaquin."

"And Melaquin," Prope said, turning back to us, "is also an approved exile world."

"That's not in the registration catalogue," I objected.

"There's a lot that isn't in the registration catalogue." Harque grinned nastily.

I tried to keep my face steady, but my stomach had been carved hollow with one sweep of an invisible scythe. The captain put on the look of a big sister who's caught you playing with yourself. "My orders from the Council mentioned that some Explorers try to . . . waive this sort of mission in various ways; but all the loopholes have been plugged, believe me. You two can choose to be banished to Melaquin as criminals with little more than the clothes on your back, or you can land as Explorers with all the preparation and equipment the *Jacaranda* can muster. Now if you want to fire, go ahead. It's five o'clock in the morning, and I could use the sleep."

Yarrun's hand touched my wrist, lowering the stunner for me. In a moment, he took my arm and nudged me out the door. As it closed behind us, I could hear Harque snicker.

Yarrun said, "I'll take the stunners back and lock them up."

I put an arm around his shoulder and squeezed lightly. "It was a childish plan anyway."

He slipped away and walked off slowly, tapping the guns against his thigh with every step. I slumped back against the bulkhead and tried not to think of how good it would feel to plunge my fist into someone's face.

Admiral's Escort

Admiral Chee poked his head out the infirmary door. He still had no pants on, just blue boxer briefs.

"Are you a guard?" he asked.

"No."

He slipped into the corridor with an ostentatious attempt at stealth. It was unnecessary—I could see that the people in Veresian's office had closed the door, leaving the admiral unattended.

"I'm not supposed to be out here," Chee said with great satisfaction. "They thought they could stop me by stealing my pants." He raised a hand to his mouth and blew a raspberry salute back toward the infirmary. "It didn't work, did it? And do you know why? Because I'm an admiral and people are more embarrassed seeing my ass than I am showing it. Watch."

He spun around and hiked up the back of his shirt to give me a better view of his skinny flanks. Reflexively, I flinched and the old man cackled with glee.

"Rank hath its privileges, Ramos! I'm not embarrassed and you are. You're blushing something awful . . . one side of your face, anyway."

I was too stunned to react, flabbergasted by what he'd

said. While I was still trying to decide whether to be hurt or furious, the admiral gestured at a blue jacaranda painted on a nearby door. "What's this tree?"

"A jacaranda," I answered, still feeling numb.

"A jacaranda . . . that sounds familiar."

"It's the name of the ship."

"I know it's the name of the ship," Chee snapped. "I was making a joke."

"Sorry, sir."

"What's behind this door?"

"I don't know, sir."

"Why don't you know?"

"I'm an Explorer, sir. We don't get to see much of the ship."

He snorted. "Can't be much of an Explorer if you've been here six years and haven't explored the ship."

Once again, I was taken aback: how did he know how long I had been on the *Jacaranda*? But he was already off on another tangent.

"Have you ever discovered where the galley is, Explorer?"

"Yes, sir."

"Let's go then; I want a snack. Mushrooms in hot chocolate . . . have you ever had that? Slice them, fry them, and float them on top. They look like fungus umbrellas in mud. You'll love it."

"I don't think we should go to the galley, sir."

"Why not?"

For some reason, it felt good to say no to an admiral, especially *this* admiral. "Your presence here is supposed to be a secret, sir. High Council's orders. If you go to the galley, you'll likely be seen by crew members—the night shift drop by the galley frequently."

"Oh, take out the pickle, Ramos!" he thundered. "Five minutes ago you're ready to mutiny, and now I can't have a snack because it's against orders? Be consistent, Explorer! That's the first rule of command: be consistent! You can be sadistic, you can be lazy, you can be stupid, but if you're

consistent, the crew will still let you sit in when they play
dominoes.''

"Admiral, about the mutiny—"

"Semi-stupid move, Ramos, but only semi-stupid. If
you'd thought a little longer, you'd have guessed the Council would plan for contingencies. On the other hand, you
still should have shot that prick Harque. He's your subordinate; at this point, he's a freebie.''

Chee winked broadly, then laughed when I looked bewildered. "Don't know how to take me, do you?'' he
grinned. "I'm not as senile as you might think. 'I am but
mad north-north-west. When the wind is southerly I know
a hawk from a handsaw.' Who said that?''

"Hamlet?''

"Damned right, and aren't you glad I pressured the other
admirals into requiring a Shakespeare course at the Academy?'' He gave me a look, and this time I could see a
glimmer of shrewdness hiding under the wild-eyed act.
"The fact is, Explorer, I am not senile. My mind may wander from time to time, but mostly I am suffering from
Don't-give-a-shit-itis. The High Council, bless 'em, think
it might be contagious, so here I am. I presume you have
some idea of how they use Melaquin?''

"Yes.''

"Well, your idea is likely wrong, but who cares? Have
you thought about the Landing?''

"We haven't had much time,'' I told him. "Or information.''

"You won't get it either. Melaquin's ten hours away,
and we've been ordered to Land within two hours of making orbit. I say we go to the galley, talk things out for the
length of time it takes to drink a cup of hot chocolate, then
get some sleep.''

"It really would be better to stay out of the galley, sir.
The orders—''

"Fuck the orders,'' Chee interrupted. "I'm in the mood
for pointless gestures of defiance. We will *occupy* the galley. We will sing dirty songs to draw attention to ourselves.

We will accost crew members in the corridors and tell them our life stories. We will write CHEE WAS HERE in soy sauce on the servery wall, and carve our names in the tabletops, using a knife whose blade does not exceed twenty centimeters in length.''

"Admiral. . . ."

"Yes?"

"Could we do all those things wearing pants?"

He heaved a mighty sigh. "Lighten up, Ramos. The best revenge is making them envy your freedom."

But he slunk back into the infirmary for his trousers.

Our Advantage

While the admiral was gone, Yarrun returned from the weapons locker. His eyes were bloodshot and his shoulders sagged.

"Cheer up," I told him.

"Why?"

"It's an order."

"Oh."

He slumped heavily onto the wall beside me. I think we were both tired enough to be glad we had something solid to lean against.

"So what now?" he asked.

"I talked to the admiral. He suggests a few minutes of planning in the galley, then sleep."

Yarrun stood a little straighter. "That sounds more . . . *lucid* . . . than I expected from the admiral."

"Chee *is* lucid," I replied. "Unstable and too damned whimsical, but I think he's healthier than the High Council suspects. Healthier on the mental scales, anyway. Physically . . . well, it's interesting that Harque and Prope are still in talking with Veresian. I suspect the good doctor found some medical condition that should legally keep the admiral out of any Landing party, and the captain is trying to convince Veresian to keep his opinions to himself."

"Who'll win?"

"Not us."

"Mmm."

Silence. The growing dizziness/giddiness of fatigue came sneaking into my brain, and it was only when Yarrun started speaking that I jerked out of near-sleep.

"If we look at this coldly," Yarrun said, "Chee's health is immaterial. He's strong enough to survive another twenty-four hours, and that's more than enough to get down and back . . . if we manage to get back. But the more clear-headed he is, the better for us."

"He'll be less of a burden, if that's what you mean."

"More importantly, he's an admiral. And the High Council of Admirals may be the only people who know anything about Melaquin. Chee is a potential source of information."

"Teams have landed with admirals before," I reminded him. "It hasn't helped them."

"But if our theory is correct, most of those admirals have been senile," Yarrun replied. "Our advantage is that this one still has brains we can pick."

The infirmary door swished open again and Chee skittered out. He had put on the top half of his gray uniform, but the trousers were slung over one shoulder; instead, he wore the baggy mauve pants used during surgery. He also wore a surgeon's mauve cap and thin rubber gloves. "Look at this great stuff!" he beamed.

I turned back to Yarrun. "Pick his brains fast—the crop's rotting on the vine."

The Admiral Proves His Sentience

[Conversation on the way to the galley.]

Chee: Do I really get to wear an Explorer suit?

Me: Yes, Admiral.

Chee: With the vanes sticking out the back and everything?

Me: Those are for ice planets. Melaquin is temperate,
isn't it?

Chee: Of course.

Yarrun: Are you sure?

Chee: If you want to get technical, it's cold on the
tips, hot in the middle, and temperate in between.
But compared to ice planets and infernos, it's
shirt-sleeve weather from pole to pole.

Yarrun: Then the admiral has some knowledge about
Melaquin?

Chee: Some.

Me: Do you have any . . . insights into what we might
find there?

Chee: Insights? Why should I have insights?

Me: The Admiralty has sent a lot of parties to Melaquin. Considering that you're an admiral. . . .

Chee: Ramos, are you suggesting I would knowingly
send a human being to her death?

Me: Not in so many words.

Chee: Look, you two: the League of Peoples classi-
fies murderers as non-sentients, right?

Me: Murdering a sentient is a non-sentient act, yes.

Chee: A *dangerous* non-sentient act, Explorer.

Me: Yes, sir.

Chee: And what's the penalty imposed by the League
for taking a dangerous non-sentient into interstellar
space?

Yarrun: Immediate execution of everyone who knowingly participates.

Chee: Have you ever heard of humans fooling the
League? Smuggling killers, lethal weapons, or
dangerous animals into open space?

Me: No.

Chee: And you won't, either. Damned if we know
how they do it, but take it from me, the League's
quarantine against homicide is absolute—a law of

the universe, more certain than entropy. Am I here?

Me: Of course.

Chee: Then I never ordered anyone anywhere I thought they were sure to die. Q.E.D.

[Pause.]

Yarrun: Rather explains why the High Council of Admirals never leaves New Earth, doesn't it?

Chee: You bet your ass, sonny. Those buggers would be vaporized if they jumped too high on a pogo stick.

In the Galley

The galley was brightly lit. Coming in from the night-dim corridors, we blinked like wakened owls.

Two ensigns lounged at a table near the door, one wearing the dark blue of the Communications Corps and the other in Life Support white. The woman in blue was laughing at something as we entered; she had her back to us. The other woman looked up with a smile on her face, saw the admiral's gray jacket, and snapped to jittery attention. The laugher swung her head around and jumped up too.

"At ease," Chee commanded, "at goddamned ease. It's beyond me why the Fleet wants people to play jack-in-the-box when an officer enters the room. This hopping around is unsettling. I could name you five Fringe Worlds where they'd think you were drawing a gun."

Under his breath, Yarrun murmured, "Herrek, Golding, Nineveh, Biscayne . . ."

"And Sitz," I offered, when it became clear he was stuck.

"Bloody Explorers," Chee complained to the ensigns. "Heads filled with trivia no one cares about." He fixed his eye on the woman who'd been laughing. "What's your opinion of bloody Explorers, ensign?"

"I don't know, sir." She ventured a worried glance at his mauve baggies.

"Of course you know. You're just too chicken-shit to say anything." He snapped around to the other woman. "What's your opinion of chicken-shit ensigns, ensign? Take your time; whatever you say will offend someone."

The woman took a deep breath. "I don't think that's a fair question, sir."

Chee clapped his hands in delight. "Quite right, ensign, I was being a prick. I can't understand why people put up with it. What's your name?"

"Berta Deeren, sir."

"Berta Deeren Sir, you have the makings of a human being. If you're ever offered a command position, jump ship. Now get out of here, the two of you—we're going to fill this place with the stink of death."

The ensigns saluted quickly and headed for the door. Berta Deeren was blushing hot red. Yarrun and I stood aside as they left.

"Sir," Yarrun said to the admiral after the ensigns were gone, "why do you do that to people?"

Chee smiled. "You could say I'm trying to wake the clods out of their rigid mental sets by forcing them to deal with unconventional behavior . . . or you could say I just like jerking folks around. For that matter, you could say anything you damned well want to. I do."

He grinned at Yarrun. Yarrun gazed back thoughtfully. I said, "The hot chocolate is over there."

Mushrooms

Mushroom slices floated on the surface of my hot chocolate like ocean flotsam. I sipped carefully so I didn't get any mushrooms in my mouth. The damned things wanted to be swallowed—they nudged my lip in their eagerness.

No one serving in deep space could avoid mushrooms for long. Huge quantities were grown on every ship, station,

and outpost. They grew quickly and cheerfully under conditions that would kill photosynthesizing plants: odd grav-
itational effects, artificial atmosphere, lack of natural
germinating agents. Mushrooms were served as "fresh
treats" in contrast to the synthesized food that made up the
bulk of our diets. The Fleet expected us to slaver with gratitude.

I did not like mushrooms. I did not dislike mushrooms.
I had long since transcended the urge to vomit at the sight
of yet another mushroom-based meal (stuffed mushrooms,
mushrooms au gratin, poached mushrooms with creamy
mushroom sauce), and had achieved a lofty plateau of indifference to the nasty gray growths.

On Landings, however, I did delight in hacking up fun-
goid matter whenever a mission required biological samples.

Hot Chocolate

The hot chocolate was lukewarm because the pressure
pot was being used for coffee.

Pressure pots were needed to compensate for the sub-
normal air pressure maintained on board ship. Low pressure
meant that water boiled at a lower temperature, and that
meant poor quality coffee, poor quality tea, and poor quality hot chocolate. To compensate, you wanted to make your
coffee, tea, or hot chocolate in a pressure pot, where the
water could reach a decent heat and your drink could pick
up a decent amount of flavor.

Of course, you could only use the pot for one beverage
at a time.

On board the *Jacaranda*, we had three complete engines
in case of breakdowns. We had two spare Sperm-field generators and five redundant D-thread computers.

We only had one pressure pot. And it was always dedi-
cated to coffee.

If you took the time to brood about that, the chocolate just got colder.

Planning (Part 2)

"You're the ranking Explorer," Chee said to me. "It's your show."

We sat casually around a table . . . or perhaps I should say we sat *expansively*. We were flagrant in our nonchalance. Chee leaned so far back in his chair that the springs squeaked every few seconds; a heavier man would have broken the clamps that attached the seat to its tracks. Yarrun sprawled sideways across his chair, one elbow on the table, the other hand toying with a napkin. I had both arms on the table, hands cupping my mug as if I were drawing heat from it. In fact, I was hoping my hands would warm the chocolate up.

"All right," I said, "we're agreed the planet is temperate?"

Both men grunted a yes.

"And it's relatively Earthlike?"

"Don't assume it's *too* Earthlike," Chee said.

"Eighty percent of an Explorer's training is aimed at stamping out such assumptions," I replied. "The specifics of each planet are different, but there are usually some general parallels. For example, do we think Melaquin has flora and fauna?"

"It must," Chee answered. "If it's an official exile world, it has to be able to sustain human life. Otherwise, banishment to an exile world would be as good as murder, and the League of Peoples would condemn Outward Fleet laws as non-sentient. No . . . there's got to be a reasonable chance for survival on any exile world—Melaquin included. It must have breathable atmosphere, drinkable water, and edible food."

"So Melaquin has all the comforts of home," I said. "Why is it so deadly?"

"Microorganisms?" Chee suggested. "A planet with life must have bacteria, and thousands of diseases for which we have no immunity."

"Unquestionably . . . but we'll breathe canned air and wear the usual protective gear," I told him. "The skin of a tightsuit can't be penetrated by the smallest virus we know; and the pressure inside is kept higher than atmospheric pressure outside, so any microbe that comes close to penetrating the suit's skin is blown right back out again."

"What about organisms that can digest tightsuits?"

"There are five different kinds of tightsuits," Yarrun explained, "each made from a different material. Standard procedure is for each party member to wear a different type of suit. It's extremely unlikely that microbes would eat through each material at exactly the same rate, so if one of us gets a suit breach, the others should have some warning before their suits go too. And of course, death by disease is not instantaneous; even the most virulent bugs we know need at least an hour to multiply to lethal levels. During that hour, our suit sensors would surely notice some sign we're in trouble—loss of suit pressure, spread of alien organisms through our bodies, deterioration of body functions—not to mention we'll know we're getting sick without any help from the electronics."

"By then it could be too late," Chee said.

"Almost certainly," Yarrun agreed. "But we would still have time to communicate with the ship and describe the problem. Sickness is a valid reason to demand immediate pickup; and then we'd only have to hold out another five minutes before we were back on the ship. Even if we died on board, our bodies *must* be sent to the Explorer Academy for examination, at which point the whole secret would come out."

"Not if the High Council suppressed the information," I muttered.

Yarrun shrugged. "Secrets are flimsy things—spread them among too many people, and they get torn. Maybe the council could suppress information about a single Landing . . . maybe even a handful of Landings. But if people go missing on a regular basis, there are too many leaks to catch. Admiral, how many people has the council has sent to Melaquin?''

Chee thought for a moment. ''Maybe one or two a year. And they've been doing this for at least forty years. They certainly couldn't suppress hard evidence that long.''

''Which means that whatever the danger is on Melaquin, it hits the party too fast for anyone to collect hard evidence.''

''Do you have any ideas what it might be?'' Chee asked.

Feeling like a cadet reciting a case study, I said, ''On Canopus IV, there's a plant that spreads its seeds by exploding violently. In the right season, the vibration from a single footstep is enough to set it off. Five parties were killed there before one team spread out and put a hundred meters between each party member. In that team, one Explorer was killed; the others reported back and Canopus IV was eventually tamed.''

''So you think we should spread out?''

Yarrun snorted a small laugh. ''The planet Seraphar has a race of semi-sentient shapeshifters who would quietly stab Explorers in the back and take their place in the party. Spreading out just made it that much easier for the shapeshifters to do their work. Six parties were killed before one stumbled on the truth.''

''Every decision is a gamble,'' I told the admiral. ''In this case, however, we don't need to tax our brains. So many teams have landed on Melaquin, they must have tried all the standard approaches by now. None of those worked, so we're free to do whatever the hell we want.''

We spent several moments of silence, contemplating the wealth of freedom presented to us.

No-Comm

"Of course," I said at last, "there's a more pleasant alternative."

"I'm eager to hear it," Chee answered.

"According to my old instructor Phylar Tobit, teams exploring Melaquin don't necessarily go Oh Shit; they just go no-comm. Suppose there's something on the planet that interrupts communications—some kind of interference field."

Yarrun looked thoughtful. "Didn't Tobit suggest that parties can broadcast for a while before being cut off? If the planet has natural interference, it should kill communications right from the start."

"Not necessarily," I answered. "Suppose Melaquin has some kind of standing interference field; but when a ship drops its Sperm tail to land a party, the tail disrupts the field. The Explorers land, the tail is withdrawn . . . and for a few minutes the party has normal communications. Then the interference reestablishes itself and the party goes no-comm."

"Wouldn't there be some warning?" Chee asked. "Static or something, as the field closed back in."

"If the field closes fast enough, it doesn't matter," Yarrun told him. "To pick up a party, the ship has to drop the Sperm tail in exactly the right spot; and the only way to do that is to lock onto the tracking signal put out by a communicator. The signal is a sort of hypermagnetic anchor that seizes the end of the Sperm and drags it to the party's location. If the signal isn't working, there's no chance a ship could ever plant its tail stably on the surface."

"So you think," Chee said, "there's some kind of field—"

"No, Admiral," I interrupted, "I'm just saying it's one possibility. There must be a dozen other ways to disrupt communications: a trace chemical in the atmosphere that corrodes D-thread circuits; bacteria that like to chew on transducer chips; semi-sentients with the equipment to jam transmissions; periodic bursts of positronic energy that are drawn to communicators like lightning rods . . ."

"You're pulling my leg on that one, Ramos."

"I hope so," I told him drily.

"The point still stands," Yarrun said. "I'd rather believe in a phenomenon that blanks communicators than one that kills whole parties in the blink of an eye."

Silently, I agreed. I could live with the thought of machines breaking.

The Poles

"You know," Chee said, "perhaps our future isn't so bleak after all. We know the planet is Earthlike. The weather won't be a problem if we pick our landing site carefully enough. We'll have food and water and breathable air—it's an official exile world, so that part is guaranteed."

I shook my head at his naïveté. "If we're really planning to survive for any length of time, we'll put down on the edge of polar permafrost and hope we can subsist on scrub vegetation."

"Why?" Chee sounded outraged.

"Because," Yarrun explained, "the colder the region, the less microbial activity there is. When we land, we'll each have twelve hours of canned air; after that, we have to start breathing local atmosphere. Our tightsuits do their best to filter microorganisms from incoming air, but don't expect a hundred percent effectiveness. Theory says we'll live a lot longer if we go where the airborne microbe count is low."

"*Theory* says?"

"Actual evidence is skimpy," Yarrun shrugged. "No Explorer has come back to tell us either way."

Kicking a Lion in the Ass

"Are we really going to land near the poles?" Chee asked with conspicuous lack of enthusiasm.

Yarrun answered for me. "Festina was joking, in her way. When we land, we want the *Jacaranda* to remain in geosynchronous position above us so they can pick us up at a moment's notice. However, the *Jacaranda* was designed as a deep-space ship, and its sublight engines are not very efficient. If it parks close enough to the planet to pick us up, it has to maintain a reasonable speed relative to the planet's center of gravity, or else expend a lot of energy trying to hold altitude. Close to the poles, a hovering flight path is just too slow for the ship to hold very long. We're pretty well restricted to the region between, say, forty-five degrees north and south latitude."

"Which gives us plenty of land to choose from," I promised Chee, "and many types of terrain. To land safely, we'll choose somewhere fairly flat. To survive the first few hours, we'll pick a place with sparse vegetation and little animal life . . ."

"But not too sparse," Yarrun added. "We don't want to find ourselves in the middle of a desert if we suddenly go no-comm."

"Close to fresh water, far from any oceans . . ."

"I like the ocean," Chee protested.

"So do thousands of other lifeforms," I told him. "We must think defensively, Admiral. We know nothing about this planet except that it's dangerous. If we set down near an ocean, we have to worry about nasty ocean things as well as nasty land things. The fewer environments and ecologies we have to contend with, the fewer variables we need to think about and the more likely we are to be here this time tomorrow, drinking lukewarm chocolate and mushrooms. All right?"

"You don't have to snap, Ramos," he pouted. "I'll bow to your expertise on every point . . . which is generous of me, considering that standard Explorer techniques work like shit on Melaquin.''

"Admiral," Yarrun said quietly, "we recognize the standard methods have proved inadequate. Even so, we shouldn't abandon them entirely. Sometimes all the procedures in the book can't protect you from the perils of a planet; but that's no reason to walk up to something that looks like a lion and kick it in the ass.''

"On the contrary," Chee answered with a gleam in his eye, "suppose the first thing I did on Melaquin was boot some large toothy animal in the butt. What would happen?''

"Depending on its ecological niche," I replied, "it would run, kick you back, or bite off your foot.''

"And what would you do?''

"Depending on the size of its teeth, we would run, laugh, or shoot it with a stunner.''

"What would happen to me?''

I threw up my hands. "There's no way to know. How fast is the animal? How deadly is its attack? How susceptible is it to stunner fire? Does it sever a major artery or just give a flesh wound? Does its saliva happen to be poisonous to human life? How fast can we get you back to the ship's infirmary?''

I stopped, realizing what I just said.

Chee nodded happily. "Standard policy says when a party member is injured, you must request immediate pickup.''

We all pondered that a moment. Yarrun said, "Suppose the Admiralty have ordered Prope not to pick us up.''

"They can't do that!" Chee snapped. "Get it through your head—the Admiralty, the Technocracy, the whole damned galaxy, is constantly monitored by the League of Peoples." He suddenly broke off. "Look," he said in a lower voice. "Let me tell you a story.''

And he did.

Chee's Story

"Off in the Carsonal system," Chee said, "there's a planet with the stimulating name of Carsonal II. And living on Carsonal II was a species called the Greenstriders. Looked a lot like six-armed watermelons the size of a man, with long spindly legs.

"Now," he continued, "the Greenstriders joined the League of Peoples long before humans did, but they aren't one of the *ancient* races. They still have physical bodies, they still have to eat and excrete . . . in other words, they're small potatoes compared to the big boys in the League. But the Greenstriders had pretensions; they did indeed. And for a long time, the only contact between them and humanity was the occasional communicator message: 'You are attempting to colonize a planet in Greenstrider territory. Please to vacate it immediately.'

"The first time that happened, the Technocracy said, 'Sorry,' and left. The second time, we said, 'All right, we'll go, but give us a map of the territory you claim, so this won't happen again.' The third time, we said, 'This planet wasn't on your map, and it's time we had a heart-to-heart talk . . . in front of League arbitrators.'

"That's where I came in," Chee told us, "because the Admiralty always sent as many people as it could to an arbitration. Not to take part, but to watch. Or to spy, if you want a more colorful word. A few were assigned to spy on the Greenstriders, but most of us kept our eyes on the three arbitrators, to gather as much information as possible about the high mucky-mucks who really hold power in the League. In this case, the tribunal was a cloud of red smoke, a glowing cube, and a chair that sure as hell looked empty. But forget it, that's not the point.

"The point is that the hearing took place, the arbitrators asked a lot of questions, blah, blah, blah, everything you'd expect; and at the end, the tribunal decided the Greenstriders had been acting too highhanded. They got a slap on the wrist, and we got rights to colonize several new planets.

"Admiral Fewkes, who was fronting for our side, tried to soften the blow in good diplomatic style. Too bad, he said, that there were misunderstandings in the past, but now the problems had been straightened out, Fewkes hoped that humans and Greenstriders could open friendly diplomatic relations. . . . You can fill in the rest. And then Fewkes held out his hand for a cordial little handshake.

"Now you have to understand," Chee said, "that as far as we knew, this was the first time humans and Greenstriders had ever been in the same place together. All previous communications were by radio and hypercom. And throughout the hearing, we had always been kept separate from the Greenstriders by order of the tribunal. Fewkes wanted this handshake to be a memorable moment, first contact, a photo-op to please the folks back home. But when the head strider chiggered over to shake the admiral's hand, the moment was even more memorable than Fewkes expected. Within five seconds, he was lying on the floor gasping, and ten seconds later, he was dead."

Yarrun and I nodded gravely. "Secretions on Greenstrider skin," Yarrun said. "Their perspiration acts as a lethal nerve toxin on human beings. We learned that in the Academy."

"Thank Fewkes for the information," Chee replied. "He learned the hard way. Looked hellishly painful too, the way he screamed just before the end; but these things happen. It wouldn't be the first time that alien lifeforms turned out to be intrinsically deadly to each other—just a tragic accident.

"But . . . the arbitrators were still in the hearing room, and the cloud of red smoke said, 'That was a non-sentient act.' Seems there *had* been previous contact between humans and Greenstriders, and the red smoke knew all the details. A pair of Explorers had met some strider scouts, when both sides were checking out the same planet for possible colonization. There'd been diplomatic handshakes back then too; the Explorers had died so fast, they couldn't report why.

"So the Greenstriders knew what contact would do to us. Or more accurately, the knowledge existed somewhere in Greenstrider society. The strider who shook Fewkes's hand didn't personally know what would happen, but the cloud of red smoke said that was no excuse. A warning should have been conveyed to all striders who might come in contact with humans. Anything else was homicidal negligence on the part of the Greenstrider government as a whole."

"Harsh," Yarrun murmured. "If the strider who shook Fewkes's hand really didn't know . . ."

"The tribunal said he *should* have known," Chee answered. "When the Explorers died that first time, it was truly an accident. But after that, someone should have passed the word. I agree with the League on this. Someone in the chain of command was blatantly non-sentient if the information wasn't deemed important enough to be conveyed through channels. Not even the Admiralty is that sloppy; every Explorer in the Corps is meticulously instructed in how to interact with known alien races for maximum mutual safety. Right?"

"We hope so," I replied.

"You are," Chee said. "If only because the High Council wants to avoid what happened to the Greenstriders. Their entire governmental system was declared non-sentient: negligently careless. The whole damned race was grounded—barred from interstellar travel until they reorganized into a more conscientious society. A few of them tried to defy the ban . . . and for the next few years, our fleet kept finding strider ghost ships drifting through space, every strider aboard killed the second they tried to leave their home star system. Not a mark on the bodies. Just dead. The League has no qualms against exterminating non-sentients to protect the rest of the galaxy."

Chee paused to let that sink in.

"One question," I said. "If the red smoke knew the handshake would kill Fewkes, why didn't the smoke do something? Even if it had just shouted 'Stop!' before the strider made skin contact. . . .''

"The high echelons of the League prefer not to interfere with the actions of lower species," Chee replied. "They say it has something to do with free will."

"Or," Yarrun murmured, "giving us enough rope to hang ourselves."

The Admiral Volunteers

"So," Chee started again, "we were talking about Melaquin . . . and I was saying the High Council has to tread carefully. They can order us to explore a planet where there's only a slim chance of survival, but they can't send us on a total suicide mission. That's why they use Melaquin so often: they've found they can get away with it. And they *can't* get away with ordering a ship to refuse aid to the injured. That's a blatant non-sentient act. The League would never let another Outward Fleet ship into interstellar space."

There was a long silence. I thought about Chee's suggestion: deliberately getting hurt as an excuse to abort the Landing. It would have to be a real injury; faking or lying was dereliction of duty and we'd all be exiled back to Melaquin. But a genuine life-threatening wound was reasonable cause to cut short a mission . . . as was the death of a party member, for that matter. Whether or not Yarrun and I could save Chee's life was immaterial.

I turned to Chee. "Are you really volunteering to take the risk? It's much greater than you may realize. Infection, for instance. Any wound exposed to alien microbes. . . ."

"Nice of you to care," Chee replied, "but I have nothing to lose. If we stay too long on Melaquin, we'll end up dead like the others. Even if we're just stranded no-comm, I can't survive long without YouthBoost—in case you were wondering, I'm fucking ancient. On the other hand, if I take a wound three minutes after we land, there's a chance we'll get back to the ship and I'll pull through. I'd get a kick out of that . . . not just living but thumbing my nose at the High Council. Think of the looks on their faces when I come back from Melaquin again. I'd give 'em a raspberry so loud it'd be heard on every ship of the Fleet. Do you want to spoil an old man's fun?''

I looked at Yarrun. He murmured, "It would be more fair if we drew lots for who takes the risk."

"I'm an admiral," Chee told him. "I don't have to be fair. Besides, if someone gets chomped, it's better to have two competent Explorers taking care of the victim than one competent Explorer and one senile old beanbag. Right?''

Chee looked to Yarrun for agreement. Yarrun shrugged and looked at me—he chose the most annoying times to defer to my rank. "All right, then," I sighed, "we'll pick a Landing site where we can expect to find large predators. Anything else?''

"I'll wear a tightsuit without the helmet," Chee said. "I may as well test the atmosphere and bacteria while I'm at it.''

"Without a helmet, the rest of the suit is useless," I snapped. "We might as well send you down naked."

"You wish," Chee smirked. "But I'm going to wear a suit anyway, because I deserve it. I'm an Explorer now, aren't I?''

"I suppose so. . . ."

"Right," he said, raising his mug. "Here's to being an ECM." He waited for us to raise our mugs too, then drained off the dregs of his chocolate in one loud slurp. In almost the same motion, he hurled the mug sideways into the galley wall. The mug shattered, scattering ceramic shards in all directions.

Chee turned back to us with a satisfied smile. "Now *that's* what 'expendable' means."

Part IV
OBSERVATIONS

Alarm

I woke to the sound of applause and distant shouts of "Brava! Bravissima!" The less restrained members of the audience let loose a flurry of sharp whistles. The cheering went on and on, louder and louder, until I kicked away the sheets and stomped to my computer terminal to enter the de-ac code.

It has long been known that if your alarm clock makes the same buzz or ring every morning, you learn to sleep through it. For this reason, all wake-up systems in the Outward Fleet produced a different noise each day.

In the preceding week, I had wakened to the hum of a million bees, the drone of bagpipes, the love songs of whales, the demolition of an office tower, the screams of earthquake victims, and the national anthem of some obscure Fringe World nation as performed by a 200-voice chorus of five-year-olds. Even worse, they all started at low volume and gradually increased, so that you might sleep through as much as a minute before truly gaining consciousness.

It made for the damnedest dreams.

Dripping

I had just shoved myself into the shower when the message buzzer hummed. For a few moments, I pretended I couldn't hear it, but the buzz increased in volume. One day in my second year on the *Jacaranda*, I had plugged my ears and hoped the buzzer would burn out its damned speaker; but before that happened, the strength of the sound vibrations broke one of my eggs, a fragile filigreed shell from Tahawni. I had to stop the buzzer back then, and I had to stop the buzzer now. Cursing, I dripped my way out of the shower, wrapped a towel around the parts most likely to get goose pimples, and stomped off to answer the call.

Harque's smirking face appeared on the screen. "Good morning, Explorer. I hope I didn't disturb you."

There was no way he could miss that my hair was streaming wet and I was only wearing a towel, but Harque was Harque. "What is it?" I asked.

"Five minutes to Melaquin orbit," he announced. "Any special instructions as we go in?"

"I have a special instruction for you, Harque, but I don't think it's physically possible."

"Goodness, Explorer! Need I remind you that deliberate rudeness is Conduct Unbecoming an Officer. Especially when I'm merely doing my duty. I don't suppose this Landing has you frightened, has it?"

"One more word, Harque, and here's what I'll do. I'll show the admiral one of my pretty little eggs, and I'll tell him he can have that pretty little egg if he immediately transfers you to the Explorer Corps. I think he'll do it, Harque, and then you'll get to visit Melaquin with the rest of us."

The screen went blank and I laughed aloud. Vacuum personnel were so susceptible to cheap theatrics.

Leave-Taking

I spent too long drying my hair and trying to get it to fluff properly. It should have been cut weeks ago, but I refused to have it done on ship—the *Jacaranda* barber felt she had the right to comment on my appearance and make suggestions to improve it. ("All it would take is the right kind of makeup, not really heavy, just some pancake, and we could soften that color a lot. What if you wore your hair over to the side like this? Well really, Festina, I'm just trying to help. If you'd just make an effort, you could hide it so scarcely anyone would notice.")

Rushing, rushing, and I was nearly out the door when it occurred to me I might not see this room again. The thought chilled me. My collection. Two thousand, three hundred and sixty-four eggs, catalogued, mounted, polished.

And if I died? Perhaps the captain would let the crew traipse through my quarters and take whatever appealed to them, manhandling my treasures, breaking them, laughing at me for collecting useless dead things.

Or perhaps Harque would come with a garbage hopper and throw in all my eggs, smash, smash, smash, and they would be jettisoned into space, shot out through the Sperm tail like trash and Explorers.

No.

No.

Surprising what can give you the will to live.

My Will

But I was an Explorer, a good Explorer, and therefore a realist. I didn't have much time, but I keyed the computer for audio input and dictated the following. "Instructions: lock the room and do not open until you register my voice print or Yarrun's. Confirm?"

It beeped once, then responded, "Confirmed."

"If anyone overrides my instructions by asserting that I

am dead or Lost on Landing, you will immediately inform
Captain Prope and Fleet Central Records that I bequeath
my egg collection and all personal effects to . . .''

To whom? My parents were dead. Yarrun would be my
second choice, but he was about to go Oh Shit with me.
Perhaps I could leave everything to my old crush Jelca . . .
but no, a classmate told me he had gone Lost three years
ago; she hadn't known the details. No other friends came
to mind. No one really. . . .

"I bequeath my collection and personal effects to Admiral Seele. Confirm?''

"Confirmed.''

There. Everything to my first Admiral, the one who wept
and tried to hold my hand. It was a bequest Prope and
Harque wouldn't dare ignore. And Seele cared for me in
her way. As good a way as any.

I wondered if she belonged to the High Council now. I
wondered if she had been the one who picked me to take
Chee to Melaquin. If so, receiving my collection would
unsettle her.

It would seem like some kind of gesture.

In the Halls (Part 2)

While I was asleep, the day shift had come on duty. The
corridors were now filled with crew members striding
along, wearing self-important airs that told the world they
had Things to Do. Most pretended to be so absorbed by
their obligations that they didn't notice me; those who
couldn't pull off such obliviousness doffed self-conscious
salutes to me without meeting my eyes.

As I passed open hatchways, I heard snippets of conversation. The crew seemed bursting to tell each other that
Admiral Chee was on board. (''A real admiral, but he's
here incognito, so keep it secret.'') Each of them had a
theory why Chee was here: Prope was going to be court-
martialled; Prope was going to be promoted; the League of

Peoples had decided humanity was mature enough to receive another technological "gift," and the *Jacaranda* was taking the admiral to pick it up.

Once in a while, the gossipers noticed me and instantly went silent. Before I passed out of earshot, their babble began again with, "I'll bet she knows."

And yet no one spoke directly to me. No one asked if I had news. It was as if I were encased in glass walls that no one could break through—not them, and not me.

Even now, that's how I remember the *Jacaranda*.

First Sighting

On the bridge, Harque sat at the pilot's console and occasionally tapped a key to make course corrections. Chee frolicked behind him in the captain's command chair, swivelling left and right as far as it would go. *Thunk*, an arm of the chair would hit the engineering monitor panel; *thunk*, the other arm would hit the communications board.

Prope clenched her fists tighter with every collision . . . which was no doubt why Chee did it.

Yarrun had already taken his place at the Explorer station, and was programming probe drones for preliminary surveys of the planet surface. This was routine work; he nodded to me as I walked by, then went back to his gauges.

On the view screen, a purple speck had begun to differentiate itself from the background of bluish stars. We were not on a direct course at the moment, so the speck drifted slowly to the left. I grabbed one arm of the command chair and stopped Chee's gyrations long enough to push a button on the chair's control pad. The purple spot blossomed to the size of a baby prune.

"I thought Melaquin was supposed to be Earthlike," Chee said. "Why is it purple?"

"Blueshift from our speed of approach," Prope answered. "I can computer-correct the color if you let me work the controls. . . ."

But Chee had already keyed in the correction, plus an extra level of magnification. He muttered, "She thinks I've never heard of blueshifting. I just forgot, is all. Too long since I've been on a real bridge. . . ."

"Anything special for the probes?" Yarrun asked me for the sake of formality. The rules of rank said he should defer to me, but his programming skills were at least as good as mine, and his planetography intuition was superb. I waved for him to proceed and he turned a knob. "Probes away."

Four projectiles appeared on the screen and sped toward the planet. They looked like ejaculated Sperm, wearing a milky film dragged off the *Jacaranda*'s own envelope. The wispy white coating hung loosely about the probes, held by the faint magnetic fields generated as a side effect of internal electronics; but within a few minutes, those Sperm coverings would lose their grip and fall away into hot little eddies of nonrelativistic spacetime that would take years to normalize. I watched as the Sperm cover slipped off one of the probes, curled, and rolled in on itself; but before the other covers did the same, the computer running the monitor lost its battle to keep the probes visible, and they vanished into darkness.

"Shot our wad, did we?" Chee asked.

Prope winced at the expression.

"Yes, sir," I told Chee. "Now Melaquin knows we're coming."

Sitting on the Edge of Immortality

Time crawled by. The probes would take five or six minutes to reach the planet and assume their initial scan configuration, then there'd be another two minutes before we started receiving data.

One of our instructors at the Academy (Explorer Commander Dendron, afflicted with a progressive muscle disorder that pulled his face taut over his bones like a rubber mask stretched on a cannonball) encouraged us to smoke a pipe of tobacco during this waiting interval. "Nothing like a comfortable pipe," he would say whenever he could manipulate a lecture in that direction. "Calms you, gives you something to do with your hands, and irritates hell out of the Regular Vacuum types. Imbues the upholstery with your presence too—you may go Oh Shit within the hour, but the smell of pipe smoke will stink up everything till the ship gets decommissioned. What other immortality do we have?"

In fact, ECMs were granted another form of immortality besides tobacco fumes: the Memory Wall at the Explorer Academy. The wall recorded the names of all Explorers who went Oh Shit in the course of duty. Perhaps it was significant that Commander Dendron didn't consider our Memory Wall as a true memorial for the Lost. You had to be remembered by "real people"—other Explorers didn't count.

Chee's Pipe

Neither Yarrun nor I had been swayed by Dendron's suggestion; we did not smoke as the probes sped toward McLaquin. Chee, however, chose that moment to pull a briar pipe and leather pouch from an inner pocket of his jacket. As he opened the pouch and pulled out a pinch of dark brown shreds, the rich brandied aroma of tobacco took command of the bridge. I had smelled pipe tobacco before (Dendron's brand if nothing else), and the odor usually had a metallic tang to it . . . like the taste of water that has been stored too long in a steel canteen. Chee's tobacco, however, had a thicker, purer scent; somehow nostalgic, though I couldn't imagine why.

Chee must have noticed me eyeing his tobacco, for he offered the pouch for me to inspect. "It's the real thing, Ramos. Rank hath its privileges."

I took the pouch and inhaled deeply in spite of myself. "What do you mean?" I asked.

"This tobacco was stolen under cover of darkness from Old Earth itself. I organized the raid personally. Five Explorers landed on the island that used to be known as Cuba, primed as much ripe leaf as they could get in fifteen minutes, then scampered back to the ship just before the Spark Lords arrived with weapons blazing."

"You risked Explorer lives for tobacco?"

"Don't squawk," Chee growled. "The High Council reamed me out enough, without you bitching too. Of course, all the council cared about was violating our treaty with the Sparks; they didn't give a flying fart for the Explorers . . . who all got back without a scratch, I might add. The council cursed and screamed, and next thing I knew, they were sending me to Melaquin. I suppose you agree with them."

"Your actions *are* difficult to understand," Yarrun replied. "Tobacco is grown on many Technocracy planets, not to mention the Fringes. It seems rather . . . extravagant to endanger Explorers and the treaty for something so easily available."

"Shows how little you know about tobacco," Chee answered. "The stuff our Technocracy grows is castrated and harmless—no tar, no nicotine, not a single carcinogen or addictive substance in the damned vegetable from flower to root. Sissy weed! On Old Earth, tobacco still has balls. It can kill you . . . *will* kill you if something else doesn't get you first. I like that in a plant."

He produced a match and swept it across the rough metal control pad set into the captain's chair. Prope and Harque drew in their breaths sharply. Ignoring them, Chee sucked on the pipe to pull the match flame onto the tobacco, then took a few experimental puffs. "I hate safe vices," he continued, shaking out the match. "Live your life on a limb, that's what I say."

"Begging the Admiral's pardon," I said, "but from an Explorer's point of view, inhaling weak carcinogens is a pretty candy-assed risk. Ultimately, you die in bed. Sir."

The bridge fell silent except for the soft hum of machinery. Prope's mouth dropped open in shock. Harque had his back to me so I couldn't see the expression on his face, but his hand stopped moving and hovered stunned over the instrument panel. Even Yarrun stared at me in surprise, his hideous face lit from below by the greenish glow of his data screen.

Chee met my gaze without rancor. "The wolf knows something the sheep will never understand. Is that what you're saying, Ramos?"

"The wolf pays for it," I answered.

"A big ante buys into a bigger pot," he said.

"The pot only grows big when there are many losers."

With a small laugh, he patted me on the arm. "Don't you just love arguing in metaphors? Makes you feel profound as a polecat. Even when you don't know what the hell you're talking about." He smiled. "Maybe we'll have this argument again someday."

"Maybe." If he could pretend we'd survive, I could pretend with him.

"Data on Melaquin coming in," Yarrun quietly announced.

Melaquin—The Story from Initial Probes

Melaquin (AOR No. 72061721)
　　Third planet in the Uffree system; one moon
　　Average distance from primary: 1.0 A.U.
　　Gravity: 1.0000 G.
　　Thermal Index: 1.0000 S.
　　Atmosphere: 21% oxygen
　　　　　　　　　78% nitrogen
　　　　　　　　　.9% argon
　　　　　　　　　.03% carbon dioxide
　　　　　　　　　Other trace gases, e.g. methane,
　　　　　　　　　　　ozone, water vapor
　　Day: 24.0000 standard hours

Orbital period: 365.25 days
Axial tilt: 23.5 degrees

Surface: 78% water; four continental land masses; many islands, some approaching continent size; poles ice-capped

Life: Abundant green vegetation in 80% of land areas; abundant carbon-based microorganisms in atmosphere; quantity of methane in atmosphere consistent with large carbon-based animal life; sightings of motion in open plains suggest movement of large animal herds

Sentients: No illuminated cities visible on night side; no industrial pollutants in atmosphere; no unnatural EM transmissions; no visible roads or constructions; no visible dams or canals

Initial Response

A summary of the initial probe data replaced the starscape on the main monitor. "It's rather like Earth, isn't it?" Prope observed. "Isn't that, uhhh, *surprising*?"

"There are two ways to look at it," Yarrun answered. "Given the vastness of the universe, it is highly probable that a close twin of Earth would exist somewhere; therefore, the mere existence of such a planet should not take us aback. On the other hand, the odds of such a twin turning up only a few thousand parsecs from the original planet . . . that is frankly unbelievable."

"Which means?" Chee asked.

"What else?" Yarrun shrugged. "There's something fishy going on."

"I just hope the continents don't look familiar," I muttered.

Conjectures

A. *Prope:* Perhaps we're really looking at Old Earth. Through some unknown phenomenon, we aren't where we think we are in space; or at least we're seeing into a completely different part of space.

   Yarrun: The stars aren't in the right places for the Sol system. And the other planets are all wrong.

   Me: Besides, Earth would show plenty of signs of sentient habitation. Cities, highways, all those nuclear waste dumps . . .

B. *Harque:* Maybe the computer is malfunctioning.

   Chee: [After banging three times on the console with his fist.] Has anything changed?

C. *Prope:* Perhaps this is just an illusion, and some unknown agency is tampering with our very minds.

   Me: So what do we do about it?

   Chee: [Closing eyes and holding fingers to temples.] I disbelieve, I disbelieve, I disbelieve. [Opening eyes again and looking at Harque] Shit.

The Globe

"I think we have enough to construct a map of the day side," Yarrun said. He tapped a few keys and a globe appeared on the screen in front of us: north pole at the top of the view, south pole at the bottom. (By convention, all planets are assumed to rotate west to east; once you determine west and east, north and south fall out automatically.)

On the left of the display, two land masses were emerging from shadow at the terminator. One lay roughly in the northern hemisphere, one in the south. The positions of the continents reminded me of North and South America on Old Earth, but the coastlines were very different. For that, I was grateful.

The daylit part of the north continent formed a breast-shaped bulge jutting eastward into a crystal blue ocean.

That sparkling blueness on the view screen was deceptive—the computer used color to represent water depth, not tranquility. On land, various colors represented types of terrain, splitting continents into patchworks of yellow desert, gray mountains, green forests. Every few seconds, a region of the map shimmered for a moment, as the colors were updated on the basis of more specific data. The effect always made planets look more cheerful than they actually were.

A narrow spine of mountains cupped the lower coast of the northern bulge, extending east into the water to form a tail of rocky islands and rounding northwest into the darkness of the night side. Inside that cup of mountains, the rest of the bulge appeared to be a grassy basin, broken by three linked lakes that emptied into a river flowing northeast.

The south continent had a concave coastline, gouged by a large bay slightly south of center. North of the bay, the land supported a tropical forest; south was a strip of hilly woodland along the ocean, but thinning to desert farther in. The lowest part of the coast offered jagged fjords, zigzagging down to the whiteness of polar snow.

"Designating those continents the western hemisphere," Yarrun announced formally.

The eastern hemisphere had two continents too. Most of the northern continent had disappeared into the night side. The remainder was an egg-shaped protrusion narrowing to a long peninsular arm that reached almost all the way down to the southern continent. The peninsula had once been mountainous, but the mountains were old and worn with erosion. The range continued back into the mainland of the continent, dividing it into plains to the south and forest to the north.

The southern continent lay more to the west, and most was still in daylight. The land was shaped like a Y lying on its side, two arms pointing west and the tail pointing east. Between the arms clustered an archipelago of hundreds of hilly islands, no more than a few square klicks each. The northwest arm of the Y held a broad patch of

desert, but the rest of the continent was a combination of
forest and meadow.

"What do you think?" Chee asked.

I pointed to the lakes on the northern continent, western
hemisphere. "What's the weather like here?"

Yarrun turned a dial. Cloud patterns became visible over
various regions of land and sea, but the sky over the lakes
was clear. "Temperate mid-autumn," Yarrun said. "The
temperature is only about ten degrees Celsius at the moment, but it's just an hour after sunrise. It could go up to
twenty degrees by the middle of the afternoon."

"Shirtsleeve weather," Chee grinned and Yarrun nodded.

"Okay," I decided. "Concentrate the probes there. We'll
see what looks good."

"Keep the probes in high atmosphere?" Yarrun asked.

"No," I answered, "send them in as low as you want.
If the place has natives, we'll give them a thrill."

Fields and Forests

In a few minutes, the lake district bloomed on the screen,
marked with fifteen-meter contour lines. Moderately tall
bluffs rose at several points around the lakes, but most of
the shore was sandy beach. Inland, the countryside con
sisted of rolling hills with plenty of streams, a few marshes,
clots of forest here and there, and wide stretches of grassy
meadow.

"Looks pleasant enough," Prope said.

"That's what you think," I told her.

"What's wrong?"

"There are too few trees," Yarrun answered for me,
scanning some figures thrown up by the computer. "All
those open fields . . . with that kind of soil and climate, you
expect forests to encroach on fields and eventually cover
them. On a truly Earthlike planet, there'd be trees everywhere unless. . . ." He turned a few dials and checked a

readout. "Well, the computer gives seventy percent chance there was a forest fire south of the eastern lake, between ten and thirty years ago . . . but the fire only took out a few dozen hectares. Not nearly enough to explain the discrepancy. I suppose Melaquin might have evolved a particularly aggressive form of grass that doesn't need much light—one that encroaches on trees, starving out their roots. . . ."

"Yarrun is grasping at straws," I told Chee. "The truth is, this terrain profile looks more like farmland than virgin wilderness. Not meadows, but cleared fields."

"Any sign of actual cultivation?" Chee asked.

"No," Yarrun replied, "but the probes are spreading their attention over a large area. They could easily miss cultivation on the scale of garden plots. Or larger fields that have lain fallow longer than five or ten years."

"Sentients!" Prope said in a hushed tone intended to be dramatic. She had assumed yet another pose, staring at the monitor through narrowed eyes, her head lifted to show the clean white edge of her jaw. "Do you suppose this could be a world of sentients, once great, now fallen? Yet even though the planet lies barren, *something* has been left behind. Something that has killed before and will kill again. . . ."

"Shit," muttered Chee. "I *told* the council we shouldn't let Vacuum officers take Pulp Literature as an elective."

The Lake

"Let's do a full workup on this lake," I said, tapping the one lowest on the view screen.

"Why?" Chee asked.

"It's closest to the equator. Winter's coming to the whole lake district, and I'd prefer not to freeze my tail off if we get stranded down there."

"Explorer Ramos grew up in an unduly warm climate," Yarrun explained to the admiral. "She is rather delicate when it comes to chills."

I did not rise to the bait. Yarrun's own home colony was snowed in more than half of each year, and his people had developed an unhealthy reverence for subzero temperatures. They ascribed all manner of beneficial properties to freezing cold: it built stamina, it built strength, it built moral fiber. As far as I could tell, all it built was an irrational disdain for those of us who had the sense to be born in environments free of frostbite.

"Yarrun," I said, "check out the south lake. The southern shore."

He rubbed a dial. Far below us, one of the four probes sacrificed almost all its airspeed as it arrowed into the water. The splash was big enough for the other three probes to register: a pimple of red marked the splash point on the viewmap, until the computer factored it out.

"The water is fresh," Yarrun reported as the sunken probe began to return data. "The usual natural trace elements; no signs of industrial pollution. Microorganism count measures a bit low."

"Does that mean anything?" Prope asked.

"Probably not," I told the captain. "Lots of simple factors could decrease the micro count in a given area—anything from a strong current, to a recent rain, to a nearby school of filter-feeders."

"Still . . . it seems a little *sinister*, don't you think?"

I ignored her.

The Bluffs

"Let's concentrate on these bluffs," I said, pointing to a line of elevation on the south side of our chosen lake.

"Why there?" asked Chee as Yarrun twisted dials to send the three remaining probes on a close flyby.

I thumbed a dial myself to magnify that area of the map. "Along the top, we have open fields . . . good visibility. If we're in for a long stay, we can get fresh water from the lake, but in the short term, we'll be far enough away that we don't have to deal with the complexities of shoreline ecologies.''

"What if something unspeakable charges the party and knocks you off the cliff?" Prope asked.

"If we see something unspeakable, I for one will *jump* off the cliff," I answered. "Our tightsuits will protect us from the brunt of the impact, and the long leap is a nice fast escape route."

Prope's expression showed what she thought of people who would jump off a cliff rather than face something unspeakable; but she held her tongue.

Pictures

"Pictures," Yarrun said; and the map on the screen shimmered to show a sunny meadow dotted with yellow wildflowers. Off to one side stood a deciduous tree, something like a maple; a bird flitted into the leaves, too fast to see clearly, but it had two wings, a small head, and a black or dark brown body. A few dozen meters behind the tree, the land dropped off at the edge of the bluffs, down to the sparkling blue lake.

The view slowly shifted as the transmitting probe moved along. We saw a gray rock outcrop, more deciduous trees, a thicket of brambles. Something darted into the brambles, and my mind said "rabbit" . . . but an Explorer had to ignore such snap judgments. The human brain is still hopelessly tied to Old Earth; it always interprets a fleeting image as something terrestrial, no matter how alien the creature might really look.

"Try it ten kilometers to the east," I said. Yarrun played with dials.

Prope sneered. "You think the meadow looks too dangerous?" she asked.

I tapped the screen. "Didn't you see that animal run into the briar patch?"

"You're afraid of a little beast like that?"

"I'm *wary* of a little beast like that," I told her. "I'm afraid of whatever the little beast was running from."

Our Choice

The picture dissolved into a view from another probe, this one hovering over the lake and looking shoreward to the bluffs. The cliffside was tangled with weeds and scrubby bushes. Here and there, swaths of bare sandy soil interrupted the undergrowth—gullies probably washed out by spring runoff. Erosion was slowly undercutting the top edge of the ridge; at one point, the rim had collapsed in an earth slide that dragged down a great strip of brush.

The probe moved toward the land, and slowly rose to give us a view of the heights: another flowered meadow, with a few lichen-covered outcrops of rock. A short distance inland, a deep ravine ran parallel to the bluffs—probably the bed of a stream on its way to the lake. Trees grew up the sides of the ravine, but none were visible on the flat land.

"This an example of what we were talking about," I said, pointing at the screen. "If you have trees growing in the ravine, you should have trees growing in the field—it has to be easier for them to root on level ground than on a slope. But it looks like the flat has been cleared."

"Is that enough to scare you off again?" Prope asked.

"Not in the least," I answered, working to keep my temper. "Cleared terrain is good for a Landing. You're less likely to hit something on the Drop, and you have an unobstructed view of things coming to eat you." I turned to Yarrun. "What about it?"

Instead of answering, he fiddled with dials, rotating the screen's view through a slow 360 degrees. The meadow seemed very peaceful . . . no motion but the gentle waving of grass in the wind. "The motion sensors are picking up a lot of animal life," he reported, "but nothing big. Mostly on the order of insects, with the occasional field mouse.

Which is to say, something warm-blooded the size of a field mouse.''

It was easy to forget this wasn't some tame terraformed world, stocked with all the species we knew, and loved, and could kill if necessary.

"Any thoughts?" I asked the room at large. Prope looked as if she wanted to say something scathing, but knew it would only delay things. "Okay," I told Yarrun. "Have the probe drop a Sperm anchor. Immortality awaits."

Part V
LANDING

Our Robing Chambers

The *Jacaranda* had four robing chambers for Explorers. This was a matter of prestige. A frigate was equipped with only two robing chambers; a light cruiser had to surpass a frigate in all possible ways, so it had three chambers; and a heavy cruiser like the *Jacaranda* was obliged to be better still, so it had four.

All three types of ship carried only two Explorers. There was no prestige in having extra Explorers.

Suiting Up

Each of us suited up alone—Yarrun and I in our usual places, Chee in one of the dusty surplus chambers.

Suiting up was a simple procedure: I stood passively, wearing nothing but a light chemise, while robot arms did all the work. Tightsuit fabric was extremely stiff and difficult to handle. Every six months, I had to go through an emergency drill where I wrestled in and out of a suit without robot help, and it always left my hands aching with exertion.

As the suit was being sealed around me, Chee shouted through the wall, " 'And from the tents, the armorers, ac-

81

complishing the knights, with busy hammers closing rivets up, give dreadful note of preparation.' What's that from, Ramos?''

"Shakespeare . . . *Henry V*," I replied, glad that I happened to remember; but I hoped Chee wouldn't quote from *Timon of Athens*. I had skipped *Timon* in the Academy Shakespeare course; Jelca had actually said yes to going on a date, and it put me in such a dither, I couldn't concentrate for three days.

The tightsuit continued to assemble around me. As it came together, robot eyes scanned every joint and seam, checking for flaws. There were eight such eyes, each as wide as my thumb, each on the end of a metal tentacle that curled through the air with the nonchalance of a cat's tail. Yarrun had given each eye a name: Gretchen, Robster, Clinky, Fang . . . I forget the rest. He swore they had different personalities, but I think he was putting me on.

The eyes swirled about on one last inspection—peering into my suit's crotch, armpits, the ring around my neck that my mother always claimed was dirty—then the tentacles retracted into the walls and the sterilization process began. I saw none of it; the visor in my helmet opaqued in response to the opening salvo of microwaves. However, I knew I was being bombarded by heat, UV, hard gamma, and several more exotic forms of energy the League of Peoples contended were necessary to cleanse all possible contaminants from the skin of my suit.

We followed this procedure meticulously whenever landing on unexplored planets—especially ones where there might be intelligent beings. It was a dangerous non-sentient act to introduce foreign microorganisms onto someone else's planet.

The sterilization bombardment was another reason why we always let the robots seal us into our tightsuits. If you touched the exterior of a suit with your bare hands, the resulting fingerprints turned a burnt-looking brown under the onslaught of the sterilization energy. You ended up looking like some smear-handed child had wiped chocolate on your crisp white outfit.

Fellow Explorers didn't tease you about that, but the Vacuum personnel always snickered.

Limbo

When the sterilization was complete, a bell chimed and a blue sign flashed PLEASE EXERCISE. For five minutes, we were supposed to get used to moving in the suit, by stretching, picking up small objects, doing deep knee bends, and so on. The Admiralty called this the "Limbering-Up Period." Explorers shortened the name to "Limbo."

It was a point of pride that Explorers never limbered up as specified. The prescribed exercises were invented by an Admiralty consultant who tried on a tightsuit and found (to her surprise) she couldn't get the hang of it right away. Never mind that Explorers spent much of their four years at the Academy lumbering around in tightsuits. Never mind that by the time we graduated, we felt more at home in a suit than in street clothes. A consultant came in for a day and found she was clumsy; therefore, the Admiralty immediately agreed that her ideas about tightsuits should be come official Fleet policy.

The *de facto* Fleet policy was more mundane: instead of exercising, Explorers used their five minutes of Limbo to empty their bladders. Tightsuits had extensive facilities for handling waste, recycling the liquids into coolant water and compressing solids into cubes that could later fertilize mushrooms; but actually using these facilities required painstaking attention to the alignment of valves, tubes, and bodily orifices. It was better to relieve yourself in the quiet safety of the ship than to try it under more stressful conditions planet-down.

Besides, thinking about the mechanics of pissing took your mind off the Landing. And if you let yourself get sloppy, your suit would stink of urine for the whole mission. An Explorer could pay a severe penalty for inattention; it didn't hurt to have that kind of reminder in your nostrils for a few hours.

One Minute Warning

The PLEASE EXERCISE light went off. That meant we had one minute left. One more minute of Limbo.

During this minute, some Explorers prayed. Some sang. Some discussed final details of the Landing over their radios. Some talked to themselves about the great or mundane regrets of their lives.

Some screamed.

I don't know what Yarrun did. He never told me. I never asked.

If he had asked me the same question, I couldn't have told him what I did. I just waited. I just waited the full minute.

The Admiral's Worth

But this time, I somehow couldn't bring myself to wait in silence. Instead, I tapped a button on my throat to turn my transceiver implant to "local."

"Admiral," I said.

"Hey! What?"

"Admiral, tell me something you've done that you're proud of."

"Christ, Ramos, you should know better than to distract a man at a time like this."

"Tell me something you're proud of. I want to know what you've done with your life. I'm going to die for you; I want to know who you are. If there were a point to any of this, would you be worth dying for?"

Chee didn't answer immediately. I could hear Yarrun's breathing over the headset in my helmet. It was a little like snoring; his lip fluttered slightly when he inhaled.

I wondered why Yarrun had his transceiver turned on. Had he intended to say something too? And would he have spoken to me or to Chee?

Something to be Proud Of

"The thing I'm proudest of," Chee said at last, "is my spy network."

"Spy network?" I repeated. "What's the point? The League of Peoples enforces peace throughout the galaxy. We have no wars. We have no enemies."

"We have incompetents, Ramos," the Admiral answered. "On every planet, colony, and Fringe World, the civil administration suffers the same malaise as the Outward Fleet: the people who rise to positions of leadership are the Propes and the Harques. Administrators like Prope funnel citizens' money into glamorous projects like erecting public buildings so big they change the course of continental drift . . . and no one remembers to order toilet paper. Or food. Or air. Administrators like Harque spend their time in petty political maneuvering, snubbing rivals, acquiring perks, and generally feathering their own nests . . . but the results are the same. No toilet paper. No air. While all the tinpot tyrants backstab each other for an office with its own pressure pot, no one minds the store. Supply schedules get botched; atmosphere plants break down; water purification levels slide into the red zone.

"So on every world of the Technocracy, I put a spy. A retired Explorer, actually. Explorers are the last bastion of competence in our civilization, Ramos, and I don't mind saying it. They're the precious few of our citizens who aren't *comfortable*—the only ones in the whole Technocracy who work completely without safety nets. Everyone else these days has the luxury of indulging in melodrama: of pretending that they're the stars in some story where there are good guys and bad guys, winners and losers.

Everyone else can pretend it's a game. The streets are safe and the government is forbidden to let people starve, so whatever non-Explorers do isn't survival. . . . At heart, it's just amusement. Explorers are the only ones who know deep down that death isn't kept at bay by luck or posturing, but by constant attention to necessary details.

"Therefore, my Explorers finked to me when the tap water turned brown, and when the air turned to smog, and when there weren't enough oranges on the shelves to prevent scurvy. Those warnings gave the Admiralty a fighting chance to do something about the situation . . . because you know what the civilian authorities are like on most planets. Power-hungry vermin whose only talent is winning elections, not making good decisions. When something goes wrong, you can be damned sure those administrators would rather see their whole worlds starve than report that they'd personally fucked up."

"You talk about your spies in the past tense," Yarrun observed.

"*I'm* past tense now," Chee answered. "When I'm gone, who'll take over for me? A Prope? A Harque? I'm going to god-be-damned Melaquin because I finally ruffled one too many important feathers. The High Council will replace me with some VIP's unemployable nephew . . . and a lot of planets will start drowning in their own sewage."

Neither Yarrun nor I spoke. Explorers never asked, "What happens next?" The question was always, "What do we do now?"

The door to the transport bay slid open.

Our time in Limbo was over.

Bold Grace

Walking comfortably in a tightsuit made a person look bowlegged—the fabric was thickened on the inside of each thigh so that one leg rubbing against the other wouldn't encourage the material to fray.

Once we were planet-down, it didn't matter what we looked like; but our walk along Sterile Corr-1 was different. The corridor led from our robing chambers to the transport bay, and Vacuum personnel watched us on monitors, every step of the way. Each time I walked that path, I felt the eyes following me. For personal vanity and for the pride of the Explorer Corps, I forced myself to stride along with bold grace.

Learning to walk so cleanly had taken three months of hard practice at the Academy. Resisting the force of the fabric required strength in thigh muscles which were rarely used for other purposes. (Rarely used by me, at any rate.)

I let myself stride into the corridor with consummate poise. Yarrun stepped out of his own chamber and matched my stride. I hoped Prope and Harque were watching... even though I didn't give a damn about either of them.

Chee, the Explorer

A moment later, Chee emerged from Chamber C. He moved with slow, straight-legged dignity. His suit showed no chocolate-colored fingerprints.

"So, Ramos," he said, "do I look like an Explorer?"

"Yes, sir."

"Well, I don't smell like one!" he snapped. "When you radioed me without warning, I fumbled my damned tube and pissed myself. Let's get down to the damned planet so I can take this helmet off."

Three abreast, we strode into the transport bay. The door closed behind us, and a metal safety hatch slid up in front of it.

With a tap, I switched my throat radio to full transmit. "Ramos to *Jacaranda*," I said. "Is the tail anchored?"

"Affirmative, Explorer." The voice coming over my headset was Harque's perpetual smirk. "Pressurizing now."

The ship's Sperm-tail was now in position at our chosen

Landing site, establishing a tube of hyperdimensional space from here to there. In effect, here *was* there; no physical space separated us from the planet's surface. The *Jacaranda* would increase air pressure in the transport bay, just enough to exceed the pressure at the planet's surface. Then, when the Bay Mouth opened, we would be squirted forward, down the tube to the planet, making the passage in a real-space time of zero seconds.

The subjective time would not be zero seconds. Human brains are perfectly conscious of the time they spend in hyperspace, even if the outside world perceives the transit as instantaneous.

Harque's voice sounded again in my headset: "Ejection in ten seconds."

I jerked my head around to glare up at the mezzanine, where Harque loomed behind the control console. He was supposed to wait for my signal before starting our ejection countdown. Insulting to the last, the petty bastard.

Yarrun nudged my elbow, and shook his head.

Fuming, I turned back to face the huge aperture in front of us: the Aft Entry Mouth, which was irised tightly closed for the moment. From this vantage point, the Mouth seemed immense—four storeys high and ready to eat us. Yarrun, Chee, and I, stood tall, shoulder to shoulder . . . and that mouth could swallow all three of us in a single gulp.

I closed my eyes. I had thought that perhaps this time, this last time, I would keep my eyes open. But I didn't.

"Ejection," Harque said.

Down

Down was the pull of ship's gravity beneath my feet.
There was a sharp hiss of sound as the Mouth opened.

Down was behind me. Down was back where my stomach still wanted to be. I flew forward like a straw in a hurricane.
The world squeezed as I plunged down the gullet of the

Worm, the Sperm. The squeezing was gentle, but unstoppable. My body compressed obligingly.

Outside the Sperm, the compression would have killed me: bones would snap and poke splinters through internal organs; eyes would burst; muscles would be kneaded to thread. Inside, however, the laws of physics were daintily overruled. I was a thing infinitely malleable.

Down was inside me, a point halfway between navel and groin. The Chinese call that point the *dantien*, the center of the soul. I fell toward my center like rain.

The center of my soul. The center of my soul. If I conceived a child, this was where it would grow. When I died, this was where I would run.

Down was everywhere around me. I flew outward. I exploded into my body. My skin snapped taut like a sail catching a gust of wind. I felt blood surging through my brain.

The world burned red outside my closed eyelids.

Down was the vector of my descent. My eyes flickered open.

I rolled with the impact of my landing. Grass lashed wet streaks across my faceplate. In that moment, I remembered how grass smelled on summer afternoons, when I was young and would live forever.

But I didn't smell the grass; I smelled only my own sweat. My tightsuit and I were a closed system.

Breathing the odors of my body, I stood up.

Down was the pull of gravity beneath my feet.

Melaquin.

Melaquin Without Stories

Overhead, a cloudless blue sky surrounded a yellow sun. Around me, a grassy field danced with wildflowers.

Black-eyed Susans. Daisies. He loves me, he loves me not.

A few paces to my left, Yarrun scrambled to his feet. Green grass stains were streaked across the white of his suit. He shrugged off his backpack and began to rummage through it.

I powered my throat transceiver to maximum strength. "*Jacaranda*, do you read?"

"Loud and clear, Explorer," Harque answered, with just the faintest tone of insolence.

"Christ, I love that ride!" Chee's voice said over the com-set.

I looked around. A few meters away, Chee lay spreadeagled face-down in the grass. He made no effort to get up, but his feet kicked enthusiastically like a gleeful child. Good—no damage to his spinal cord. "*Jacaranda*," I said over the radio, "the Drop was successful. Proceed to record."

"Roger. Recording."

Idly, I wondered if Harque was lying; but I had stopped caring. I would do my job, I would make my reports, and I would be professional to the very end.

Formally, I announced, "Explorer First Class Festina Ramos, *TSS Jacaranda*, reporting initial survey of Melaquin, AOR. 72061721, Inter-date 2452/9/23. Other party members: Explorer Second Class Yarrun Derigha and Admiral Chee. Any comments for the record, Admiral?"

"The High Council of Admirals can kiss my—"

"Thank you, Admiral. On a more immediate note, Melaquin appears to be an extremely Earthlike planet with local weather and flora similar to the temperate zone of New Earth . . . the Lake District of Novatario, I'd say. Thick grass growing calf-to knee-height. Wildflowers highly reminiscent of daisies and black-eyed Susans. About a hundred meters away, this meadow falls off into a ravine with deciduous trees on its side. And in the opposite direction, we have bluffs descending to a sizable freshwater lake.

"There is a good deal of insect activity apparent here: I can see several on the wildflowers around me. They are highly reminiscent of terrestrial bees.'' In fact, they were exactly like terrestrial bees, big fuzzy bumblebees in yellow and black . . . the kind we all ran from as children, even though adults told us not to make sudden moves. ''I can also see three butterflies not too far away. Two are a green-ish-white, wingspan about three centimeters; the other is highly reminiscent of a Monarch butterfly.''

It *was* a Monarch butterfly. Orange and black, landing on a milkweed plant whose pods spilled creamy floating seeds.

''In short,'' I said aloud, ''one's immediate impression of local flora and fauna is that they are visual duplicates of Earth species. Do you concur, Admiral Chee?''

''The High Council commits unnatural acts with poodles.''

''Duly noted, Admiral. Thank you.''

The Bumbler

''Bumbler operational,'' Yarrun said with exaggerated diction. (He was always self-conscious about having his voice recorded. A typical exploration report from the two of us consisted of a steady stream of blather from me, with infrequent one- or two-word interjections from Yarrun.)

The Bumbler—officially our ''Portable Wide Spectrum Amplification and Analysis Datascope'' but only called that by quartermasters—was a hand-held scanning device about the size and shape of a flat-topped coffee pot. It served two functions:

A. Its screen could be tuned to display any range of the electromagnetic spectrum in a visible form . . . handy if you wanted to check the neighborhood for the IR glow of warm-blooded fauna, or take an X-ray shot of some animal specimen's skeleton.

B. The machine was constantly analyzing incoming data for hints suggesting the approach of hostile lifeforms.

The Bumbler broadcast an alarm if it detected anything moving toward us. It had saved my life at least twice, and I was grateful; I was not, however, overwhelmed with the Bumbler's acumen. It was a kindly little machine that meant well in its bumbling way, but it was not as bright as one might hope—it took so long to do a risk analysis that the alarm sometimes went off *after* the first attack.

Surveying

"Infrared scanning," Yarrun said, turning a careful circle with the Bumbler in front of him. "Cat-sized creature," he said, suddenly pointing off to my right; but almost immediately, he lowered his hand and muttered, "Went down a hole."

"Another rabbit?" Chee asked. He was sitting up now, working at the release catches of his helmet.

Yarrun didn't answer. He completed his sweep, then reported, "Negative warm-bloods now."

"Then we'll begin standard sampling," I told him. I reached into my own backpack. On top of everything else lay my stunner, and I slid it into my hip holster. In entertainment bubbles, donning a weapon is always a portentous affair; but that's because in entertainment bubbles, weapons have a more tangible chance of stopping whatever is trying to kill you. In my case, I was only moving the stunner out of my backpack because it lay in the way of the plastic bags we used to hold samples.

Yarrun traditionally took plant samples while I dug up packets of soil. I wasn't particularly interested in dirt, but I had sat through four soil analysis electives at the Academy because geology was one of Jelca's majors.

My own major was zoology. It meant that whenever we shot an animal, Yarrun made me decide what to do with the carcass.

"Ahhhh!" Chee sighed, inhaling deeply as he removed

his helmet. The sight of him, naked to the planet's microbes, filled me with envy and anger . . . like the time when I was a teenager, and watched girls with normal faces go skinny-dipping as if it were the height of erotic sophistication. I knew it wasn't, and I knew it was.

"It smells wonderful out here!" Chee cried in delight.

"Could you please describe the smell, sir?"

"It smells real. Grass. Air that hasn't been through anyone else's lungs. Glorious."

"And you feel well?"

"Better than I have in months." He arched his back in a happy stretch. "Forget the damned samples, Ramos. Let's go for a walk."

"Begging the admiral's pardon," I replied, "but we are conducting a survey mission here."

"You're conducting an execution, Ramos. The survey is nothing but horseshit."

"Any information we gather may assist other parties who land here," I insisted. "No Explorer is an island."

"Don't give me that John Donne crap," Chee grumbled. "Do you know what he said about Shakespeare?" Turning his back on me, the admiral headed in the direction of the lake, taking ostentatiously deep breaths.

"Admiral," I called out, "please don't wander off. You don't understand how risky—"

"I understand fine! I'm just going to look at the water."

I considered tackling him. Or shooting him. But the edge of the bluffs really wasn't far for him to wander. If our goal was to use him as bait for whatever danger lurked on Melaquin, I had to give him his lead.

It took real effort to watch him walk away from me. Explorers don't let go easily.

The Worm

The first soil sample I took contained an earthworm. Technically speaking, I suppose it was a Melaquinworm, but it looked like an earthworm to me: brown, annelid, roughly ten centimeters long, with the familiar thick clitellum band partway along its body.

"Greetings," I said to it, feeling ridiculous. "I am a sentient citizen of the League of Peoples. I beg your Hospitality."

"Find something?" Yarrun called.

"A worm," I told him.

"You're talking to a worm?" Chee cackled over the com-set.

"I am talking to an alien lifeform that may prove to be sentient. Don't be so narrow-minded!"

"I bet it's just a worm."

Almost certainly, Chee was right. On the other hand, you never know when you might be scoring goodwill points with the League. They supposedly keep constant watch on all human activities.

I let the worm crawl for a moment, then nudged a stone into its path. It bumped its nose into the stone and seemed confused.

Proof enough for me. It was stupid; it was just a worm.

I shot it with my stunner and put it in a plastic bag.

The Bird

As Chee walked toward the cliff, a bird suddenly dashed out of the grass near his feet with a great panicked chirping. Yarrun and I both drew stunners and aimed. But the bird simply scuttled several meters away and made no gestures we could interpret as a threat.

In fact, it ran clumsily, one wing drooping.

"I didn't touch it!" Chee said with aggrieved innocence.

"I'm sure you didn't," I told him. "Stay where you are, please."

Carefully, I walked toward Chee. The bird flopped about, squawking loudly.

"What's wrong with it?" Chee asks.

"It's a . . . it displays the appearance and behavior of a mother killdeer. She's pretending she has a broken wing. She wants us to chase her rather than snoop around her territory." I searched the grass near Chee's feet. Autumn seemed late in the year for what I expected to find, but every species has individuals who are out of step with the times.

Two paces away, I found the nest the killdeer was protecting. There were three eggs in the nest, their shells dirty white with brown speckles.

Three beautiful eggs.

Eggs

I took the Bumbler from Yarrun and crouched beside the nest. Melaquin's atmosphere blocked most of the X-rays emitted by the local sun, Uffree; but the Bumbler was extremely good at amplifying what little there was.

Inside each egg was a tiny bird. (Their mother squawked frantically at me from a distance.) The Bumbler showed only their skeletons, curled into positions that seemed impossibly cramped. The little birds filled the eggs completely; within hours, they would hatch.

"Greetings," I whispered softly to them. "I am a sentient citizen of the League of Peoples. I beg your Hospitality."

The mother squawked in anguish, dashing back and forth with her feigned broken wing.

Gone

"Where's Chee?" Yarrun asked suddenly.

My head snapped up. Yarrun and I were alone in the meadow.

"Admiral Chee, come in, admiral," I called over the radio, keeping my voice calm.

No response.

"Maybe he fell off the bluffs," Yarrun suggested.

"You check." And while Yarrun hurried toward the edge of the bluffs, I switched the Bumbler to IR, and did a fast circle. Nothing showed up anywhere near Chee's size. He wasn't hiding in the grass. "Admiral Chee, please respond. Admiral Ch—"

A force closed on my windpipe like a strangling hand. I stopped talking mid-syllable. I could not breathe, I could not speak.

Oh shit.

Oh Shit

My throat transceiver. Was that it? Was that all?

Oh shit.

It was something in my throat implant. It was killing me. How stupid. How mindlessly stupid. Shit.

No monsters. No sentients. No deadly physical phenomena. Just crude treachery.

And I was fool enough to feel disappointed. I had a little Prope inside me who thought death should come glamorously. How juvenile. How stupid.

Shit.

Where had Chee gone? Over the bluffs? Did it matter?

A few paces in front of me, Yarrun was ripping off his helmet. He hadn't figured it out yet; he must have thought his suit had a malfunction.

I turned the Bumbler on him, its sensors still keyed to read X-rays. Yes, his transceiver had twisted itself around his windpipe. And now he understood—he turned to me with a look of bitter sorrow.

Shit.

They must have built the implants to kill us. Did the choking mechanism activate in response to some natural transmission generated on planet? Or did someone somewhere turn a dial? Had Harque pushed some button, just following orders? Did he know what he'd done?

Shit.

Yarrun's hands reached for his throat. I wondered if he would try to pull off the transceiver assembly. No good, I could see that on the X-rays—the mechanism was wrapped so tightly in place, he'd just rip out his larynx.

Shit. Oh shit. Yarrun was tapping out SOS in Morse code. Tapping on the transceiver itself. Gazing hopefully at the sky. And he couldn't know if the transceiver was still broadcasting, and he couldn't know if any of those goddamned Vacuum assholes on the bridge had even *heard* of Morse code, and he was still trying the only thing he could think of to save our lives.

Shit.

I blasted him with my stunner and he went down in a spiraling slump, as if he was turning to look at me one last time.

Forget it, forget it. I dropped to my knees beside him, upturning my whole backpack in search of the scalpel from the medical kit.

Maybe I could stay conscious long enough to perform an emergency tracheotomy. Cut through Yarrun's throat into his windpipe, below the point where the transceiver was strangling him. Open a new breathing passage.

I had done a tracheotomy once before. At the Academy. On a cadaver. I couldn't remember what grade I'd received.

The first cut had to be vertical—less chance of hitting a major vein or artery. Blood spurted as I worked the knife, but after that it slowed. I hoped that was a good sign.

My vision was clouding. Didn't matter. If I screwed this up, what was the difference?

No. There was a difference.

The medical kit contained no tracheotomy tube, but it did have an esophageal airway. The airway was so wide. Who had the nerve to cut a hole that big in someone's throat?

I did. I had the nerve.

My head was spinning. My eyes wouldn't focus. I pulled

what I hoped was an ampoule of blood coagulant from the medical kit and sprayed it around the incision. I didn't know if I'd killed my friend. I'd die without knowing.

I thought, *Yarrun, don't hate me. I don't want to be hated.*

Then I thought, *Shit, here I go.*

Oh Shit.

Part VI
AWAKENING

Up

Up. Fight.
Fight. Harder.
Up. Up.
Light.
Here.

Ow. Shit

My head was pounding.
My throat felt raw and shredded.
Swallowing was like being clawed by some angry animal. As soon as I swallowed, I felt the urge to swallow again; surely, it couldn't hurt as much as the last time.
But it could.
Ow. Shit.
I was alive.

Alive

I was sprawled facedown, still in my tightsuit. The suit stank of urine and worse, but the blue OK light still glowed

on the inside of my visor: no breach in the suit's skin, and
at least an hour of canned air left. For what it was worth,
the suit's monitors considered me in perfect health.

Monitors are stupid. I tried swallowing again, and regretted it.

Sloshing inside the suit, I pushed myself up to my hands
and knees. My body cast an elongated shadow across the
grass of the field; sunset was coming. We had landed an
hour or two after sunrise and the season was early fall, so
I'd been unconscious nine or ten hours.

And nothing had eaten me all that time. What a wimp-
ass planet.

A moment later, a stab of memory jolted me. In a panic,
I scrambled to my feet and looked left, right, all around.

Yarrun was gone.

Searching

The Bumbler and the medical kit still lay where I'd
dropped them. The scalpel . . . the empty drug ampoule . . .
even the esophageal airway I thought I had inserted into
Yarrun's throat . . . everything was there except Yarrun.
Flecks of dried blood dotted the grass where he had lain,
but he was nowhere to be seen.

From reflex, I tapped my throat transceiver and called,
"Yarrun! Yarrun!"

My words stayed muffled in my suit. Usually, I heard
some trickle of feedback on my audio receiver, a tinny echo
of my broadcast voice. This time, there was no such echo.

Radio silence. No-comm. My transmitter had gone Oh
Shit.

Perhaps that was why I was still alive: the effort of strangling me had been too much for my throat implant. It had
blown its circuits before finishing the job. Equipment burn-
outs were not a novelty in the Outward Fleet; the Admiralty
tendered supply contracts to the lowest bidder.

That still didn't explain Yarrun's absence. If the tracheotomy worked, he might have woken before me. Had he pulled out the airway, then wandered off? He might have done so if he was dazed. With his helmet off, he'd been exposed to local air for hours—plenty of time to get infected by an alien microbe and go delirious.

Damn. How long would he stagger about before he fell off the cliffs into the lake?

Fighting the urge to race forward, I picked up the Bumbler and walked slowly to the edge of the bluffs. Rushing wouldn't help Yarrun, especially if I tripped over the edge myself.

The gathering shadows of sunset didn't make it easy to scan the scrub brush between me and the lake. However, the Bumbler showed nothing as warm as a human body on the cliffside or the shore below.

I refused to consider the possibility that Yarrun's body was no longer warm.

Carefully, I tracked along the bluffs a hundred meters in both directions. The Bumbler showed no significant heat signatures. Added to that, the face of the bluffs was sandy loam, and reasonably moist; if Yarrun fell over the edge, he would have gouged deep scuffs in the dirt on his way down.

The soil showed no marks of any kind. Nothing human-sized had tumbled over since the last rain.

Poison Ivy

I could have continued searching along the bluffs; however, there was still the ravine on the opposite side of the meadow and I wanted to check it before daylight faded. Searching the ravine would not be easy—the trees were losing their leaves with autumn, leaving a layer of red and gold thick underfoot. I hoped the Bumbler was sensitive enough to discern Yarrun's body heat if he lay under a day's worth of fallen leaves.

The weakening rays of sunlight didn't penetrate much

distance into the woods. From the treeline, I could make out a spindly creek running along the bottom of the ravine, but beyond that was only shadow. The Bumbler saw farther, but not well; its effective range was a hundred meters, and the ravine was wider than that. For best coverage, I would have to trek to the bottom and follow the creek, scanning both sides as I walked.

Grimly, I started down. The undergrowth was ankle-height and patchy—low-light greenery that could survive in the shadow of the trees. Given the Earthlike look of the vegetation, maybe the plants brushing my legs were poison ivy; I couldn't tell. With all my Explorer training, I had never learned what temperate-zone poison ivy looked like— the Academy could not imagine I would ever face genuine Earth flora.

Not that I should fall into the trap of believing this world was terrestrial. The trees looked like maples, the worms looked like worms, the insects looked like bees and butterflies, but none of that meant anything.

This was an alien world. A hostile alien world.

IR Anomaly

I reached the creek and stopped by the shore, briefly checking the water for dangerous lifeforms. There were only a few small fish, barely the length of my thumb and as slim as whispers; they darted away when the reflection of my tightsuit fell across the surface. I watched them go, then lifted the Bumbler, turning a slow circle in search of heat traces.

Halfway around, I found exactly what I wanted: a human-sized blob of bright glowing warmth. The figure was crouched and working at something low to the ground—I didn't understand what he could be doing, but I was so relieved to see he was moving, I called, "Yarrun! Yarrun!"

On the Bumbler's screen, the figure jerked its head

around. Then it put on a spurt of effort shoving at something, pushing, heaving.

Why?

Suddenly fearful, I slung the Bumbler under my arm and set off at the fastest trot I could manage, the confinement of my tightsuit slowing me down . . . like the nightmare where you can't run fast enough to outrace the monster. Fallen leaves thrashed with the sound of surf as I barged through them. Shadows clustered thick under the trees, but the pale white of a tightsuit soon became visible in the twilight in front of me.

A white tightsuit. A head of white hair.

Admiral Chee stood and came quickly toward me. His face was red with exertion. He had the overly bold look of someone blocking something with his body.

"Ramos," he said, with forced heartiness. "Glad to see you're finally awake—"

I pushed past him without a word. He tried to grab my arm, but was neither fast enough nor strong enough to hold me.

A few paces farther on, Yarrun lay motionless on the ground. Chee had been trying to hide him by stuffing the body into a hollow log. Yarrun's feet and legs were inside the log now, but his top half was clearly visible.

His arms limp.

His face drained of blood.

His throat butchered.

So dead he had not even been warm enough to show up on the Bumbler.

No Weapons

"I killed him," I whispered.

Silence from the admiral.

"Didn't I?" I insisted. "I killed him, didn't I?"

"You were trying to help," Chee mumbled. "Emergency tracheotomy, right? And in the heat of the moment—"

''I killed him because I tried hacking at his throat when I couldn't see straight. If I'd just left him alone, his implant might have burned out like mine.''

''Burnout!'' Chee exclaimed. ''Is that what you—'' He stopped himself. ''Yes, burnout,'' he said. ''You were lucky.''

What did he mean by that? It *was* pure luck, wasn't it? Unless the implants weren't designed to kill us at all.

I groaned as the truth came to me. Of course they couldn't have killed us. That would have violated the one unshakeable law of space travel: no lethal weapons on a starship. The League of Peoples *never* let such weapons through, no matter how well concealed. ''The implants weren't made to kill,'' I said aloud. ''Just to knock us out for a while.''

''You didn't have time to think that through,'' Chee said sharply. ''You responded to an emergency, that's all.''

''I didn't respond to an emergency—I killed my partner!'' My face felt hot. ''And you were trying to hide the evidence, weren't you? Stuff him into a tree so I wouldn't find him. What were you going to tell me? That he'd been dragged off by predators?''

Silence.

''I don't know,'' Chee finally answered. ''I just thought it would be better if you didn't have to confront . . . if you didn't have to wake up with him right there.''

''Right there,'' I repeated. ''Lying in the grass. Where I killed him.''

And I began to cry.

Hell

Hell is weeping inside a tightsuit.

I wanted to cover my face with my hands. The helmet was in the way.

My nose ran. I could not wipe it. Dribbling and hot, untouchable tears poured down my cheeks.

I hugged my arms across my chest. The suit's surface was like iron; no matter how hard I tightened my grip, I couldn't feel my own touch. My arms squeezed against unyielding fabric, never making contact with the me inside.

Alone, alone, crying alone. I could not even reach myself.

My Helmet

In time, the sobs wore themselves out. The misery didn't. The taste of my running nose was salty on my lips.

Chee had his arms around me, trying to give comfort. I couldn't feel *him* through the suit either.

He was saying things, meaningless things. "You didn't know, how could you possibly think clearly, don't blame yourself. . . ."

Stupid things. I shoved him away. "Leave me alone."

He was looking at me. I wanted so badly to turn away from him that I stared him straight in the eye.

"Ramos," he said, "take off your helmet and wipe your nose before you drown."

"I can't take off my helmet," I sniffled. "There are germs."

"How much air do you have left?" Chee asked. "An hour? Two hours? We're going to be here longer than that."

"I'm going to be here forever!" The words came out before I even knew what I was saying. "I'm a murderer now. A dangerous non-sentient. I'm no different from that Greenstrider you talked about—it doesn't matter what was going through my mind, I should have known."

"Look, in the heat of the moment . . ."

"No!" I almost screamed the word. "I should have figured it out. I *should* have. I don't deserve to be called sentient if I can kill my partner so stupidly."

"Ramos . . ."

"I can never go into space again," I said. "Even if a

rescue ship arrived this minute, they couldn't take me away. The League would never let me leave Melaquin. They'll call me non-sentient, and they're right.''

"Take off your helmet," the admiral ordered. "I refuse to argue with a person who has snot all over her face.''

In another time and place, I might have been obstinate. I might have played the steely Explorer, sternly adhering to Fleet policies no matter how runny her nose was. But just this once, I didn't have the energy for willpower. With two sullen taps of my finger, I hit the helmet release button and the safety catch. It took five more seconds for the interlocks to disengage and for the pressure regulator to equalize with external atmosphere. My ears popped just as the helmet swung back on its hinges and exposed me to extraterrestrial air for the first time in my life.

Without a second's hesitation, I wiped my nose on my sleeve.

"Good," said Chee, "you aren't an utter idiot after all.''

A Tomb

We interred Yarrun in the log Chee had chosen—there was no better place for him to go. The miniature shovel in my pack was only adequate for skimming soil samples, not for burying bodies; it would have taken hours to dig a hole deep enough to hold my partner, hours of staring at his throat. I couldn't bear that.

The admiral couldn't do the work either. Whatever strength let him carry Yarrun into the woods had dissolved the moment I arrived. Now his face looked like brown chalk; his breathing sounded too deliberate, as if he was forcing himself to keep control. I gave him some excuse about wanting to deal with Yarrun myself and he didn't object. He simply sat against a tree and watched with weary eyes as I did what had to be done.

Pushing Yarrun into the log.

Forcing his helpless body inside, among the ants and beetles and fungus.

Smelling the odor of punky wood strong in my nostrils, the scent mixed with the tang of Yarrun's blood and my own stink.

Toward the end, it occurred to me to lock my own helmet onto Yarrun's tightsuit, encasing him completely so that carrion-eaters would not sniff him out. Then I finished cramming the corpse into the shadows, stuffing the end of the log with dead leaves until I could no longer see him.

When it was all over—when I had done what I had to, and what I could—I turned away and threw up.

"That's what fucking 'expendable' means," I said as I wiped my mouth. "That's what it really means."

Impeccable Timing

Chee took my arm as we walked back to the landing site. I thought he was going to try to comfort me again; but he simply needed the support.

"You shouldn't have carried him all that way," I said.

"It seemed like a good idea at the time," he said. "The kindest thing."

"But it took too much out of you."

He shrugged. "It gave me something to do. I woke up hours before you did."

"You got knocked out too? How? You don't have a throat mike."

"They must have planted something on me earlier," he answered. "Maybe they slipped it into my food back on the *Golden Cedar*. A little radio-controlled capsule no bigger than a grain of salt—the High Council loves to develop crap like that. Those bastards desperately need toys; and if the League of Peoples won't let them build guns, they build nonlethal junk instead. Same time they triggered your throat-set, they put me to sleep too."

"Mm." Of course, the Admiralty would have to silence

all of us at the same time; otherwise, there would be calls for help . . . demands for rescue. The *Jacaranda* would not be able to refuse a direct mayday, but if we all went off the air at once, Fleet policy was clear and precise. *Don't send more people into unknown danger. Report the situation and let your superiors decide what to do.*

Our wonderful, benevolent superiors.

Chee's grip around my neck tightened. "Ramos? I've been thinking of a lot of things since I got here. Old times." He shuddered. "Maybe the council was right to dump me. My memory comes and goes—a lot of the time, when I'm making a spectacle of myself, it's because I suddenly can't remember who I am. It's not like I forget my name, but I forget . . . important things in the past. You know? Things I sure as hell should have told you. But sometimes the memories just weren't inside my head; and sometimes the memories were there, but the courage wasn't."

"Courage?" I thought he was rambling.

"It's hard admitting past . . . failures. Ignoble surrenders. The times you should have been smarter, or braver . . ."

He stumbled over a stick hidden by leaves. I kept him from falling, but it took all my strength—he hadn't made any effort to save himself.

"Are you all right?" I asked.

He didn't reply.

A thought struck me. "When was your last Youth-Boost?"

"Two weeks, Ramos. One thing you can say for the council, they have impeccable timing."

"Shit."

"*Oh* Shit," he corrected.

At Chee's age, two weeks was the longest he could go between Boosts. Without a shot, he'd go downhill fast . . . and it didn't help that he'd been drugged into unconsciousness, then wasted his strength carrying Yarrun a couple hundred meters. His entire metabolism must be stressed to the limit—a metabolism that would soon start feeling its full century and a half.

"How can they do this to you?" I demanded. "Sending you here in this condition was . . . sorry, but it was a death sentence."

"The League won't permit outright killing," Chee answered, "but they accept the principle of letting an organism die when its time has come. Not much of a difference for someone in my position; but the League are experts at splitting hairs. Obviously, they do let the High Council get away with this. Otherwise, Melaquin wouldn't be such a time-honored dumping ground for used admirals."

"And now you're here."

"Now you see me, soon you won't." His hand, lying across my shoulders, ruffled my hair for a moment. "Sorry to leave you on your own."

"I'll survive," I said lightly.

"Make sure you do," he answered, with full seriousness. "Make sure you do."

"Do you think I'm going to kill myself? I can't—I'm programmed not to. In the early years of the Explorer Corps, the Fleet had too high a suicide rate. Isn't that a surprise? Explorers becoming depressed just because they're unloved freaks, shunned by the regular crew and as expendable as toilet paper. Why would that bother anyone? So the Admiralty started protecting its investment by indoctrinating us. It made sure we died on official missions rather than choosing our own place and time."

"I know how you're programmed," Chee said. "And I know people can overcome their programming. Maybe not the first time you try and maybe not the second; but eventually, you wear down the mental blocks. Determination is a powerful thing. But I want you determined to live, not determined to die."

"Why?" I asked. "Living well is the best revenge?"

"No. The best revenge is getting back to New Earth and cramming the council's misdeeds down its throat."

"I'm a murderer. I can't leave Melaquin."

"God damn it, Ramos!" Chee roared. "You may feel guilty, but you are not a—"

That was when he had his stroke.

Suh

We were almost to the top of the ravine. A few paces ahead, the trees gave way to the meadow where we had landed. Off to the west, I could see the last thin yellow of sunset fading into the purple of night.

Chee slumped like deadweight, slopping off my shoulders and falling into the crackle of forest leaves. I was so busy looking at the sky, I didn't react fast enough to catch him.

"Suh," he said, face down in the leaves. "Suh."

I knelt quickly and turned him over. Already, the left half of his face was dead. The Explorer paramedic course had talked about this, but it had just been words: *Loss of control over one side of the body . . . a telltale symptom of stroke.* But now it wasn't a symptom, it was something that had happened to someone sprawled in my arms.

The right half of the face still had Chee in it. The left half was empty—unoccupied flesh, controlled by nothing but gravity.

"Suh," he said urgently. His right hand grabbed my arm. "Suh!"

Last Wishes

"Admiral," I told him, "try to be calm. I might have something in the first aid kit—"

He slapped his palm over my mouth . . . a fumbling clumsy swipe that would have hurt if he'd had any strength left. "Suh!" he shouted. "Suuuuh!"

I leaned back, just far enough to dislodge his hand. It fell limply across his chest. "Admiral Chee," I said with choked self-control, "you have had a stroke. It has affected your left side, so it probably happened in the right lobe of your brain. Most people have their speech nodes predominantly in the other lobe, so there's a good chance you can still speak if you relax." I didn't know if that was true, but

I said it anyway. "Imagine you're speaking with the right half of your mouth. Maybe that will help you focus."

"Suhhhh . . . suuuhhh. . . ." He pursed his lips with great effort, then tried again. "Suhhhhh. . . ."

"Something about the sun?" I asked. "Sand? Soil? You're sorry?"

His hand flopped across my mouth again. If he hadn't done it, I would have stopped myself in another word or two. This was not the time for guessing games. The man had suffered a stroke thirty light-years from the nearest med-center. That was bad enough; but this was the start of YouthBoost meltdown—it would only get worse. And what could I do about it? Grab my scalpel and see if I could make it two-for-two?

"Suhhhh. . . ."

He lifted his hand to point. For a moment, it aimed toward the ravine—south. Was that it? But then his whole arm spasmed and pointed the other way: toward the lake. The lake? Or did his confused brain think it was the sea?

"The sea?" I said. "Is that it? Do you want to be buried at sea?"

His whole body sagged. I couldn't tell if he was relaxing because he'd got his message across or collapsing because his strength had run out. His grip on my arm went slack, and he sank back into the leaves.

One leaf drifted over his face, covering his nose and eyes. He didn't even twitch.

More Expendability

It took Chee another hour to die.

I sat with him, his head cradled in my lap as I stroked his hair with my hand. His eyes fluttered open now and then, but I don't think he was really seeing anymore. Occasionally he would grimace and grunt; then his face would relax once more into apparent calm.

From time to time, I used the Bumbler to check his vital

signs. Eventually, the readings came up negative. No heart-beat. No EM activity in the brain.

As planet-down deaths go, it was more gentle than any Explorer expected.

More gentle than Yarrun.

To take my mind off that, I asked myself why it had been so important for him to be buried at sea . . . if that really was what he wanted. I knew some religions believed strongly in the practice—the Last Baptism, they called it, a return to the mother of us all. Did Chee belong to one of those faiths? Or had he perhaps come from a waterworld, an oceandome, a sargasso habitat . . . some birthplace near the sea, that would now gather him home?

I never found out.

I never found out.

I never learned why he had asked to be buried at sea . . . or if he had been trying to say something entirely different, and had died in frustration at not being understood.

For a while, I continued stroking his hair. ''That's what 'expendable' means,'' I whispered, over and over again.

Then I began dragging his body toward the lake.

Part VII
MOONRISE

Moons

I stood at the edge of the bluffs and looked down at the water. The sky was clear and perforated with stars; to the southeast, a large white moon hung a hand's breadth above the horizon.

The moon was the color of Old Earth's moon. Ancient and melancholy.

I liked white moons—they had a subduing effect on their planets. When a world has a red moon in the sky, nights tend to be desperate . . . you're fighting angry, or you scramble for someone, anyone, to lie sweat-slick entangled with you, till the morning comes and you're exhausted enough to sleep. Greenish moons can make you happy on the right day in spring, but any other time they look fetid and sickly; when a planet's dominant moon is green, the people are whiners, filled with petty resentments. As for blue moons. . . .

Blue moons are rare for populated worlds. The only one I'd ever seen loomed in the skies over Sitz, the planet where all cadet Explorers got sent for inoculations that everyone knew were pointless. To avoid reactions with the shots, you had to abstain from all other medications . . . which meant that my memories of Sitz were centered on fierce menstrual cramps, unaided by the usual swatch. I passed my single night on Sitz huddled on the floor of the cadet hostel, staring at the bluish glow in the sky and outraged that something so mundane could hurt so much.

In the back of my mind, I wondered how many swatches I'd find in the first aid kit. Not enough to last a lifetime on Melaquin. How long until my next period? Twelve days, unless the stress of the last few hours threw my chemistry off . . . which it probably would.

Suddenly, the moon rising before me was more ominous than it had been.

Still, it was a white moon, and that was a point in its favor. White moons are aloof and formal—like a bachelor uncle who will leave you alone when you need to cry. People born under white moons know how to be silent; they don't feel the need to fill every quiet moment with conversation.

Then again, most people aren't born under moons at all. Most people are born under roofs—at least their souls are. And they sluggishly live their lives under roofs. At night they pull the curtains for fear some moon will shine in and infect them.

I liked moonlight. Even colored moonlight.

Moonlight was forgiving when I looked in the mirror.

Down the Bluffs

Chee's body was at my feet. I had clamped his helmet back in place on his suit so that crickets and grass wouldn't go down his collar as I dragged him across the meadow. It wasn't clear whether I should take the helmet off again when I finally got him to the lake. If this burial at sea was a matter of religion, maybe it was important for him to be in actual contact with the water. (And in contact with the fish who would chew his flesh . . . who would eventually float in the darkness of his picked-clean ribcage, as if he were a skeleton of coral.)

Stupid, Festina, I chided myself, *keep it together a bit*

*longer. Be hard, be hard, until you've done what needs
doing.*

So I pulled my gaze away from the moon and started
hauling the admiral down the bluffs.

The slope was steep but not forbiddingly so. I could dig
my feet into the sandy soil and keep my balance by hanging
onto the weeds that grew on the slanting face.

Burdock. Nettles. Thistles.

Stumbling down in the dark, I didn't like so many thorns
clustered around me . . . but the tightsuit was as tough as
plate mail, proof against anything a milquetoast terrestrial
weed could dish out. Chee was protected, I was protected,
and gravity was in our favor; so we proceeded down the
bluffs in a controlled slide, me on my feet tugging Chee
on his back, headfirst so he didn't get caught in bushes.

I was also lugging the Bumbler, which I refused to leave
back at the Landing site: a slow-witted proximity alarm was
better than no alarm at all. I had no partner now to watch
my back.

At the bottom of my climb, the weeds ended abruptly at
the beach: a wet, narrow beach, littered with driftwood,
clam shells, and half-rotted fish. I could see the place
clearly, thanks to the moon . . . and I could smell it clearly
too, with the air moldering breezeless in the shelter of the
bluffs. Ocean shores smell of salt; fresh water smells of the
day's decay.

With the admiral safely down from the bluffs, I rewarded
myself with a rest, sitting on a driftwood log: a time to
catch my breath, to listen to the waves, to debate whether
I should leave Chee's suit open or closed. If he stayed helmet on, he would float—the air in his suit would buoy him
up like a life preserver. Floating, he would soon drift to
shore; so perhaps I had to take off his helmet and fill his
tightsuit with rocks . . . enough to weigh him down until the
water had its way with him.

Was that what he would have wanted? I didn't know. I
didn't want to make the decision.

I might have sat on that driftwood a long time, if a glass coffin hadn't risen out of the lake.

Glass

The coffin surfaced silently, sending out ripples under the moonlight. Its glass had a mirror polish, dappled with drops and trickles of water; the sheen reflected the shadowed bluffs, making it impossible to see inside. As smooth as a swan the coffin slid across the waters, until it nudged the beach only twenty meters away from me.

I held my breath as the coffin lid opened. A woman lying face down inside pushed herself up and stepped onto the sand.

A nude woman made of glass.

The glass was clear and colorless. I could see right through her, the beach beyond distorted by a woman-shaped lens.

She was my height, but she looked like an Art Deco figurine. Everything about her seemed sleek and stylized— the long sweep of her legs, the slim torso, the high-cheekboned face. Her hair was not hair but the *suggestion* of hair: smooth glass swaths which were not differentiated into separate strands. That went for both the hair on her head and the tasteful implications of hair on her pubis . . . nothing so earthy as real genitalia, but an artistic rendering which hinted at some platonic ideal.

What was she doing here? On a planet with real worms, real butterflies and real killdeer, how could there be such a patently unreal woman? She was out of place, disturbing. Alien.

And so beautiful, she filled me with shame at my own flaws.

The woman walked onto the beach the way glass would walk if it could—smoothly, strongly, boldly. The muscles of her legs and arms slid silkily with the movement; whatever she was made of might resemble glass, but it was not brittle. After a glance that didn't come around far enough to see me, she faced back to the coffin and called out something in a resonant alto voice. The words were no language I had ever heard, but they were obviously commands to her vessel. Its lid closed silently . . .

. . . and in that moment of quiet, the Bumbler finally noticed her. Its alarm chittered *Beep, beep, beep!* in the still night air.

The woman's head whipped around. She couldn't help but see me. Lit by the full moon, her mouth and eyes flew open in horror.

"Greetings," I said as I kicked the Bumbler's SHUT-UP switch. "I am a sentient citizen of the League of Peoples. I beg your Hospitality."

With an agonized howl, the woman spun away from me and sprinted for the coffin.

Submergence

By the time she reached her vessel, the coffin lid was fully shut. That didn't stop her—she threw herself onto the top and hammered at the mirrored surface. Glass fists clacked sharply against the glass lid; but the coffin showed no sign of opening, no matter how hard she pounded.

Slowly, the craft slipped back into the water . . . and the woman hung on, shouting words I didn't understand but could easily guess: "Help, help, a monster!" How else would she react to a purple-faced stranger, dressed in bulky white? The coffin paid no attention to her screams. With increasing speed it withdrew from the shore, fast enough to throw spray in its wake.

Wet glass fingers clung to the wet glass lid—and as water sprayed in the woman's face, her grip slipped with the squeal of glass on glass. The coffin's surface was too slick to offer purchase; and when the sarcophagus started to submerge, a thickening onrush of water pushed the woman clean off, coughing, spluttering . . . and sinking.

"Bloody hell," I muttered. Could she swim? Could she breathe under water? Did she need to breathe at all?

If she really was glass, she'd be heavy as an anchor.

"God damn it," I said. But I knew I would have to play lifeguard.

Emergency Evac

I couldn't rescue her in my tightsuit: with the helmet off, it would fill with water and drag me down as soon as I started swimming. Growling profanities, I dug my thumbs under the twin flaps protecting the emergency release buttons, then pressed down hard. It was something I'd never done before, not with an active outfit—all our escape drills were performed with deactivated gear to avoid destroying valuable equipment. This time, however, the suit was live . . . and it stayed that way for precisely two seconds, just long enough for me to splay out my legs and throw my arms wide over my head.

Then the suit exploded off my body.

It went in pieces, splitting along seams invisible to anything less than an electron microscope. The gloves rocketed into the sky while the sleeves peeled themselves back like bananas, then ripped free from my shoulders as tiny charges of plastique blew them away. The breastplate had plastique of its own: enough to blast the front half five paces down the beach and the back half ten centimeters deep into the sand of the bluffs. The crotch slumped away without force—the males on the tightsuit design team must have been squeamish about high-powered explosives near that part of their anatomy—but the leg releases had enough plastique to compensate, spraying a confetti of fabric over a radius of ten meters and leaving me with nothing but shin-high white boots . . . that and the sweaty cotton chemise I wore to protect against the tightsuit chafing.

"Mmmm," I said, in spite of myself. No matter what other things I had on my mind, it's hard to stay focused when all your clothing is blown off in a single zipless whirlwind.

"Mmm. Mmm-hmm."

And you are left standing on a moonlit beach, exposed to the soft night air.

"My oh my," I said.

Then I saw that some of the fabric tatters had slapped like useless bandages onto Admiral Chee's corpse. And I thought of the woman, maybe with the ponderous density of glass, sinking over her head in lake water.

There'd been too many deaths already. I refused to permit another.

Lifeguard

Clasping the Bumbler's strap to my shoulder, I hit the lake running, took one bounce, then knifed out in a shallow dive while I still had momentum. For a woman brought up in the steamy tropics of Agua, the water temperature here was an education. No doubt, an ice-colony boy like Yarrun would have claimed the lake was balmy, but this was still mid autumn at forty-one degrees north latitude. My muscles did not seize up with the cold; my lungs continued to gasp up air whenever I lifted my head from the water; but I could feel my skin pebble into gooseflesh, and had to grit my teeth to keep them from chattering.

Ahead of me, the glass coffin was nothing more than a V-shaped disturbance under the water. Before it vanished completely I took a sighting on it, trying to estimate the difference between its position now and where it was when the glass woman slipped off. Was I getting close to her? The water was certainly over my head. Trying not to think about undertows, sharks, or water-borne parasites, I swung the Bumbler around and pushed its scanner under the surface.

A visual scan would only waste time; the water was black, the target transparent. I set the sensors to look for heat and cranked up the gain. There was no guarantee the woman would be warm-blooded—who knew if glass had blood at all?—but even if her metabolism just matched air temperature, she had to be warmer than the frigid water around me. The Bumbler would pick her up if she was within ten meters.

The screen flickered then bloomed with something hot right beneath me—something alive, close and moving. My heart choked tight with fear before I realized I was seeing my own legs, treading water. Oh. Tilting the scanner outward, I swung myself in a slow circle . . . and tried to force from my mind the memory of doing the same when I was searching for Yarrun.

"Where are you?" I muttered. "Come on, come on. . . ."

A bright blob flared on the bottom, only a few meters from me. Steady, steady; and in another few seconds, the Bumbler had sufficient data to resolve the image into a human shape, its arms and legs struggling futilely.

Okay. Okay.

Sling the Bumbler over my shoulder.

Take a deep breath.

Dive.

Even with the heat trace sighting, it wasn't easy to find a transparent woman in night-black water. I swept my hands blindly for at least ten seconds before I made contact: smooth slick skin, warm but diamond-hard. Before I could decide what part of her I was touching, an arm lashed out and grabbed me, catching hold of my hair. She nearly yanked out a handful. Then we were wrestling, unable to see in the dark—the woman wild with the fear of drowning and me trying to get her in a good rescue hold.

It was a match too evenly balanced for comfort. Explorers are trained in every conceivable rescue technique, and I had the added advantage of my martial-arts work, breaking free from people who wanted to grapple. On the other hand, the glass woman was strong and desperate, with a hide like blastproof plastic. When a flailing hand caught me in the stomach, it felt like a hammer—if the water hadn't slowed it down, the blow might have knocked the air out of me.

The slipperiness of her skin was a mixed blessing. It made things easier for me to wriggle away when she grabbed me, but she could also slip from my grip whenever I tried a rescue hold. My only edge was that she had been underwater longer than I had; and once, I even got away from her for a moment, long enough to surface for breath. I didn't worry about losing her in my brief moment of departure—she might be hard to see, but I wasn't. She grabbed me the second I came back within reach.

Little by little, she weakened. After a long confusion of thrashing limbs, I managed to loop an arm around her neck and drag her to the top. We both gasped, spitting and sputtering; then she lapsed into uncontrolled gagging which gave me time to haul her to shallow water. At the edge of the beach, I let her go and we both collapsed, side by side— half in, half out of the lake, propped up on our elbows and sucking at the air.

Out of the corner of my eye, I studied her: sleek and elegant, even when coughing up lake water. I could see right through her to a gnarl of driftwood on the beach beyond her; everything about her was transparent except for her eyes. As she turned toward me, I saw they were silvered like mirrors.

"You can't understand me," I told her, "but you have nothing to worry about. I saved you, didn't I? I mean you no harm."

The woman gazed at me for a moment, then let her head slump back onto the sand. "Fucking Explorers," she said. "Always *Greetings, greetings, I mean you no harm.* But you only make people sad. Go away, fucking Explorer. Go away now."

And she covered her eyes with her hand.

Part VIII
ACQUAINTANCE

Shocked and Hurt

Without a millisecond's pause, I spun away from her, rolling across the sand and tucking up to my feet in a fighting stance. My mind was scarcely aware what I was doing; the reaction had been programmed into me along with so much else.

It was an ongoing experiment by the Admiralty. In situations of total shock, when the conscious brain was too surprised to make a rational decision, some Explorers were trained to assume an aggressive posture, some to become passive, and some to freeze in whatever position they happened to be. The Fleet wanted to determine if any of the three approaches offered better survival prospects than the others.

If the study had drawn any conclusions, no one bothered to tell us Explorers.

With an effort, I forced myself to lower my fists. The woman's hand was over her eyes—maybe she hadn't noticed my reaction . . . although if I could see through her hand, why couldn't she? I looked carefully through her glass fingers and saw that her eyelids were an opaque silver, shut tight and trembling.

"You've met Explorers before," I said after a moment. "How else would you know my language? And since dozens of Explorers have come here over the past forty years, it's not completely improbable that an earlier party landed in this neighborhood. They may have followed the same chain of reasoning as we did." I was talking to myself, not her. "But what did they do to you? Why are . . . how did they upset you?"

She opened her eyes and raised herself on one elbow so she could look at me; she didn't lift her gaze high enough to meet my eyes. "They made me sad," she said. "Fucking Explorers."

"Did they hurt you?" I knelt in the sand so I wouldn't loom over her. "If they hurt you, it must have been an accident. Explorers are programmed . . . Explorers are taught very strictly never to hurt the people they meet."

"Yes," the woman said, "they are taught many things." This time her gaze met mine for an angry second before dropping away. "Explorers know so much, and it is all *stupid*!"

I stared at her, trying to decide how to read her. She looked like a grown woman, perhaps in her early twenties; but she talked with the words of a child. Did she only have a primitive grasp of English? Perhaps she learned the language as a child and hadn't used it since. A team of Explorers might have passed through this area when the woman was young, spent a few months, then moved on. Children learn languages quickly . . . and they form crushes quickly too. Maybe the Explorers had done nothing worse than leaving an overfond child who wanted them to stay.

"I'm sorry," I said, "that the other Explorers made you sad. I'll try not to do the same thing. If I ever make you sad, you tell me and I'll try to fix it."

"Fucking Explorers." She turned away and tucked up her knees, hugging them to her chest. "Your face is very ugly," she said.

"I know." I told myself I was speaking to a sulky five-year-old. "And I look even worse in daylight."

"Why do fucking Explorers go places when they are so ugly? Other people do not like seeing ugly things." She took a deep breath that was bordering on a sob. "Fucking Explorers should just stay home."

"No argument from me," I murmured. In a louder voice I said, "If you want, I'll go away."

She ignored my offer. "Why is the other Explorer so stupid?"

"What?"

"He just lies there. He doesn't talk. Does he think he is smarter than me? Does he think I'm dirty?"

I had forgotten about Chee. His body lay a short distance up the beach, his tightsuit glistening in the moonlight.

"The other Explorer is dead," I answered softly. "He was very old, and he just—"

"He is not dead!" The woman was suddenly on her feet, glass fists clenched in fury. "Do you think you are sacred? Do you think you are holy? Fucking Explorers are not such things as can die!"

And she stormed over to Chee's corpse and kicked it hard in the side.

Sad

My kung fu master would say the kick showed incorrect foot formation—if *I* kicked a tightsuit like that, I'd have broken my toe. The glass woman showed no sign of injury; and when she pulled her foot away, I saw a shadowy dent in the suit's fabric, as if someone had smashed it with a sledgehammer. The force of the kick had been enough to scuff the body back several centimeters over the sand.

"Are you asleep?" the woman shouted at Chee. "Wake up! Wake up!"

She kicked him again.

I stepped forward to stop her, then held myself back. She couldn't hurt Chee now; and if there was an afterlife, the admiral would be amused to watch a beautiful nude alien try to wake up his corpse.

After three more kicks that didn't quite breach the suit,

the woman dropped to her knees right on the admiral's chest and screamed in his face, "Wake up! Wake up!" She shook his shoulders, then clapped her hands on both sides of the helmet with a thud.

Panting and puzzled, she turned back to me. "He cannot hear me inside of his shell."

"He can't hear you," I agreed, "but it's not because of the suit."

"Do not say he is dead!" She buffeted the helmet with more smacks of her hand.

"Wait," I said at last. "Wait."

Kneeling by Chee's head, I fumbled with the clasps on his helmet. My fingers were clumsy after the dunk in cold water; wearing clammy wet underwear didn't help my condition either. I'd have to build a fire soon, before hypothermia set in.

The glass woman's face was close to mine as I removed Chee's helmet—I could feel her body heat on my skin. As soon as the helmet was off, she reached down and pinched his cheek. When she got no response, she shook him by the chin, then pulled on his ear. I placed my hand over hers and pulled her gently away from the corpse.

"He *is* dead," I told her. "Really."

I laid the back of my hand against the admiral's forehead. He was beginning to cool.

Hesitantly, the glass woman peeled open Chee's eyelid. The pupil did not react. She suddenly snatched back her hand and pressed it to her chest, as if she could hardly breathe.

"He is truly dead?" she asked.

"Yes."

"Explorers can die?"

"They're famous for it," I said.

She stared at me; her expression was so intense, I came close to flinching. "*You* can die?" she asked at last.

"As far as I know. It's not something I want to test anytime soon."

The woman peered at my face a moment longer, as if

searching for some sign I was lying; then she turned away, her troubled gaze moving toward the lake's dark water. After a moment, she said, "Now I feel very sad."

"I feel sad too." My hand still lay on Chee's forehead.

Oar

I told her, "Before my friend died, he asked me to put his body into the lake."

"Yes," the woman agreed. "We will hide him in the lake. We will use rocks to make him heavy so he will go to the very bottom; and he will be safe forever and ever."

I wondered what was going through her mind: why she used the phrase "*hide* him in the lake," what she meant by "safe," why the ability to die meant so much to her. Possibilities leapt to mind, but I shoved them away; Explorers shouldn't jump to conclusions.

We both began collecting rocks—mostly just pebbles, since neither the beach nor bluffs offered stones of any great size. I stuffed what I gathered into Chee's belt pouches, but the woman deposited hers directly inside his suit. She placed them there one at a time, working with care and delicacy. Once, I thought I saw her lips speaking silent words as she pushed one pebble after another through the suit's open collar. I wondered what she was saying . . . but her face had such a look of concentration, I didn't interrupt.

There came a time when we were both kneeling beside Chee's body: the woman inserting pebbles through his collar and me filling his pockets. After a full minute of silence, the woman said, "My name is Oar. An oar is an implement used to propel boats."

"I'm pleased to meet you, Oar," I answered solemnly. "My name is Festina Ramos and I take . . . my name is Festina. According to my mother, that means 'the Happy One.'" I didn't mention how Mother held that against me. *You're supposed to be happy, Festina; you have everything a little girl could want. Why must you be so deliberately miserable?*

"Your mother," Oar said. "That is the woman who gave you birth?"

"Yes."

"Have *you* given birth to a child, Festina?"

"No. Not me."

"Do you think you will some day?"

"No."

"Why not? Would it not be interesting to have a child come out of you?"

"I suppose so."

"And since this man here has . . . died," Oar continued, "should you not produce a new Explorer to replace him?"

"It's not that easy."

She looked at me, waiting for me to explain. I shook my head, too tired to belabor the details. Would she understand if I explained that women received tubal ligations upon joining the Fleet? The operation could be reversed on request after ten years' active service; but I doubted I would find a surgeon to do the job here on Melaquin. Children were impossible for me. Someday, when I was past the numbness of Yarrun and Chee dying, I wondered how I'd feel about being permanently barren.

After waiting for me to answer, Oar came up with an explanation of her own. "Oh yes," she said, "you cannot have a child here and now. You need a man to supply his juices."

"That's certainly a consideration," I agreed.

Oar fell silent. I fastened the snap on one of Chee's belt pouches, then looked up. Her silvery eyelids were closed.

"I know a man," Oar whispered.

"Yes?"

"I know an Explorer man." Her eyes opened. "I have not seen him in three years, but I am sure he is still such a man as would give his juices to any woman."

There was bitterness in her voice.

"Oh," I said. "Oh, Oar."

And I understood why she said, *Explorers only make people sad.*

Fucking Explorers.

"Who was this man?" I asked.

She closed her eyes again. "Explorer First Class Laminir Jelca."

My Heart

Jelca.

Jelca.

I'd heard he'd gone Oh Shit a few years ago—nothing in the official records, just a rumor. I should have realized there was only one place you could disappear without leaving records in the Fleet archives.

Jelca was here on Melaquin. And not just on the planet—he was somewhere close by. He had not landed on a different continent; he had not landed on some isolated island; he was *here*. At least, he had been here three years ago. How far could he have traveled since then?

My heart beat faster, though I knew it was foolishness. I scarcely knew Jelca—after that night we carried Tobit to his quarters, we had gone on two dates, no more. There was every chance Jelca had treated Oar badly . . . and yet, I was already making excuses for him in my mind. *She had misunderstood mere friendliness; and perhaps Duty had forced him to leave.*

Never mind that my excuses didn't make sense. In the heat of the moment, "making sense" was my enemy.

I had killed Yarrun. Chee had died. But if Jelca was here, I was not alone.

In that moment of weakness, I thought Jelca would save me.

Jelca's Partner

"Where is Jelca now?" I asked as calmly as I could.

"He went away with *her*," Oar replied. She made the word "her" sound like excrement.

"Her?" I repeated.

"The ugly woman who blinks."

"Ullis? Ullis Naar?" My old roommate with the permanent twitch in her eyes.

"Yes, Explorer Ullis Naar. She blinks and blinks until you scream at her to stop. She is so *stupid*!"

I said nothing. Ullis was not stupid; she had a good brain and a better heart. In our years rooming together at the Academy, I had never heard Ullis say an unkind word about anyone. Sometimes   sometimes we avoided her, when the stress of our studies exhausted us so much, we didn't have the strength to put up with her blinking; but she never made us feel guilty afterward. If she had become Jelca's partner after graduation, he was lucky.

So was she.

I tried not to think of her alone with Jelca on this planet. It gave me a hollow feeling in the pit of my stomach.

Away

I asked, "Where did they go, Oar?"

"Away." She pointed in the direction of the bluffs—south. "They said they had to join with other fucking Explorers, but that was just an excuse. Jelca left because he wanted to go."

Other Explorers . . . Jelca must have contacted some of the others marooned here. He could have cobbled together a radio, possibly by cannibalizing his Bumbler—he came from a Fringe World where children learned electronics from the age of three—and he'd managed to contact other Explorers on the planet.

"Oar," I said, "you have to believe Jelca wasn't making

up excuses. If he found out about other Explorers, he'd have to. . . ."

I didn't finish my sentence. Oar's fierce expression told me she wouldn't believe a word in Jelca's defense. "Okay," I conceded. "Okay." There was no point in angering her. She sniffed a bit, then went for another handful of pebbles.

Visible Light

In time, Chee's pockets bulged with rocks. The interior of his suit was less full, but it would do—when I gave his body an experimental shove, I could barely move him. No amount of ballast would weigh him down forever, but we'd done enough to keep him submerged for a good long time, provided we started him out deep enough.

Getting him away from shore was the trick. I could drag the body as far as I could wade, but it was too heavy to swim with—smart Explorers don't dogpaddle while carrying an anchor. Oar had shown she couldn't swim at all, and the wrinkled curls of driftwood on the beach were too small for building a raft. For a moment, I considered giving up on the burial at sea and just digging a grave in the sand; but then I thought about Chee's last desperate attempt at speaking. "Suh . . . suh . . ." Although I had no confidence he really wanted to be committed to the water, I wanted to do something that felt like granting his final request.

"Oar," I said, "do you have any ideas how to take my friend out into the lake?"

She answered immediately, "We will carry him on my boat."

"You have a boat?"

"It will come when I call. Stay here."

She walked away down the beach, giving me the chance for something I'd been longing to do since she appeared. Casually activating the Bumbler, I aimed the scanner at her

smoothly sculpted back and did a quick run through the
EM band.

In the visible spectrum, she was transparent; but at every
other wavelength, she gauged very close to *Homo sapiens*.
IR readings showed her body temperature was less than a
degree warmer than mine—or what mine would have been
if I weren't shivering on an open beach in a wet cotton
chemise. On UV, she looked just as opaque as I did; and
on X-ray, she actually showed a skeleton and the ghosts of
internal organs. To my untrained eye, the images of bone
and tissue looked entirely human . . . except that none of it
showed up with visible light.

An invisible heart, beating in her chest.

Invisible lungs, processing air.

Invisible brain, glands, liver, gall bladder . . . all wrapped
up in a glassy epidermis that let light through unimpeded.

Could she possibly be a machine? Unlikely. Machines
tend to have IR hot spots: power packs, transformers, things
like that. Oar's body temperature was more evenly distributed—like mine, to be honest, with head and thorax warmer
than the extremities but none of the sharp gradients you see
in androids. Organisms also emit waves in the radio band
with a completely different pattern from machines; nervous
systems transmit their signals in ways wires can't imitate
. . . not even biosynthetic wires made from organic mole-
cules.

No—Oar was not built on an assembly line. That still
didn't make her "natural" . . . most likely, she was the result of DNA tinkering. She or her ancestors had been pur-
posely altered. More important, she'd been altered for the
benefit of eyes like mine. No other species in the League
of Peoples perceived exactly the same set of wavelengths
as humans. If other sentient beings looked at Oar, they'd
see her IR glow, or perhaps a full X-ray layout. They certainly wouldn't see the perfect transparence that greeted my
human eyes.

The only plausible explanation was that humans had
lived on Melaquin, either now or in the past. The planet

had worms, killdeer, and monarch butterflies; why not *Homo sapiens* too? And for some reason, those humans had fabricated this new transparent race . . . transparent to human eyes, if not to the eyes of extraterrestrial species.

Of course, I had no idea why they'd do such a thing. Why make yourself hard for your fellow creatures to see? Were they trying to hide from each other? But Oar still showed up on IR, UV, and other wavelengths. She couldn't conceal herself from high-tech sensors . . . and surely her culture had such gadgets. They were sophisticated enough to engineer themselves into glass; they must understand basics like the EM spectrum.

Maybe turning to glass was simply a fashion statement. Or a religious practice—implementing some teaching that glassiness was next to godliness. *No*, I told myself, *that was too easy:* too many sociologists threw up their hands and said, "It's just religion," when they found a custom they didn't understand at first sight. An Explorer doesn't have the luxury to dismiss anything.

I had to be scrupulously honest: I didn't understand why people would make themselves glass . . . and perhaps this whole train of thought was merely jumping to conclusions. Melaquin showed no roads, no cities, no signs of technology—scarcely consistent with a culture that could engineer people into near-invisibility.

Unless . . .

. . . at the same time they made a race so hard to see, they also removed all signs of their presence on the planet.

Unless these see-through bodies and the dearth of development were all attempts to hide that this planet was inhabited. Even if they showed up on IR, glass bodies were still harder to see than normal flesh and blood.

And if that was true, what were they hiding from?

I shivered; and this time it had nothing to do with air temperature or damp clothes.

Radio, Boat

Oar walked twenty paces, then crouched beside a shadowed tangle of thornbush washed up on the sand. She glanced back and gestured that I should turn my head away. I complied, but tucked the Bumbler's scanner behind me so I could watch while my back was turned.

A few moments passed while she checked I wasn't looking. Then she stretched her arm into the tangle, methodically pushing away one branch after another as she moved her hand inside. I played with the Bumbler's dials, trying to see what Oar was reaching for; and suddenly, the image glowed with a flare of bright violet.

Hmmm.

On the Bumbler's current setting, violet corresponded to radio waves. Somewhere in the bushes, a concealed radio transmitter had sent out a signal.

Oar stood and began walking back to me. I clicked off the Bumbler's display and pondered how long I should pretend to be unaware of her approach. Before I was forced to decide, I was saved by the lapping of waves offshore— the glass coffin had reappeared, and was slipping in toward the beach. I watched it a moment, then turned to Oar. "Your boat?"

"Yes. It comes when it is wanted." Her voice had a self-satisfied tone, as if I should be impressed by the boat's "magical" response to her whim. The magic was surely the radio signal she'd just sent . . . but perhaps Oar didn't know that herself.

"It must be good to have a boat like that," I said. "Where did you get it?"

"I have always had it," she replied, as if my question was nonsense. "Would you like to ride in it with me?"

"Both of us?" The boat's size was generous for a coffin, but getting two people inside would be a squeeze. "It's a bit small," I said.

"Two can fit," she started to say . . . then she stopped, suddenly stiff and distant. "You are right, Festina," she said in a voice that was meant to sound casual. ''The boat is very small.''

Ouch, I thought; and I imagined Jelca and Oar enclosed there together, arms and legs entwined, sailing impassioned through the lake's silent dark.

Half of me was sick with jealousy. The other half pictured myself in the same position with Jelca; and that half was not sick at all.

The Last of Chee

Oar began to tell me her plan, and in a moment, I collected myself enough to listen. She would board the boat and I would drape Chee's body over it. At Oar's command, the boat would sail slowly out into the lake. When they were far enough out, she would tell the boat to submerge and let the admiral slump off into the water. I had a hunch the boat's glass was so slippery, Chee might slide off sooner than expected. Still, if they only got a stone's throw from shore, it would be better than I could do wading; so I nodded and complimented Oar on the cleverness of her plan.

She smiled like a queen acknowledging the adoration of her subjects.

After Oar got into the coffin, I was left alone to heave Chee onto the lid. The rocks made him damnably heavy . . . and he was beginning to stiffen as well. Getting him into position took all my strength, plus leverage from sticks of driftwood; but at last I spreadeagled him face down on the glass, his arms dangling on either side of the coffin and his toes hooked over the forward edge. I wanted to send him out feetfirst, hoping he would stay in place longer— headfirst, there would be nothing to stop him from sliding backward, and the open collar of his suit would catch spray as the boat glided forward.

Oar could never be described as a patient woman. I had scarcely arranged Chee's limbs when the boat pulled away, backing into the lake. This was the first close view I'd had of the coffin while it was moving; I saw nothing that looked like a propulsion system, nothing that told me how it pushed itself through the water. Whatever engines it had were completely silent. With no exhaust, no bubbling of hidden propellers, the boat quietly withdrew and glided off along the surface.

Soon I could see nothing but Chee's tightsuit glistening in the moonlight. He lay quite still, his head toward me as he moved away. His thin white hair was slick with lightly splashed water; and I thought of Oar inside the boat, looking up through the glass at Chee's lifeless face. He was just a stranger to her. . . . And yet, his death seemed to mean something profound to her.

The moon went behind a cloud and I lost sight of the body. Was that it? Was Chee gone forever? But the cloud passed and the moonlight sparkled again on white fabric far out on the water.

I raised my hand in the only heartfelt salute I ever gave an admiral, and held it there till he was out of sight.

Part IX
ADAPTATION

Seamstress

I don't know how long I stood there; but I came to myself with a sudden shake, realizing I had been slipping into a daze that could not be healthy. Hypothermia is sly—it creeps in so gradually, you may never realize you're dying. "And wouldn't the other Explorers laugh?" I said. "Festina Ramos getting Lost so tamely."

Then I added, "Wouldn't my face be red?"

Getting giddy—definitely time for a campfire.

Tinder was easy to come by: brush from the bluffs, dead and dry as straw with winter coming on. Much of the driftwood was dry, too; I chose sticks from high up the beach, on the theory they'd arrived with the lake's spring peak and had baked in the sun ever since. The hardest thing to find was my jar of matches. They'd been in a pouch of my tightsuit . . . and since the suit lay in hankie-sized pieces all over the sand, it took time to track down the right hunk.

Five minutes later, I had a fire: warmth, light, salvation. I cuddled up to it till I'd steamed off my immediate chill, then began to make short forays out to retrieve more scraps of my tightsuit.

I had accumulated a pile of fabric beside the fire when I found the pouch I was looking for, impaled on the thorns of a bush whose species I didn't recognize. A brief struggle pulled the pouch loose, and I opened it immediately. I counted six plastic vials inside, all still intact. "Thank you," I said to the sky.

The Admiralty loved toys—people in positions of undeserved power always do. And since the Admiralty loved toys, the High Council allocated generous funds to the development of Explorer equipment. Not that the council gave a damn about Explorers themselves; but the demands of Exploration raised fertile engineering challenges that the research department found irresistible. As a result, ECMs were truly equipped to handle almost anything . . . like trying to put Humpty Dumpty back together again after an emergency evac blew him to bits.

Three vials in the pouch contained solvents. The other three contained fixative.

With work, I could glue the tightsuit patches into a usable garment—not as strong as the original, but better than spending the rest of my life in my underwear. Creative tailoring might even give this new suit advantages over the old; I could, for example, remodel the pants to make walking easier. Blimp-shaped thighs might be best for maintaining positive pressure against incoming germs, but now that I'd been exposed to Melaquin's air . . .

I didn't want to think about that. Concentrate on being a seamstress.

First, the top—that was easy. The breastplate and back had come off as single pieces, simple to fit back together. With the torso reassembled, attaching the arms was no worse than gluing together strips of banana peel. The result was as bulky as a stiff cable-knit sweater, and had the same degree of blessed warmth. There were too many seams now to match the original suit's insulation to forty degrees below zero; but that didn't stop me from diving into the garment as soon as it was done, or shuddering with bliss as my gooseflesh started to recede.

The bottom part was more difficult. The basic delta of the crotch hadn't been damaged, but the individual pouches of the belt had blown away separately. Putting them back together used up most of my chemicals, because I wanted an arrangement that would fit my real waist, not the bulbous girth of the original suit. After much trial and error, I jury-rigged a two-tiered pattern that worked well enough; but that left me low on solvent and fixative, too low for constructing pantlegs. The path of least resistance was to glue my remaining scraps to the foundation of the crotch, building a skirt from a spiral patchwork of cloth until I exhausted my supply of adhesive. The result came just to my knee—higher than I liked with winter coming on, but I had flared the skirt wide to give my legs freedom of movement. Cold knees were one thing; not being able to deliver a good side kick was something else.

I had fabric left over when I ran out of glue, plus a lot of spare gadgetry—air tanks, pressure pump, life-sign monitors, etc. They could stay on the sand where they were; I doubted I'd need them again. Carting them around the countryside would just waste energy . . . unless, of course, Jelca could strip them down and use the parts for something.

Jelca. Jelca was here on Melaquin.

I might have thought about that for a long time if Oar's boat hadn't appeared again.

The Scalpel

Chee's body was no longer sprawled on the boat . . . and when the glass lid opened, Oar was gone too. The boat stood empty on the sand like a plundered sarcophagus. I could almost *feel* it waiting: waiting for me to get in so it could carry me away. It must have come back to take me to Oar's home—an underwater habitat like the ones on Attulpac, or perhaps something subterranean . . . a hidden place, undetectable from orbit.

Did I want to board a glass coffin and ride off into dark water?

Yarrun was dead. The admiral was dead. For a moment,

I couldn't think of a reason to move forward or back. Then reflex took over and I found myself packing things into the boat.

Always do the next necessary thing.

The Bumbler had to go, of course . . . and Chee's backpack, which I'd removed before sending him off forever. I'd also have to retrieve my own pack, still lying amidst the daisies on top of the bluffs. Oar would be impatient for me to join her, but I refused to abandon things I might need later.

Climbing the bluffs was easier than I expected—Chee's body had flattened a trail on its way down. The gloves of my tightsuit were still intact, so I could catch hold of weeds and pull myself up, without worrying about thorns and burrs. Apart from a run-in with stinging nettles on my bare right calf, I reached the meadow unscathed.

Everything was where I had dropped it: my pack, my stunner, Yarrun's helmet . . . and the scalpel, black now with Yarrun's dried blood. I didn't want to touch it. I wanted to leave it there forever, rusting in the rain.

But it was probably made of rustproof metal.

And it would be cruel to leave something so sharp where animals could injure themselves.

And a true Explorer doesn't abandon a useful tool just because she's squeamish.

Carefully, I wiped the blade on the grass.

Carefully, I put the scalpel away in the first aid kit.

Then I threw the kit into my backpack and fairly ran back down the bluffs.

Thunks

With so much equipment stuffed into the boat, I had to wriggle to get in myself. The boat waited motionless for me to settle; since Oar had given it voice commands before, perhaps I had to say something to get it started.

"Okay," I announced. "I'm ready to go."

The boat didn't react immediately; but after I'd lain still and silent for five seconds, the lid slowly lowered. It came to within a centimeter of my face—any jostling, and I'd bump my nose on the glass. I hoped we weren't going far . . . not just because the space was cramped, but because it wouldn't take long to exhaust the scant air inside the coffin.

Smoothly the boat moved out. Black water lapped on both sides, inching up the walls until it eased over the top: the craft was submerging. I had one last glimpse of the moon and stars—my sky, the night sky—and then they were swallowed by blackness. A hand's breadth of water above me was enough to cut off all light coming from the outside world.

Whatever propelled the boat worked silently. The only sounds were my careful breathing and my heartbeat. A drop of water fell against my cheek and I felt sudden panic—was the boat leaking? But it was only the moisture of my breath, condensing on the glass so close above me and dripping back down.

Something thumped against the boat near my feet. I jumped enough to clonk my nose on the glass, watering my eyes . . . but nothing else happened.

A fish—it must have been a fish, rudely surprised by colliding with a nearly invisible submarine.

And where there is one fish, there are many more.

Thunk. Thunk. Thunk.

Sometimes the hits were direct, sometimes soft glancing blows. The impacts had no pattern—whole minutes could go by in total silence, then two jolts one after another, like the proverbial water torture, never knowing when the next drop will come.

At least it kept my mind off the stuffiness of an unventilated coffin sailing with tons of water overhead.

I didn't think about that at all.

Austere

The ride ended in a sudden bloom of light, beginning at my feet and sliding swiftly up the length of my body as the boat glided into an illuminated space. I had not looked at my watch before starting out, so I can't say how long the voyage lasted . . . perhaps ten minutes, though it felt like an hour. It was lengthy enough that my eyes had adjusted to the total underwater blackness; even squinting, I could see nothing against the light now beating on my eyes.

The boat's lid opened and I heard Oar's voice. "Why did you take so long? Did you not understand to enter the boat? Are all Explorers stupid?"

Nice to see you again too, I thought. But the next moment I realized she must have stood there waiting, wondering if I had abandoned her the way Jelca had. In a conciliatory voice, I said, "Sorry—I needed time to pack my gear. Where are we now?"

"This is my home, Festina. It is the most beautiful home in the universe."

My eyes were beginning to adjust to the light . . . not the fierce light it seemed when I emerged from total blackness, but a grayish glow like an overcast day. Oar stood beside me, hands on hips, keen for me to stop squinting and admire her home.

Beyond her lay a village of glass. Why should I have been surprised?

We stood near the edge of a space two hundred meters in circumference, covered with a hemispherical dome. The dome was either jet-black itself or transparent to the lightless water of the lake. Underneath the dome stood two dozen buildings, all glass: high Moorish towers where the dome offered enough headroom, and squat rectangular blockhouses out on the periphery. Boulevards separated each structure from its neighbors; and looking to the middle of town, I saw a plaza where two glass fountains sprayed water high into the air.

Clear water. Clear glass. I found myself searching for

any hint of color, a tint to the glass or a prism-effect that broke light into spectra; but the glass was as pristine as crystal, and the sky too muted for rainbows. I couldn't even tell where the lighting came from—it was simply there, so pervasive it didn't allow my eye the relief of shadows.

"Is my home not beautiful?" Oar asked.

"Austere," I replied.

"What does that word mean?"

"Pure," I said. "Clean."

"Yes." She sounded pleased. "Very very clean."

Clean of everything—the streets were empty. Oar and I were the only people in sight.

A Tour

"Do you live here alone?" I asked.

"Do not be foolish," Oar answered. "I have many many ancestors."

"And they're here?"

"Yes."

I looked around. Certain Fringe Worlders believed their ancestors remained participants in their lives—ghosts who walked beside them unseen. The living would leave an empty seat at dinner so great-great-grandma could sit among them; and on Sitz, they took water spritzers with them into the bath, to squirt phantom uncles who might sneak in for a peek. Did Oar believe the same thing? I could think of no tactful way to ask. Oar was easy enough to offend without opening the topic of religion.

"Why don't you give me a tour?" I suggested. "Show me the things I should see."

"You should see everything, Festina. And I will show you everything."

I nodded and put on a smile. Mentally, I reviewed my repertoire of facile compliments for all occasions—enthusing about architecture and other curios did not come naturally to me. Entertainment bubbles may portray Explorers as zealous to investigate alien cultures, but that wasn't our job; we only established a secure foothold, after which the Fleet unloaded an army of xeno-ethnologists to do the true fieldwork. Right now, Oar's tour was a chore, one more job between me and thinking about. . . .

I had killed Yarrun.

I had watched Chee die.

"Lead on," I told Oar. "I'm sure I'll enjoy this."

Food

"This makes food," Oar said.

We stood in a one-storey blockhouse, not far from the access port where I had entered the city. The blockhouse consisted of a single room, with no furniture, no decorations . . . just a single glass pillar in the center of the floor, as thick as the trunk of a redwood. The surface was smooth, but dusty—all except a spotlessly clean niche half a meter deep, cut into the pillar at waist height.

"How does it work?" I asked.

"You say what you want, and the machine makes that for you." She didn't call me stupid this time, but her tone implied it.

"I doubt if your food synthesizer understands my language," I said. "Unless the machine learned from Jelca and Ullis the same way you did."

"The woman taught it some of your dishes," Oar answered. "She said it was not hard to . . ." Oar paused, straining to remember an unfamiliar word. After a moment, it came to her: "Not hard to pro-gram."

Good old blinky Ullis, I thought. Like many Explorers, she had been a superb programmer—the result of feeling more comfortable with machines than humans. I sympathized; I too had been a teenage hermit. As a farm girl, however, I had passed the solitary hours working with our livestock, not tinkering with circuit boards. At the Academy, Ullis tutored me in computing, and I helped her with exobiology.

"So," I asked Oar, "what did Ullis program this machine to make?" I hadn't eaten since leaving the *Jacaranda* that morning; my pack contained emergency rations, but their taste was so cloying no one would eat the stuff *except* in an emergency.

"I did not learn the names for Explorer dishes," Oar answered. "I did not want to learn. When the fucking Explorers ate, I went away so I would not be sick. Explorer food is very very ugly."

"What do you mean by ugly?" I wondered if Jelca and Ullis followed strange Fringe World diets—I couldn't remember what either of them ate at the Academy.

"They ate sauces the color of animal blood. Grains as white as maggots. Vegetation that looked as if it was pulled straight from the ground!"

"Oh." Marinara sauce, white rice, and salad . . . apparently not Oar's kind of food. "Maybe I'll come back later," I said. "It'll take time to experiment with what Ullis programmed." I was not ravenous yet; and if worst came to worst, I could nibble on rations when Oar wasn't looking.

"Then let us go," Oar replied, starting toward the door, "and I will introduce you to my ancestors."

Oar's Ancestors

She led me into one of the central towers. It was twenty storeys tall. Each storey was filled with bodies.

The bodies were all clear glass, lying placidly in rows on the floor. Some were male; some were female. The women looked like Oar—perfect copies as far as I could tell, though my eyes may have missed tiny distinguishing characteristics. The transparent glass made it hard to see the faces at all, let alone make out subtle differences from one woman to another. The same went for the men: they were clean-shaven, with hair and facial structures similar to the women. If not for their breastless chests and demure genitalia, I could scarcely have told male from female.

Not that it mattered in a functional way: male or female, all of these people were dormant. Breathing and warm to the touch, but comatose.

Oar stood in the midst of those unmoving bodies, waiting for me to say something. I botched it. ''Are they . . . what happened . . . is this some . . . so, Oar, *these* are your ancestors.''

''Yes,'' she said. ''Not all are *direct* ancestors; but they have lived in my home from the beginning.''

''And, uhh . . . what do they do here?''

''They lie on the floor, Festina. They do not want to do anything else.''

''But they could get up if they wanted to?''

''When the other Explorers came,'' she said, ''my mother and sister got up. They were curious to meet strangers, even though the Explorers were so ugly. After a day, my mother grew bored and came back here—that is her, lying over there.'' She gestured in the direction of a glass wall. At least five women lay in that neighborhood, all of them twins to Oar. If one was truly Oar's mother, she showed no sign of being older than Oar herself . . . nor did any of the women show evidence of motherhood. Glass stomachs must not get stretch marks, glass breasts must be immune to the demands of nursing. And gravity.

''What about your sister?'' I asked. ''Did she eventually get bored too?''

''I am sure she is very bored now,'' Oar answered haughtily. ''She is bored and sad and stupid.''

''Oh?''

''She went away with the fucking Explorers. They took her and not me.''

Oar loosed a furious kick at the body closest to her—a man who skidded across the floor with the force of the impact. He opened his eyes to glare at Oar, said a few unknown words in a grumbling voice, then shifted back to his former location.

Oar immediately kicked him again. "Do not call me names, old man!" she snapped.

He glared at her once more, but said nothing. He didn't try to move this time, but settled where he was, folding his hands across his chest and closing his eyes. I wondered if he would shift back to his original place after Oar left.

"They all have tired brains," Oar told me. "They are old and tired—and *rude*," she added, raising her voice pointedly. "They have nothing else they want to do, so they lie here."

"Don't they eat or drink?"

Oar shook her head. "They absorb water from the air ... and absorb the light too. My sister said the light in this building is nutritious—good enough anyway for people who do nothing. I do not understand how light can be nutritious, but my sister claimed it was true."

Having lived with solar energy all my life, I had no trouble appreciating how light could "feed" an organism; but clear glass was not a good photo-collector. It's better to be opaque to the light you're trying to absorb ... and then it occurred to me, these bodies were opaque to most nonvisible wavelengths. A quick Bumbler check confirmed it—the deceptively muted light inside this building was laced with enough UV to bake potatoes. I shuddered to think what other radiation might be flooding the air ... say, microwaves and X-rays.

"Let's go outside," I told Oar briskly. "You've probably never heard the word 'melanoma' ... but I have."

The Surrender

The light outside was not so lethal—the Bumbler certified it fell within human safety limits. Obviously, the tower containing Oar's ancestors was shielded to keep all that juicy radiation inside ... which only made sense. If you devoted so much wattage to feed solar-powered people, you didn't want energy spilling uselessly through the walls.

Whatever the tower was made of, it certainly wasn't ordinary glass; it held in everything but visible light, making a high-band hothouse for photosynthesizing deadbeats.

"They really just lie in there all day?" I asked.

"Most have not moved in centuries. That is what my mother said her own mother claimed. As long as I have lived, only my mother and sister have moved."

"But now your mother is dormant and your sister left with Jelca?"

"Yes. I have been alone the last three years."

I felt the urge to touch her—pat her shoulder, give her a hug, pass on comfort somehow. But I didn't; I didn't know the right thing to do.

"It's hard being alone," I finally said. "It's a wonder you haven't laid down with the others."

"I do sometimes," she told me. "Sometimes I go into the tower to be with people. Once in a while . . . once in a while, I see if I can lie with a man and get him to give me his juices; but it never works and I just get sad."

She spoke in a halting voice. I didn't know how to answer. Finally I said, "You can't die, can you? Your species can't die."

"We are not such things as die," she whispered. "We do not get damaged. We do not grow old and sick like animals. If you had left me in the lake, Festina, I would have lived and lived . . . under the water, too weak to move, but still alive.

"Our bodies live forever," she continued, "but our brains slow down after a time. When people's brains grow tired and there is nothing else they want to do, they just lie down. It is called the Surrender. Some people surrender outside—in the grass, on the sand, or in the water—but most come home to this tower. It is pretty and comfortable here; and the light gives enough strength that you can always move if you want to. My mother said that was good: she felt she could get up any time she had a reason. She just couldn't think of a reason."

I couldn't meet Oar's gaze. "I'm proud of you," I said, finding it hard to force the words out.

"Why are you proud of me, Festina?"

"Because you aren't in there with everyone else." I grabbed her arm to pull her away from the building . . . or rather to touch her in the only way I could justify. "Come on—you were showing me the sights. Let's keep going."

And we did.

By the Fountain

We stood in the central square of the village, directly in front of the glass fountains that chattered in the middle of the plaza. Oar walked up to one, spreading her arms and watching her skin mist up in the humid air. The look she gave me, back over her shoulder, suggested she considered such behavior daring.

"My mother called this *The Fountain of Tomorrow*," Oar said. "The other is *The Fountain of Yesterday*." She paused. "They look very much the same, do they not?"

"Too much." I wondered if that was the fountain-builder's point. "Oar," I asked, "what do you do all day?"

"Why do you ask, Festina?"

"You don't have to work to survive. You can get food just by asking the synthesizer, you don't wear clothes, and this village clearly runs itself automatically. You must have done things with your sister while she was here; but how do you fill your days now?"

Oar didn't answer immediately; she stayed motionless in the fountain's mist, water beading on her skin. It made her easier to see—like the glass of a bathroom mirror, fogged after a long hot shower. Finally, she turned and sat on the edge of the fountain. Her movement shook loose the larger droplets, sending them trickling down her body.

"I clear fields, Festina. That is what I do."

"Clear fields? Why? Do you grow crops?"

"I just clear fields," she answered. "Jelca said it should

be done. He said that civilized races always cleared fields on their worlds. When I asked why, he refused to tell me. He said he should not have mentioned it in the first place—that Explorers were not supposed to influence the people they met. He told me to forget it. But I did not forget. And if he ever comes back, he will see that I am a civilized person, not stupid at all.''

"So you . . . clear fields."

"Yes." Her voice was proud. "In addition to the machine that makes food, this city has machines for making many other things . . . if you know how to ask. I asked a toolmaking machine for such a blade as could cut down trees. The machine gave me a good blade indeed. So now I cut down trees every night, when no one is watching. I cut the wood into pieces that I can carry away, then I cover the stumps with grass and leaves.''

"You've been doing that ever since Jelca left?"

"Yes. It is hard work, but when he comes back, he will be sorry he did not understand how civilized I am.''

"I'm sure he will."

Our probes had reported this area was too clear of trees. All the work of one woman? Could one person cut enough forest that it was noticeable from space? Amazing. And all on the strength of a slip of Jelca's tongue.

Oar sat on the edge of the fountain, dribbles of water pouring down her arms, her shoulders, her face.

"My sister has never cut a tree in her life," she said.

"Which proves she isn't civilized?"

"That is correct." Oar smiled. "Come, Festina. I will show you Jelca's house.''

Prototypes

"This is where Laminir Jelca chose to live," Oar said. But she didn't have to tell me that.

While touring the village, I had peeked into several glass buildings, all bare of any adornment except dust. The blockhouse we had just entered was different: strewn with discarded circuit boards, coils of wire, and stripped insulation. A small fraction of the material must have come from the Technocracy—I recognized a familiar D-thread chip, straight out of a tightsuit pressure monitor—but most of it was native to Melaquin.

It was easy to tell the difference: all the Melaquin components were clear and transparent. Nudging a see-through cable with my toe, I wanted to growl, "Haven't you people heard of copper?"

Jelca probably felt the same way—after all, he had to work with the stuff. Many of the glasslike parts were labeled in thick black letters from the marker pen all Explorers carry: RESISTOR, 10 OHMS . . . FUSE, AT LEAST 15 AMPS . . . BAD TUNNEL-TUBE, DO NOT USE! How he had identified these things, I couldn't imagine; but as I said before, Jelca came from a line of dabblers in electronics. With the aid of his Bumbler, he could analyze almost anything, given enough patience . . . and enough duplicate parts for the times he guessed wrong.

"Did he explain what he was making?" I asked Oar.

"Foolish things," she answered. "He claimed he could make a machine to talk to people far away . . . and a version of our food maker machine, only small enough to carry."

Practical thinking on Jelca's part: a radio and a nutrient synthesizer. That gave him a way to contact other marooned Explorers, and the means to feed himself while he traveled to wherever the others were. After a moment, I corrected myself—the means to feed himself and Ullis, plus Oar's sister if she was traveling with them. It would take a big synthesizer to produce enough food for three people . . . but if Oar's sister was as strong as Oar, she might have no trouble carrying heavy equipment for hours on end.

Carefully I prowled the room, examining everything Jelca had made during his time here. I recognized several nutrient synthesizers, the kind that take leaves and other organic material as input, then produce compact food cubes: not fine cuisine, but enough to keep you alive. There seemed to be a progression of prototypes, from one that must have weighed a hundred kilos down to something much less bulky. Jelca had obviously worked to produce the smallest equipment possible so he and Ullis could travel light. Naturally, they'd taken the most compact version with them; but sizing up the best one they'd left behind, I thought I could stand hauling it five or six hours a day, if I built a good carrying frame.

Thank you, I whispered to the air. Jelca had left me the means to follow him.

The Picture Box

"This box makes pictures," Oar said behind my back.

She pointed to a crystal screen embedded in the wall . . . or more accurately, embedded in what was left of the wall. Jelca had ripped away much of the material around the screen so he could get in behind it—into a mass of fiber-optic cable and circuits feeding the screen. By the looks of it, this was a native Melaquinian television; and Jelca had either tried to repair it or plunder it for parts.

"The screen showed pictures?" I asked.

"Yes. Pictures of ugly Explorers."

"Jelca and Ullis?"

"No, different Explorers."

"Different . . ." I forced myself not to lunge for the TV. If other Explorers could broadcast television signals, they must have developed a substantial technological base—either that or they had drawn upon existing Melaquin resources. Now that I thought about it, normal TV/radio waves could never reach here under the lake. The dome must have a concealed antenna or cable feed reaching up to the outside world. Perhaps the planet supported hundreds of hidden villages like this one, connected by a shielded cable network: a network that would allow communication from one village to another, but whose transmissions would not be detectable from space.

And my fellow Explorers had tapped into that system.

"Oar," I said, "I'd like to turn on the machine."

"You may not see anything," she answered. "The pictures only come for a short while, then go away. And they are always the same stupid Explorers saying the same stupid things."

It must be a looped signal saying, "Hello new arrivals, here's where everyone else is." With clumsy fingers, I clicked the TV's switch. The screen lit with a display of static. For some reason, I had convinced myself it would show a picture immediately; but ten minutes passed (Oar tapping her toe impatiently) before a picture snapped into view.

"Greetings," said a man on the screen. "I am a sentient citizen of the League of Peoples and I beg . . ."

I was too shocked to pay attention to the words. The man on the screen was Chee.

Part X
COMMUNICATION

Ears

The Chee on the screen looked younger—not so many lines on his face and only a few gray streaks in his black hair. He wore the hair down to his shoulders; but it couldn't hide the huge misshapen ears sticking out from his head like purple-veined plates.

Those ears looked like botched engineering: some ill-conceived project to achieve God knows what. Even though it was illegal, there were always fools who tinkered with their offspring's genes, failing to understand that a change in enzyme A might affect how the body used proteins B, C, and D. Most of the time, such alterations killed the child *in utero*; but occasionally, the fetus lived to full term, emerging from the womb with deformities like the man on the screen.

A man with the ears of a cartoon caricature. Or an Explorer.

Yes. Those ears would make him a prime candidate for the Academy . . . if he could still hear. If the malformed ears handicapped his hearing, Technocracy medicine would leap to the rescue: reconstructive surgery, prosthetic replacements, targeted virus therapy—whatever it took. But if the ears were merely grotesque, and the child was intelligent, healthy, psychologically *pliable* . . . on to the Academy.

Chee. An Explorer.

Was it really him? Could it just be a close relative, a brother, or even a clone? All were possibilities; but I could feel in my gut this was the real Chee.

Chee had known more about Exploring than any normal Vacuum admiral. When suiting up, for example, he had known to empty his bladder during Limbo.

An Explorer. An Explorer who somehow became an admiral.

How long ago had this recording been made? The signal could have looped for decades if it ran off a reliable power source. If Chee had been one of the first marooned here, some forty years ago . . . yes, I could believe it. The Explorer on the screen was a veteran, probably taking YouthBoost every few months. Forty years would bring him almost exactly to the Chee who had died a few hours ago.

Forty years.

Plus ear surgery.

And some way to escape from Melaquin.

Chee's Speech

With an effort, I forced myself to concentrate on his words, not his appearance. (Chee's voice—it was definitely Chee's voice.)

". . . fully expect that more of us will get shanghaied here over time. If you are in that position, I invite you to join my partner and me in the enclave we've found. It's an underground city, fully automated and self-repairing . . . centuries old. The people are humanoid but glassily transparent; all seem dormant, though we cannot guess the cause. We have had no success in rousing them to consciousness for more than a minute at a time.

"We've had better luck with the technical facilities here: this broadcasting station, for example. If we've analyzed its structure correctly, our transmissions should be going out over a high-capacity network, perhaps reaching all around the world. We have also discovered very old machines capable of space flight . . . or at least they *were* capable of flight centuries ago. If we can restore one of these ships to working condition, we might use it to get off the planet. We have yet to find a ship with FTL capacity, but we don't need to get as far as another star system—we just have to escape the restricted airspace around Melaquin, then send a mayday.

"Therefore, fellow ECMs, I invite you to help us with this project. We may not be space-tech engineers, but we're smart and resourceful. In time, we can rebuild a ship and get out of here—if we work together."

Chee suddenly grimaced straight to the camera. "Shit, that sounded pompous, didn't it? But you know what I mean. We can get our asses out of here if we don't fuck up. Some of you must have landed way to hell the other side of the ocean and you'll never make it here under your own steam; but look around, see what you can scrounge up. This civilization had sophisticated goodies before it went to sleep. Maybe you can find a starship of your own . . . if not, maybe a boat or a plane that'll bring you to us, even if you're thousands of klicks away.

"And where is here, you might ask? To answer that, I'll turn the floor over to my partner who's drawn up a map to show exactly where this city is . . ."

Chee reached toward the camera, his hand looming in front of the lens before the shot swivelled to a new angle. In a moment, a woman came into view. She was holding a map, but that wasn't what I was looking at.

Her left cheek had a fierce purple birthmark, twin to mine.

And beneath that birthmark was the face of Admiral Seele.

My First Admiral, Again

Admiral Seele. My first admiral. The one who spent several days with me on the *Jacaranda*.

The one who paid me so much attention, I thought she wanted into my bed.

"Shit," I whispered. "Shit, shit, shit."

"What is wrong, Festina?" Oar asked. She glanced at the screen. "Are you angry this woman has copied your ugliness?"

Yes, that's why I'm angry, I thought. *I'll sue her for stealing my trademark.*

Admiral Seele. No wonder she took such interest in me. My mark was on the right, hers on the left; we were mirror images. On screen, as she pointed to her map and blathered about landmarks, she even looked the same age as me . . . but the recording was made forty years ago, give or take. I could well imagine those forty years had aged the woman I saw now into the admiral who cried for me.

But how had Seele lost her birthmark? How had Chee lost those monstrous ears? And how had they both become admirals?

I could think of only one explanation. The two of them *had* resurrected a spaceship. They had escaped, returned home, and reached a deal with the Council. What kind of deal? I could only think of one: Chee and Seele wouldn't blow the whistle on Melaquin, provided they were boosted up the chain of command and got the medical treatment needed to make them look like real people.

What else could it have been?

"Bastards," I whispered. "Traitor bastards."

They'd sold out their fellow Explorers in exchange for an admiral's gray uniform and plastic surgery. They'd had a chance to expose the High Council, but held their tongues. Forty years later, Explorers were still getting tossed onto Melaquin like trash.

"Damn it!" I growled. "How could you do it, Chee? How could you treat us like we were . . . expendable?"

The screen gave no answer. In time, the faces were replaced by static.

A Selfish Thing

I felt a touch on my shoulder. "Why are you sad, Festina?"

Oar looked at me earnestly.

"I'm sad," I told her, "because someone I thought was my friend did a selfish thing."

"That is bad," Oar said, her hand still touching me. "It hurts when people just do, do, do, without caring. It is very wrong."

"Yes, well . . . I don't have all the facts." I took a grudging breath that immediately let itself out again in a sigh. "It's been a long day for me, Oar; and getting choked unconscious for a few hours isn't as restful as you think. Is there a place I can sleep?"

"Jelca's bed is in the next room," Oar replied. She pointed toward a door. I felt like saying no—refusing to spend the night under the same roof as the television, as if hostility could punish Chee and Seele from afar. But it couldn't. And if Jelca had a perfectly good bed within a stone's throw, why go someplace else?

Why not spend the night in Jelca's bed?

"Damn, I'm a basketcase!" I muttered. "How many emotions can you squeeze into a minute?"

"I do not understand the question," Oar replied.

"Just talking to myself," I said. Without waiting for her to respond, I walked into Jelca's bedroom.

The bed was clear and transparent—a water-filled sack on the floor, with a hard plastic frame around the outside to prevent you from rolling off the edge. I wondered if Jelca had made this himself or if the bed was standard issue for Oar's people. Did Oar need to sleep? The engineers behind her glassy genes may have designed her to stay awake twenty-four hours a day.

"Do you sleep?" I asked her.

"Yes, Festina . . . whenever I want to. I could sleep now, for example."

The hint in her voice was not subtle.

And so we slept the night together in Jelca's bed: chastely, but not apart. She was lonely for company. And I had lost so much in one day, I wanted to hold something warm and solid.

Sick

I do not remember dreaming that night; but I woke in a dreamlike state, hard-pressed to believe my surroundings were real.

My arm was draped over Oar's quiet back. On the other side of her body, my hand looked as big as an inflated glove, magnified by a lens effect from her breasts. The sight disturbed me, as if my flesh was bloated with native microbes. Flustered, I untangled myself from her and rolled away; the water bed gurgled as I moved. After a moment, I settled onto my back and stared at the ceiling, trying to force back a sense of reality.

Reality.

How could I grasp reality when everything had a see-through, not-really-there quality? The walls, the bed, the woman beside me . . . all so elusive. I was marooned on a planet too much like Earth, I had killed my partner, I had watched Chee die, I had slept in Jelca's bed—but all of it felt so disconnected: details of some other woman's life. My mind floated, unattached to my body or my past; closed up, walled off. The sensation was neither pleasant nor unpleasant. I had no interest in judging it; I simply let it wash past me.

After a while, a thought occurred: *Maybe I'm sick.*

Everything would be all right if I were sick. I could let the germs take responsibility for the coming hours . . . days

... weeks. Sick people don't have to participate in their own lives.

I found myself visualizing the microorganisms that coursed through my bloodstream. Specializing in exobiology had its benefits; I could imagine some *great* microorganisms.

My favorite ones looked like eggs.

Metabolisms

Oar lifted herself on one elbow and asked, "Are you awake, Festina?"

"Hard to tell. Do awake people lie around, picturing needle-shaped microbes perforating their capillaries?"

"Perhaps you should ask my ancestors," she said. "You may have to tell them what a capillaries is, for they are not so wise as me."

"I think I'm sick," I said.

Oar put her hand on my forehead. "This is what my mother did when I was sick." She waited a moment, watching me solemnly. Then she removed her hand and asked, "Do you feel better now, Festina? Or shall I touch you again?"

I smiled. "I'll just lie here for a while."

"Are you sure? Would you like some food or water? Do you want to go to the bathroom?"

Hmph. If her goal was to get me out of bed, her words had more effect than a hand on the forehead. Suddenly, I was aware of intense hunger, thirst, and the urge to urinate. For a few seconds, I tried to return to my former comfortably dazed dislocation; but no matter how sick or emotionally overloaded I might be, I hadn't lost any basic bodily needs.

"Help me up," I muttered. "Please."

She rolled off the bed and held out a hand. As soon as I took it, she pulled me strongly to my feet, the water bed galumphing beneath me. Some part of me wanted to feel dizzy when I reached the vertical; but the clawing in my bladder focused my attention too effectively to allow light-headedness. "Show me the toilet," I growled.

There was a small one in the building's back room—a clear glass bowl with a conventionally-shaped seat. Oar entered the room with me and showed no sign of leaving . . . not that I'd have any privacy anyway, with walls of glass. I sat; I went; Oar wrinkled her nose. "It is yellow, Festina," she said.

"I suppose yours is clear?" Then I answered my own question. "Of course it must be—otherwise, I'd see your bladder floating inside your body. You have one hell of an eerie metabolism if even your wastes are see-through."

"I have a consistent metabolism," she sniffed. "And if you are finished. . . ."

As I got up, I wondered if she had talked this same way with Jelca, three years ago in this very room. I didn't really want to know.

Three Days

When we were both finished in the bathroom, Oar volunteered to get food from the synthesizer. I warned I might be too sick to eat, but I knew it was a lie—I wasn't sick, I was merely wrecked. Shipwrecked, soul-wrecked, brain-wrecked.

And I stayed that way for three days.

Why did it hit me then—in those minutes when Oar was getting food? Why not earlier or later? I suppose it was being alone for the first time since landing on Melaquin: truly alone with nothing to do. No one to help, no bodies to bury . . . no orders, no mission, no agenda. It was the first time in years nothing was dragging me into the future—I had no duties to keep my mind off what I'd done. I could almost feel things letting go inside me: not the pleasant easing of burdens, but a dismaying loss of cohesion, bits of myself slipping out of place.

Alone, alone, alone. Alone in a colorless village, all the inhabitants as good as dead except for one childlike woman who could never understand my ugliness, my pettiness, my pain. . . .

Three days passed. I won't describe them. I could say I don't remember them, but that's dodging the truth. Even if I can't list what I did, I remember every hour deep in my bones: grieving, raging, raving. I can return to that darkness anytime I want; stand over the pit and look down, shivering with the same furies and regrets. Now and then I deliberately turn back to those days—lift the lid to reassure myself I have not forgotten. At other times the memory rises unbidden; I find myself blurting out, "I'm sorry!" in the silence of an empty room.

The taste is still bitter.

Oar took care of me in her way: alternating between earnest attempts to comfort me and annoyed impatience when I wouldn't "stop being foolish." Sometimes she would storm off, calling me a stupid fucking Explorer who was very, very boring. Later she would come back and hold me, rocking me in her arms as she searched for words to bring me back from wherever I was. She fed me; she told me when I had to wash; she slept beside me after I fell into bed from exhaustion.

When I awoke the fourth day . . . I won't say I was better or over my breakdown, because that makes me sound stronger than I was. I felt as fragile as an eggshell; but a tiny part of me was ready again for the future.

By the time Oar woke up, I was rewatching the broadcast from Chee and Seele. This time, I paid attention to the maps.

Geography

As I had seen from space, the lower half of this continent was a wide prairie basin, bounded to the south by an arc of mountains and to the north by the three-lake chain stretching well into the heartland. The more I thought about the layout, the more it reminded me of Old Earth's North America: the Great Lakes in the middle of the continent with forest-covered shield to the north and grassy plains to the south. The parallels weren't exact, but they were disturbing, as if someone had superimposed Earth's ecology onto another planet's plate tectonics.

In terrestrial terms, I was close to the south shore of the lowermost Great Lake—call it Lake Erie—and the city Chee and Seele described lay several hundred klicks to the south, somewhere in the mountains along the "Caribbean" coast.

The trip from here to there looked suspiciously simple. The region immediately below the lake had a good growth of forest (slightly thinned by Oar); but a few days travel would bring me to open grassland, and from there it was an easy walk all the way to my destination.

No doubt there would be difficulties—rivers to cross, wild animals to avoid—and winter could start snowing down in a few weeks. By then, however, I'd be substantially closer to the equator. If Melaquin's weather patterns were comparable to Earth's, I might miss the snow entirely.

As the broadcast ended, I finished scribbling in my notebook: Seele's description of how to find the entrance to the subterranean city. Between now and the next broadcast, I would check the best food synthesizer Jelca left behind and get the rest of my gear together. Then I'd listen to the loop one more time to make sure I had all the details correctly. Within an hour, I'd be ready to head south . . . except for one loose end.

"You are writing, Festina," Oar said. "Does that mean you are no longer crazed?"

Seeing the World

"When you are crazed," Oar continued, "you are a very boring person, Festina. You nearly drove me to lie down with my ancestors forever and ever."

"I'm glad you didn't," I told her. "I still feel three quarters crazed, but at least I've cried myself out. How are you?"

"I am not such a person as has difficulties," she answered, "except when you fucking Explorers make me bored or sad."

"Lucky you," I murmured.

She gave me a look of wounded dignity.

"All right," I sighed, "let's talk about important matters. Have you ever wanted to see the world?"

"I can see the world now, Festina. It is not invisible."

"See *more* of the world. How far have you traveled from your home here?"

"As far as far." She lowered her eyes. "When the other Explorers left with my sister—for some time I was crazed like you. Later, I tried to follow them; perhaps I was crazed then too. I walked for many days in the direction they had gone, until finally I came to a river that was very wide and deep. It was not such a river as I could cross, but I tried anyway. That is how I know what drowning is like, Festina. It is very unpleasant. I was lucky the river had a strong current—it carried my body along till I washed up on shore. The same shore I left. I thought about trying to cross again, but I lacked the courage."

She glanced up quickly, as if to check whether I was sneering at her as a coward. "You made a wise decision," I assured her.

"I did not feel wise. I felt sad and lonely. I sat on the bank of that river for many days, wondering how my sister got across. We are not such creatures as swim. But perhaps Explorer Jelca pulled her through the water, just as you pulled me out of the lake. He might have wrapped his arms around her and helped her away."

For a moment or two, we both brooded silently over that mental image.

My Native Guide

"All right," I said at last, "you've traveled before. Would you like to do it again?"

"What do you mean, Festina?"

"I know where Jelca and Ullis went. I want to go there too, and I'd like you to come with me. My native guide."

"We would see Explorer Jelca?"

"And Ullis and your sister," I added, too sharply. "What's your sister's name anyway?"

"I call her Eel," Oar answered. "An eel is an unpleasant kind of fish."

"Is that her real name?" I asked suspiciously.

"Yes," Oar replied. In a lower voice she added, "At one time, I did not think eel-fish were so bad."

I hid a smile. "Would you like to go with me, Oar? I could use your help."

"Is that true? *I* would be helpful to an Explorer?"

"Absolutely. You've helped me the past few days, haven't you?"

"That is different, Festina—you were crazed. Now that you are an Explorer again, you are not such a person as needs help from me."

I looked at her closely. Her head was lowered, her posture crumpled. Hesitantly, I patted her shoulder; today, her skin felt cool under my fingers. "The other Explorers made you feel useless . . . is that it?"

"You do too, Festina." She didn't lift her head. "You know many clever things. Even when you are being stupid, you make me fear *I* am the one who does not understand. You can swim and make fires; you can use your seeing machine. And you know the names of plants and animals— you talked about them when you were crazed. I have lived here all my life and do not know such names. You know more about my world than I do." Suddenly, she raised her eyes and looked straight at me. "How do you think I will help you, Festina? Do you just need someone for bed games? That is the only thing Explorers do not like to do by themselves."

"Oar . . ." When I met Jelca, he was going to have a lot of explaining to do. "Oar, I need you to help carry things. It's not glamorous, but it's important—you're much stronger than I am. And I'll teach you other things as we go along. Besides," I added, "I'll be lonely and sad if I go on my own. I need company, and I'd like it to be you."

"Festina," Oar said, "are you telling the truth? Maybe you just feel bad about going away, and you say, 'Come along, Oar,' because you are sorry for me. I do not want to burden you, Festina. It is sad being alone, but it is worse being with someone who hates you."

"I don't hate you now, and I won't hate you ever. Listen, Oar. If I went without you, I'd be alone with my thoughts for weeks on end. I couldn't stand that—not right now. With you along, I'll stay sane . . . probably moody as hell, but I'll cope. Besides, Explorers never set out alone if they can help it. Solo missions are a hundred times more dangerous than taking a partner."

Oar's face brightened. "I will be your partner? Your real partner?"

I closed my eyes against a stab of heartache. *Oh God, Yarrun!* I thought. But he would be the first to tell me, *Let go, let go.* "Yes," I said, "you'll be my new partner . . . if you want to be."

She leapt forward and seized me in a bear hug so fierce it had a serious potential for cracking my ribs. I might have been squeezed to a pulp if a sudden thought hadn't struck her. Releasing her grip, she stepped back a pace and asked, "Now that I am an Explorer, do I have to make myself ugly?"

I didn't know whether to laugh or cry.

Part XI
TRAVEL

Weeds Transformed

Riding back to the beach in Oar's glass coffin was more pleasant than my previous trip. This time there was a hint of brownish green light, dimmed by fathoms of water but enough to show where the boat was going. I lay on my stomach and looked through the forward wall, watching for fish crossing the bow. There were several collisions on the trip—smallmouth bass who glanced off and scuttled away in terror—but the thumps of impact weren't so loud when I knew they were coming.

The boat opened up as soon as it landed, and I hurried to unload the equipment I'd been lying on: my pack, the Bumbler, and Jelca's food synthesizer. The last was a heavy brute—it took all my strength to wrestle it out of the boat, even using the carrying straps that I'd attached to it. If I carried the machine myself, I'd only manage a few klicks a day before dropping from exhaustion. Oar, however, claimed to have no trouble hauling such a weight. When her ancestors engineered themselves transparent and immortal, they'd obviously thrown in the strength of gorillas as a bonus.

And Oar felt inferior to me?

After two minutes, the boat closed itself and slipped back into the lake, returning underwater to pick up Oar. In the meantime, I busied myself testing the food synthesizer. If it didn't work, we'd still press on with our trip—I could shoot game with my stunner, or forage for nuts and berries—but spending time as hunter-gatherers would reduce the distance we could travel in a day, and increase our chance of being caught by winter. Added to that, I preferred not to eat local flora and fauna. Everything might *look* like Earth species, but they still could turn out poisonous. Even if they were fully terrestrial, that was no guarantee of safety. What if I cooked a rabbit for supper and later found it had rabies?

Since the synthesizer was solar-powered, I set it in the sun and loaded the hopper with weeds from the face of the bluffs. Grinders whirred immediately, turning the plants to puree: a good sign. There was no way to guess how long the machine needed to do its job, breaking the weeds into basic aminos, then reassembling the components into edible blobs: maybe five minutes, maybe several hours. In the meantime, the day was fresh, and placidly warm outside the shadow of the bluffs. I took off my top to air after wearing it four days straight . . . or perhaps just to feel the autumn sun on my skin.

For a few minutes, I had the planet to myself.

Alone

I had never been alone before . . . not in this specific way. Often I had been one of only two sentient creatures on a planet—the other being Yarrun, of course. But a planet-down mission was different, with goals to accomplish, checklists to work through, and a shipload of Vac personnel listening to your transmissions. Even as a little girl, I never felt truly alone. I was constantly accompanied by responsibility: the schoolwork heaped upon potential Explorers from the age of three, plus the chores I had to do on the farm. Now and then, our family took vacations; now and then, I played hooky or ran off to sulk in "secret hiding places'' my parents likely knew from their own childhoods. But wherever I went, I was shadowed by what was expected of me. You don't free yourself from duty by running away. That only increases the weight on your shoulders.

Now, I *was* free—forcibly cut loose. If I stayed on this beach forever, what difference would it make? How would anything change? Jelca wasn't expecting me. He might not even be glad to see me: just some kid who made a spectacle of herself, mooning after him at the Academy.

Ullis would be happy if I showed up—we got along well as roommates. Even so, I remembered one night in the dorm, when she complained after hours of study, "Who *cares* about zoology, Festina? Cataloguing animals is as pointless as stamp collecting. There's only one classification system that interests me: things that can kill and things that can't." Even as Ullis hugged and welcomed me, she might be thinking, *A zoology specialist . . . why couldn't it be someone with useful skills?*

Why force myself on them? It might be better just to lie in the sun. I could keep Oar company, and give her English lessons till she felt brave enough to use a contraction.

And then what, Festina? Help clear fields to prove you're both civilized? Play "bed games" with her out of sheer boredom? Endure it as long as you can, then go lie down with her ancestors? That would be a vicious way to die: withering up with radiation sickness, while the glass folk around you fed on the rays.

"I'm an Explorer," I said aloud. The words had no portentous echo—they were just words, spoken as waves lapped the shore and bushes rustled in the breeze.

I touched my cheek. "I'm an Explorer," I repeated.

As a duty, it was stupid; but as an open opportunity. . . .

Some maudlin urge made me want to address a speech to Yarrun—an apology and a promise. But the only phrases in my mind were too banal to voice.

The sun continued to beam warmly on my skin. A gull launched itself from the top of the bluffs and I watched it soar into the cloudless sky.

Oar's Axe

Ten minutes later, Oar's boat slid onto the sand. She stepped out, and with rehearsed casualness, swung a gloss-silver axe onto her shoulder. It looked deadly heavy, but not metallic—perhaps plastic, perhaps ceramic. Whatever it was, I'd bet my favorite egg the blade was sharp enough to shave a balloon; a culture that could make a see-through woman could certainly produce a monofoil cutting edge.

"On our trip," Oar announced, "we should clear trees now and then. Then we can tell the Explorers we traveled in a civilized way."

"Let me guess," I said. "When Jelca taught you our language, he never explained the word 'ecology.'"

Oar Food

Before I could lecture Oar on environmentalism, the food synthesizer gave a subdued chirp. I looked at my watch: eighteen minutes since I pressed the machine's ON button. Jelca might be lax on conservation, but he made admirably efficient gadgets.

When I opened the drawer at the bottom of the synthesizer, it contained two dozen blobs of jelly, each the size of my thumb. They came in several shades: light pink, frost green, and dull brown, with a few clear colorless ones too. I lifted a pink blob and smelled it; the fragrance was generically fruity, like cheap candy that simply tastes red.

"What are those, Festina?" Oar asked.

"Food."

Her nose wrinkled skeptically. "Explorer food?"

"And Oar food."

During my three days of breakdown, Oar had fetched us both food from the big village synthesizer, so I knew what she usually ate. Most dishes had the shape of common terrestrial foods—noodles, wafers, soups—but of course, each morsel looked like glass. The jellylike output from Jelca's synthesizer was at least translucent; but I had to admit it didn't resemble Oar's normal cuisine.

"Try that clear one there," I pointed. "I'll bet it tastes good."

"I cannot put that in my mouth," she objected. "It has touched the green one. It is *dirty*!"

"This is special food," I said. "It doesn't get dirty." I took the clear blob myself, making sure it hadn't picked up any color from adjacent blobs. "See? It's pretty."

"Now *you're* touching it."

"My hands are clean . . . and my skin color doesn't rub off, you know that. Otherwise, you'd be smeared and smudged yourself."

She didn't look convinced.

"Oar," I said, "if you don't like food from the synthesizer, what are you going to eat? Do you want me to kill animals for you? Or rip up plants I think might be edible? Do you want to eat raw fish? Or bright red raspberries?"

Her eyes widened in horror. "I will try machine food," she said quickly, and plucked the clear jelly from my hand. With the get-it-over-quick air of a woman taking medicine, she plopped the blob in her mouth, and swallowed without chewing . . . as if she was hurrying to get it down before the taste made her gag.

Seconds ticked by silently. "How was it?" I asked.

"I do not know," she answered. "I shall wait to see if I become sick."

Good enough, I told myself. If I could eat her food, she could probably eat mine; but let her work up to it gradually. In the meantime, the sun was bright—she could photosynthesize, like her ancestors back in the village.

"We're ready," I said. "Let's head south."

We Begin

Our climb up the bluffs proved Oar had ample strength to carry the synthesizer—with it strapped to her back, she walked as if its weight were barely there. I worried the straps might chafe her bare shoulders; but as time passed without a peep of complaint, I concluded her skin really was as tough as glass . . . and hardened safety glass at that.

From the top of the bluffs, our way south ran into the wooded ravine. I veered off the most direct route to avoid passing the log that held Yarrun's corpse; instead, I led Oar along the ravine's spindly stream, traveling southeast according to my compass. Walking wasn't easy—undergrowth tangled thickly along the stream bank—but I stuck with it for ten minutes, till we were far past my partner's shabby burial site. Then we turned due south again, climbing out of the ravine and into more level woodland.

For a long time after that, I still made wide detours around any logs that lay in our path.

Walking (Part 1)

Here is what I remember from that first day.

The peaceful stillness of the forest . . . and sudden compulsions to break that silence, babbling trivialities to cover the noise of guilt in my brain.

The quality of Oar's voice as she replied to me—the way the surrounding trees absorbed the sound and muted it.

The slash, slash, slash of our feet through fallen leaves.

A covey of quail which suddenly flushed from cover as we approached.

A flock of geese flying south in a lopsided V, their honking distant and piercingly autumnal.

Topping a rise and seeing a great open marsh in front of us, sparkling in the clear sunlight.

The small nose of a muskrat weaving along the edge of the creek in the marsh's center.

Oar fastidiously cleaning her feet after picking her way across mud. ("It is brown and ugly, Festina; people will think I am stupid if my feet are brown and ugly.")

Watching a great blue heron balance on one leg as it scanned the water for prey.

Borrowing Oar's axe so I could cut down a cattail, then pulling the plant's fuzzy head apart as we continued through the swamp.

The maddening suspicion that there were eggs all around me: heron eggs hidden by bulrushes, turtle eggs buried in the mud, frog eggs globbed just beneath the creek's surface. I knew better—on Earth, few species laid eggs so soon before winter—but still I was seized by impulses to look behind patches of reeds or kick the dirt with my toe . . . as if I had acquired some mystic intuition of eggs calling to me.

I hadn't. I found nothing. And in time, twilight closed around us as we reached the far edge of the marsh.

My Sleeping Bag

Beyond the marsh was forest; we built camp just inside the trees. More precisely, Oar went to gather firewood, while I pulled handfuls of marsh greenery as input for the food synthesizer. Once the machine had begun digesting the plants, I went to my backpack and debated opening my sleeping bag.

Like most Explorer equipment, standard-issue sleeping bags were compact. They had no bulky padding; an open bag looked like a sheath of tin foil, shiny side in. The foil didn't have the weight of a nice down comforter, but it was a good insulator for all its thinness—the glossy interior reflected back most escaping body heat. Surprisingly, the entire bag could be folded into a package no bigger than the flat of your hand.

It could be folded that way exactly once: at the factory where the bag was manufactured. Once you broke the shrink-wrap containing the bag, you would never fold the damned thing neatly again. It turned into a crinkly cranky mess of foil, billowing unmanageably in the slightest breeze

and smooth enough to slip from your hands unless you held
it in a death grip. The best refolding job I ever managed
produced a lumpy wad as big as a pillow. Try jamming
that into your rucksack when the original package was the
size of an envelope.

So: to open or not to open the bag, that was the question—whether it was worse to spend the night unprotected,
huddled against Oar for warmth, or to open the bag now
and spend the rest of my life on this planet, fighting with
a misshapen clump of surly tin.

To hell with it. I'd sooner shiver.

Around the Campfire

We ate around the campfire, Oar picking out the clear
jelly blobs and me eating the rest. It took several courses
to fill our stomachs. We would stuff the synthesizer with
biomass, wait eighteen minutes, then eat the results while
the machine whirred away on another batch.

While we ate, we talked . . . which is to say, Oar talked
and I asked enough questions to keep her going. I wanted
to learn all I could about her background, especially what
she knew about the history of her planet.

She knew almost nothing. The far past was a blank; even
the recent past was vague. Oar couldn't remember her father—her mother had pointed him out in the Tower of Ancestors, but he had been dormant Oar's whole life.
Sometime during the pregnancy, he had simply decided
enough was enough.

That was forty-five years ago.

It unsettled me that Oar was forty-five: she was almost
twice as old as me. On the other hand, I had seen that her
people didn't show their age . . . and why should I think of
her as childlike, just because her English was simplistic?
How's your grasp of her *language?* I asked myself.

It brought up an interesting question.

"Oar," I said, "how *did* you learn to talk like Explorers? Did Jelca and Ullis teach you?"

"Yes."

"They taught you to speak this well . . . and how long were they here?"

"A spring and a summer, three years ago."

"You learned this much English in six months? That's fast, Oar."

"I am very smart, Festina," she answered. "Not stupid, like Explorers."

It struck me she might be right. Bioengineering made her stronger and tougher than me; why not smarter too? Admittedly, Earth's attempts at building smarter people had seldom met with success: tinkering with the brain was so complex, most intelligence enhancement experiments ended in tragic failure. Even "successful" research projects had a ratio of ten thousand dead or near-vegetable infants for every child who turned out a cut above normal. Still, Melaquin had succeeded in so many other DNA modifications, why not heightened learning ability? It could work with the right approach—nothing crude like a mere increase in skull capacity, but exploring how humans truly differed from other animals. . . .

Neotony. Maybe that was it.

"Neotony" was a biological term related to a prolonged period of childhood. Humans were the winners in that category, at least on Earth; some species took longer to reach sexual maturity, but nothing required parental care as long as *Homo sapiens*. From time to time, zoologists hypothesized that neotony was a prime factor in human intelligence. After all, children learn enormous quantities of knowledge in a short span of time—much more than the greatest genius manages later in life. Some experts thought that the length of human childhood kept our brains in a state of accelerated learning for years longer than anything else in the animal kingdom . . . precisely what put us ahead of other species in terms of thinking capacity. If you keep acquiring knowledge at high speed for ten to fifteen years, you're just naturally going to beat animals who hit their plateau at two months.

Suppose the Melaquin engineers extended the childlike learning phase even longer—decades past us normal-flesh humans. Suppose a forty-year-old could learn languages with the wide-open ease of a toddler. And keeping these glass people childlike wasn't a safety hazard: they were practically invulnerable and had all their needs supplied by machines like the food synthesizer.

On the other hand, childlike brains might have their drawbacks in the end; after decades of operating at top speed, burnout might easily set in. Was there a neural chemical responsible for feelings of interest, curiosity, wonder? To construct childlike minds, the engineers may have pumped that chemical up to intense levels—levels that just couldn't be sustained forever. After years of high-capacity effort, the gland that produced the chemical might simply succumb to overwork. Result? Motivational shutdown. A deep metabolic lethargy.

It was all guesswork, but the logic held together. I gazed at Oar, seated across from me with the campfire's reflection flickering on her face. A sting of tears burned in my eyes. *Pity is stupid,* I told myself. *Every organism breaks down eventually. My father's heart broke down . . . my mother's liver. Why feel unbearably poignant that Oar's weak spot is her brain?*

But the tears did not stop stinging.

Walking (Part 2)

We slept the night in spoon position, with the Bumbler keeping watch for prowling bears. Only my legs got cold—the rest of my body was protected by the insulated remains of my tightsuit. An hour before dawn, I heaped fallen leaves over me from thigh to ankle, so I wasn't directly exposed to the breeze. The improvement was immediate; I kicked myself mentally for not doing it when I first lay down. Something had frazzled my survival instincts, and I couldn't allow that to continue.

The day dawned cloudy, and by noon it was raining. The good news was that we were walking through forest; the bad news was that the trees had shed enough leaves for rain to get through anyway. Little dribbles trickling down Oar's body looked like drops on a windowpane.

The drizzle continued intermittently for a day and a half. It started warm but turned colder on the second morning: a drop of five degrees according to the Bumbler. I hoped this wasn't the tip of the icestorm . . . but the temperature stabilized during the afternoon of our third day of travel, and the clouds thinned enough to let the sun glimmer through whitely. By then, we had reached the end of full forest and were picking our way through patchier groves down into the great prairie basin.

The next day we had to detour around an enormous herd of buffalo grazing directly in our path. Oar was surprised we didn't walk straight through them; but large bull ruminants are notorious for nasty tempers, and I had no intention of getting trampled. It took four hours to circle to a point where we could turn south again, which tells you how big the herd was . . . several thousand animals in total, all of them shaggy with winter fur.

In midafternoon, with the herd still visible behind us, we came upon a dozen wolves. No doubt, the pack was shadowing the buffalo; I couldn't remember whether wolves were day or night predators, but they would attack when they were ready, running in to pull down a calf or an elderly animal too weak to defend itself. In the meantime, they eyed us from a judicious distance of a hundred meters, sizing up our food potential.

"Clap your hands," I murmured to Oar.

"Are we expressing admiration for those dogs?"

"Just do it!"

Oar slapped her hands together several times: glass on glass, each impact as loud as a hammer blow. The noise hurt my ears; and the wolf pack vanished like mist at dawn, slipping silently away through the tall grass.

We had no more trouble with animals that day. Most wildlife stayed away from us through the entire journey. As the terrain flattened out, it became easy to spot ground mammals a long way off—prairie dogs, rabbits, coyotes— but they always disappeared before we came near. Birds let us get closer; they stared at us suspiciously from trees or bushes, or flew overhead in vast migratory flocks. It was late the same day we passed the buffalo that I looked up at one flock and said, "Holy shit!"

"Do Explorers revere shit?" Oar asked with interest.

"It's an expression," I said, still staring at the sky. "Do you know what those birds are?"

"No, Festina."

"I can't be sure . . . but I think they're passenger pigeons."

The Pigeons

"Do those pigeons carry passengers?" Oar asked. "I should enjoy flying on a bird."

"I don't know why they're called passenger pigeons," I told her. "They've been extinct for five hundred years."

"Extinct means dead?"

"Yes."

Oar burst into giggles. "Dead things do not move, Festina. You are very, very stu—confused."

I didn't answer. Over the past few days, I had grudgingly accepted Melaquin as Earth's near-twin; but the sight of an extinct species jolted me. There weren't even passenger pigeons on New Earth—when the League of Peoples built humanity its new home, they could only duplicate what was still alive on. . . .

"Damn, I'm stupid!" I said, hitting my head with my palm.

"No, just confused," Oar insisted generously.

Duplication

In all my time on Melaquin, my mind had been too lost in dismay and distraction to put the pieces together. The League of Peoples had already proved it could duplicate Earth—after the schism that divided humanity, the League had built New Earth as a refuge for those who agreed to respect the galactic peace. Humans who refused to give up armed violence were quarantined on their old planet, stuck with the legacy of pollution and war accumulated over the centuries; but those who abandoned their weapons were given a clean new planet: Earth without the garbage. New Earth was a "Welcome to the Universe" gift from the League of Peoples . . . along with star drives, YouthBoost, and other goodies no sentient race should do without.

Why had it taken me so long to remember New Earth was artificially constructed? Stupid, Festina: very stupid. But now that my eyes were open, everything made sense.

Some time far in the past—long enough ago that history didn't record it—members of the League must have visited Old Earth. They made the same proposal then that they made to humanity in the twenty-first century: prove your sentience by renouncing violence, and we will give you the stars. As in the more recent contact, some prehistoric people must have said yes while others said no . . . and those who agreed not to kill were given a new home elsewhere in the galaxy.

Here on Melaquin.

This planet must have been built by the League to duplicate Earth at that long-ago time . . . including the presence of passenger pigeons. Somewhere Melaquin must also have dodos, moas, and other species that hadn't survived recent times on *our* Earth; unless the humans who came to Melaquin had killed those animals all over again.

No, I thought to myself. *They didn't kill the animals, they killed themselves.* Either they developed bioengineering on their own, or they received it as a gift from the League; and they had turned themselves into glass creatures like

Oar—tougher, stronger, smarter, and a complete evolution-
ary dead-end.

"Festina," Oar said, "are you becoming crazed again?"

I must have been standing frozen, thinking it all through.
"No," I answered, "I'm not crazed . . . although you may
think I am when I tell what I want to do."

"What?"

"We're going to find rocks and look for creatures that
probably aren't there."

Paleontology

There is one simple difference between Old and New
Earth: the original planet has fossils; the duplicate does not.
When the League gave New Earth artificial deposits of
sandstone, limestone or shale, they didn't enliven the rock
with simulated remnants of ancient life. For the sake of raw
materials, they *did* create fields of petroleum, coal, and
other fossil resources . . . but not the fossils themselves.

I bet Melaquin didn't have fossils either.

The most promising excavation site within view was the
shore of a creek half an hour ahead of us. Water cuts down
into soil, exposing stones that would otherwise require digging to bring to the surface. The creek bank should have a
good sample of easy-to-pry-out rocks; if I checked a few
dozen without finding fossils, I could be fairly confident
my hunch was right.

"We're going to that creek," I told Oar.

"Yes, Festina," she answered patiently. "Going around
it would take a long time."

Creeks were plentiful in that part of the prairies. Most
were a few paces wide and barely thigh-deep, so crossing
them was no challenge—just cold and wet. The one we
approached now was larger than average, but still too small
to deserve the name "river": thirty meters across, sluggish
and barely over our heads in depth. In spring, it might be
deeper; but now the water level was low enough to leave

a healthy sweep of gravel uncovered on the near shore.

"Perfect," I said. "As good as we're going to find on short notice."

"Do you want me to clap in admiration of the creek?" Oar asked.

"No need." I climbed down the dirt bank to the gravel and stared around appraisingly. The top layer of stones were worn smooth by water action—whatever fossils they once contained could have eroded to invisibility. Still, I might find better samples underneath; and there were other places to look for exposed deposits.

"Oar," I said, "can you please walk along the bank and see if there are any rocks sticking out of the dirt? I'm looking for rocks with edges . . . not smooth like these pebbles."

"What shall I do if I find one?"

"Bring it to me."

She looked at me dubiously. "You want me to touch dirty rocks, Festina? That is not very nice."

"You can wash your hands after—the creek's right there."

"Is the creek water clean?"

"Clean enough," I said, stretching a point. It was actually a bit muddy, thanks to silt washed down by the previous day's rain. No doubt, it also contained the usual disease-causing microbes one finds in untreated water: typhoid perhaps, and a cornucopia of viruses for intestinal flu. However, Oar had little to worry about—along with the other improvements in her body, she probably had a nigh-impregnable immune system. Why not? Her designers had built in everything else.

I envied her for that. Since the start of our trip, I'd carefully purified the water we drank, boiling it on the campfire and filling enough canteens to last us through the next day. I also had water purification tablets if the canteens ran dry, but I preferred to use those sparingly, since I could never replenish my supply. Still, I worried about infection. If this planet really was a duplicate of Earth from millennia ago, it might have smallpox, diphtheria, pneumonic plague: famous diseases, extinct in the rest of the galaxy, but possibly still thriving here on Melaquin.

Maybe Oar was right to worry about getting dirty.

With the air of a woman who hopes she doesn't find anything, Oar started walking slowly along the water's edge. I turned my attention to the gravel flat and began to dig down. Sure enough, the stones were not so eroded a few centimeters below the top surface. I was just beginning to examine them for fossil evidence when the Bumbler's alarm went off.

EM Anomaly

I did my programmed roll-and-tuck, having the good fortune to dive in the direction of the Bumbler rather than throwing myself into the nearby creek. With fists ready for trouble, I kicked the Bumbler's SHUT-UP switch and scanned the area.

I saw no threat, but standing on the creek-bed, I was three meters lower than the main level of the prairie. Anything could be up there, lurking just out of sight.

Not far away, Oar opened her mouth to say something. I held up a hand and held my finger to my lips. She closed her mouth and looked around warily.

Think, I told myself. *What could the Bumbler detect from here?* It might be a false alarm—Bumblers did make mistakes—but Explorers who dismissed such warnings soon had their names entered on the Academy's Memory Wall.

Maybe the Bumbler had suddenly decided to complain about Oar again: unknown organism, help, help. Still, I had programmed the machine's tiny brain to accept her as a friend; her presence hadn't bothered it for days. Best to assume the problem was something else . . . something I couldn't see.

What could the Bumbler detect that I couldn't? It had a small capacity for peering through the creek banks, but not well—its passive X-ray scans could only penetrate ten to fifteen centimeters of dirt. Naturally, it could see farther if something was emitting large quantities of X-rays . . . or radio waves. . . .

Radio. Someone nearby might have transmitted a radio message. Quickly, I backtracked the Bumbler's short term memory and looked at the radio bands. Yes: it had picked up a coherent short-wave signal lasting only fifteen seconds. Did that mean an Explorer in the neighborhood? Or someone else?

Silently, I turned to Oar and pointed to the creek. Without waiting to see if she understood, I hefted up the Bumbler and headed for the water. We could hide there, just to be on the safe side—the middle of the creek was deep enough to be over our heads. My pack had a tiny scuba rebreather, only two minutes of air, but enough to stay submerged in an emergency. I'd give that to Oar; for myself, I'd have to make do with. . . .

Shit. I'd have to snorkel with the same esophageal airway I'd used on Yarrun.

The Peeper

After whispered instructions to Oar, I lowered myself into the water. It was cold; it was also murky, but that was good. The slight cloudiness would make it hard for someone to see me poised just under the surface. Oar, of course, was invisible as soon as she submerged.

I found a depth where I could stand on the bottom and keep the tip of the airway just above the surface. The taste of it was sour in my mouth. I had washed it since the Landing, washed it over and over again; but I still imagined I could taste the rusty flavor of blood on the plastic.

Trying to refocus my thoughts, I aimed the Bumbler's scanner straight up at the outside world. In the muddy water, I had to amplify the Bumbler's brightness before I could make out the screen; but my eyes adjusted soon enough to give me an adequate view above the surface.

The sky. The creek banks.

Thirty seconds after we had hidden ourselves, a head peeked over the south bank.

At first, it looked like a fully human head: smooth brown skin; darker lips. But as I stared more closely, bile rose in my mouth. The head had no hair—or rather it had an abstracted glass simulation of hair, like Oar's but a slightly different style . . . and the eyes were also like Oar's, silvery globes with mirror surfaces.

The lips drew back in smile . . . or maybe a grimace. Inside the mouth, the teeth were clear as glass.

Sickened, I realized what I was seeing. This was a glass person just like Oar; but he or she had glued strips of skin onto cheeks, forehead, and throat.

Strips of human skin.

Part XII
SKIN

Hiding

The skin-covered face peered down a few seconds more, then withdrew. I stayed put, hoping Oar would do the same—she was under orders not to come out until I gave the okay. Still, she had only a brief supply of air, and was inexperienced using a scuba breather; I gave the signal to surface at the two minute mark, even though I would have preferred to stay under much longer.

Oar emerged silently and kept her mouth shut. Good; no matter how she might be given to outbursts, her cultural heritage placed priority on not being noticed. They built their villages underwater, they made themselves transparent, they cleaned all trace of their presence from the environment . . . no wonder Oar had the instinct to stay quiet when strangers were near.

I wondered if Skin-Face was the reason Oar's people were so good at hiding.

For five minutes we remained in the water with only our heads showing. All that time, some devil's advocate in my mind kept asking why we should cower. The skin on that glass face was probably just animal hide—perhaps leather from a buffalo carcass, scraped clean of fur and worn for harmless adornment. Believing it was human skin was mor-

bid imagination . . . that and the blurriness of looking at the
Bumbler screen through muddy water.

But if it *had* been human skin, it came from an Explorer,
not someone with a glass body. And perhaps the accompanying radio transmissions had come from Explorer equipment: equipment stolen from my fellow ECMs along with
their skins.

I made myself get out of the water when I could no
longer control the chattering of my teeth—not fear, but the
physical chill of a creek in waning autumn. For a while I
shivered on shore, until the sun warmed me back to a tolerable temperature. Thank heavens R&D made the tightsuit
from quick-dry fabric; I would only stay soggy for half an
hour, after which the material's natural insulation would be
as good as a dry parka. In the meantime, I had to hug
myself for warmth and wonder if Skin Face would reap-
pear.

He didn't . . . or possibly *she* didn't, although I was in-
clined to think of the stranger as male. Some atavistic prej-
udice in my subconscious still believed men were scarier
than women.

Say it was a man, a glass man of Oar's species: he must
have heard the Bumbler's alarm beeping and came to investigate. It had taken him more than a minute to arrive,
so he hadn't been nearby . . . close enough to hear it, but
far enough away that he hadn't recognized the sound as
unnatural. When he saw nothing out of the ordinary, he
must have decided the noise was just bird cry. One quick
look, then he went back about his business.

What was his business? It was time to find out.

It was also time to get the stunner out of my pack.

Three Spears

Motioning Oar to stay put, I swam the creek with the
stunner in my mouth, in case I might need it quickly. The
afternoon continued quiet and undisturbed—the chirp of

birds, the light hiss of breeze ruffling the prairie grass. On
the far side of the water, I climbed the dirt bank: steep, but
only three meters high, the damp earth providing plenty of
purchase. When I was almost at the top, I dug my feet
firmly into the soil and did a quick scan with the Bumbler,
X-raying through the last few centimeters of bank to make
sure Skin-Face wasn't lurking above. The screen was clear
except for pebbles and roots; so with straining caution, I
lifted my head over the edge for a look.

No Skin-Face close at hand; but a kilometer downstream,
three humanoid figures tracked along the bank, walking
away from me. The Bumbler gave me a telescopic view of
the trio: three males, all carrying spears and shoulder bags,
all wearing strips of skin on their faces. They had skin on
their genitals too, carefully wrapped around penis and testicles. One also had a patch of skin on his chest—I could
see it through his transparent back.

Perhaps that was the chieftain: the man who could com-
mandeer the largest share of a kill.

Still hoping I was wrong, I magnified the view a few
notches higher. Maybe the skin strips were some kind of
harmless ornamentation. . . .

No. In extreme close-up, there was no mistake. It was
brown human skin, complete with wisps of hair, fastened
to the underlying glass flesh.

One man lifted his hand and pointed at the creek ahead
of them. The chieftain nodded, and all three started down
the bank toward the water. My guess was they had reached
a point shallow enough to ford; they were obviously reluctant to cross where the creek was over their heads.
That gave me useful intelligence about the enemy . . .
and already I was thinking of them as enemies, although
they had showed no sign of hostility toward me or anyone
else.

Explorers habitually regard strangers as threats. Shaking
hands is for diplomats.

Simple Prairie Hunters

The men appeared on the far side of the creek a short time later and continued north. On their present path, they would run into the buffalo herd we had seen that morning . . . and that might be their goal. They might be simple prairie hunters, searching for food to feed their families.

Simple prairie hunters who carried radios.

I shook my head to clear it. Explanations would come eventually . . . or else they wouldn't. Unsolved puzzles were a permanent frustration of the job.

At last the spearmen disappeared behind a copse of trees and I waved for Oar to join me. She crossed the creek with the scuba breather in her mouth, even though it couldn't have much air left in it. I didn't say anything—if she was happier to get air from a machine rather than holding her breath for the few seconds the water was over her head, so be it. The little tank was self-charging, given enough solar energy and access to air; in twenty-four hours it would be usable again.

From the top of the bank, I led us straight to the nearest clump of trees, to make sure we were shielded from the spearmen's eyes—even though they were more than a klick away, the prairie allowed for long sight-lines. The men had come from this direction; we found their footprints in the dirt when we stopped to collect ourselves.

One good thing about people as dense as glass: they leave deep, clear footprints.

"Who *were* those people?" Oar blurted when we were safely under the trees.

"I was going to ask you the same question," I answered. "You don't know who lives in this area?"

"No. I thought . . ." She stopped herself. "I thought something very foolish."

Her face was troubled; I suspected I knew why. Oar might have believed she and her ancestors were the only people in the world. She had seen the transmission from Chee and Seele talking about another city to the south, but she had dismissed that as an Explorer lie. The three Skin-Faces may have been the first strangers she'd seen . . . the first non-Explorers anyway. Their presence upset her more than they upset me. They were proof she wasn't unique.

I didn't belabor the subject. "You said you came this way once before . . . when you decided to follow the other Explorers. You didn't see the Skin-Faces?"

"No."

"But you did get this far?"

"Yes, Festina. The great river where I stopped is still ahead."

I frowned. Why hadn't she seen Skin-Faces on her last trip? Had she just been lucky? Or were the three spearmen outside their usual territory? Maybe they were the only people of their kind here on the plains; or maybe there was a tribe of thousands, but they usually stayed south of the great river Oar talked about.

Maybe we were walking straight into the arms of a horde who had already killed one set of Explorers and now wore their skins.

Jelca? Ullis?

I gritted my teeth. "Let's get moving," I said. "But keep your eyes open for trouble."

"I am ready, Festina."

She swung her silver axe to her shoulder. I couldn't tell if the gesture was meaningful, or if she was simply getting ready to move out. Did she understand that her axe could be a weapon, or did she only see it as a tool for clearing trees?

I shivered. Spears. Axes. Weapons.

Feeling the weight of the stunner in my hand, I headed off at Oar's side.

Night on the Plains

The footprints of the spearmen had come from the south-west; therefore I headed southeast, setting a brisk pace until the depths of dusk. We camped for the night in a stand of a dozen trees—large enough to conceal us from prying eyes, but small enough that we still had a clear view in all directions.

Before we went to sleep, I tuned the Bumbler's intruder scan to cover the maximum possible area. With so much ground to cover, the Bumbler wouldn't be as sensitive—it would probably overlook snakes, for example, especially ones moving slowly—but it would detect glass spearmen at almost a klick away.

Frankly I didn't give a damn about snakes that night . . . even rattlers.

When sleep finally came, my dreams were ugly: Yarrun as a Skin-Face, tattered flesh hanging from his disfigured jaw. He tried to kill me with a spear, or maybe it was Oar's axe; I couldn't keep my attention on the weapon with that ravaged face in front of me. As sometimes happens in dreams, it kept repeating itself ineffectually—Yarrun would lunge and I would dodge, much too slowly. The weapon came in, but nothing happened, as if my mind didn't care whether the blow actually landed. The moment passed, then the whole thing started again: Yarrun attacking again and again, with both of us sluggish, as if slowed by water.

It was a tiring dream . . . like doing hard work hour after hour. Eventually I woke, still in darkness. I lay on my back and stared at the stars for a long time. Maybe the dream really happened then: when I assembled the random non-sense floating through my mind and interpreted it as Yarrun attacking. Some psychologists claim that's the way dreams work—invented after the fact, when you try to impose order on the mental chaos. Perhaps I owed it to Yarrun to dream about him. Who knows?

If I thought about Yarrun, I would cry. If I thought about Chee, I would probably cry too. If I thought about Jelca . . . I wouldn't cry, but it wouldn't help my mood.

In the end, I passed the time devising ways to fight people made of glass. How to punch them without breaking my hand. Where to kick for maximum effect. Whether their

greater density made them harder or easier to take down
with a leg sweep. And the perennial question of any martial
artist raised under League of Peoples's law: how to batter
opponents into unconsciousness without the risk of killing
them.

No one has ever answered that question to my satisfaction. That made it a good topic for thought in the restless
night . . . letting my mind swirl around the possibilities until
finally, sleep took mercy on me.

Dragons

There was frost the next morning—a white feathered
coating across the broad green of the prairie. Oar considered it an aesthetic improvement; she also enjoyed the way
her breath turned to steam when she huffed out.

"I have become a dragon," she told me. "Haahhhhh! I
am breathing fire."

"How do you know about dragons?" I asked.

"My sister told me."

"Before or after she met the other Explorers?"

"I cannot remember."

Idly, I wondered if her sister heard about dragons from
Jelca and Ullis, or if the dragon myth was so old, these
people remembered it from long-ago days on Earth.

Less idly, I wondered if dragons *weren't* a myth on Melaquin: if there really were fire-breathing creatures, created
by bored bioengineers. Exposed out here with open space
in all directions, would we suddenly see a flying giant in
the sky?

Sometimes I hate the way an Explorer's mind works.

The River

We reached the great river shortly after noon, having
seen no further sign of glass-people. Although the day had

started clear, gray clouds stole in throughout the morning, making the sky morosely overcast. The river was none too cheerful either: half a klick wide, muddy, and festooned with deadfalls. Every dozen meters or so, bare branches protruded from the water, remnants of trees that had fallen upstream, floated a while, then run aground in shallows. Here and there, larger logs lurked under the surface, their slime-coated wood a jaundiced yellow.

"I do not like this river," Oar said.

"Because it came close to drowning you?"

"It is also mean and spiky."

The spiky bits—the deadfalls—worried me too. Before seeing the river, I had planned to cross using some suitably floatable log: Oar would cling to the log, while I dog-paddled to push it from one bank to the other. Now I realized that was easier said than done. Finding a log wasn't the problem; we could chop down a tree from the many stands dotting the shore. However, threading the log through the erratic palisade of deadwood, without running afoul of sunken obstacles . . . that would take luck.

I hated relying on luck. When it worked, it made me feel so damned eerie.

To give myself time to think, I led Oar east for a while, tracking the shoreline to see if we'd find somewhere better to cross. Three bends of the river later, nothing had changed: deadfalls in the shallows and sunken trees farther out. Worse, I hadn't any new ideas and the longer we dithered on shore, the more chance we might be spotted by people we wanted to avoid. The clincher was the sky darkening minute by minute. Rain was coming: rain that would fill the river with fast-running mud.

"Here's a good place," I said, trying to sound chipper. "A good straight stretch of open water." It was only half a lie: the river did run straight for a klick, but it was just as congested as everywhere else.

It took fifteen minutes to find a fallen tree, trim its branches with the axe, then drag the trunk to the river. Oar's glass muscles did most of the work. Soon we were in the water, positioned on the upstream side of our "boat"—if we did run into a sunken log, I didn't want us squeezed between the log and our tree trunk. For final preparations, I held the stunner in one hand and slung the recharged scuba device around my neck. Oar wasn't happy I kept the rebreather for myself, but it was the rational thing to do. She couldn't die by drowning; I could. The rebreather would also give me a chance to pull us both out of trouble if something went wrong.

The water was not as cold as the stream we'd hidden in the day before, or maybe it just seemed warmer because the air had turned cool. Clearing the shore proved easy enough—we only snagged once on a deadfall, and Oar chopped us free within seconds.

Good axe.

The current was slow but strong, moving about a meter per second. As I flutter-kicked us forward, the far shore slid dreamily sideways. Oar kept up a steady chatter of encouragement. "We are doing very well, Festina. We are going to miss that log there . . . yes, see? And if we go a little faster . . . yes, we have cleared that one too. We are doing very well. Very, very . . ." She stopped. "What is making that beeping sound?"

"The Bumbler," I panted. "Proximity alarm."

"Is this where we say *Oh shit*, Festina?"

"Let me get back to you on that."

Scanning for Trouble

The alarm scan was still set on its longest range—at least we had ample advance notice for whatever the Bumbler had detected. There were no Skin-Faces on shore, no hypothetical dragons soaring through the sky. That suggested the danger might be in the water with us . . . and a scary suggestion it was. On this setting, the Bumbler wouldn't notice anything as trifling as a lamprey, piranha, or water moccasin; it had to be something bigger.

If we were lucky, it might be a freshwater dolphin. If we weren't. . . . I told myself the river was too cold for alligators, and snapping turtles seldom bit anything larger than pickerel.

"Keep as still as you can," I told Oar. "If you don't move, your legs are almost invisible in the water. You won't look like anything's supper."

She said nothing—her "stay quiet, don't be seen" instincts had kicked in again. I fumbled with the Bumbler, trying to locate what it was beeping about.

Radio first. No signals.

Visual scan. Nothing.

IR . . . and immediately it showed a strong heat source in the water, one hundred meters upstream.

The temperature was too high for a reptile; it had to be warm-blooded. That suggested a dolphin; but the heat trace on the screen looked bigger than any fresh-water dolphin I'd heard of. In fact, the bogey looked as big as a killer whale, and as hot as a gas-powered engine.

Holding the Bumbler high out of the water, I dialed "Visual telescopic" and aimed the scanner in the direction of the IR blob. A moment later, the screen showed a sharklike fin cutting the surface in a straight line toward us.

The fin was made of glass.

The Glass Fin

"Have you heard of glass dolphins?" I asked Oar.

Her answer was barely audible. "No."

I scowled. Possibly, the engineers of Melaquin made glass versions of higher cetaceans as well as humans—the animals were, after all, sentient in their own way. Even so, the blob on the Bumbler's screen had a furiously bright IR signature. Hotter than Oar. Hotter than any blubber-insulated orca built to avoid leaking body heat into cold surrounding water.

The fin continued straight for us.

Still working with the Bumbler, I tried to resolve a better picture of the thing—particularly its tail. Cetaceans have horizontal tail fins; fish have vertical. The image on the screen was still too blobby for me to be certain, but this tail looked vertical. And the thing's body wasn't moving properly: no undulations to provide propulsion. The body stayed completely rigid, more like a submarine than a living organism.

I thought of Oar's glass coffin boat. Perhaps Skin-Faces had boats too, built with intimidation in mind.

"Shit," I said.

"Oh shit," Oar murmured, like the response in a litany.

Raising my voice, I shouted at the onrushing fin, "Greetings! I am a sentient citizen of the League of Peoples, and I beg . . . aw, fuck it."

Lifting my stunner, I shot the beast right in the dorsal.

Accidental Music

Hit by sonics, the fin sang like a glass harp. The sound reminded me of the hum from running a wet finger around the rim of a wine glass. I could actually see the vibrations, strong on the fin's tip, damped down where the fin entered the water.

Without hesitation, I shoved the stunner into the river and fired again.

Ouch.

My hand tingled with numbness—in water, the tight sonic beam didn't hold its cohesion, and a fraction of it radiated back at me. My grip didn't loosen enough to drop the gun, but I couldn't pull the trigger again till my fingers got over the shock. Still, the incoming bogey took a hard hit too: water conducts sound better than air.

A moment later, the fin disappeared.

On the Bumbler screen, the bogey's heat signature veered to one side and angled into a steep dive. If it used sonar, it would have quite a headache—maybe enough to

send it running in pain. For that matter, it looked like it
was going to....

I swear I felt the jar of impact as the bogey's nose hit
the river bottom. The heat blob on the Bumbler dimmed to
half, as muck bloomed up from the collision site and fuzzed
the IR scan. Still, I could see the bogey reverse its way out
of the mud and angle off in another direction, only to run
into a sunken log as it neared the surface.

The log cracked. I hoped the bogey did too.

Our tree trunk rocked wildly as waves swept across us,
hard and fast. For a moment, my attention was occupied
with keeping hold of the Bumbler and the stunner; to avoid
losing the weapon, I transferred it to my other hand. That
left only my numb arm for clinging to the tree trunk. Awk-
wardly, I slung the arm over the tree, not holding on but
only propped up with the trunk snug under my armpit.

I was just turning back to look for the bogey when it
jumped straight out of the water.

It was a shark the size of a killer whale, but clear as
glass and just as stiff. As it soared upward, head clearing
the water, then fins, then tail, I could see its nose was
starred with cracks from its collision with the log: the beast
wasn't invulnerable. Without hesitation, I raised the stunner
and shot straight at its cracked snout while it still sailed
through the air.

The sonics struck the glass like a gong. For one brief
moment, the bogey reverberated—a pure deep tone of
whale song. Then the arc of its jump brought it splashing
into the river, more than a ton of glass bellyflopping in front
of me.

Tsunami time.

Submerged

One moment my numb arm was propped over our tree
trunk; the next I was hammered by a wall of water, knocking me loose and burying me under its weight. It drove me

deep below the surface, battering my head and shoulders, almost stunning me. Instinct was all that kept me holding my breath. I was left disoriented, dizzy . . . which way was up? And even if I could figure out the direction to swim, could I do it with one bad arm and the Bumbler weighing me down?

Yes, I could. I could do it.

The rebreather was still around my neck. I shoved it into my mouth, cleared it, and took a breath. Air. Yes. I was in control.

Light meant up, dark meant down. The light looked a long way off, but I could make it. I just had to take it easy. Once I found air again, I could search for Oar. Probably she was still afloat; with strength like hers, it would take more than a tidal wave to knock her off our tree trunk.

I swam upward, filled with the calm that comes when survival demands it. Up toward the light. I could see it better now. I could. . . .

Bump. My outstretched hand touched glass.

The whale-shark floated between me and the surface.

Around the Belly

Maybe it was dead. No, it had to be a machine; say that it was broken, not dead. But I had shot it three times, it had smashed into the river bottom and the log, then it had suffered the crashing smack of bellyflopping into the water after its jump. All that buffeting must have taken its toll.

The machine lay still now. I prayed it was too damaged to move. Keeping my hand against the thing's hull, I began to feel my way around it: under its belly, up to fresh air.

Clang.

The sound was soft. I didn't hear it so much as feel it through my fingertips. Something had shifted inside the glass machine.

Just broken equipment, I told myself, *banging together.*

I didn't believe it. I gave a good kick, trying to hurry to the surface.

Whir.

An engine spun into life. I could feel that through my fingers too.

Shit.

I was still palming my way along the hull when the whale-shark started to move. The motion was jerky—damaged. I wanted to press my stunner against the machine's glass belly and keep pulling the trigger till the gun's battery was exhausted; but there might be an echoing backwash that left me unconscious in the water. My arm was still numb from that earlier bounce-back. All I could do was hurry, and hope Oar and I got out of the water before the glass monster came to its senses.

The hull under my hand was starting to curve upward. I was around the bulge. Pushing off, I swam hard toward the light. Beside me, the machine moved forward, its wake pulling me around in a spiral. Ignore it—up was up, and I was almost at the surface.

For some reason, I thought I'd be all right if I could reach fresh air again.

My head emerged into the light. Some distance away, Oar still clung to the tree trunk, her body frozen, not looking in my direction. I was about to swim toward her when something grabbed my leg.

I was dragged under again, fighting and kicking. There was time to see glass tentacles stretching from the whale-shark's mouth to my ankle. Then I was pulled inside.

Jonah

For such a big machine, the interior was cramped—too cramped to bend and loosen the glass grip on my leg. The Bumbler pressed hard into my kidneys, the pain stinging sharp; so I wriggled and squeezed to roll the other way, facing the Bumbler instead of having it at my back. Having a Bumbler jammed against my stomach wasn't comfortable either, but I could stand it for a while. With less than two minutes of air in the rebreather, I had worse troubles.

The whale-shark's mouth began to close. I tried to hold it open, tried to grab its jaw and pull myself free; but the hold on my ankle was as strong as iron, chaining me in place.

Better to stop fighting. My air would last longer that way. *Concentrate*, I told myself. *Slow breaths. Wait.*

I had no idea what I was waiting for; but no one builds a river-shark just for the hell of it—not one with tentacles for grabbing passersby. This machine was designed to capture people . . . and I hoped it took them alive.

Yes. Of course it must want me alive. If its purpose was to eliminate intruders, it would have killed me by now. It could have zipped out a knife to slit my throat the second I was immobilized.

Unless it wanted my skin intact. Unless the machine's job was to supply the Skin-Faces with fresh Explorer pelts.

Concentrate! I growled mentally. *Slow, slow breaths.*

Somewhere inside the shark, machinery started grinding. It was an unhealthy, damaged sound—the stunner had shattered some part of the glass mechanism. Slowly though, slowly, the water around me gurgled away. The shark was pumping water out, and (I hoped) pumping breathable air in.

Taking a chance, I raised my head into the clear space and inhaled shallowly through my nose. So far so good. I completely filled my lungs and waited.

No dizziness, no sudden rush of blackness. The shark wasn't even doping the air with knockout gas.

What a wimp-ass planet.

Pumps Clanking

The water level dropped till half the interior was filled with air. I expected the water to continue receding; it didn't.

Why did that bother me?

The whale-shark contained no light source, but it swam close enough to the surface that weak daylight filtered through the machine's glass hull. The dim illumination showed why the water level wasn't dropping anymore: as fast as the pumps sucked water away, more water seeped through the cracks where the shark had hit the log. It looked like the glass bent slightly inward up near the snout—as if the water pressure outside had enough strength to buckle the hull, now that the inside was half air.

"Okay," I said aloud, "I am now officially worried."

Minutes passed. The grinding noise in the tail section got worse, punctuated occasionally by soft electric crackling. If that was the sound of the pumps, they wouldn't last long.

I held the rebreather in front of my face. The gauge was hard to read in the dimness, but the little tank still held sixty seconds of air. Careful breathing could stretch that out, but not forever.

Lifting my head into the air space, I filled my lungs as deeply as I could. By the time I finished, there was no doubt possible: the water level was back on the rise.

Arrival

In an entertainment bubble broadcast, I'd be saved at the last second—just as the chamber was completely full, just as my rebreather gasped out its last molecule of oxygen. Life doesn't match that standard: you do not find a job just as you run out of money, a couple's orgasms seldom arrive simultaneously, and salvation may not sweep to the rescue at the point of peak drama. For me, salvation arrived with some minutes to spare—better than mistiming its cue in the other direction.

To make a long story short, the whale-shark's gullet still held a few fingers of air at the end of the machine's journey.

My first hint we were close to our goal was a sharp dive:

I couldn't tell if we were going down intentionally or some
new breakdown was sinking us at speed. The dim and distant daylight from the river's surface faded to darkness.
After half a minute, I asked myself how deep the river
could be. We hadn't traveled far enough to reach the ocean.
Perhaps we had come to a lake whose bottom was lower
than the river feeding into it.

Down and down and down. I was glad the water level
had risen now—it helped balance the fearsome pressure
pushing on the shark's broken nose. Even so, the damaged
area creaked in protest . . . and perhaps it *was* in the nick
of time that the machine passed through an airlock into
bluish-silver light.

The shark's mouth opened, spilling water onto a concrete
jetty.

The tentacled grip on my ankle eased. Stiffly, I pulled
myself past the Bumbler (still pressed against my stomach),
and crawled out of the shark's mouth. Thirty seconds later,
I was on my feet, the Bumbler strapped to my back, and
my stunner in hand.

Silence.

No one rushed to attack me. The entry chamber was
small and empty, with blank concrete walls. At the far end
was a metal door with a red pushbutton beside it.

Enter freely and of your own will, I thought to myself.

The Colored Town

There was no way to go back the way I came. Even if I
could start the whale-shark again, I'd drown on the return
journey. That left two choices: sit where I was, or move
forward. Staying put just avoided the future. Better to head
out now, and find cover before anyone came for me.

I walked straight to the door and pressed the button. With
a rusty whine, the hatch opened toward me. I stepped
through.

Glass towers. Glass homes. Glass blockhouses.

It was larger than Oar's village, but built on the same model. A black hemispherical dome loomed overhead, no doubt holding back a million tons of water. The buildings on the perimeter were low-built, while the ones in the middle reached high into the air, stretching more than halfway to the roof. Like Oar's home, the place had an abandoned air: quiet and unpeopled.

But it had color.

Red plastic streamers lay in the street, like the unswept remains of a Mardi Gras. Purple and orange banners had been fastened above many glass doorways—banners now fuzzed with dust, and corners dangling dog-eared where the glue had lost its stick. The tallest spire in town sported a droopy yellow flag with a smudged black crest in the middle; and other towers had flags of their own, bile green, dark blue, stripes of brown and fuchsia.

It all looked so sad. Dirt-specked attempts to brighten the place up. Deliberately garish yet futile.

Wherever I looked was glass, as sterile as distilled water. The scraps of blousy fabric only heightened the austerity of the barren backdrop. How can a meter of cloth enliven a wall twenty storeys high? And from the clashes between adjacent colors, I could tell the decorators had no sense of what they were doing. They had no particular effect in mind—they only wanted to disrupt the sameness of glass on glass.

I thought of the spearmen I'd seen, wrapping skin on their faces and genitals. Did that come from a similar impulse? Plastering skin on their bodies to break up the sterile sameness?

But there was no reason to assume this town belonged to the Skin-Faces. For all I knew, the banners around me might be centuries old. The red plastic in the gutters might be that old too. With no rain under the dome and no animals, with air that was likely filtered free of most bacteria, the fallen streamers might last a lifetime. A flat and weary lifetime.

It might be helpful to see whether this place had its own

Tower of Ancestors filled with dormant bodies. If the bodies wore scraps of skin, it would tell me something.

Cautiously, I walked to the middle of town. Like Oar's home, this place had an open square, a square featuring four fountains, not two. The colored debris was more abundant here: mostly on the ground, but with scraps of colored plastic thrown over the fountains and festooned clumsily above doorways.

The heavyhandedness of it all weighed drearily on me. I sat on a glass bench and tried to will myself into seeing the color as sincere celebration, not a vain roaring against the bleakness.

Silence. The emptiness of a place whose spirit had died.

Many Happy Returns

With a swish, a door opened in a building behind me. Four Skin-Faces marched out, two men, two women, all holding spears. They fell into position beside the doorway, men on one side, women on the other—like an honor guard lining up to welcome a VIP.

"Attention!" one of the men called. *Attention*: the English word. All four spear-carriers slammed the butts of their weapons on the ground and snapped rigid in perfect Outward Fleet form.

I didn't move. If I ran, they might chase me; and where could I hide in a city of glass?

Two imperious hand-claps sounded sharply from within the building. I couldn't see who'd clapped—the Skin-Faces blocked my line of sight. Very slowly, I adjusted my grip on the stunner, in case the clapped command was an order to attack.

It wasn't. One of the women cleared her throat, hummed a musical tone, then began to sing: *Happy Birthday*. The others joined in.

On the third line ("Happy birthday, lord and master"), a figure emerged from the building: a person in tightsuit.

its fabric smeared with grass stains, brownish sludge, and clots of rust-red. The suit's helmet had its visor set to one-way opaque; I couldn't see whether the face inside was flesh or glass.

Walking slowly, bowlegged, the tightsuited figure passed between the lines of Skin-Faces and continued across the plaza—straight toward me. I raised the stunner, ready but not aiming it directly at the approaching stranger.

The figure stopped, then spread its arms wide, showing its hands were empty: an obvious "I'm unarmed" gesture.

I didn't lower the stunner. I did, however, say the words. "Greetings. I am a sentient citizen of the League of Peoples, and I beg your Hospitality."

A chuckle sounded within the suit—a male chuckle. "Hospitality?" The figure reached up, popped the releases, and took off its helmet. "A lot you know about hospitality, Ramos. You haven't even wished me happy birthday."

"All right," I said. "Happy birthday, Phylar."

Part XIII
GIVEAWAYS

The Tip

Phylar Tobit's face spread into a grin. One of his front teeth was vividly whiter than its yellowed siblings. I assumed the clean tooth was false.

"Bet you didn't expect to see me," he chortled.

"*Happy birthday* was a dead giveaway," I replied. "So the Fleet finally pulled you from the Academy teaching staff?"

"Eight years ago," he nodded. "Something about setting a poor example." He opened his mouth and loosed a belch; trust Tobit to be able to do that at will. "I think we both know how the council handles embarrassments to the uniform."

"And what a delightful coincidence," I said, "that on a planet the size of Earth, we happen to run into each other. What are the odds?"

"Damned good," Tobit replied. "Assuming you got the tip."

"The tip?"

Tobit shrugged. "If you didn't get it, maybe your partner did. Or whatever turd of Admiralty shit you escorted here. The tip."

"What tip?"

"The tip that you should land on this particular continent. Best chance for survival and escape."

I stared at him. "Someone told you that? Before you landed?"

"Told my partner." He held up his hand to stop my next question. "No, I don't know how the tip was delivered— my partner didn't share confidences . . . especially not with me. We were assigned to each other for this mission only; she knew the council wanted me Lost, and was pissed as hell to get dragged down with me. Selfish bitch. All she said was someone passed the word: land in this neighborhood if you want to save your ass."

Chee or Seele, I thought to myself. *The tip had to come from Chee or Seele.* They'd already visited Melaquin; and their looped broadcast claimed there were spaceworthy ships in that city to the south. Now that I thought about it, Chee had said he ran a spy network throughout the Technocracy. He might have used it to find out who was due for marooning . . . and to tip off the Explorers who'd be sent along for the ride. It almost made me think fondly of the old bastard again—even if Chee had sold out to the council, he directed fellow Explorers to the same escape route he'd found.

Of course, he hadn't tipped off Yarrun or me—we'd chosen the Landing site ourselves. If we'd picked the wrong continent, would Chee have talked us out of it? Or were his brains so scrambled that he'd forgotten all about Melaquin? YouthBoost meltdown does ugly things to memory; Chee had said so himself. It would have been ironic if we were the one party to land on the wrong continent, because Chee couldn't remember his own advice.

Tobit was still talking. "Think about it, Ramos. Once you've decided on this continent, where are you going to land? West of the prairies, you've got mountains all the way to the coast—ugly terrain for touchdown. So you either pick the plains themselves, or go for a clear space in the lake country up north. Nothing else makes sense."

"True enough," I admitted. And maybe that explained

why Jelca and Ullis had put down in the same neighborhood we did. Plains vs. lake country was a fifty-fifty choice; and if you chose the lakes, Explorers would then start looking for a region of bluffs, to get the advantage of a height of land. "Still," I said, "this continent must have a million square klicks of landable area. I find it remarkable we should just run into each other. . . ."

"Run into each other?" Tobit laughed. "I don't know about you, Ramos, but I got ambushed by a fucking glass shark. There's dozens of those things patrolling the river; they've got the whole watershed covered, hundreds of klicks upstream and down. Anyone crossing the water stands a good chance of getting captured—you think you're the first Explorer I've seen in eight years? You're number thirteen, sweetheart, and piss off if you're superstitious."

I stared at him. "You mean there are twelve other Explorers in this town?"

He made an exasperated sound. "Not *now*, Ramos. One look at me, and they took off like gassed rabbits. Shows what loyal friends I made at the Academy."

"So there's a way out of this town?"

Tobit grimaced. "You just set a record, Ramos. Shortest effort at small-talk before you brought up the subject of leaving." He gave a jaundiced grin. "Even at the Academy, you were famous for your people skills."

"So were you," I said.

People Skills

One of the Skin-Face women trotted up to us. "Lord Tobit," she said with a worshipful bow, "the bell just rang again."

"Hot damn!" he replied, rubbing his hands together like an enthusiastic host. "The sharks have brought another visitor, Ramos. Your partner, no doubt."

"No. My partner is dead."

"Dead?" Tobit stared as if I'd made a joke. "An Explorer dead? On a candy planet like this? What'd you do to him?''

I returned Tobit's gaze till he flinched.

"The new visitor is probably a friend of mine," I said coldly. "A local. We'd better go reassure her. She gets upset easily."

"A local," Tobit repeated. "All glass?"

"Yes."

"Eloi," snarled the Skin-Face woman, her lips curling into a sneer.

"None of that," Tobit snapped. "No one starts a fight on my birthday. Take the squad back to base, lieutenant."

"Yes sir," she answered immediately. With a brisk salute, she pivoted away and returned to her three companions. A moment later, they disappeared into the nearest building.

"Eloi?" I asked.

"My own terminology," Tobit replied. "The solid glass layabouts are Eloi; the ones with skin are Morlocks. It's from a book."

"And you've trained your cadets to say *Eloi* with hatred? Very nice, Phylar. I love when Explorers spread enlightenment to the people they meet."

"The Morlocks hated the Eloi long before I got here," he answered. "It's a religious thing; but I've reined them in." His words would have been more convincing if he hadn't tossed a glance over his shoulder and added, "We'd better greet your friend before someone gets too upset."

He strode off quickly in the direction I had just come. I followed, saying nothing. It was tempting to take this chance to ask where the Morlocks got the skin for their faces; it was tempting to ask whether the Explorers who previously visited this town had really left in one piece. If, however, the Morlocks' false flesh had come from flayed Explorers, Tobit was in this mess up to his bloodshot eyeballs. Calling him on it would bring the issue to a boil; and I preferred to delay any confrontation until I knew Oar was safe.

When we were almost to the edge of the town, Tobit asked softly, "Your partner . . . who was it?"

"Yarrun Derigha."

"The kid with the jaw?"

"Without."

"Same thing." He walked in silence a few more steps. "Oh well," Tobit said at last, "that's what 'expendable' means."

He gave me a sideways glance, as if trying to decide whether to pat my arm reassuringly; but he did nothing.

Welcoming Oar

"This will be the first Eloi I've seen down here," Tobit said as we approached the door to the shark-machine dock.

"Didn't Jelca and Ullis pass this way?" I asked.

He nodded. "Three years ago."

"They were traveling with my friend's sister."

"Not when the sharks picked them up," Tobit shrugged. "The sister might have dodged getting caught; but the other two didn't mention traveling with another person. And they stayed a few days, like they weren't in a hurry to make a rendezvous."

I had no chance to pursue the subject—we had reached the door to the dock. Tobit pressed the OPEN button . . . and I barely managed to pull him from the entranceway before Oar leapt out, her hands bunched into fists.

It was a creditable imitation of my own response to surprise. These people certainly were fast learners.

"Don't worry, Oar," I said, "no one's going to hurt you."

"I did not like it inside the fish," she said with an injured tone.

Glancing into the dock area, I said, "No kidding." Oar's shark was more of a wreck than the one I'd blasted . . . except that the glass on hers was cracked from the inside, where she must have tried to punch her way out. "I see you found a way to amuse yourself on the trip."

Oar ignored me—she had noticed the town and was viewing it with a steely eye. "What is this place?" she asked. "Why is it so stupid?"

"Stupid?" Tobit asked.

"It is stupid to copy someone else's home," she sniffed, "and if you *must* create a copy, it is stupid to make so many mistakes." She waved her hand dismissively. "It is too big. It has ugly things attached to it."

"Those are flags!" Tobit said. "My friends hung them to celebrate my birthday."

"Get smarter friends," she told him, and turned her back pointedly.

Home-Brew

"What is a birthday?" Oar whispered to me.

"A commemoration," I replied. "A remembrance of the day a person was born." I tossed a glance at Tobit. "Phylar remembers his birthday with great regularity."

"No need to be rude," Tobit said. "I'll have you know, this is my *real* birthday, Ramos . . . on some pissant planet whose name escapes me. I'll look it up when I get back to my quarters."

"You brought your birthday calculator to Melaquin?"

"I knew I'd get marooned here," he answered. "I made sure to bring everything I need. Speaking of which . . ." He reached into a tightsuit pocket and withdrew a silver brandy flask. "Want a sip?"

The thought made me shudder. "An Explorer never drinks on planet-down missions."

"Here's some news, Ramos—this stopped being a mission as soon as the High Council choked you unconscious. And I stopped being an Explorer long before that." He raised the flask and took a swig. When he lowered it again, he sighed with pleasure . . . a sigh that reeked of rotgut alcohol.

"Home-brew?" I asked, trying to control my gag reflex.

"My own recipe," Tobit answered proudly. "You can't get booze from the local food synthesizers, but they produce some superbly fermentable fruit juices. The only hard work was programming the maintenance-bots not to throw out what I produced: they thought it was lemonade gone bad."

He laughed. I didn't. "What do your skin-faced friends think?" I asked. "Do they like a lord and master who drinks himself into a stupor?"

"Ramos," he answered, still chuckling, "they *adore* a lord and master who shares his liquor. Like I said, their food synthesizers don't make the stuff. They didn't know what they were missing till I came along." He gave me a leering smile. "How do you think I became their lord and master in the first place?"

"If you are anyone's lord and master," Oar said, "they are very stupid people. You are ugly and you smell." She slipped her arm into mine. "Let us go now, Festina."

"You ain't going nowhere yet, girlie," Tobit told her. He didn't sound offended; calling Oar 'girlie' might have been his attempt at rakish charm. "The only way to leave is inside a shark . . . and frankly," he waved toward the dock, "neither of those is seaworthy anymore."

"Can you summon other machines?" I asked.

"Nope. They show up on their own when they need to refuel. One docks in every few days. In the meantime . . . you can both be guests at my birthday party."

I said nothing; but Tobit must have seen how undelighted I was. "Cheer up!" he said, giving my arm a light slap, "you'll like my parties. I give presents to my guests, not the other way around. And I've just thought of a doozy for you."

HAPPY

We walked back to the central plaza, Oar still holding my arm to keep me between her and Tobit. Every so often she sniffed pointedly; she could smell the liquor on him. In her mind, he must be the epitome of *dirty*.

As we drew near the Morlocks' building, I made sure my stunner was ready for a quick draw. Tobit might claim to control his "subjects" but I had my doubts; I had my doubts about everything Tobit said. If those Skin-Faces attacked, I had to be ready to knock them out. . . .

I stopped in the street as a thought struck me. What would sonics do to a glass person? They weren't real glass . . . but the shark machine rang like a chime when I shot it. I wondered if the Morlocks would resonate too. That might be a vulnerability of people who were hard instead of soft. Could sonics from a stunner seriously injure them? The blasts had damaged the machine; or maybe I had just scrambled some sonar guidance system and the real damage happened when the shark ran into that log.

Impossible to say—but I pushed the stunner back into my belt so I wouldn't be tempted to use it. For a moment, I had imagined Oar's body shattering, like a wineglass breaking under an opera singer's voice. I couldn't do that, even to a Skin-Face.

No more killing. No more killing.

Tobit led us into the building where I'd first seen him—a building smelling of booze mixed with vomit. Oar convulsed in a coughing fit as soon as the odor reached her. I held down my gorge with memories from the Academy: waking on the floor after an end-of-term bash, the arms of other Explorers draped over me, everyone's breath so flammable the air purity sensors blinked yellow. Why had we done it? Because we were young and tongue-tied; getting drunk together was the greatest intimacy we would dare attempt.

And the Morlocks? They were engineered to have the minds and openness of children; once Tobit brewed his booze, they didn't stand a chance.

I could see them now, through the glass walls ahead of us: the same quartet as before, helping themselves to a brownish concoction that must be Tobit's hootch. It ran down their throats and pooled darkly in their stomachs, sloshing slightly as they moved. Oar's grip tightened on my arm—she had seen too, and for once her face showed none of the haughty superiority she usually assumed when confronted with the unfamiliar. More than anything, she looked hurt . . . like a sick little girl who can't understand why pain exists.

"Right this way!" Tobit boomed, waving us into the room with the drinking Morlocks. Oar moved forward mechanically; I went with her, squeezing her arm.

Unlike most rooms I'd seen on Melaquin, this one had furniture: glass chairs, and a glass table supporting something like a cake. The cake must have come from a local food synthesizer, since it was clear and transparent; but someone had spelled the word HAPPY across the top, in scraps of grubby red plastic.

Either there hadn't been enough plastic to spell out BIRTHDAY, or nobody cared enough to bother.

The Gift

The Morlocks glared at Oar with the owlish blinks of drunks everywhere. They had not consumed much liquor yet—I could tell just looking at their stomachs—but already they showed its effects.

Tobit gestured toward the Morlocks. "These are my faithful comrades: Mary, Martha, Matthew, and Mark. Perfect names for disciples, don't you think?"

The Morlocks didn't move to acknowledge their names. They continued staring at Oar.

"My name is Festina Ramos," I said to them, "and this is Oar."

In a whisper, she said, "An oar is an implement used to propel boats."

The Morlocks remained motionless. Tobit looked from them to us, then gave an exaggerated sigh. "Am I the only one on this goddamned planet who knows how to party?

Fun! Festivity! Falling down dribbling spittle! You hear me?''

Every Morlock said, ''Yes, lord.'' They didn't mean it.

Another tense silence. Tobit groaned. ''All right. I was going to leave this till later, but we have to do something to get people in the spirit. Ramos . . . time for your present.''

''I don't need a present.''

''Everyone needs presents. And I have the perfect one for you. Something you could search for from one end of the galaxy to the other, and lucky me, I have some right here. Damned good luck, considering I didn't know you were coming. If you had any sense of courtesy you'd have called ahead—''

''Phylar . . .'' I sighed.

''All right, leave it be. No sense pissing you off when I can win your everlasting gratitude . . . not to mention showing how smart I am to think of this on the spur of the moment.'' He drew himself up with counterfeit dignity. ''Explorer Ramos, have you noticed my disciples' bodily adornment?''

''The skin?''

''Yes, the skin. Have you wondered where they got it?''

''I'm hoping from animals.''

''Wrong!'' Tobit grinned in triumph. ''It's artificial: comes straight out of a synthesizer down the block.''

''Obviously not a food synthesizer.''

''No,'' Tobit agreed. ''This town has lots of different synthesizers, programmed with manifest goodies from the League of Peoples. You guessed that, right, Ramos? You guessed that the League relocated these folks to Melaquin from Earth?''

I nodded. ''The League must have made the same offer they made us four hundred years ago—renounce violence and get a new planet.''

''Right,'' Tobit replied. ''I get the feeling they only made the offer to selected tribes . . . maybe those who were already peaceful enough to convince the League they were sentient. Anyway, your ancestors and mine stayed back on Earth while the chosen few got a free ticket to Melaquin. The League built these towns, the synthesizers, the communications systems . . . and they also arranged that all future generations would be strong and healthy.'' Tobit pointed at Oar. ''God knows why the League decided to make them of glass, but I suppose people got used to it. This all happened about four thousand years ago; folks from those days must have been so glad their kids didn't die in infancy, they didn't care what the babies looked like.''

''My mother was proud of how I look,'' Oar said defensively. ''I happen to be extremely beautiful.''

''Yeah, you're one in a million,'' Tobit sniggered. ''Anyway,'' he turned back to me, ''I was talking about my Morlocks' skin. The League whipped it up for the first generation to come here—the non-glass humans. It's a bandage material: covers cuts, bruises, pockmarks . . . those people must have been a sorry-looking bunch when they came here, what with disease, malnutrition, and all the other crap of 2000 B.C. Artificial skin must have been damned popular with them.

''Of course,'' he continued, ''the glass kids were next to undamageable, so the skin wasn't used once the first generation died; but a few hundred years ago, some wise man from this town—''

''The Prophet!'' one of the Morlocks shouted. For a moment I thought she sounded angry, but then she raised her drink and chugged it in a toast.

''Yes, the Prophet,'' Tobit agreed, then turned my way, rolled his eyes, and mouthed the word *whacko*. ''The Prophet,'' he said, ''received a revelation that the Morlocks should return to the ways of their ancestors: hunting animals and living off the land.'' He lowered his voice. ''Once every few years anyway—most of the time they just sponge off the food dispensers like everyone else.''

Raising his voice, Tobit went on, ''The Prophet also had an insight about the ideal state of the human body: covered with skin like the first generation. Skin good, glass sinful. You see, Ramos, being invulnerable and immune to disease is ignoble. Far better to suffer and bleed and get bitten by insects. . . .''

I tried to silence him with a sharp look. The Morlocks were drunk, but they still might recognize sarcasm . . . and I could guess their reaction if someone mocked their prophet.

"Sure, okay," Tobit said grudgingly. "The point is, the Prophet found the synthesizer that could make artificial skin; and he devised a scheme for bestowing skin on Morlocks who deserved it. Like merit badges. You get skin for your face at birth—that's a freebie—then on your crotch when you pass puberty rituals, on your chest for killing a buffalo, on your hands if you kill a mountain lion . . . that sort of thing. And if you are worthy and brave, eventually you get to look like . . ." Tobit did a mock curtsy. "Me. Skin from head to toe. I'm their fucking ideal."

"They are fools," Oar said.

A male Morlock tried to struggle to his feet, but Tobit waved him down. "Stay! Sit!" The Morlock slumped again. "You see what having skin means?" Tobit smirked at me. "I have clout. I'm fucking elevated. And that means I can bestow certain honors on my friends."

He reached into his belt pouch and pulled out a hand-sized scrap of brown tissue: thin and limp, like a cloth bandage.

"Skin, Ramos," he said. "Do you think this chunk is big enough to cover that splotch on your face?"

Part XIV
TRANSITION

Camouflage

For a moment, my mind went blank. I wish I could say I wanted to hit him, kick that stupid grin off his face; but I was too stunned even for anger. The limp flap of skin lay in his dirty glove like a rag of brown linen . . . and he thought I should put that on my face?

"I can see you're pleased," he said. "And I promise, it's everything you hope for. Self-adhesive . . . porous to let sweat out and air in . . . even designed to adapt to your skin color like a chameleon."

"My . . ." I swallowed hard. "Yes, Phylar, that's just what I want. A scrap of synthetic I can put on my cheek and watch turn purple. The height of entertainment."

"Ramos, the League designed this stuff to *hide* crap like that shit on your face. Hiding is what Melaquin's all about. Let me tell you, I had one fuck of a lousy scar as a memento from an old exploration mission. Now it looks as smooth as a baby's bottom." His voice was loud with booze, and he must have realized it. In a softer voice he said, "Listen—Festina—maybe it'll work, maybe it won't. Who knows how the skin will respond to your . . . condition. But when I use it to cover a bruise, it doesn't turn the color of the bruise. And I'll tell you a secret: I put some of this fake skin on my nose. It hides the. . . ."

He waved his hands vaguely—too squeamish, I suppose, to say that his nose had once been the ravaged red of a drunkard, florid with prominent blood vessels. Now that I looked, Tobit's nose *was* a healthier color than at the Academy: smooth, not pitted or flushed. It was still unnaturally bulbous, but the skin itself looked . . . good.

"See?" he said, proudly turning his head to show off his physiognomy. "Maybe the skin can help you too."

He pushed the pathetic brown tissue toward me. I didn't take it.

"What's wrong?" he demanded. "You aren't the sort of woman who uses her face as an excuse, are you? The kind who blames every little problem on an accident of birth, and won't try to fix things for fear it might work. You can't be worried that without the birthmark, you won't have reason to bitch and moan—"

"One more word," I told him, "and the skin I take off you won't be that piece in your hand."

The Morlocks roused themselves stewishly and made a show of brandishing their spears. Their attempt to look threatening was pathetic. I felt like showing what a tiger-claw strike could do to someone's face, fake skin or no. But Oar put her hand lightly on my arm, and said, "Do not be foolish, Festina. This man says you can be less ugly. It would be better if you were less ugly. People would not feel so sad when they look at you."

"Do you feel sad when you look at me, Oar?"

"I am not such a person as cares how others look," she answered. "But there may be people who see you and feel like crying, because it is wrong for the only nice Explorer to look so damaged."

Ouch.

Ouch.

"All right," I said, holding out my hand to Tobit. "Give me the skin."

Shading

It felt like a scrap of silk stocking—a mesh so fine and smooth, I wanted to stroke it with my fingers. The color was close to my own skin already: a shade darker, that was all. Even if it stayed the same color when I put it on, I could have a whole face; I'd just have to darken the rest of my skin with a modest amount of makeup.

That assumed the skin didn't turn magenta to duplicate my birthmark.

"How fast does it change color?" I asked, not looking at Tobit.

"About an hour."

"I'll see you in an hour," I said, and left the room.

Punch Gently

Oar trotted at my heels. I didn't really want company, but it was safer this way—if the Morlocks turned belligerent with liquor, she'd be in trouble on her own.

Once we had left the building, I set a fast pace across the plaza toward the outskirts of the town. "Where are we going?" Oar asked.

"To find a mirror." As if I needed one, surrounded by so much glass; if necessary, I could put on the patch using my slight reflection in Oar's own body. But I wanted to put distance between me and Tobit, to leave his leers behind. If this worked, his smugness would be obnoxious; but if I didn't even try, he'd be utterly unbearable.

If I didn't even try. . . .

Listen. My stomach had the same nervous flutters as the night I decided to lose my virginity: balancing on a razor's edge of desire and fear. I wanted to see myself whole. I yearned for that. Yet I was afraid of being disappointed, and even worse, of being *changed*. My life sometimes felt like a war to hold on to what I was; to remain *me*. I was terrified of turning into something different—of losing my definition.

It sounds childish. It sounds glib. I only have words to describe the superficial issues. Even to myself, I can't express the depths of my fear. Nor can I express the depths of my longing. You'd think it would be easy to explain why I wanted to cure my disfigurement; that's obvious, yes? Obvious why I'd want to look like Prope and Harque and everyone else whose glances of fascinated revulsion had humiliated me all my life. Why should I feel ashamed of wanting to look like them?

And Jelca . . . pathetic to think of him at a time like this, but how would *he* react? Would he be delighted to find a real, unblemished woman on Melaquin? Or would he regard me the way Explorers always regarded the unflawed: as shallow and vain, pretty objects but unworthy of deep attention.

"You look sad," Oar said. "Why are you sad, Festina?"

"Because I'm foolish," I replied. "Very foolish. I want to be me, but I also want to be some other woman I'm afraid I won't like."

"That *is* foolish," Oar agreed. "If you turn into an unlikable woman, I will punch you in the nose; then you will know you have to turn back into my friend."

Laughing, I kissed her on the cheek. "Thanks. But punch gently, okay? My face has enough trouble without a broken nose."

In Front of the Mirror

We found a blockhouse, much like the one where Jelca had made his home in Oar's village—the same layout anyway, but without the clutter of cannibalized electronics. The bathroom had a mirror. After asking Oar to wait outside, I stared at my reflection.

Memorizing a face I'd often wanted to forget.

"This may not work," I said.

"I can always take it off," I said.

"This patch may be too small," I said.

It was big enough. In fact, it needed some trimming. I used the scalpel from the medical kit, but I spent a long time washing the blade first.

My Appearance Revisited

The skin eased down onto my cheek. I patted it into place. For a moment I could feel its light touch, but the sensation slowly vanished—like the residue of water after washing your face, disappearing as it dries into thin air.

When I first laid out the patch, its edges were visible. I spent a minute trying to smooth them down; but as I watched, I could see the outer fringe knit itself into my own skin, bonding, becoming part of me. I brushed the intersection with my finger: it was barely discernible. It was still possible to see where the patch ended and my own cheek began—the patch was darker—but within minutes all trace of a join was gone.

Like a parasite affixing itself to a newfound host.

Yet I did not feel any revulsion. My cheek had the texture of smooth, perfect skin. When I looked closely, I could see fine hairs peeking out of it. Were they my own hairs, protruding through the mesh? Or did the material have hairs of its own, mimicking real tissue?

I didn't know. I couldn't remember if hairs had grown up through my birthmark. After only three minutes, I was forgetting what my birthmark looked like.

I shivered.

With sudden energy, I snapped myself away from the mirror and strode into the next room. "Let's go for a walk," I told Oar.

"May I touch it?" she asked.

"No. Walk."

Hard

We began to stroll the circumference of the habitat dome—keeping to the edge of town let me avoid being surrounded by glass buildings. In an hour, I would look at my face; before then, I didn't want to catch any chance reflection. Therefore, my gaze was turned toward the black dome wall as we walked. There was nothing to see, and that was good.

From time to time, I could feel Oar glancing at me. I was deliberately walking on her right, so she could only see my good cheek; her furtive peeks were attempts to watch the new skin change. Or perhaps she was only trying to gauge my mood. After minutes of tentative silence, she finally asked, "How are you feeling, Festina?"

"I'm fine." The words came out automatically. "I'm always fine," I said.

"You are not fine, you are troubled. Must I punch you in the nose so soon?"

I gave her a rueful grin. "No." It was tempting to face her, but I didn't. I could feel nothing special in my cheek, yet it seemed to be the center of all my consciousness. "This is just hard," I said.

"Why is it hard? Either you will stay the same, or you will look less ugly. You cannot lose."

"I might have an allergic reaction."

"What is an allergic reaction?"

"It's . . ." I shook my head. "Never mind, I was just being difficult." I turned my gaze to the crisp white cement beneath our feet. "This is hard," I said again.

We walked another minute in silence. Then Oar said, "I know how to stop you being sad. We can find the Tower of Ancestors in this place."

She looked at me expectantly.

"And that would cheer me up?" I asked.

"It feels good inside the Hall of Ancestors."

"Only if you feed off UV and X-rays," I told her. "I'll pass."

"But if we go to the Tower of Ancestors," Oar insisted, "we can find the foolish Prophet those Morlocks follow. Then we will walk up to him and say, 'Pooh!' Just like that: 'Pooh!' Someone should have spoken to him a long time ago. 'Pooh!' "

I smiled. "You have a knack for theological argument. Good thing you didn't try it with the Morlocks themselves."

"The Morlocks are all very foolish," she replied. "It does not make sense to wear skin when it only looks ugly. Ugliness is bad. You know that, Festina. You will never be beautiful, but you are trying to look better. That is wise. That is correct."

"Thank you," I answered drily. "But even if the new skin works, I may not wear it forever. I just put it on for curiosity's sake. An experiment, that's all. No self-respecting woman places much value on mere appearance . . ."

Such babble. Even Oar knew I was talking for my own benefit. She gazed at me with gentle pity . . . and perhaps I would have prattled on to greater depths of humiliation if a naked man hadn't materialized two paces in front of us.

The Naked Man

He didn't step from behind a building. He didn't rise out of the ground or appear in a puff of smoke. One moment the space in front of us was empty, and the next it was occupied. As instant as a scream.

The man was short and brown and hairy. His head was thatched with crinkly salt-and-pepper hair, and his mouth surrounded with a bushy silver beard. Graying curls dappled his chest, arms, and genitals. Beneath all that hair was a wiry body marked liberally with scars—wide slashes of whitened tissue, the kind you see on Opters fanatical

enough to refuse stitches, no matter how serious the wound.
His eyes had a yellow tint to them, but were still bright and
alert. He looked straight at me for a moment, then slammed
his fists on his stomach and spoke in a melodious language
I didn't recognize.

I looked at Oar to see if she knew what he was saying.
She returned my gaze in bewilderment.

"Okay," I sighed to the little man. "Greetings, I am a
sentient citizen of the League of Peoples, and I beg your
Hospitality."

"Why do Explorers always say that?" Oar muttered. "It
is very annoying."

"Blame it on boundless optimism," I told her. "Someday I'll say it to someone who doesn't run screaming or
try to kill me."

The man did neither. Instead he spoke again, this time
guttural words with phlegmy rasps in the throat. It sounded
so different from his first speech, I guessed he had changed
languages in an attempt to find one I understood. *Good
luck*, I thought to myself. No Explorer bothers with lin-
guistic training; it's taken for granted we'll never understand the native tongues of the beings we meet. If they
don't understand our "Greetings" speech, our only re-
course is to play charades . . . very careful charades, trying
to avoid gestures that would be misunderstood as hostile.

Accordingly, I lifted my hands, palms out, facing the
man. "Hello," I said, more for Oar's benefit than his. "I
am unarmed and friendly." To back my words, I smiled,
making sure to keep my mouth closed: for many species,
baring the teeth means aggression. The man in front of me
appeared to be one hundred percent *Homo sapiens*—the
kind with real skin, not glass—but it would still be a mistake to assume too much cultural common ground.

Before the man could respond to my gesture, Oar took
her own stab at communicating: a gush of words in her
own native language, a flood of syllables that went on for
more than half a minute before she paused for breath.

The man blinked once, then turned back to me. His at-

titude said he didn't understand Oar, and had no interest in
trying. He ventured another smattering of syllables, this one
a type of singing that reminded me of Gregorian chant. The
words, however, weren't Latin—I don't speak the language, but a zoologist knows enough scientific names for
animals to recognize Latin when she hears it.

"Listen," I said, keeping my voice soft and friendly,
"we aren't going to understand each other this way. Maybe
if we . . ."

I didn't finish my sentence. At that moment, the man
flickered in and out of existence like heat lightning.

Flicker

The effect only lasted a second: his image breaking into
a moiré pattern of optical interference, then righting itself
again into a seemingly solid man. It didn't matter how brief
the disruption was—it told me two things.

First, the man was a hologram: a *good* hologram, since
it's extremely difficult for projections to fool the eye at a
range of three paces. Nevertheless, I knew he was just a
constructed image . . . something I half-expected already,
since corporeal men don't appear out of nowhere. (Some
members of the League are rumored to have perfected tele-
portation, but no one with that technology has ever contacted humans.)

The second thing I knew was that Melaquin had started
to live on borrowed time. The flicker in this image could
only mean some machine somewhere had acquired a fault.
It might only be a small malfunction in a nonessential system—the hardware for projecting pictures of naked men
was unlikely to be crucial for survival—but even a tiny
glitch meant things had begun to break down. No one, not
even the League of Peoples, could build equipment that
lasts forever; all the automated repair systems in the universe can't hold back the patient creep of entropy. If four

thousand years was the lifetime for the systems here on
Melaquin . . .

. . . the lifetime of the people wouldn't last significantly
longer.

Fluent Osco-Umbrian

The man in front of me behaved as if nothing unusual
had happened. He launched into another speech in another
language—no language I knew, no language I cared about.
I bided my time till he finished, then held up my hand to
stop him from trying again.

"Don't bother," I said. "Whatever message you want to
convey, it's four thousand years too late. You're a simulation, right? Probably the interface projection for an artificial
intelligence that oversees this town. Computer-controlled
and designed to relate to the first people who came here. To
them, you must have looked like a wise old man . . . someone they'd naturally respect. But to me, you're evidence of
the AI's imminent breakdown. Trying to reach me with languages four millennia old; you can't understand Oar, so you
haven't kept up as the people here changed. Anyway, I've
never liked talking to AIs—they're always smarmy and unctuous."

The man said nothing. He stared intently, as if sheer
force of will could make my words intelligible.

"Oar," I said, "you'd better fetch Tobit. He might know
how to deal with our friend. If Tobit has lived long enough
in this town, maybe he's learned Osco-Umbrian."

"Tobit . . ." the naked man whispered.

"Ah," I said, "a name he recognizes."

"Tobit," the man repeated.

"You're friends with Tobit, right?" I said. "Maybe you
two get lit up together."

"Tobit," the man answered. "Tobit. Toe . . . bit . . . toe
. . . bee . . . or not to be, that is the question. Whether 'tis

nobler in the mind to suffer the slings and arrows of out-
rageous fortune—"

"Shit," I said. "Or rather, *Zounds*."

Speaking Trippingly From the Tongue

"Hail and well-met!" the man said with a flourish of his
hand. "I have in timely manner found your tongue within
my mind."

An ugly anatomical image, I thought. Aloud, I replied,
"You've finally identified my language in your data
banks."

The man nodded. "This blessed talk, these words, this
speech, this English."

"What is *wrong* with him?" Oar asked in a whisper. "Is
he simply foolish, or is there something chemically wrong
with his brain?"

I shook my head. "The League of Peoples obviously
drops in now and then to update the local language databases. The good news is that the records are recent enough
to include English; the bad news is—"

"It is a foolish kind of English," Oar finished.

"Let me not to the intercourse of true minds admit im-
pediments," the man replied. "My tongue may be rough
and my condition not smooth—"

"Enough," I interrupted. It annoyed me he understood
my contemporary English but continued speaking his Eliz-
abethan version. That's an AI for you: probably trying to
"uplift" me by setting an example of "correct" speech.
"Let's keep this to yes-or-no questions," I said. "*Are* you
a machine-created projection?"

"Yea, verily."

"So I'm essentially talking to an artificial intelligence?"

"Aye, milady." The little man displayed a smile of
delight—the indulgent smile a pet-owner wears when the
family dog rolls over. As I said, AIs are all smarmy.

"And there's some good reason you've approached me?" I asked.

"E'en so."

"What reason?"

"To lay this thy kingdom at thy feet. To bid you take up the scepter. To hail you as lord, and queen hereafter."

And he knelt before me, lowering his head to the pavement in respectful submission.

The First of My Kind

I had never been offered the title of queen. I did not want it now.

"Do you say this to everyone who comes by?" I asked.

"Only you," the man replied. "You are the first of your kind to walk here since the dawn of this era."

"He means you have occluded skin," Oar said helpfully.

"A diplomatic turn of phrase," I told her. Turning back to the man, I said, "I'm not the first of my kind to come. What about Tobit? Or the other Explorers who've visited this town?"

"Pretenders have been legion," the man admitted. "Many a child," he gestured toward Oar, "has tried to usurp the throne, clad in borrowed rags." I realized he meant glass people wearing artificial skin. "Another who dwells in this place appears to have the proper bloodline, yet has knitted himself to unliving metal and is therefore discounted." That had to be Tobit, "knitted" to his prosthetic arm; the League disapproved of cyborging, and had obviously programmed the AI to disqualify anyone equipped with any augmentation.

"Some too," the man continued, "have arrived with unverifiable claims, hidden as they were behind impenetrable armors."

"Ahh!" The other Explorers to pass this way had all been wearing tightsuits. The suits must be sufficiently shielded that the AI couldn't tell whether the wearers were fully human. I, on the other hand, in my knee-high skirt. . . .

"Why are you laughing, Festina?" Oar asked.

I answered, "How many women ever became queen because of their legs?"

Probably a lot, I reflected. Especially if kings had anything to do with it.

The Powers of the Queen

"What does being queen entail?" I asked the little man.

"All this realm's resources lie at your command," he replied.

"Which realm? This dome? Or the entire planet?"

"All that lies beneath this most excellent canopy, look you, this brave o'erhanging firmament, this majestical roof—"

"The dome," Oar explained.

"I got that," I nodded. "Not much of a kingdom," I told the man-image. "And not much of a distinction either. What can a queen do that a commoner can't? Anyone can work the synthesizers to get food, artificial skin, you name it. What else is there?"

"Only one thing more. Follow me, your majesty."

I shrugged. "Lay on, Macduff."

The man rose gracefully from his knees and after a courtly bow, led us forward, keeping to the circumference of the dome. Although his legs were half the length of mine, he had no trouble walking at our pace, since his image could skim over ground as quickly as necessary.

As we walked, I passed the time scanning the area for the projectors creating the man's image; but I soon realized my search was pointless. Whether the machines were mounted on the dome, on a tower, or shining straight through the walls of nearby buildings, it didn't make a real difference. He was here. He was projected. Everything else was a technicality.

After another minute of walking, the man turned to the

outside wall of the dome and threw up his arms, shouting, "Behold, O Queen!" A moment later, a section of dome wall thirty meters wide and twenty high popped backward with a soft hiss. I tensed, fearing a deluge of water might suddenly pour through the breach. No such flood occurred; and as we watched, the wall dropped back four more paces, then slid sideways on guide tracks, revealing a large, well-lit chamber.

Or more accurately, a large, well-lit aircraft hangar.

Daggers Before Me, Handles Toward My Hand

Five fliers stood in a perfect line before me, each fashioned to look like a chiseled glass bird. The closest was a goose, wings and tail outspread, head stretched straight forward; it ran twenty meters long, with space for two riders, side by side in the middle of the bird's body. The next plane was an eagle, then a jay, then an owl, and lastly a generic songbird which the little man said was a lark. All were stylized, their feathers mere suggestions, their shapes trimmed and streamlined for better aerodynamics . . . but then, the same was true of Oar. Like her, these craft were Art Deco versions of living creatures.

Yet they were also working airplanes: jets, by the look of them, though the tiny engines were artfully incorporated into the wing structures to look like fluffed regions of feathers. I counted four such engines on each wing, plus two more on the tail. Each was small, but their combined power must pack a kick if you really needed propulsion.

Only one thing spoiled the planes' sleek, birdlike appearance: each had four charcoal-gray cylinders mounted on their bellies. *Fuel tanks?* I wondered. No—they were impractically long and slender. Rockets for extra boost in emergencies? Sensor arrays?

Then the explanation came to me—an archaic concept dating back to the earliest days of aviation. The cylinders were *missiles*. Weapons. Designed to be shot at other planes or ground targets where they would explode on impact.

"Bloody hell," I murmured. "Where did those come from?"

"Fashioned at behest of the first generations," the AI-man answered cheerfully.

"That's hard to believe," I snapped. "The first generations must have been primitive hunter-gatherers. They didn't wake up one morning, saying 'We'd like some warplanes, please.' "

"You have the right of that," the man conceded. "But the League took in hand the education of those who came to this place. One generation followed hard on another; and within a handful of centuries, they advanced to devices like these."

He waved proudly at the killer birds.

"You actually *built* them weapons on demand? Of course, you did," I went on without letting him answer. "The synthesizers made that axe for Oar. As long as no one took weapons offplanet, the League didn't care."

"They cared, O queen," the man replied. "All violence cuts them to the very quick. Yet they grant each species the right to choose its course, within the containment of its proper sphere."

"So you helped this town build . . . wait a second. I thought you only followed instructions from people with skin. After the first generation, wasn't everyone made of glass?"

"By no means," he answered. "Though many firstcomers chose to be so altered that their children gleamed with health, others held to the frailty of flesh. That path was hard; what mother can watch her child ravaged by fever without vowing her nextborn shall not suffer? What father can bear the bitter spectacle of his children continually bested by those swifter of mind and foot? Pricked by such thorns, more chose the way of glass with each passing year; yet not all. Not all. And those who walked with hollow-eyed Death bedogging their steps like a shadow, those stubborn folk of deliberately mortal flesh . . . why, they saw devils in every dust mote and knives in every open hand. What wonder that they demanded fearsome engines of war? Death was the currency of their lives: the only coin they had to spend, the only coin they could demand of their enemies. And so it continued until the last such purse was emptied.''

I stared at him. "You mean the people of flesh warred themselves into extinction?"

"That overstates the matter," he replied. "They fought but little, for their numbers were small. Yet they forged their arsenals with the diligence of fear; and fear, more than all, became their undoing. Frighted people yearn to protect their families. What better protection could they find than immortality? Wherefore, as voices of war grew clamorous, more among their number claimed the gift of alteration . . . until there came a day when every child was glass, and no new flesh was born. The drums of anger fell into silence; and if the crystal children wished to continue their parents' hates, I stopped mine ears to their cries. I and my kind do not serve them—they need no such service. But you, mi-lady . . . you shall I serve and right gladly.''

My mouth was open, ready to snap back a retort—as if I wanted an AI to put killer jets at my disposal!—but I stopped myself from hastiness. With a flier, Oar and I could reach the southern mountains in short order: no long days carrying packs, no frigid river fords, no confrontations with wolves.

And (my stomach fluttered) I might be face to face with Jelca before nightfall.

"Which plane can I take?" I asked.

The AI-man beamed. "The lark, milady; the herald of the morn.''

The First Farewell

Short minutes later, I stole past the dirt-worn banners of Tobit's home, hoping I could sneak in and back without being noticed. Through the glass wall ahead, I could see our equipment: my pack and the food synthesizer. I could also see the four Morlocks and Tobit, sprawled in comatose luxuriousness, passed out from drinking. It was just the way I wanted to leave them.

Not that I expected them to stop us from getting away—they'd let the other Explorers go—but I didn't want them to know *how* we went. The AI had kept the hangar secret because its planes were only intended for flesh-and-blood human use. But Tobit was as much flesh-and-blood as I was; if he detached his prosthetic arm, he could command the AI like a despot. Melaquin had enough troubles without a souse in charge of a fighter squadron.

My pack was close to the door of the room; also close to a Morlock woman with a slosh of booze in her stomach. Tendrils of brown extended threadlike through her abdomen, the alcohol slowly becoming part of her, diffusing into the background transparency. The zoologist in me felt fascinated, curious to stay and watch the complete process of digestion—but the prospect made me queasy. How could these people watch such a thing happen to themselves?

But they *didn't* watch it. They were out cold.

Or so I thought.

"Leaving so soon?" asked Tobit as I lifted my backpack.

He lay spreadeagled on the floor. He had not moved a muscle except to open his eyes.

"I have the chance to go," I told him. "I thought I might as well."

"Another shark came in?" he asked. "Or is it two sharks: one for you and one for your . . . friend."

"Something like that," I said.

"You can keep the sharks from leaving if you want to spend more time resting from the road. There's a toggle-switch on the airlock door; flip it and the machines won't go till you're ready."

"Still . . ." I said.

"You want to leave," he finished my sentence. "Of

course you do. There's nothing that interests you here.''

He lowered his gaze to the floor. A good actor could have made the moment poignant, but Tobit was too drunk for that. The line between tragic and maudlin is too thin.

"You can leave too," I told him. "Hop a shark. Go south. The other Explorers will be happy to see you."

"You think that, do you?"

"Phylar," I said, with a trace of anger, "don't blame the world for your own sulkiness. If you're feeling lonely or hard done by, it's because you deliberately choose to isolate yourself. There's nothing genuinely wrong with you. You're perfectly all right. Stop bitching about your lot in life if you never make an effort to fix things."

He stared at me for a moment. Then he broke into deep gut-busting laughter, not mean or forced, but sincerely spontaneous. "What?" I demanded; but that just sent him into fresh gusts, long and loud—as if this was the first time in his life he'd been totally delighted.

I couldn't understand it. With burning cheeks, I heaved up my pack and stormed out the door.

Essential Maintenance

By the time I returned to the hangar, the place buzzed with service drones of all types: everything from an automated fuel truck filling up long-dry tanks to a bevy of chip-checkers no bigger than my thumbnail, crawling like beetles over the lark's hull in search of structural flaws. A gray haze around the craft showed there were nanites at work too, microscopically reconstituting any systems that had rotted or corroded since the last time such repairs had been made.

I wondered how often this flurry of maintenance had taken place over the past four thousand years. Once a decade? Once a month? High-tech equipment has a half-life comparable to fast-decaying radioactive elements—even in a sealed, climate-controlled storage chamber, components willfully break down as soon as you turn your back. Still, the AI in charge must have done its best to keep the craft functional over the centuries: replacing a circuit here and a rivet there, until each plane had been rebuilt completely several dozen times. The service checks taking place before my eyes were a matter of form, not necessity . . . I hoped.

(In the back of my mind, I couldn't forget how the AI's holographic projection had flickered that once. There *were* glitches in the system. I crossed my fingers that the nanites clouding around my plane were repairing faults, not causing them.)

Something beeped impatiently behind me. I stepped quickly out of the way of a flatbed dolly that wheeled itself under the glass goose. Already waiting there were a frame-mounted pair of robot arms, patiently holding a missile they had detached from the plane's belly. With commendable gentleness, the arms lowered the payload onto the dolly then went to work on the next missile. As newly anointed queen, I had given strict orders to the AI: no more weapons, now or ever. The missiles were to be removed and dismantled as fast as safety allowed. For all I knew, their firing mechanisms might already be dead—a team of nanites could gut several kilos of wiring in seconds.

The naked man bloomed into existence in front of me. "All proceeds apace, milady. You and your daughter may soon depart."

"And you're sure I'll have no trouble piloting?"

"Do you but speak your smallest wish, and on the instant, your craft will obey."

"Good." I had no objection to voice-controlled flight. My teachers at the Academy claimed there was no technical barrier to creating an automated starship that would outperform human operators on every scale. However, the Admiralty would never allow such a ship to be developed. If you did away with Vac crews, you couldn't help seeing that the only essential personnel in the Fleet were Explorers.

ECMs. *Essential* crew members. I liked the sound of that.

Flightworthy

Oar stood against one wall of the hangar, her eyes wide at the sight of so much hustle and bustle. I walked over and said, "Impressive, isn't it?"

"I do not like machines that move," she answered. "Especially the small ones. They are like stupid little animals."

"They aren't so stupid," I told her. "They're making sure we can fly."

"We will fly inside that bird?"

"Yes."

"How far can we fly, Festina? Can we fly to your home in the stars?"

"These craft look strictly atmospheric," I answered, "but you bring up an interesting question." I motioned to the hologram man. "If I asked you to build a starship, could you do it?"

"Nay, good queen. That is forbidden me. Those who dwell on this planet are rightly granted dominion over their native land and seas; but to step beyond, into the vasty deeps of night, you must make your own way."

"Pity," I said, though his answer didn't surprise me. The League views interstellar space as sacrosanct—closed to undeserving races. If you weren't advanced enough to reach space on your own, it was only logical that the League wouldn't help you. Transporting ancient humans to a safe haven on Melaquin was one thing; giving them the means to gad about the galaxy was something else.

"How much longer before the bird can take off?" I asked.

"But a moment's time," the hologram replied. "Mayhap you would care to enter now, that your departure can be more swift."

I gave Oar a look. "Ready to get in the plane?"

"Will we truly fly?" she asked.

"I hope so."

"Milady," the hologram said with a chiding tone, "how can you doubt me? My heart beats to the rhythm of the League of Peoples; shall I then place sentients in harm's way?"

I didn't answer. An AI of the League would never invite a sentient to board a plane that wasn't safe . . . but did that really guarantee anything? The AI was not in perfect repair. Would it even know if the aircraft was flightworthy after four thousand years? Or would the sculpted glass wings fall off before we hit cruising speed?

As if you ever expected to die in bed, I told myself. "Come on," I said to Oar. "Let's board."

Straps

The cockpit had two swivel seats, with enough space between them that passengers wouldn't block each other's view through either side of the glass fuselage. To aid in sightseeing, there were no clunky controls to get in the way: no steering yoke, no pedals, no levers or dials or switches. That lack disturbed me; voice operation was one thing, but no manual backup was something else. I had no skill flying aircraft, but if we were crashing, I wanted the chance to wrestle blindly with the controls.

It would give me something to do.

Oar plopped into the right-hand seat; I helped buckle her in before I took the other chair. "These belts are interesting," she said, plucking at the X-shaped bands crisscrossing her chest. "Can I make them very tight?"

"If they're too tight, you won't be comfortable."

"How tight is too tight?" She yanked on the drawstrap hard enough to jerk her back against the seat. "Is this what wearing clothes feels like?"

"Depends on the type of clothes," I answered diplomatically.

"Perhaps I should have some clothes. The other fucking Explorers said that clothes were a sign of civilization." She gave another yank on the drawstrap.

I swiveled my seat away. Although I tried to concentrate on the activities of the maintenance bots outside, from time to time I heard a soft grunt as Oar jerked the straps tighter.

Ventilation

The hologram man suddenly appeared beside me, hovering a centimeter above the floor. *Bad sign*, I thought: evidence that the AI hadn't accurately calibrated the image to match the height of the cockpit.

"Gird ye for takeoff," the man said. "All is in readiness."

"How is this going to work?" I asked.

"Thy carrier bird will ride chariotlike to the next chamber," he answered, pointing toward the far end of the hangar. A set of doors had begun opening down there; the room beyond was pitch black. "From thence you will pass into the waters that surround this, mine abode."

Obviously, the far room was an airlock—a staging point before plunging into the river beyond. "How well does the lark work underwater?" I asked.

"It was fashioned for that very purpose. Your craft will ascend full fathoms five 'til, cresting the surface, it cleaves the air and soars on high. Once safely borne upon the wind, you may speak to it, guide it, wheresoever you will."

"Good," I nodded. "You'll shut the door to the main dome once we're gone?"

"As you have commanded."

"You can't close up any earlier?"

"Alas, no. This your conveyance exhales fierce vapors which must be allowed exit into the larger space beyond."

"Ventilation—fair enough." I glanced out the window and saw maintenance bots scurrying away. "Looks like we're ready to launch."

"Just so," the man bowed. "Now prepare thyself. The lark is ready and the wind at help, thy associate 'tends, and everything is bent for the Southland."

He winked out instantly. The next moment, the room erupted with the roar of engines.

An Open Door

The sound was enough to deafen granite. Instinctively I slapped my chest, right where the MUTE dial was on a tightsuit. If I'd been wearing my helmet, it would have begun generating a similar roar 180 degrees out of phase with the original, canceling the thunderous noise. Without that protection, all I could do was cover my ears and yawn in an attempt to equalize pressure.

Oar had her mouth open too. I think she was screaming, but I couldn't hear.

I prayed for the lark to start taxiing toward the airlock chamber. Once we were surrounded by water, the din would be muffled to a more tolerable level.

But the lark didn't move.

It's just warming up, I told myself. I tried to remember if jets had to reach a certain heat to operate or if that was some other type of engine. Too bad the Academy avoided giving us even a rudimentary introduction to aviation. Vacuum personnel wanted to keep their monopoly on aeronautics knowledge.

The roar continued. It must be raising an unholy ruckus in the main part of the habitat—a booming clamor echoing off the dome, reverberating in the closed space.

"Shit," I said without hearing my voice. "Tobit will wake up for sure."

I faced the main door, my hands pressed hard against my ears. Maybe Tobit would dismiss the sound as a delusion— some DT nightmare, to be avoided, not investigated. But the Morlocks would wake too, asking, "What's that noise?'' in whatever language they spoke. Tobit would *know* he was missing something.

"Close, damn it," I told the door. "Close."

The lark moved: an unhurried circle to aim its beak toward the airlock. I swiveled my chair to keep watch on the other door. If it closed before Tobit arrived, he would never figure out what had happened—he would shrug it off and take another swig from his flask. But if he saw a previously hidden door in the side of the dome. . . .

He was a drunk, but he was also an Explorer. He had a good brain, no matter how many neurons he'd pickled. In time, he'd find the truth . . . especially since the solution was as easy as detaching his prosthetic arm. The AI would acknowledge him as completely flesh and kowtow to him, laying the town's resources at Tobit's feet.

Tobit with an air force.

If he came to the door now, he might even catch sight of the missiles. It wouldn't matter that the weapons were disarmed. He could just instruct the AI to make more.

Maybe the next Exploration Team to visit Melaquin wouldn't find the surface quite so unspoiled.

The Second Farewell

Languidly, the lark wheeled forward. The light of the hangar gave way to the darkness of the airlock area. *At least we're clear*, I thought. *No matter how angry Tobit may be that I kept this a secret, he can't catch us now*.

The airlock door started to close.

We might make it, I thought.

Stupid.

Tobit and his disciples raced into the hangar. A Morlock pointed her finger at our plane—the source of the noise. Tobit's face twisted with fury. I had let him believe Oar and I were leaving in sharks, not a flier. He fumbled out his stun-pistol and pointed it in our direction.

His hand shook. I couldn't tell if it was a meaningless tremor or if he had pulled the trigger.

I remembered what my stunner did to the shark.

The lark vibrated. It had been vibrating all along, trembling with the roar of its engines.

Had he fired? Had we been hit?

The airlock door squeezed shut, cutting off the light from the hangar. We were in darkness.

The jet noise choked to burbling as water flooded into the airlock chamber. The roar in my ears faded to a damp hiss—not a real sound but an aftermath of the aural onslaught, my eardrums stunned into a bruised sensation of white noise.

I lay back in my seat panting. Behind me, Oar moaned; my hearing was so battered, I couldn't tell if her whimpers were loud or soft.

Should I unbuckle myself and go to her? That was dangerous . . . especially if the lark suddenly shot forward when the other airlock door opened.

"Please," I said aloud to the plane. "Can we have some light? I want to see how Oar is."

A soft blue glow dawned around the edge of the floor—a ribbon of illumination barely the width of my finger.

It was enough; tears trickled down Oar's glass face, but she gave me a look of determined bravery. I almost laughed—she sat bolt upright in her chair, strapped in so tightly she could only move her head.

She would be all right. She was built to be immortal.

I turned away. With dim light inside and blackness out, I saw my reflection in the cockpit's glass.

My face was perfect. My cheek was perfect.

I was whole.

Part XV
BEAUTY

My Blindness

It was my face. It was not my face.

I did not know how to look at myself when I wasn't disfigured.

Was I now beautiful? Was I now merely normal?

What would other people think?

What would Jelca think?

It was ridiculous to ask such questions. I refused to be so weak that my self-image depended on others.

But I didn't know how to look at myself. I didn't know how to see myself. I didn't know how to *assess* myself.

Not that the reflection in the glass was truly Festina Ramos. I was wearing a mask: an invisible mask, but underneath there still lurked my purple "pride."

The real me: damaged . . . deformed.

But I couldn't see the real me. I didn't know what I was seeing.

A woman with clear brown skin. Strong cheekbones. Green eyes you could actually look at, without your attention being dragged downward in guilty fascination.

I couldn't remember ever looking into my own eyes—not beyond searching for fallen lashes and my few attempts at using kohl.

241

Were they beautiful eyes? What does it mean to have beautiful eyes?

What does it mean to be beautiful?

Up Revisited

The lark gurgled forward. "Lights off," I said—partly so I could see outside, partly to hide my reflection. Prope and Harque might gaze dotingly on their faces; but I wouldn't.

I refused to think about it. I refused to acknowledge it. I refused to be changed by it.

The glow at the base of the cockpit faded, leaving a dim aftershine still rimmed across my vision. There was nothing outside but blackness—a blackness that bubbled as our jets churned the water. At some point we must have passed out of the airlock into open lake, but I couldn't sense the transition: just a steady motion forward that gradually assumed an upward arc.

Rising out of the waters . . . born again with a new face.

I dug my fingernails into my bare arm as punishment for such thoughts. *How banal can you get?* I chided myself.

When the light finally came, it arrived quickly: from a glimmer far over our heads to a diffuse glow, then rapidly looming down on us until we broke through into late afternoon sunshine. Like a jumping trout, the plane shot out of the water then slapped down hard on its belly, not flying fast enough yet to stay airborne.

The impact jarred my teeth together, and Oar gave a yelp; then both of us gasped in unison as our swivel chairs locked into forward-facing positions and the engines kicked in with full jet power. A hammer of acceleration slammed me back with at least five Gs, pressing on me with such ferocity it emptied my brain of all but one thought: *This better not rip off the skin.*

Water tore away beneath us as the lark skimmed the water surface; then we were climbing at a sharp angle, still accelerating, still crushed back by the force. The pain was worst in my knees—they were propped over the edge of the chair as both my thighs and feet pressed backward, making a straining, two-way stretch. It was only a matter of time before soft tissue tore under the stress . . . but before that happened, the engines eased and the wrenching ache subsided.

Lightly, I touched my cheek. The skin still seemed in place.

I let myself breathe.

Altitude

Below I could see a modest lake a few kilometers across—not much more than a widening in the long fat river that lazed its way from one horizon to the other. I tried to memorize the look of the area in case I had to come back: in case Tobit made such a nuisance that I had to talk some sense into him. With luck, he would simply retreat into wounded inebriation. He would poison the Morlocks with his rotgut and it would never matter to the world that somewhere under the lake was a dome housing sullen drunkards.

"Festina!" Oar said excitedly. "We are flying!"

"Yes we are."

"Like birds!"

"Yes."

"We are high above the ground!"

"Yes." In fact, we weren't far up at all: enough to clear any slight hill in the prairie, but at a much lower altitude than I was used to flying. For anyone below, the noise of our engines would punish the eardrums; however, there was no one down there but rabbits and gophers. From this vantage point, Melaquin looked pristine—an unspoiled natural world, devoid of messy civilization.

"Turn south," I told the lark. "Set whatever airspeed gives the most distance for the fuel we have. And let's gain some altitude, shall we? There's no point in scaring the animals.''

Cruising

The plains rolled away beneath us. Oar had loosened her safety straps for more freedom to delight in the view—to squeal happily as we passed over a stampeding herd of bison or to ask why no river ever ran in a straight line. I responded as politely as I could, but my mind was elsewhere.

What would I say when I met Jelca? What would he say to me?

We had gone on a total of two dates, one real, one virtual. I paid for both.

The real date was the usual thing—four hours of volunteer patrol for the Civilian Protection Office. As Explorers, we were qualified for assignment in a tough neighborhood: tough enough that we got into two separate fights with the same Purpose gang. Like most gangs, they fought fists only; they dreamt of leaving New Earth one day, and were smart enough to know armed violence would ruin their chances. On the other hand, they couldn't ignore Jelca and me on their turf. They mistook my face and his scalp condition as evidence of ''alien miscegenation'' . . . genetically impossible, but then, the Purpose didn't ask for a C-level in biology as an entrance requirement.

I considered my evening with Jelca a bonding experience. How can you help but feel closer when you've protected each other's backs in a brawl? And we fought well. Like all civilian volunteers, we had a cloud of sentinel nanites watching that we didn't get in over our heads; but we never needed their help. Jelca had brought an Explorer stun-pistol with some customized enhancements he'd made for the occasion. With that and my kung fu, we held our own. We didn't break heads indiscriminately—at the end of the night, we received a commendation for staying completely within policy—but Jelca and I worked well together. We had a good time. We did something useful and demanding, after which we could smile at each other.

When the action was over, we did not leap into bed. That may be the usual pattern—get blazed on your own adrenaline, then burn off the aftershock of tension and triumph in the age-old way. But Jelca and I were Explorers. Partnering another person through danger touched deep feelings; it seemed cheap to exploit it as a mere stimulant for heavy breathing. Therefore we parted, feeling warm and close, but in control . . . despite (on my part at least) a ferocious urge to fuck and fuck and fuck until I passed out.

Two weeks passed after that first date. Jelca and I talked often, but made no plans. I wanted to; but I had to wait for him to make the next move. My home planet had an inviolable rule of etiquette: never force yourself on someone twice in a row. If Jelca didn't offer his own invitation, I should quietly accept he had no interest in further developments. Of course, different cultures have different customs; and I agonized whether he might be waiting for me just as I was waiting for him. Perhaps where he came from, women instigated *every* date . . . or perhaps whoever started the "courtship" was expected to initiate everything from then on. There's no database summarizing such customs—they're too vague to quantify. So, after many earnest conversations with myself, I (the freshman) timidly asked out Jelca (the senior) a second time.

He said yes.

This time we chose a fantasy walk through a haunted VR forest—a temperate forest, because Jelca said he liked those best. I would have preferred a rainforest like those back home, so I could show off my jungle-girl competence; but since Jelca was a city boy I thought I could still hold my own with him, even if I couldn't tell a sugar maple from a Lanark.

As always with fantasy walks, I had a panicked urge to rip off the interface helm as soon as it began extracting my archetype. Intellectually, I knew the scan only skimmed the

surface of my subconscious; it avoided exposing too much
of my psyche. Still, I shuddered at the thought of stripping
myself spiritually naked in front of Jelca . . . of my subconscious vomiting up some loathsome dung-smeared monster
to be my VR alterego.

Of course, that didn't happen. Fantasy walks are wish
fulfillments: daydreams, not nightmares. I materialized in
the virtual forest as a ghostly feline . . . my paws pale and
terrible as I held them in front of my eyes, their milky
ectoplasm translucent as smoke. My body faded in and out
of existence, sometimes invisible, sometimes lethally solid.
Strong and elusive, impossible to pin down—the archetype
truly was an intimate personal fantasy, a reflection of deep
desires. I felt a sexy kind of vulnerability to show myself
this way. Not disguised, but *revealed*.

And Jelca . . . Jelca appeared before me as a whirlwind—
a bodiless force of nature, a black funnel cloud stretching
as tall as the trees. He could not talk; but his sound could
sweep from the barest whisper to a deafening roar, uproot-
ing giant oaks or slipping through the woods without rustling a leaf.

He excited me.

The programmed session was conventional fare: defeat-
ing a cadre of demons who gradually increased in power
until we faced The Supreme Evil In Its Lair. It was a blessing my archetype couldn't speak any more than Jelca's;
otherwise, I might have spoiled the mood with deprecating
comments on the creators' lack of imagination. Without
words, however—without the ability to remind each other
this was only a simulation—we had no choice but to enter
the spirit of the piece, to vanquish our enemies with wind
and claw, until the final fiend lay bloody at our feet.
Then. . . .

Then. . . .

Then the Supreme Evil's lair turned into a glittering pal-
ace; Jelca and I found ourselves in a sumptuous bedroom;
the knowledge came into our heads that we could remain
as we were or be transformed into the prince and princess

we deserved to be. Crassly put, we were invited to celebrate victory with a virtual fuck, either as cat and tornado or human beings. All things were possible. Soft music filtered out of nowhere, the bedsheets pulled themselves back, candles lit themselves, the walls turned to mirrors. . . .

And in that moment, I saw my archetype fully. The mirrors showed a phantom jaguar: evanescent and fierce, pure ghost white . . . except for a lurid purple disfigurement on the right half of its face.

That was the "fantasy" dredged out of my mind.

That was what Jelca had looked at all night.

I never asked him out again. I avoided him in the halls. I scarcely took an easy breath until he graduated and was posted into space.

Peaks

An hour after our lark had taken off, the southern mountains appeared on the horizon—grassy foothills first, then thickly treed slopes, and finally stony snow-capped peaks. It was a young range, geologically speaking: its crags were sharp, untouched by erosion. Good climbing if you had the right partner. . . .

No. Stop that train of thought. I was tired of bleeding.

Fingering my cheek, I searched for the first landmark Chee and Seele talked about. The lark had been traveling blind, without charts; we could have been several hundred klicks off course. However, I sighted our target after only half an hour flying above the foothills—a steamy area of geysers and hot springs, simmering with enough vapor to be visible for thirty kilometers. After that, the route was easy to follow: up a winding river valley that snaked its way through the foothills and on into the mountains. Within minutes I ordered the plane, "Land wherever you can . . . as safely as possible."

For once, things went without a hitch. The lark had vertical landing capability; it touched down on grass beside the river we'd been following, only half a klick from the entrance to Chee and Seele's city. Not that we could see the entrance—like everything else on Melaquin, the doorway was hidden—but I was sure we were in the right place.

"This land is strange," Oar said as we clambered out of the cockpit. "It is very tall."

"You've never seen mountains before?" I asked.

"Oh, I have seen many, many mountains," she replied quickly. "I am not such a one who has never seen mountains." She affected an air of blasé sophistication, waving her hand dismissively. "I have seen much better mountains than these. Pointier. Snowier. And ones that did not block the light so unpleasantly. These mountains are very gloomy, are they not, Festina?"

I didn't answer. Our landing site *was* shadowy, when contrasted with our flight in the bright sunshine—we were at ground level now, and the sun was low enough to be blocked by a peak to the west. Still, a little shade didn't mean the place was gloomy . . . or even very dark. Four nearby peaks still glistened with sun on their snow, filling our valley with a reflected light of heartbreaking quality. The world was clear and quiet: nothing but the murmur of the river and the tick-tick-tick of the lark's engines cooling.

Peace.

For ten seconds.

Then a man strolled out of the forest, wearing nothing but a red tartan kilt.

A human man. An Explorer.

We looked at each other for a long moment. Then we said in unison, "Greetings. I am a sentient citizen of the League of Peoples . . ."

We both broke up laughing.

One of the Family

He told me his name was Walton: Explorer Commander Gregorio Walton, but he disliked his given name and hated his rank. At first, I thought he'd become an Explorer because of his face—the most wrinkled face I'd seen on a human, a droopy deep-pile face with the jowls of a basset hound. It was only later I noticed that his fingers were webbed like duck feet. *That* was what made him expendable; the wrinkles were recent developments, the result of decades on Melaquin without benefit of YouthBoost.

Walton had been here twenty-six years. He was only eighty, but appeared twice that age. His general bearing looked healthy enough, but his webbed hands trembled constantly. I had to force myself not to stare.

He used one of those trembling hands to pat the lark's fuselage. "Nice plane," he said. "Noisy, though."

"You heard it coming?" I asked.

"Long before I saw it," he nodded. "Eyesight's not what it was."

"The lark's made of glass," I said. "Hard to see at the best of times."

He smiled. "I like a woman with tact."

"I have tact too," Oar announced.

"Good for you," Walton said.

"For example," Oar continued, "I will not talk about how ugly you are."

"I appreciate it," Walton answered with a smile.

"So are there others nearby?" I asked, to change the subject.

"I'm the only one who comes outside much," he replied. "Meteorology specialist. Put in a small weather station up the mountain a bit—thermometer, anemometer, simple things like that. I was tinkering with the equipment when I heard your engines." He gave me an appraising look. "Don't suppose you know anything about fuzzy circuits? I've got a glitch in my barometer."

"Sorry," I answered. "I'm a zoology specialist. The best I can do is identify the species if something's been nibbling your wires."

He chuckled. "Maybe I should go back and play with the equipment while there's still some light. Getting close to the big day, and we wouldn't want to launch our ship into the teeth of a blizzard.''

''You have a ship ready for launch?''

''Depends who you ask,'' Walton said. ''Some'll tell you it's been ready for months. Others say it needs months more testing. Damned if I know—only aviation I understand is weather balloons.''

''Is it . . .'' I paused to think of how to put my question. ''Is it a big ship?''

''Don't worry,'' he replied. ''There's room for everyone. Won't be long before you're heading for home.''

Walton smiled. I'm sure he expected me to smile back, overjoyed at the prospect of getting off Melaquin. But I wasn't leaving—a murderer couldn't. I tried for a smile anyway, but it didn't fool Walton. ''What's wrong?'' he asked.

''Nothing,'' I answered quickly. ''Just . . . bothered that I've dropped in at the last moment when the work's nearly all done.''

''No one will hold that against you,'' he assured me. ''You're one of us, Ramos. You're an Explorer.'' He took my hand and gave it a friendly shake. His skin felt grizzled against my fingers. ''Welcome to the family,'' he said. ''Whatever hard times you've had on Melaquin, you're not alone anymore.''

I smiled . . . and felt alone anyway. Suddenly, I didn't know why I'd come here. To see other Explorers? To see Jelca? Walton's manner was sincerely warm, but I found I could not return it. Any day now, he'd be leaving. They'd all be leaving.

And what would I have then?

On the Ride Down

Walton gave directions to the city entrance, then headed back to his weather station. I couldn't help feeling I'd disappointed him: I was too clenched to respond to his calm cheerfulness. Still, I was not so numb that I didn't feel a stir of excitement as we left the lark and the river behind. We followed a short trail through pine forest, then came to an open area of rock and gravel, just as Walton described.

A concealed doorway lurked behind a rock outcrop. PRESS PALM HERE was scratched onto the stone. I pressed, and the door opened.

An elevator lay beyond the door. Someone had painted UP and DOWN beside two buttons embedded in the wall. I pressed DOWN.

The elevator began to descend.

"We're here," I said to Oar.

"And there are many fucking Explorers here?"

"I promise they'll treat you kindly."

"They will not whisper about me? They will not look at me as if I am stupid?"

"Walton didn't, did he? And if any of the others do, I'll punch them in the nose."

I smiled, but Oar didn't smile back. It occurred to me I'd barely paid attention to her since we boarded the plane. I had spoken more to the plane than to Oar.

Moving to her, I took her arm and patted her hand. "It'll be all right . . . really."

"I am scared," she said in a small voice. "I feel strange in my stomach."

"Don't be afraid. Whatever happened between you and Jelca—"

She interrupted. "Will he want to give me his juices again?"

Ouch. "Do you want him to do that?" I asked.

"I am not such a one as needs Explorer juices!" she snapped. "I just do not want him to think I am stupid."

"No one thinks you're—"

"They left without telling me! All of them: Laminir Jelca, Ullis Naar, and my sister Eel. I woke one morning and they were gone. They took Eel with them, but not me."

I studied her for a moment. "You're angry at Eel?"

"She was my sister. She was my sister but she went with
the fucking Explorers and left me alone."

"Oar . . ." I wrapped my arms around her. "You aren't
alone now. You're with me. We're friends."

She hugged me, crying, her head on my shoulder. That
was how we were standing when the elevator opened . . .
and damned if I didn't try to pull away, for fear Jelca might
see us like that.

Oar's grip was too strong for me to escape. Anyway,
there was no one waiting on the other side of the door.

Reflections on the City

Beyond the door lay a city.

A city.

Oar's home had been a village; Tobit's a town. Here, in
a cavern hollowed out of a mountain, there was space for
thousands of buildings, perhaps millions of people.

All glass. All sterile. All empty and sad.

Listen. When you think of a glass city, do you imagine
a crystal wonderland, bright-lit and glittering? Or perhaps
something more mysterious, a glass labyrinth dreaming in
permanent twilight? Then you don't understand the ponderous monotony of it all. No color. No life. No grass, no
trees, no gardens. No friendly lizards basking in the plazas,
or pigeons strutting across the squares. No smells of the
marketplace. No playgrounds. No butterflies.

Nothing but a vast glass graveyard.

I don't know what the League intended on Melaquin. To
build a refuge? A zoo? How had those humans of four
thousand years ago reacted when they saw this new home?
They had food, they had water, they had medicine and artificial skin; they even had obedient AIs to help and teach
them. With all those comforts, it would be hard to walk
away . . . but it would also be hard to live here, eternally
colorless and odorless.

Or perhaps I was wrong. Perhaps those ancient people

filled these streets with music . . . held dances, played jokes,
painted murals on every glass surface. They were finally
free from fear and want; their beautiful glass children
would never starve down to skeletons, or cough themselves
bloody from TB. Those first people might have lived joy-
ously and died in comfortable peace, convinced this was
truly a paradise.

That was four thousand years ago: the early ages of what
humans call civilization. If those first generations painted
these walls, the paint had long since flaked away. If they
sang and danced, the tunes were forgotten. Human roots
ran shallow on this planet; when the people of flesh died,
their works crumbled, leaving only immortal glass.

Glass buildings. Glass children. Children who seemed to
make no artworks, no songs, no sloppy messy life.

Was the problem physical . . . some lack in their glands,
something the League left out when making these new versions of humanity? Or was the problem social? When the
fear of death was gone, when offspring were rare, did you
lose the incentive to achieve something beyond yourself?

I still don't know. Whatever went wrong on Melaquin
happened in every settlement on the planet—an astounding
thing in itself—and it happened so long ago that no evidence remained of the loss.

All I saw was glass. A glass city.

Oar no doubt thought it beautiful. She too was glass.

Signs

The elevator was set into the outermost wall of the city:
a wall of rough-hewn stone, striated with geological layers
slanted twenty degrees to the horizontal. I have never liked
caves—I can feel the weight of all that rock pressing down
on my head—but the cavern was so huge, my misgivings
were small. Besides, there were veins of pink quartz, green
feldspar, and other tinted minerals deposited through the

stone, providing welcome variations in the bleak color scheme.

Another variation was a sign painted in loose black letters on the nearest building:

GREETINGS, SENTIENT BEINGS
WE'RE IN THE CENTRAL SQUARE
WE'LL SHOW THEM WHAT EXPENDABLE MEANS!

"What does that say?" Oar asked.

"It says hello," I told her. "And that we've come to the right place."

"It is a very big place," Oar said, staring out on the forest of towers, domes, and blockhouses.

"Be brave." I gave her a squeeze, telling myself not to feel awkward about touching her "Walton said we should walk to the center now."

It was a long walk; it was a big city. I wondered how many ancient humans had been brought here . . . certainly not enough to fill the place. After living in grass huts or wattle-and-daub, the people must have been intimidated to have so much space at their disposal. Then again, they were used to living outdoors; maybe with a roof over their heads, they actually felt confined.

Our route led straight down a broad boulevard, its surface smooth white cement. A few buildings had words painted on their walls: KEEP GOING . . . NO U TURN . . . BE PREPARED TO MERGE . . . the indulgent signs people write to amuse themselves in empty cities. SIGNAL YOUR TURNS . . . DEER CROSSING . . . ALL CARS MUST BE RUNNING ELECTRIC. . . .

I didn't translate them for Oar. Some jokes aren't worth explaining.

Dirt

The closer we got to the center, the more dirt I saw. First it was just thin dust on nearby buildings; then bits of grit accumulated at the edge of the boulevard; then spills of grease or electrolyte darkening the pavement.

"This is a filthy place," Oar said with self-satisfaction. "My home would never become so dirty."

"Do you clean your home?" I asked.

"No." Her voice was offended. "Machines attend to such matters."

"This city has the same kind of machines. Otherwise the place would be buried in grime. The Explorers must have kicked up more mess than the systems could handle; either that or my friends have commandeered the cleaning machines for other things." *Most likely for spare parts*, I thought. Someone like Jelca wouldn't hesitate to sacrifice a janitor-bot in his drive to restore a spaceship.

"So the Explorers make this place dirty?" Oar asked. "Hah! Fucking Explorers."

"Maybe you shouldn't use that phrase," I told her. "You want to get along with the others, don't you?"

"I do not know them yet," she replied. "If they are very stupid, I may want to kick them."

"Please, Oar, you're my friend, and they're my friends. It will make me sad if you pick fights."

"I will not pick fights unless they deserve it." Her tone of voice suggested they *would* deserve it.

"Oar, if you get jealous that I have other friends—"

"Festina!" shouted a voice behind me.

Jelca.

Changed

He had no hair. Wasn't that strange? Just the bald skull I remembered, covered with the scabby patches that would grow inflamed and bleed if he tried to wear a wig.

For some reason, I had thought he'd have hair. I don't know why—I hadn't said, "Melaquin tech helped me so it must have helped him too." I hadn't thought about it logically at all; I had just assumed Jelca would have hair . . .

that he would be dashing and handsome and muscular.

I had assumed he would be perfect.

He was not perfect; he looked gaunt and twitchy. Jelca had always been thin, but now he looked positively ravaged, as if he hadn't eaten or slept for days. It didn't help that he was wearing a badly-fitted long-sleeved shirt . . . a shimmery thing of silver fabric that probably came from the local synthesizers: something like spun glass, but a fine enough mesh that it was opaque. I doubted Jelca wore it for the sparkle—more likely it was the only cloth the synthesizers would produce—but the shirt was so glitzily out of place, it looked like voluminous silver lamé hung around the bones of an anorexic.

"Festina?" Jelca said.

"Yes."

"You're here too?"

"Yes."

"You've changed."

"Have I?"

"Yes."

He spoke flatly—no grin of welcome for an old friend, or even a courteous smile for a fellow Explorer. Walton had been happier to see me, and Walton was a complete stranger.

Jelca's eyes stared fixedly at my cheek. God knows, I was used to stares, but this one unsettled me. I couldn't read his face. Was he simply surprised? Or was he disappointed with me, maybe even repelled?

I noticed that his hand had dropped onto the stun-pistol holstered at his hip—not a purposeful gesture, I thought, just a reflex, just something he was in the habit of doing. Everything about him seemed as tight as wire.

"You look good," he said at last. It did not sound like a compliment.

"You look good too," I responded immediately.

"You both look very ugly," Oar announced in a loud voice. "And you are so stupid I want to scream."

"So scream," Jelca said. "Who's stopping you?"

"I am too civilized to scream," she answered. "I am very cultured, I have cleared many fields, and I do not—"

"You're Oar," Jelca interrupted, obviously making the connection for the first time.

Oar shrieked. "You recognized ugly Festina but did not recognize me?"

"You all look alike," Jelca shrugged. There was no apology in his voice. "Why are you here?"

"My friend Festina needed my help to come to this place! That is the only reason. She wanted me with her so I came, because she is my *friend*."

"Friend," Jelca repeated with pointed intonation. "Oh."

My face burned. I wanted to blurt, *It isn't what you think* ... and I hated myself for feeling that way. I hated Jelca too. Why didn't he smile? Why didn't he run forward and sweep me into his arms?

Why didn't he think I was beautiful?

"How's Ullis?" I asked, just for something to say.

"Fine," he said. "Busy. You haven't seen her yet?"

"We just got here. We saw Walton outside."

"Oh. Well." He took his eyes off my face long enough to look at his watch. "It's almost suppertime. I'll show you where the others are."

He still didn't smile; but suddenly he held out a hand to me as if I remained a silly little freshman who'd leap forward at the first opportunity. Maybe I would have. I didn't run to him immediately, but maybe I would have given in after a few seconds, telling myself that this was the start of whatever I wanted.

Who knows?

Before I made up my mind, Oar darted forward and took the offered hand, lacing her fingers with his. Jelca stared at me a moment longer, then shrugged. "This way," he said.

Monstrosity

We walked to the central square. It was a huge space, several hundred meters on each side ... and almost completely filled with a giant glass whale.

"The spaceship," Jelca said.

I winced. A spaceship that looked like a whale? And a killer whale at that, an orca, with lines etched into its exterior skin to suggest the usual pattern of black and white coloration. It stood on its tail at the very center of the city, as tall as any nearby skyscraper. Its bulbous body no doubt contained living quarters, engines, and so on, but all of it was glass, glittering with prismatic refractions.

Could it fly? Like any whale, it looked streamlined enough. Still, it was a far cry from Technocracy starships. They were simply long cylinders with a "Sperm head" at the front—an oversized gray sphere that generated the Sperm-field back along the hull. The orca had no such sphere: nothing more than a huge glass parasol sticking out of its snout ... as if the whale had a beach umbrella clenched in its teeth.

"So that's our way home," Jelca said.

"You're going into space in a whale?" I asked.

"It's a *ship*, Festina." His voice flared with hostility. "Why should appearance matter?"

"It doesn't," I answered. "How are you going to get it out of here?"

"There are roof doors." He looked up briefly, then shook his head. "You can't see them from here. Can't see them from outside either. A whole section of the mountain just opens up."

"And off you go in an orca."

I meant to sound lighthearted and teasing, but Jelca didn't take it that way. "The whale was all we had to work with," he snapped. "A remnant of the Melaquin space program, whenever that was. This city has all kinds of ships, each stupider than the last. Birds, bats, insects ... even a rabbit, for Christ's sake. The people here didn't care. They scarcely worried about trivialities like aerodynamics, or tradeoffs between weight and strength of materials. Ninety-nine per cent of each ship was built by the city's AI, using League of Peoples technology. Oh no, the AI wouldn't actually build a working starship; but if you ask for a hull as strong as steel and a thousand times lighter, there's no problem with *that*! So the locals built a whale, probably because it was *romantic*."

"It is an excellent whale," Oar said approvingly. "I have seen pictures of such animals, but I did not know they were so large."

"It's a ship, that's all," Jelca replied. "And it happens to be the biggest in the city—the only one with enough room to house all the Explorers here." He turned to me. "Sixty-two Explorers now, counting you."

"Sixty-two?"

"And five non-Explorers," he went on, "who haven't got around to dying yet. Admiralty officials who got 'escorted' here—two embezzlers, two addicts, and a pedophile, all of whom the High Council preferred to have disappear rather than go through the messy embarrassment of a trial." He gave me an angry look. "Isn't that great? Getting banished here with the likes of them? The admiral Ullis and I came down with was a total piece of shit . . . took bribes from a contractor so the guy could keep selling shoddy equipment to the Fleet. God knows if anyone was hurt because of it; the admiral never asked. Never tried to learn what damage he'd done. And the council condemned Ullis and me to the same fate as a man like that!"

I said nothing. Jelca's words sounded like a rehearsed speech: a sore that had festered inside him so long, he was happy to have a new listener to hear. I knew the feeling. On the other hand, it had never occurred to me that most Explorers came to Melaquin in the company of criminals and other genuine undesirables. Somehow, I'd thought the exiles would all be people like Chee—out of control but not vicious. *Naïve, Ramos*, I thought; *too quick to romanticize the High Council as tyrants and their victims as he-*

roic political prisoners. No one was as good or as bad as I might like to believe.

"What happened to your admiral?" I asked.

"YouthBoost meltdown," Jelca answered with a shrug. "The usual fate of the scum who are sent here—they're old and fat and ready to fall apart as soon as they're cut off the teat. They keel over and problem solved . . . except for us Explorers, stuck in this hellhole."

"It is not a hellhole," Oar growled. "Melaquin is an excellent planet!"

"Sure," Jelca said. "Everything a man could want." He gave me a sideways glance. "That's why the council gets away with it, you know . . . why the League *lets* them get away with it. To an alien, there's nothing wrong with dropping Explorers on Melaquin; what other planet in the galaxy is better suited for human life? Depositing us here is damned safer than assigning us to explore a subzero ice-world or thousand degree inferno. Melaquin is a paradise for our species. When the council maroons us here, the League probably thinks it's a *favor*. Forget that we're cut off from civilization, forget that we'll never see our friends and family—"

"Your friends and family are probably very stupid," Oar interrupted. "Festina is very bored with the way you complain and wishes you would talk about something else."

Jelca gave a humorless laugh. "Sorry to bore you, Festina." He turned to Oar. "What do you think Festina would rather talk about?"

"She would rather talk about my stupid sister, Eel."

"What about her?" Jelca asked.

"Where is she?"

"She's your sister," Jelca said. "If you don't know where she is, why should I?" Before Oar could react, he gave her hand an ungentle tug. "Enough talk. I can smell supper and it's making me hungry."

The First Supper

The next few hours were an exhausting jumble.

I met the other Explorers—some familiar to me, but many stranded on Melaquin long before I was drafted into the Fleet.

I let people go through my pack: the candy rations I hadn't yet touched, the entertainment bubbles I'd brought because I had room, the odds and ends of equipment that might be used in the spaceship. There are no words to describe the joy of the female Explorers when they found my first aid kit contained two dozen menstruation swatches.

I told my story: the parts I wanted to tell anyway. I did not describe how Yarrun died; besides, the others were more interested in the lark-plane we'd left outside. One of the older men, a gray-haired Divian named Athelrod, headed out immediately to inspect the craft . . . on the hunt for spare parts he could cannibalize.

I vacillated between the urge to distance myself from Oar and the desire to keep her in close check. She was the only Melaquin native now in the city, apart from numerous towers of dormant ancestors. All other natives had left years earlier, peeved at some unspecified quarrel with the Explorers. ("You don't want to hear about that," scoffed a woman called Callisto.)

I asked about Chee and Seele. None of the other Explorers had been in the city that long ago, but they'd learned from the glass populace that two "uglies" had flown away in a glass bumblebee.

Lastly, I toured the orca ship. As Walton said, it was close to completion, especially if my lark-plane contained the parts they were looking for. "Then again," said Callisto, "it's been close to completion for the past twenty-eight years."

Or for the past four thousand years—the sticking point was what you required as an acceptable level of safety. No one doubted the ship could successfully take off; the only question was how far it would get. Out of the atmosphere?

Certainly. But far enough into space to be rescued by a League vessel? That was the crucial point of debate.

How much food and air would you need to get to the nearest trade lanes? How much fuel would it take? No one knew. So the Explorers had passed their time tinkering: an enhancement here, an increased efficiency there, but no breakthrough so overwhelming that they could state with confidence, "Now we stand a good chance of making it."

Then came Jelca: resourceful, angry Jelca. Like other Explorers, he had received what Tobit called "the tip"—a hint he would soon be marooned on Melaquin and a suggestion of which continent he should choose for a Landing. Jelca hadn't wasted time in brooding or futile attempts at mutiny. Instead, he had taken direct action. While other Explorers reacted to the tip by packing more supplies or personal keepsakes, Jelca had stolen a Sperm-field generator.

Every ship carries two extra generators, in case of malfunction. They are not large as ship equipment goes—black boxes the size of coffins, each weighing two hundred kilos. With the aid of a robot hauler, Jelca smuggled a spare generator out of the engineering hold and into a planetary probe drone. Of course, he had to remove most of the drone's sensing equipment to make room for the generator; but he considered that an unimportant tradeoff. He barely finished the work in time; almost immediately, he and Ullis received orders to escort the bribe-taking admiral on an "investigative mission" to Melaquin.

From that point on, Jelca's theft was easy: he sent out the rigged probe as part of the preliminary survey; and he arranged that the probe landed softly in a spot he could find later. Some time after the Landing, when he had reached Oar's village and heard the looped message about the city in the mountains, Jelca reactivated the probe and flew it south by remote control. He and Ullis still had to travel to the city by foot, but when they got there, the stolen generator was waiting for them.

As easy as that. A Sperm-field generator meant FTL

flight—it meant the difference between limping out of the
system after five to ten years of relativistic travel, or getting
home in two weeks. It was still an engineering challenge
to mount the generator on the whale; but with so many
Explorers in the city, they had ample brainpower to focus
on the problem. They also had an AI here like the one I'd
met in Tobit's town: a source of tools and components,
even if the AI occasionally decided the Explorers had to
manufacture particular pieces of equipment themselves.

Three years had passed since Jelca arrived with the gen
erator; now the ship was ready. Some people talked as if it
might take off tomorrow. Others contended the ship needed
months of shakedown before departure. Within a few
minutes, both camps were appealing to me as a disinter-
ested party: someone who hadn't talked herself hoarse in
the go-now-or-wait debates that had dominated every meal-
time for a dozen weeks. Before I could say stop, I was
barraged with measurements and test results, pages of figures and diagrams which both sides claimed would prove
their point. . . .

Then Ullis said, "She's a zoology specialist," and the
debaters lost interest in me.

Ullis

Unlike Jelca, Ullis Naar had greeted me warmly when I
arrived at the Explorers' mess. She hugged me; she recognized Oar immediately and hugged her too. Since Jelca
looked like he wanted to run off and eat by himself, Ullis
took me around to meet everyone. "This is Festina Ramos
and yes, she's one of us even if she looks gorgeous."

(I had explained about the artificial skin. She said she
was happy for me, and she meant it. Her own problem was
still much in evidence: blink, blink, blink every second or
so, some blinks so heavy they twitched all the way to her
shoulders. I found myself feeling sorry for her . . . feeling
pity. It was a patronizing, "Oh the poor dear" kind of pity,

and it scared me. I'd never before felt condescension for another Explorer.)

Ullis was the one who described how Jelca had obtained the Sperm-field generator; Jelca stood by silently as she spoke, as if the story were about someone else. Later, when lights throughout the city dimmed to dusk, Ullis explained that the dimming was Jelca's work too. He wanted a true day/night cycle rather than the city's eternal glimmer, so he had tracked down the control center and rewired some circuits. Perhaps, I thought, that change had been the impetus which spurred the glass populace into leaving. People who photosynthesize may not take kindly to strangers turning the lights off.

The arrival of night didn't quiet the Explorers' mess. The others were eager for news from home, gossip about the Fleet, updates on the lives of friends they had once known . . . but at last Ullis said, "Enough. Festina needs sleep. We all do."

I agreed. With good-nights all around, Ullis and I detached ourselves from the company and went into the silent city. I might not have been so quick to go if Oar and Jelca had been there, but they had left much earlier—Oar bored with Explorer talk, and Jelca because Oar took his hand and pulled him away. I had not been able to read the expression on Jelca's face as he walked out with her: neither happy nor sad, neither fearing time alone with her nor looking forward to it. Whatever Oar wanted from him, I doubted she would get it.

Ullis led me away from the central square, a few blocks' walk to a tower where she had claimed an apartment on the sixtieth floor. The city was dark now—only a few distant lights showing where Explorers had staked territory in other buildings. The lights were widely spaced from each other: people who live in glass houses don't want close neighbors. On the other hand, solid glass walls give a breathtaking view from sixty storeys up.

Ullis came in beside me as I stood on her glassed-in balcony, looking out over the city. "So," she said. "Home sweet home." She paused. She blinked. "You're welcome to stay here if you like. Roommates again."

"I don't want to put you out."

"No trouble." She blinked, then laughed. "I may get sick of you eventually, but at the moment I'm nostalgic for Academy days."

"Isn't everyone."

She turned to look at me. Her shoulder leaned against the exterior glass; beyond her, the city was as black as space. "I'm sorry about Yarrun. I liked him."

"Me too."

She waited. I said nothing more.

Finally she said, "I'm also sorry about Jelca."

"What about Jelca?"

"That he's become such a prick. I know you used to like him."

"That was just a schoolgirl thing," I muttered.

"He liked you too," she said. "When he and I were partners on the *Hyacinth*, he talked about you. A bit. He never opened up, but I think he regretted . . . you know, not seeking you out. But he didn't understand why you ran from that second date, and he was too proud to chase after a freshman. . . . Well, too proud, too shy, what's the difference? Testosterone, one way or the other. But he did think about you after."

I shrugged. "That was a long time ago."

"Sure." She regarded me sympathetically. "I saw the look on your face when he and Oar left together. . . ."

"I didn't have a look on my face."

Ullis blinked several times. Maybe she was doing it on purpose. Finally she said, "The hard thing for Jelca was being so close to normal. You understand? If he put on a wig, he was there. Not for long, maybe four hours before the lesions started bleeding, but for those four hours, he *had* it. He could walk down any street without stares. He could go on dates with real people. Yes, his scalp took weeks to heal, but if he wanted those four hours, he could have them. He could get clear. And that made him a little crazy—like he wasn't in the same boat as the rest of us. He never said it in so many words, but I was his partner; I could tell. Jelca never identified himself as an Explorer. I think sometimes he wanted to. Maybe if things had gone differently between the pair of you . . . but that was all part of it anyway. He couldn't bring himself to *connect* with another Explorer.

"I know that makes him sound arrogant," Ullis added hurriedly, "but it wasn't that way. Not at first. He just felt out of place. Miscategorized. And then, when he learned he'd be marooned on Melaquin—treated like an Explorer, and like a criminal—he felt unjustly betrayed. Like someone had personally spit on him. That's why he had the nerve to steal the Sperm-field generator. I've never asked what he did to get it, but I think he hurt someone. You know what it's like in Ship's Engineering; there's always someone around. They wouldn't let Jelca walk off with important equipment like that. I don't know for sure—maybe he took down some people with that souped-up stunner of his. But he was just so *wounded* that the council would treat him like any other Explorer . . . just as worthless, just as expendable. . . ."

"Ullis," I said, "didn't you feel wounded and betrayed too?"

"Sure. But I *am* an Explorer—and Melaquin is where Explorers end up. In a weird way, I feel fulfilled. I did my job. I stayed true. And because of that, I am *fiercely* connected with every other member of the corps."

I wanted to deny what she was saying; but I couldn't. However furious I might be with the High Council, some part of my mind whispered it was *fitting* to get dumped into the disposal chute called Melaquin.

An Explorer's life has only one proper ending: Oh Shit. And Melaquin was the Oh Shit you could walk away from.

Bad Times

"So," Ullis continued, "when Jelca woke up on Melaquin . . . no, I shouldn't pretend I can see inside his head. I just know it was bad. He came close to killing Kalovski— that was the admiral we were escorting. I had to talk Jelca into going away for a few days, until he cooled off. In the meantime, I dealt with Kalovski . . . which means I watched him die. That was pretty awful."

"Yes," I murmured.

She waited for me to say more, but I didn't.

"Anyway," she went on, "by the time I rendezvoused with Jelca, he'd already met Eel and Oar. You can imagine how I worried about that—not that I cared how he ran his love life, but two women, with minds like children . . ." She shook her head. "And back then, they couldn't even speak our language. I tried to talk some scruples into him, but he wouldn't listen. He said he was *exploring* what the planet had to offer. Whenever I could get the women alone, I tried to find out how they felt about the whole business; frankly, I may have taught them more English than Jelca did. But it was obvious they were infatuated with him. He was the first non-dormant male they had ever met. And they were so bored and lonely before he arrived, they were putty in his hands."

"Both of them?" I asked. "Oar tells the story differently now."

"She would," Ullis replied, "considering how Jelca walked out on them. When we were ready to head south, I was willing to take Eel and Oar with us—not that I thought it was healthy for them to stay with him, but if they wanted to come, I wouldn't leave them behind. Jelca wanted to disappear without a word . . . selfish bastard. So I grabbed Eel, told her what was happening, and left her alone with Jelca so the two of them could work it out. I would have done the same with Oar, but I couldn't find her; she was probably out clearing fields to impress him." Ullis shook her head morosely.

"What happened between Eel and Jelca?" I asked.

"I don't know—I stayed down on the beach while they talked up on the bluffs. Eventually, Jelca came down alone and announced neither Eel nor Oar were coming with us. They preferred to stay in their home village. There had to be more to it, of course; he'd probably screamed at Eel until she let him go. But I decided the women were better off without him, and maybe it was best to leave before they changed their minds."

"So Eel didn't go with you?"

"No." Ullis looked at me, puzzled. "Why would you think that?"

"Oar said you took her. Oar believed the three of you went away together."

I pictured Eel and Jelca alone on the bluffs that day three years ago. Jelca spurning her. Eel no more than a broken-hearted little girl . . . and never seen again.

Oh Shit.

Part XVI
Mania

My Attempts to Help (Part 1)

The next day, I tried to help with the spaceship. There was little for me to do; the ship was almost finished, and the few tasks outstanding were one-person jobs that required "technical sophistication" . . . which is to say, someone who knew what she was doing.

No matter where I went in search of something to do, people ribbed me for being a zoology specialist. Everyone brought it up. After a while, it took an effort to smile at the jibes. I told myself I was just new—oldtimers often tease new arrivals as a gruff form of welcome. It didn't help that I'd shown up after the hard work was done. "Oho, here's the animal lover, just in time to play inspector." They said it jokingly; I tried to hear it that way too.

I told myself there was no genuine resentment under the laughter: resentment for a woman who didn't look like an Explorer.

At meals, I felt people staring.

Three times Ullis told me, "You look really good, Festina."

The one time I saw Jelca during the day, he said nothing at all.

Stop imagining things, I told myself. *They don't care*

269

*what I look like . . . and even if they do, it's their problem,
not mine.*

Sure.

To pass the time, I outfitted another cabin inside the
whale: carrying in a cot, bolting it to the floor, stashing
unneeded equipment from my backpack into a locker. It
was all for appearance's sake—I couldn't escape with the
others. If I caught a ride in the ship, the League would stop
my heart in flight, the same way they terminated any non-
sentient creature trying to escape into space. They might
even take retribution on the other Explorers for helping me.
On the other hand, I had to go through the motions, or
someone might start asking questions.

Anyway, another furnished cabin wouldn't hurt anything;
the whale had plenty of space. Ullis said the life support
systems could handle two hundred people indefinitely, and
the food synthesizers had even more capacity. No one knew
why the early generations of Melaquin had bothered making a ship so huge. Had they wanted to leave the planet en
masse . . . maybe even return to Earth? Or had they simply
fancied a jaunt into space: a sightseeing tour around the
moon and back?

The other Explorers had no interest in speculation. Even
Ullis excused herself after breakfast, saying she had programming to do—simulation tests and so on. No, she didn't
need help . . . it would take too long to get me up to speed
on what she was doing.

By midafternoon, I felt glumly extraneous: sorry for myself and irritated at that weakness. Rather than mope where
someone might notice, I slipped away from the launch site
and headed into the city. Athelrod and others were still
going over the lark-plane; maybe they needed help carrying
back salvaged components. I began to retrace the route Oar
and I had taken in from the elevator . . . but I had only
reached the point where we first saw Jelca when I came
across Oar herself.

She sat huddled in the doorway of a glass blockhouse,
her arms wrapped tightly around her legs and her face

pressed against her knees. The skin of her glass thighs was rainstreaked with half-dry tears.

My Attempts to Help (Part 2)

I sat beside her and put my arm around her shoulders. For a while, neither of us said a word. Then she whispered, "I am very sad, Festina."

"I know."

"It is not fair to be so sad."

"No. It isn't."

"Nothing is the way it should be."

"I'm sorry."

She didn't speak again, but leaned in toward me. I let her rest her cheek against my chest. I could see straight through the back of her head to the tear-stains dribbled down her face.

"Eel is not here," she said at last.

"So I heard."

"And Jelca does not care. He does not care about Eel or me or anything."

I leaned over until my lips touched the hard glass hair on the top of her head. "Jelca is quite the shit, isn't he?"

"He is extremely much the shit," she agreed. "Shitty fucking Jelca."

"To hell with him," I said.

"A very deep hell. With flames and *everything*."

"That's the spirit."

I gave her shoulders a squeeze. She reached down and patted my knee. After a moment she said more softly, "I would like to punch him in the nose."

"Yes?"

"I would like to make him feel very bad."

"I know," I told her. "But civilized folks like us don't hit people."

"What do we do?"

We brood, internalize, and make ourselves miserable, I

thought. Aloud I said, "We give ourselves permission to indulge. Like eating something rich, or buying something we can't afford, or making excuses to get out of work. . . ."

She looked at me without comprehension.

"Okay," I admitted, "maybe those things aren't right for you. Is there someplace you want to go, something you want to do?"

"We could go visit ancestors," she said with sudden interest. "They live next door."

"Really."

"Yes. It is very fitting that Jelca lives beside the ancestors of this place. They both have bad brains."

"And you want to visit . . ." I didn't finish my sentence. It would be rude to describe the ancestors as senile near-corpses.

"It is pleasant inside the ancestors' home," Oar said. "It is warm and good."

"Ahhhh," I nodded, understanding. "You realize I can't go in with you?" I asked.

Her face fell. "Then maybe . . ."

"No," I stopped her, "you go. If it feels good, you deserve it. I'll wait outside."

"You will not go away?"

"I promise."

We got to our feet and walked arm-in-arm to the next building: an enormous tower, even taller than the sixty-story building where Ullis lived. Unlike other buildings in the city, this one had glass walls I couldn't see through; they had been opaqued to prevent the radiation inside from leaking out.

"I will not be long," Oar promised.

"Take your time," I called as she disappeared within. Oar looked eager for time in the tower; I didn't want her cutting the experience short because of me. It must be like a sauna, I thought—hot and steamy, the chance to lie around languidly. . . .

Oar barreled out the door, mere seconds after she'd entered. "There is a problem, Festina. The ancestors are very upset."

"At you?"

"No. At you. Come inside."

Talking with the Ancestors

It took some time for Oar to understand that going inside would damage me. I doubt if she really believed it; but she grudgingly agreed to act as intermediary, carrying messages between me and the ancestors to learn what was wrong.

Me: Why are the ancestors upset?

    [A pause while Oar ducked into the building, asked the question, and got the answer.]

Oar: Because a fucking Explorer is bothering them.

Me: Bothering them how?

    [Pause.]

Oar: Walking over them. Pushing them around. Stacking them against the walls.

Me: Deliberately trying to hurt them?

    [Pause.]

Oar: I do not think so, although some of the ancestors pretend they were grievously assaulted. Ancestors are stupid. I think the Explorer was merely clearing them out of the way. There is now a wide path down the middle of the room where the ancestors have been moved aside.

Me: Where does the path go?

    [Pause.]

Oar: I followed the path to the central elevator.

Me: Which means the Explorer was using the elevator for something.

    [Pause for me to think.]

What did the Explorer look like?

    [Pause.]

Oar: They say the fucking Explorer was shiny all over.

Me: I thought so. Look around inside, Oar . . . close to the door but maybe hidden. See if you can find a shiny suit.

[Pause. Oar returned with a bundle of silver fabric in her hands.]

Oar: How did you know this was there? What is it?

Me: A radiation suit.

I didn't mention that the glittery fabric looked like the same material as Jelca's silvery shirt.

Into the Tower

The suit was a sloppy fit on me. Tailored for someone taller: Jelca's size. It also had a holster attached to the belt. The holster was empty, but it looked like a perfect fit for Jelca's stun-pistol.

Unlike other radiation outfits I had worn, this one was comfortably light—no heavy inner lining of lead or one of the transuranics. Still, I had no doubt it would protect me from the tower's hot-bath of radiation. Jelca must have persuaded the local AI to construct the suit for him—a machine programmed by the League of Peoples would never endanger a life by building inadequate protective gear. Best of all, I knew Jelca was still alive; if he could go inside without being fricasseed by microwaves, I could too.

Radiation burns might not be a concern but vision was: the suit had no visor, no break at all in the hood covering my head and face. I could see very dimly through the semi-transparent fabric, like looking through a window bleary with rain. My view was at most three paces, and then just directly in front of me. I would have to move carefully and hope no one rushed me from the side.

For caution's sake, I checked the suit seals one last time, then stepped into the tower. The ancestors had indeed been moved to clear a path into the building—unlike the neatly ordered rows I had seen in Oar's village, these bodies were piled on top of one another, limbs dangling into each other's faces. No wonder they were annoyed.

"It is rude to treat ancestors like this," Oar whispered. I remembered that back in her own village, she had blithely kicked an ancestor in a fit of pique . . . but perhaps there was one set of rules for people inside the family and another for those outside.

"Ask them," I said, "how long they've been like this."

She spoke a few words in her native language, enunciating loudly and distinctly as if the ancestors were hard of hearing. Barely audible whispers drifted back from the clutter of bodies.

"They say a long time," she told me. "They probably do not know how long. Their brains are too tired to judge such things."

A long time . . . yet none of them had made an effort to move back to their original positions. And Jelca hadn't moved them back either. *Sloppy*, I thought—a conscientious Explorer would cover his tracks.

I turned to Oar. "Tell them we'll put them back properly in a little while. First, I want to investigate what Jelca was up to."

Oar conveyed my message. Meanwhile, I lumbered along the cleared path, wishing I could see better through the suit fabric. Glass bodies were difficult to discern; I worried about stepping on one I had overlooked. That, I supposed, was why Jelca hadn't dragged everyone back into place. He had unfinished business in the tower, and didn't want to trip over bodies every time he came in.

The path led through one room after another, three rooms of blurred body heaps, until I reached a single elevator in the heart of the building. Its door was open, ready for business; I stepped inside and waited for Oar to join me.

"Which floor do we want?" she asked.

"Start at the top and work down." Whatever Jelca was doing, he seemed to be keeping it secret from the other

Explorers. If so, he'd avoid floors near ground level—too much chance of passersby hearing any noise he might make. The city was quiet as death and filled with hard surfaces perfect for echoes; even a small sound carried surprisingly far.

The elevator closed and we began to ascend—slowly, as if anyone who took this ride had no reason to hurry. People came here to die—not literally perhaps, but that was only a technicality. Those who rode up almost never rode down.

Cheerful thoughts, Festina. To take my mind off the elevator's funereal pace, I said to Oar, "You can see better than I can. Could you please check the floor for marks?"

"What kind of marks?"

"Any kind. The path Jelca cleared was quite wide— more than he'd need just walking through himself. He might have brought in equipment. Maybe heavy equipment."

"Explorers are not strong enough to carry heavy things," Oar replied smugly.

"But Explorers can have the local AI build robots to do the work—I saw several suitable haulers at the launch site. Just check, would you?"

Oar got down on all fours and crawled around, sweeping her fingertips lightly across the floor. "There are some dents here," she reported. "Not very deep."

"Sharp-edged or rounded?"

"Rounded."

Wheels, I thought. That didn't tell me much; but the marks had to be recent. Like other machinery in the city, this elevator must undergo regular maintenance and rebuilding, courtesy of automated repair systems. Even small dents would warrant attention—otherwise, they might become starting points for rust.

"All right," I said, "Jelca brought something here. The question is what."

The Second Spare

The answer was a Sperm-field generator. We found it on the top floor, pushed tight against the wall of the building. I recognized it from a distance, even with my blurred vision: a black box the size and shape of a coffin.

"Holy shit," I whispered.

"Amen," Oar answered dutifully.

This had to be a second generator. The first was still installed in the orca starship—I had seen it mere hours before. Callisto had been running diagnostics on the device; it had actually spun a short thread of Sperm for her tests.

What was Jelca doing with another generator?

I had no doubts where the machine had come from—it was the second spare from Jelca's former starship. He must have stolen both generators from the engineering hold, then installed them into separate probes and sent both down to Melaquin. Ullis told me Jelca had flown one probe south by remote control. He must have done the same with the other probe, picking a time when Ullis was busy or asleep. Later, he had retrieved the first generator and turned it over to the Explorers . . . but he'd kept the other for himself, smuggling it here when the others weren't watching. (Jelca had been the one to instigate the day/night cycle in lighting. Clever. It ensured the Explorers would all sleep at the same time, thereby giving him a chance to fetch the generator under cover of darkness.)

But why did he need a second generator? Why did he want it badly enough to steal it, leaving his ship with no backup in case of breakdown? Of course, angry people do strange things; maybe Jelca liked the idea of the Vac crew drifting in space until someone answered their mayday. He might have thought it would give them something to think about after abandoning him on Melaquin—a few weeks of being stranded themselves.

But if that was his rationale, why hide this generator here? Why not load it onto the whale, as a replacement in case the first generator malfunctioned?

No. Jelca had plans for this second generator. I just couldn't guess what those plans were.

Hampered by my obstructed vision, I examined the black coffin. It was wired into another piece of equipment: a waist-high glass box with wing panels attached to the top. "Photo-collectors," I murmured. "Curiouser and curiouser."

"What is a photo-collector?" Oar asked.

"These panels," I told her, "soak up light and other radiation that hits them . . . which must be a hefty dose of energy, considering the output of this building. The panels obviously transfer power to a battery inside this case, and the battery supplies the Sperm generator; but damned if I know why. What's the point of generating a Sperm field on a planet?"

"Jelca is very very stupid about sperm," Oar answered.

I gave her a look she couldn't see through my suit.

Cursed with Hope

Minutes later, we were back on the street. Oar had replaced the suit where she found it, and my skin was rediscovering the joy of breathing; wearing the suit had been like being wrapped in plastic, close and sweaty.

I had decided not to move the ancestors away from the walls just yet. Oar assured me they were all getting enough light and air, and would scarcely notice a few more hours of overlapping each other. Putting the people back would tip off Jelca that he'd been discovered . . . and I didn't want that until I was ready to confront him. At the very least, I had to talk with Ullis first. Maybe the other Explorers needed to know too; but maybe not.

Maybe Jelca had a sensible explanation for everything.

I know. I was being foolish. How much more evidence did I need that Jelca had degenerated into a self-centered bastard? Toying with Eel and Oar, then callously discarding them . . . hiding the generator from his fellow Explorers . . .

giving me the cold shoulder as if I were a Vac-head. . . .

And yet. . . .

Since Oar had first told me he was here, I had dreamt about him. Thought about him. Imagined us together. Even earlier, during my years on the *Jacaranda*, he had crossed my mind now and then . . . especially when I lay beside some snoring substitute I had taken to bed because desperation got the better of me. Alone with my eggs, I invented fantasies about Jelca: a fellow Explorer I could make love with, not just a convenient Vacuum crew member to slick myself down.

I had such hopes. Stupid hopes—I knew that. But I had hoped that maybe, losing myself to Jelca would sear off my guilt, burn it away with white heat for just a few seconds. Whom else could I turn to? If I threw myself on another Explorer, or Ullis, or Oar, it would be so hollow, nothing more than drugging myself with sex. But with Jelca it could be different . . . couldn't it? He was not just someone within arm's reach, he was someone I'd thought about, dreamed about. . . .

I'd even dated him. Twice.

This sounds so banal now. It embarrasses me. I'd say I was lying to myself, but the lies were so obvious I didn't believe them, even at the time. Yet I wanted to believe. I wanted to have something with someone somewhere. Who else did I have but Jelca?

I wondered if Oar was thinking the same thing as we walked down the street in silence: patently false hopes, because the alternative was despair.

Transport Tunnels

We found Ullis in her cabin on the whale. She had jacked in to the ship's system and was programming with fervid intensity.

"Jelca's got a second Sperm-field generator," I said. "Did you know?"

She blinked without speaking for several long seconds. Then she shook her head.

It took some time to give her the full story. When I was finished, she could offer no explanation of what he might be doing. "There's no reason to generate Sperm tails on Melaquin," she said. "Even if he wanted to set up a transport tunnel . . . no. What would be the point?"

"What is a transport tunnel?" Oar asked.

"A way of sending things very quickly from one place to another," I answered. "A Sperm tail is a long tube of hyperspace . . . which means it's really outside our normal universe. Physical laws are very different there. If you stuck your arm in one end of the tube, it would immediately emerge at the other end, even if the ends were thousands of kilometers apart. If you anchored one end here on Melaquin and another on the moon, say, you could reach through, pick up a handful of moon dust, and bring it back just like reaching through an open window."

"I wouldn't reach through that window if I were you," Ullis said. "If you're standing with normal Earth air pressure behind you, and the moon's vacuum in front, you'd go shooting straight through mighty fast."

"Which is how we usually transport things along Sperm tails," I told Oar. "When we go from one ship to another, we drop the pressure at the receiving end so things shoot through from the sender. When we go from the ship to a planet, we increase the pressure in the Transport Bay so that it blows us down . . ."

"This is very boring," Oar interrupted.

"Also irrelevant," Ullis said. "If Jelca wants to use a Sperm tail at all, he has to anchor down the far end. Otherwise the tail whips around at random."

"We all carry anchors," I reminded her. Landing parties needed anchors to attract the tail when they wanted to leave the planet. Anchors were small enough to fit in the palm of your hand; I had one in my belt pouch, and no doubt Ullis did too.

"So Jelca has an anchor," Ullis conceded. "What's he going to do with it?"

"He brought the Sperm generator to this city with a remote-controlled probe drone. If the probe still has fuel, he could load an anchor on board, and fly the probe anywhere on Melaquin."

"So what?" Ullis asked. "Yes, he can set up a transport tunnel anywhere on planet, but what's the point? Why would he want to go somewhere else when he'll be going home anytime now?"

"Unless he's not going home." The words were out of my mouth before I gave them a second thought.

"Don't be crazy, Festina. We all want off this rock. Jelca may be a turd but there's no reason he wouldn't—"

"Shit," I blurted out. The light had dawned at last. "Shit, shit, shit!"

"What?" Ullis asked.

"She is worshiping," Oar told Ullis in a low voice.

"Oar," I said, "stay here with Ullis. Ullis, I have to find Jelca for a chat. If I don't come back in a reasonable time, tell the others everything I've told you. And whatever you do, don't let Jelca onto the spaceship!"

"What's wrong?" Ullis asked bewildered.

I threw a tense glance at Oar, then grabbed a scrap of paper from Ullis's work area and scribbled a message.

Ullis gaped when she read it. "What does it say?" Oar demanded.

I didn't answer; I was already running out the door.

Out of the City

No one working on the starship knew where Jelca was. Someone suggested he might have gone to help with the lark-plane.

I jogged down the boulevard toward the elevator, each footfall echoing off nearby buildings. As I passed Jelca's quarters—the place where Oar had been crying—I stopped to see if he was there. He wasn't . . . but his room contained more clothes of the silvery fabric used in his radiation suit: shirts, pants, even socks and gloves. I wondered if he'd tried piece-by-piece radiation clothing before he made the full suit; or perhaps he wore these as a second layer of protection under the main suit. If nothing else, having ''street clothes'' made of the same material would help reduce the radiation he soaked up while putting on the full suit inside the tower.

The temptation to search Jelca's quarters was strong—a thorough search, ripping the place apart if necessary—but I doubted I'd find anything. Besides, I felt an urgent need to confront him. *And give him one last chance*, said a voice in my head . . . as if there was still hope he could explain away all his actions. I hadn't figured out everything yet; the purpose of the second Sperm generator was still a mystery to me. However, I thought I had many of the answers I needed. I just hoped I was wrong.

Athelrod and Walton met me as I approached the elevator to the outside world. They carried glass holdalls containing parts they must have removed from the lark-plane. ''Too late!'' Walton called cheerfully as he approached. ''We're all done.''

''Not much there that we needed,'' Athelrod said. ''Still, we got a few design ideas. . . .''

''Have you seen Jelca?'' I asked.

''He came by the plane outside, maybe two hours ago,'' Athelrod answered. ''Didn't stay long.''

''So he came back down here?''

''No,'' Walton said. ''I asked him to see if he could fix the glitches in my weather equipment. He's very good at that sort of thing.''

''So he's up at your weather station now?'' I asked.

Walton nodded.

''How do I get there?'' After getting directions, I headed out at a run.

Walton and Athelrod stared after me with bewildered expressions.

The Coming Cold

The air outside was cooler than the day before—enough to prick up goose pimples on my bare legs. At the west end of the valley, the sun had already dipped below the far peak, though the sky was still coldly bright. Trying not to shiver, I hurried up the forest trail that led to the weather station. The world smelled of damp pine and winter.

I found Jelca sitting on a high rock looking down on the river that wound along the base of the mountain. The water ran fast and shallow; even though it was dozens of meters below us, I could hear the rattle of it running over its gravel bed. The sound was cold. The world was cold. In the forest behind us, each tree felt closed in on itself, withdrawing into its own thoughts as winter approached. The stone everywhere—under Jelca, under my feet, under the snow caps of the mountains—looked like it had been dark gray once but was now bleached pale with disappointment.

Jelca turned to look my way. He said nothing. Behind him, a small anemometer rotated listlessly as its cups accepted the wind.

I waited for him to speak.

"Ullis told me it was artificial skin," he said at last.

"Yes."

"Really just a bandage."

"That's right."

He stared at my cheek a few more seconds. "So that's it then. You've made it."

"Made what?"

"Full human status."

"Don't be stupid."

He said nothing for a moment. He wasn't even looking at me. Then: "You know what the strange thing is? When I thought of you, I pictured you this way. Without the birthmark. I would have said it wasn't part of my mental image of you; the birthmark made no impression on my mind. But I was wrong. When I saw you yesterday, you looked like one of *them*. The bastards who banished us here. It was like they'd stolen one more thing from me."

He thought of me, I told myself. I wanted to ask him a hundred questions about what he'd thought, when it happened, everything that had passed through his mind.

No. I refused to let down my guard with him. Not now. Probably never.

"I'm being ridiculous," he said. "Why should I mind that you look so beautiful?"

Beautiful. He found me beautiful.

"Jelca," I said. "Did you kill Eel?"

He was silent a moment, then nodded.

Accidents and Reality

"It was an accident," he said.

I sat down on the rock, separated from him by only an arm's length. The stone was cold beneath me . . . very cold, despite its exposure to the long day's sun.

"An accident," he repeated. "A mistake right from the beginning." He glanced at me. "You probably think I'm shit."

I didn't trust myself to say yes or no.

"There's no point trying to justify myself," he said. "When I met Eel and Oar, I was just looking to vent myself. Vent everything I felt about being heaved into exile with a piss-hole like Kalovski . . . and there were Eel and Oar. Looking so perfect it made me furious. Artificial people—like all the artificial people in the Fleet and everywhere. So I. . . ."

When he didn't finish his sentence, I said, "You either raped or seduced them."

He shrugged. "I either raped or seduced them. Couldn't tell you which. They didn't put up a fight, but they didn't understand what was going on either. It happened, the two of them together that first time, because I couldn't stop myself. Well, no—because I couldn't *bother* to stop myself.

I couldn't think of any reason that made it worth the trouble.''

"Eel and Oar themselves should have been enough reason."

"You'd think so," he admitted. "But the truth is, they weren't *real* women. None of them are real human beings. They're glass models of human beings ... or what the League of Peoples believes humans should be. Beautiful dead ends, just as most people in the Technocracy are beautiful dead ends.

"You know what I once thought?" he went on. "I thought the whole Explorer Corps was a training program for real people. Everyone else was pampered and spoiled, but we were *real*. The Admiralty wouldn't let doctors cure our problems because they wanted us to develop strength of character; they needed a small band of individuals who had to fight for respect so that we'd gain *depth*. Then one day someone would tap us on the shoulder and say, 'Congratulations. You've made it. Everyone else is useless, but you've learned all the painful lessons of life. You've won. Now we'll cure your trivial little scalp condition and make you someone important, because you've earned it.' You see? I had this daydream that everything was planned. That all the crap we've suffered had a *point*, and we'd be properly compensated in the end. Not dumped on a planet populated by empty people with nothing to *contribute*.''

"You're underestimating the people of Melaquin," I said. "They may be different from humans, but—''

"Save it," he interrupted. "I know all the arguments. And you're right, I shouldn't dismiss them. Eel and Oar deserved better than I gave them. But I didn't have it in me. They kept reminding me of all the shallow 'beautiful people' who make the Fleet a hell. So I used them and used them and used them until I couldn't stand the sight of them anymore.''

"Then you killed Eel," I said.

"That was Ullis's fault," he replied. "If she'd just let me leave quietly ... but she grabbed Eel and forced me to *explain* things. I tried rational discussion, I really did. I told Eel that Ullis and I had a *duty* to join the other Explorers; I told her that she and Oar would feel out of place if they came with us. Eel wouldn't listen. She had the mind of a child. She didn't want to be left out. Finally, I had no option but to. . . ."

He lapsed into silence, so I finished the sentence for him. "You shot her," I said. "And even though the regs made you carry a standard-issue stunner when you landed, you must have amplified the pistol as soon as you knew you were stuck on Melaquin."

"True," he admitted. "Everyone knows the guns are underpowered. . . ."

"They're underpowered because anything more could be deadly," I snapped. "I can imagine what high intensity sonics did to a woman made of glass."

"You think she shattered like crystal?" He shook his head. "Nothing so dramatic. These people aren't real glass; you know that. Eel stayed on her feet a long time. I kept shooting and shooting and she wouldn't fall down. And I swear I didn't believe the gun would really damage her; she was so tough, you could pound her with a sledgehammer without making a dent. But something inside her body was vulnerable to sonics. Something must have . . . cracked. Maybe her brain, maybe her heart, I don't know. But the instant she fell, she was dead." He shook his head as if this was an incomprehensible mystery. "So I dragged her into the woods and stuffed her under a pile of brush."

"And now you're a murderer," I said. "A dangerous non-sentient being."

"Maybe." He didn't sound convinced. "But it was just an accident. Sometimes I think it'll be all right if I get on the starship with everyone else. I didn't mean to kill her. And if I don't go on the ship, I'll be stuck on Melaquin, won't I? No better than the criminals and other scum the council banished here. . . ."

"I won't be leaving either," I said. "I'm a murderer too."

And I told him everything.

Releasing Pressure

I confessed because of the pressure to tell someone. I confessed because he was Jelca. I confessed because we were both unforgivable.

He had killed a sentient woman for the sole reason that she was inconvenient. Don't think I was deceived by Jelca's excuses. He shot Eel because he didn't want to face the fallout from exploiting her for six months. Maybe he hadn't expected the stunner to kill her. He should have considered the possibility, but maybe he didn't. Instead, he blasted her again and again until her glass vitals cracked into shards.

Jelca was a murderer and so was I. I had butchered my partner and left him to rot in a log. That was a fact, and intentions be damned.

I told Jelca the facts as clearly as I could without choking up. Neither of us could possibly leave. I didn't know how I felt about staying with him, but we owed it to the others not to jeopardize their escape.

When I finished my story—when I had told him how I sliced Yarrun's throat with my scalpel and spilled his blood over my hands . . . when I had reminded him that League of Peoples laws are more inescapable than entropy—after all that, Jelca laughed.

He laughed.

"What a wimp-ass murder," he sniggered. "What a wimp-ass excuse for a homicide."

I was speechless.

"You think the League will bar you from space for that?" He snorted in disgust. "You think surgeons are labeled murderers if they lose a patient? Wake up, Festina! You tried to help, and it didn't work. That's all."

"He would have lived!" I insisted. "If I'd left him alone, he would have lived. But no. I tried to be a hotshot, performing emergency surgery when I couldn't see straight. He died because of me!"

"Yes he did," Jelca agreed. "So you think you should be punished. You want to believe the League regards you as non-sentient, that you deserve exile. But that's just guilt talking, not common sense. You thought you were doing what had to be done to save Yarrun's life. That's blatantly *sentient*, Festina . . . and it would be ludicrous for you to stay on Melaquin and die because of it.''

Something in his tone caught my attention. "What do you mean by that?" I asked.

"Nothing." He looked me straight in the eye. "It's just stupid to spend the rest of your life in this hellhole."

I met his gaze. It was the first time he'd looked at me and not my cheek. I knew it meant he was lying. Some people are like that—naturally evasive until they put on an act of being forthright.

"What are you up to, Jelca?" I asked.

"Nothing," he repeated . . . again, looking straight into my eyes.

"Whether or not I'm a murderer," I said slowly, "I don't know that I want to leave Melaquin. It's pleasant here. Peaceful."

"Stagnant," he sneered. "Comatose."

"If I go back, I'll have to be an Explorer again." I watched Jelca's face closely. "They'll assign me another partner—how could I live with that? And I'll be sent on one mission after another until I go Oh Shit. Frankly, Melaquin sounds like a better life. Safer."

"I wouldn't recommend it," he said evenly.

Why? Something to do with the second generator. What did he have in mind? Something that would make it dangerous to stay on Melaquin. . . .

"You're going to do something to the planet, aren't you?" I said. "Something that makes it impossible for the council to maroon people here."

"How could I possibly damage something as big as a planet?" he asked.

"I don't know," I replied, "but that has to be it. You said it yourself—the League lets the council send people to Melaquin because the planet is hospitable to human life. We have as good a chance of surviving here as anywhere else in the galaxy. But suppose Melaquin stops being a paradise. Suppose it becomes deadly. Then the council can't use it as a dumping ground anymore because that would be real murder. The League wouldn't allow it . . . and you'll be able to say you beat the council at its own game."

"That would be nice," he admitted. "That would be a good *revenge*." He growled out the last word. "But it's too ridiculous to contemplate. If I worked hard I might pollute some land . . . but how much? A few hundred square klicks at most, even if I spent my whole life spilling radioactive waste on the ground. That's hardly hurting the planet as a whole. What do you think I could do, Festina? What's my nefarious plan?"

He was playing a game now, taunting me. Maybe he wanted me to think it was lighthearted teasing; maybe he saw my unblemished face and forgot I had the brains of an Explorer.

All right, think: he had a Sperm-field generator. It generated Sperm tails. What was a Sperm tail? A tube of hyperspace; a ship riding inside the tube could circumvent the limitations of relativity. The tube could also be used for instantaneous transport—as I'd told Oar, it was window from here to there. A window. . . .

Then I thought of what Ullis had said. If one end of the window was open to the planet's surface and the other ten thousand klicks straight up into the sheer vacuum of space . . . everything would go flying out the window.

The whole damned atmosphere.

How big a tail could one generator make? A klick in diameter . . . maybe more. With one end at ground level and the other trailing off into space, the Sperm would be like a giant firehose, free end whipping back and forth, spraying air into the void.

The first result would be the biggest storm this planet had ever seen: a tornado centered on the base of the Sperm tail, sucking up wind. And the storm would never stop— not until it reduced the air supply to negligible pressure.

"How long," I asked, "would it take to drain Mela-quin's atmosphere through an unanchored Sperm tail?"

Jelca looked startled. Then he answered, "18.6 years. But the surface will be uninhabitable long before that."

Part XVII
CONFRONTATION

Ego

"Jelca," I said, "there are people on Melaquin. You'll kill them."

"I'll wait for the ship to take off," he replied.

"I don't mean Explorers!" I snapped. "You'll kill people like Oar!"

"They'll be all right," he answered with a vague wave of his hand. "Their homes are safe underwater and in caves."

"They don't all stay in their homes! They come out for walks on the beach—you know that. And I doubt their habitats are so self-contained they can withstand the whole planet losing atmosphere. When the air pressure drops far enough, the lakes will boil away; what happens to underwater cities then? And how do you know the caves are so airtight they won't leak? You don't know. You can't."

"All right," Jelca shrugged, "there may be problems. So what? This planet is dead, Festina; it may look viable, but it's not. There's no civilization here. There are no *people*. No one but glass zombies too stupid to know they're extinct. The ancestors do nothing . . . even creatures like Oar do nothing. They don't deserve to be called sentient. But Explorers *are* sentient, and it's time to stop treating them like rotten meat."

"Jelca," I said, "ask the other Explorers if their lives are worth genocide. You know they'd never accept it."

"They don't have to," he replied. "I accept it for them. I take the responsibility. If someone doesn't do this, you know what will happen? When we reach Technocracy space, the Fleet will load us all onto a ship and send us straight back to Melaquin. This is where they send their embarrassments, and we'll be the biggest embarrassment of all! For everyone's sake, I have to make sure Melaquin is no longer an option."

"You aren't doing this for *everyone's* sake," I told him. "It's only for your sake. The council was mean to you, and you want to hit them back. This is so unworthy of an Explorer, Jelca. Flamboyant gestures are for people who think life means beating the other guy. That's not life, that's ego. It's what you do when you're too scared or stupid to build a life on your own terms. Demanding revenge, Jelca . . . I'm ashamed of you. It's just so *adolescent*!"

"Adolescent?" he roared. "Adolescent!"

"Juvenile. Revenge always is."

And that's when I hit him.

Fight or Flight

It was a simple punch, straight to the jaw—a sucker punch, and I had no qualms about using it. Now that I knew Jelca's plan, I was dangerous to him; he may already have decided I would have an "accident" and topple off the mountain. One shot of his stunner would take me out, so I couldn't give him a chance to draw.

The punch should have fazed him long enough to let me close for a few more strikes; but maybe I didn't put all my strength into it. Maybe some subconscious softness balked at knocking out Jelca's teeth. . . . I don't know. I just know the impact didn't completely rattle him. Before I could follow up, his emergency programming kicked in: he dove, tucked, and rolled, exactly the way I did when taken by surprise.

Pity he couldn't have been trained with one of the other responses—freezing or backing off passively.

Before he stopped rolling, I was diving too: diving for the cover of the trees. I had no chance of crossing the ground between me and Jelca before he could draw his gun. My only chance was to get out of range, preferably with sturdy pine trunks at my back. Standard-issue stunners are only effective at close quarters, but with an amplified weapon like Jelca's, I wanted all the insurance I could get.

I reached the woods a split second before he fired. My whole head buzzed for a second as if it were clamped in a vibrating vice; but momentum carried me forward, and I stayed on my feet for a few stumbling steps till the trees walled off the sound. Thank heaven they were pines—their needles rustled fiercely under the hypersonic barrage, absorbing the sound and muffling it. With each step my vision cleared, until I allowed myself to accelerate into a full run along the uneven trail.

"Festina!" Jelca yelled. "Come back. Let's talk."

What kind of idiot did he think I was? I didn't waste my breath answering. The trail had bends in it, but not many; there were long stretches where he would have a clear shot at me if I didn't stay far enough ahead. Silently, I cursed my lack of foresight for not bringing my own stunner ... but I had never expected to need it. At worst, I thought Jelca might deny killing Eel; the idea that he might have a greater lunacy planned never crossed my mind.

You're too civilized, Ramos, I told myself. *All that Explorer training, and you still aren't prepared to deal with non-sentients.*

No. I just hadn't been prepared to accept that *Jelca* was non-sentient. He was: a dangerous non-sentient, and now he was after me. His footsteps pounded the trail some distance behind. I didn't look over my shoulder—it would only slow me down, and Jelca's legs were longer than mine.

Could I hide? Take cover behind a tree and ambush him as he came by? Too risky: the tree trunks were no more than a hand wide, and here in the depths of the wood, their branches didn't reach low enough to offer concealment. The best tactic was to leave the trail, leave it now before Jelca came into sight. I might not have brought my stunner, but I sure as hell had my compass—I wouldn't get lost in the woods.

Jelca would get back to the elevator ahead of me, but that didn't matter. If he decided to wait there, blocking my way back to the city, I had more time than he did. When I didn't return, Ullis would organize a search party—after all, I had left her that note:

I think Jelca killed Eel. I'm going to talk to him about it. You keep an eye on Oar, and don't tell her a thing.

Ullis would come, I knew she would . . . and given the circumstances, she and the other Explorers would come armed.

I veered off on the first side trail I came to: a narrow track used by deer and bear. As soon as I was out of sight of the main trail, I stopped and crouched, keeping quiet. Jelca was a city boy—he wouldn't notice my tracks had turned. In a few seconds he thudded by, running hard and muttering inaudible words under his breath; I hoped they were curses. Then he was gone.

The sounds of the forest filled the silence: pine needles brushing each other, squirrels squawking as they foraged for winter supplies. When I felt the coast was clear, I moved forward, paralleling the trail but keeping a good distance off in case Jelca backtracked.

In time, the open area around the elevator entrance came into sight. I stopped at the edge of the woods, keeping low to stay hidden. Jelca could be lying in ambush, inside the entrance itself or behind the nearby rocks. Carefully I scanned each possible hiding place—no sign of him, but that only meant he'd concealed himself well. I found some cover of my own and settled down to wait. A search party would come.

Half an hour later, the hum of the elevator reached my ears. I smiled . . . and my smile grew wider at the thought of Jelca gritting his teeth in consternation. While I'd been waiting, I had silently collected a pile of stones suitable for throwing if Jelca showed his head. That would keep him busy while the search party got out of the elevator; after that, it would be over for him.

The elevator stopped. The door opened. Only one person emerged: Oar, carrying her silver axe.

"Laminir Jelca!" she shouted to the mountains. "Come out and let us see the color of your juices!"

"Okay," I sighed. "This would be the rescue party I *didn't* want to see."

Battle

Somehow Oar had learned what I wrote in my note. I had hoped she couldn't read English; but maybe she could. It didn't matter, Oar was here now with hate in her eyes . . . and that made her a prime target for Jelca if he was nearby.

He was. A trigger clicked; then came the soft whirr a stunner makes to tell you it's fired. The sonics made no sound themselves—they were too tightly focused on Oar to spill in my direction. Oar staggered and looked around wildly, unable to understand what had happened to her.

"Festina!" Jelca shouted. "Now would be a good time for you to surrender."

The way Jelca's voice echoed off the mountain made it hard to pinpoint his position, but I could narrow it down. He had to be hiding behind one of three rocks on the far side of the elevator entrance. Hugging half a dozen throwing stones to my chest, I worked my way through the forest, circling toward him.

Oar shook her head to clear it and raised her axe. "Where are you, fucking Explorer?"

The trigger clicked, the gun whirred. Oar shuddered but held her ground.

"Festina," Jelca called, "you know I can kill her. If you don't come out, her death is on your head."

I didn't answer. The fool was living some dream now—picturing himself as a desperado who could beat the world through sheer ruthlessness. What had happened to his Explorer training? I felt ashamed any ECM could blind himself with such romantic notions.

Oar jumped from where she was, hit the ground, and rolled up against a rock: an imitation of my own defensive move. The maneuver took her out of the immediate line of fire; I heard a clatter of scree as Jelca moved over the mountainside to draw another bead on her. This time I glimpsed his head for a split-second—not long enough to nail him with a stone, but now I knew where he was.

"This is ludicrous, Festina!" he shouted. "Are you going to let her die to save your own skin? Not very sentient of you." More rocks clattered under his feet. "You know," he continued, "she's the closest thing you've got to a partner now. You want to lose another partner, Festina?"

You are such a bastard, I thought. But I was an Explorer; he couldn't goad me into doing something rash. Anger is unprofessional.

The stunner whirred again. Oar groaned, then called, "It only tickles, fucking Explorer! You are stupid and boring and your gun is weak!"

Her voice sounded raspy. I pictured crystal fragments lying ragged in her throat as bits of broken glass splintered off her tissues. Other attacks might bounce off her hide, but the sonics were killing her. Was she dying already? I pressed forward as fast as I could; Jelca would soon be in my sights.

He was moving again—moving for a better shot at Oar, but also moving into clear view. It was a gamble on his part . . . but he must have thought I was still on the other side of the forest, back where the trail came out of the trees. The rocks gave him adequate cover in that direction; he might think he was safe.

I'd teach him otherwise.

Slowly I cocked my arm back, ready to hurl a stone into the side of his head. His concentration was centered on Oar; he wouldn't see it coming. But before I could throw, Oar surged to her feet yelling hoarsely and brandishing the axe. Jelca shied away, and lifted his stunner. I could imagine his finger tightening on the trigger . . . so I heaved the stone with all my strength, a shot aimed at his body rather than his head, because I couldn't afford to miss. Maybe Oar could withstand another blast and maybe she couldn't.

The stone hit him on the upper arm— not his gun hand, but I prayed it was enough to foul his aim. Without waiting to see, I sprinted forward, grabbing another rock from my arsenal and hurling it in Jelca's direction. He spun toward me, ready to fire . . . but the incoming stone made him duck and then Oar was screaming, racing at him with the axe. Jelca shot her again, pointblank range, then flinched as my next stone caught him on the shoulder. I had swung out wide, far enough that he would need to turn away from Oar to aim at me; and she was still standing, still holding the axe, even if the last shot had temporarily numbed her.

With a cry, Jelca fled toward the elevator. I held another rock ready in case he turned around, but he didn't. He ran straight to the hidden entrance; a moment later, the door whisked open, then closed. Still wary, I kept my grip on the stone in my hand as I approached Oar.

"Festina," she whispered, "I do not feel good."

She fell into my arms.

Damage Assessment

I dragged her to cover in case Jelca was being tricky; he might be waiting to leap out of the elevator and shoot us both. The safest place I could find was just inside the edge of the woods: far enough to be out of stunner range, but with a clear view of the elevator entrance if Jelca tried to sneak out.

Once we were safe, I examined Oar. She was bad. Fluid dribbled out of her ears, thin fluid with a smell like vinegar. Her breathing crackled each time she inhaled. After her collapse, she had wet herself; I mopped up as best I could with a handful of soft-rotted pine needles.

There were no wounds on the outside of her body—no chance for me to feel useful by applying bandages. I pulled the first aid kit from my belt pouch and looked for anything else that might be useful. Nothing. Antibiotics and disinfectants intended for a human metabolism, not hers.

And the scalpel, of course.

I wished I had brought my Bumbler—at least I could have used it to scan her on various wavelengths. As it was, her body was as clear as ever, internal damage invisible.

Oh well, I thought, *this time I won't be tempted to operate.*

Camping Out

Unable to help Oar, I turned to the problem of Jelca. With due caution, I approached the outcrop hiding the elevator entrance . . . and he was gone, back down to the city.

When I pressed my palm against the plate that opened the door, nothing happened. I tried it again. And again.

No luck.

Jelca must have shorted out the controls. He didn't want me chasing after him. More importantly, he didn't want Ullis or a rescue party coming up to find me and the truth.

I wasted several minutes smashing the door with rocks, then trying to pry it open with a stick. Even before I started, I knew the effort would prove futile. The door was thick metal, its frame embedded deep into the mountain itself. Nothing I could do would budge it.

Back in the woods, Oar was still unconscious, still

breathing. The shadows under the trees had thickened; only the peaks of nearby mountains caught any sunlight. I would need a fire soon to drive off the chill . . . and perhaps fire-light would be good for Oar too. The IR from the flames might be like giving her intravenous nutrients.

In case Jelca tried to bushwhack us during the night, I built the fire in front of the elevator entrance. If he tried to come out, we'd see him immediately. I had also leaned a pile of stones up against the door. If it started to move, the pile would topple down with enough noise to raise the alarm.

Once I had propped Oar in front of the fire, I warmed myself a bit, then set out for the lark-plane, only half a klick away. If it was still in one piece, I could fly Oar home—back to her own village, where I could lay her out in the Tower of Ancestors and let her absorb a full spectrum of energy. That was the only way I could think to help her; if she drank in enough strength, her body might repair it-self. Even better, Oar's mother was there in the tower . . . dormant yes, but she might stir herself if she saw Oar was seriously injured. For all I knew, Oar's mother might tell me about some miraculous med-tech machine that could fix Oar in seconds.

When I got to the lark, I saw it was not going anywhere. Athelrod's crew had ripped out circuit boards, left wires dangling, even cut away part of one wing. The plane looked like the victim of vandals; and perhaps it was. I was be-ginning to think that the High Council's greatest crime was not committed against Explorers, but against the people of Melaquin. We were cultural pollutants, contaminating an otherwise pristine environment. Think of Tobit and his homebrew . . . think of the people who had been forced out of this city by Explorer activities . . . think of the glass lark in front of me, kept intact for four thousand years, but torn to useless junk as soon as it fell into Explorer hands.

And that was ignoring what Jelca intended to do.

Back at the campfire, I sat beside Oar as night drew in. My belt pouch still contained protein rations—the flavorless kind that supply your nutritional needs but give you constipation if you eat them more than two days in a row. I munched on a cube and wondered if I should try to feed Oar too . . . dissolve a chunk in river water, then feed it to her like gruel. Not yet; I wasn't sure rations intended for humans would sit well with her digestion. Besides, her voice had been so raspy before she passed out. I didn't want to make her swallow if her throat was filled with broken glass.

Hours trickled by. I kept the fire burning brightly. Once, as I gathered more wood, I came face-to-face with a deer buck displaying a majestic rack of antlers. He went on his regal way without paying me the least attention. Other animals occasionally appeared as beady eyes reflecting the firelight, but none came closer than that.

With nothing else to occupy my thoughts, I replayed my conversations with Jelca. What should I have said? What could I have done to change his mind? I had an immediate answer: I hadn't been able to reach him because I didn't look like myself. I didn't look like an Explorer. If I hadn't covered my birthmark, Jelca would have taken me more seriously. He may have softened, allowed himself to be drawn back to sanity. Instead of destroying the planet in a fit of pique, he might have considered the possibility of a future here . . . a future with me.

But no. I looked like an empty version of the woman he knew. Sanitized. Made cosmetically acceptable. That only added to his anger . . . maybe pushed him over the edge.

Listen. I knew I was being ridiculous: putting the blame on my face, as always. Ugly face, beautiful face, it was always in the wrong. Loudly and clearly, I told myself, "You've really got to work on self-esteem, Festina."

I stared into the fire a long time. It felt hot on my cheeks.

A Gray Morning

I slept three or four hours over the night. Nothing happened. Nobody came . . . not Jelca and not a search party.

That bothered me. Ullis must know I was missing. Even if Jelca had sabotaged the elevator, all those non-zoology majors should have been able to repair it by now. Where were they?

Dawn arrived diffidently, easing itself into a chilly gray. Clouds had crept in overnight—a high overcast that misted the top of the tallest mountains. It would rain before the end of the day . . . either that or snow. I threw more wood on the fire and huddled against Oar for comfort.

Her comfort or mine. Both.

My watch read 10:05 when I first heard the distant whine. I snatched up a handful of throwing stones . . . but the sound did not come from the elevator. It was somewhere outside. Was the city opening its roof doors? Could the Explorers be launching the whale? I tried to imagine a way Jelca could trick the others into leaving without even looking for me. Nothing came to mind.

As I listened, I realized the sound was not coming from the mountain; it came from the sky.

"Don't I have enough trouble?" I groaned.

I debated moving Oar to safe cover, but she'd already been moved too much for a patient with internal injuries. Anyway, if something happened to me, I wanted her in plain sight where searchers could find her.

Better to leave well enough alone.

I stood. I waited.

A glass eagle set down on the rocks in front of me. It had missiles mounted under its belly.

The cockpit slid open and a man clambered out. "Saw your fire!" he shouted.

"Happy birthday, Phylar," I said.

Yet Another Reunion

He was no longer wearing his tightsuit. In fact, Tobit had stripped to his underwear, giving a more revealing view of his hairy torso than any woman could wish. The only piece

he had retained from his uniform was the helmet, carried
under his arm: his good arm. His other arm, the prosthetic
one, now hung from a cord around his neck, its fingers
gripping the rope like a chin-up bar. Oddly enough, the
false arm's skin was several shades darker than the rest of
Tobit's pale body. I wondered if the prosthetic surgeons
had been careless in matching his complexion or if years
of drunkenness had leached the color from the rest of his
flesh.

"That was a shabby trick, Ramos," he complained.
"Running out on me like that." With a look of wounded
dignity, he grabbed the free end of his artificial arm and
clapped it into the receptor housing that Fleet surgeons had
hollowed into his shoulder. A few hearty thumps hammered
the connector jacks into place. "You make me feel unloved," he said as he flexed the prosthetic fingers experi-
mentally. "You have something against amputees?"

I sighed with relief. He was only irritated, not angry. For
all his faults, Tobit was a true Explorer—not like Jelca,
overreacting to tiny slights.

"You were busy with your friends," I answered lightly.
"It would have been rude to interrupt the party." I glanced
at the eagle's cockpit. "You didn't bring anyone with
you?"

"There was room for only one Morlock, and I didn't
want to pick favorites." He made a dismissive gesture with
his hand: his artificial one, which now seemed fully functional. "To tell the truth, they were such pathetic sots I
didn't *have* a favorite. Except you, of course, Ramos." He
threw a smacking kiss in my direction. "You're looking
good."

"If one more person says that to me, I'll rip the damned
skin off."

"Don't rip off your cheek to spite your face." He gestured toward Oar. "What's wrong with your friend?"

"Jelca shot her."

Tobit's eyebrows raised.

"It's a long story," I said, "and I don't have time to tell it. Do those missiles of yours work?"

"Yes. No thanks to you." He looked at me warily. "Are you thinking of blasting Jelca?"

"No. I'm thinking of blasting a door."

The Blast Radius

Neither Tobit nor I could guess how much damage the missile might do. We didn't even know what payload it contained. Chemical? Nuclear? Matter-antimatter disintegration? "Phylar," I said, "before you mount weapons on a plane, shouldn't you find out how much bang they have? It might help to know whether you should keep back a hundred meters from your target or a hundred kilometers."

Tobit scowled. "I never intended to *use* the bombs, Ramos; I just wanted them there for completeness."

"Completeness," I repeated.

"I liked the look of them; besides, flying an eagle is so damned gauche, I needed something to make me look less precious. As soon as I figured out how to command the AI, I had the missiles reactivated and put back."

"So you armed the plane as a fashion statement?"

"Stop bitching, Ramos. You're the one who wants to blow up a mountain."

Difficult though it was, we loaded Oar into the eagle with us, sitting her up on my lap like a limp heap of laundry. She wouldn't be safe on the ground; there was no way to gauge the blast radius. Anyway, if the missile was nuclear or worse, she'd have to be dozens of klicks away to avoid damage, and we couldn't carry her that far on foot. Better to have her with us, and simply order the plane to remove itself an adequate distance from the explosion.

Before boarding the plane, Tobit got a fistful of dirt and smeared a huge brown X on the outcrop that hid the elevator door. The mark would be easy to see at a distance of at least five kilometers. Hitting the mark was another matter—we had no idea what guidance mechanisms the missiles had. Since the eagle possessed no controls, all we could do was say, "Shoot that," and let the plane do all the aiming.

Oar and I perched in the right-hand seat, strapped down as best I could manage. Tobit climbed in beside us and stuffed his head into his tightsuit helmet. "Why are you wearing that?" I asked.

"So I don't get blinded by the sun," he replied.

I looked dubious. The helmet's visor was clear, evidence that the overcast sky was no danger to anyone's eyes. If there had been any excess brightness, the visor would have automatically tinted itself.

"We don't have any sun today," I told him.

"There might be a break in the clouds. Or," he muttered in a lower voice, "there might be a nuclear fireball of apocalyptic proportions."

"Oh," I said. "I better close my eyes."

"Nah," he answered with an airy wave. "Just hide behind your girlfriend. She'll soak up the rads better than forty meters of lead." Then before I could respond, he told the plane, "Up. Let's get this show on the road."

Boom

The eagle rose straight up on its wing-jets, a smooth vertical liftoff. "Keep track of that X mark," Tobit said to the plane, "that's our target. Fly to a safe range, then blast it."

The plane banked away neatly, then angled into a steep climb on a straight line course away from target. Acceleration squashed me lightly between Oar and the back of my chair, but not painfully so. A small distance short of the cloud ceiling, the eagle leveled off and continued on the same heading, cruising comfortably short of Mach 1.

"Can you still see the X?" Tobit asked.

I turned around. The entrance was now far behind us. In

the overcast light, I could make out the rocky area where we'd fought Jelca, but not the X itself. "The plane must see better than we do," I told Tobit. "Telescopic sights or something."

"Bet you also believe admirals are your friends," he muttered.

I opened my mouth for a retort . . . but at that moment, the plane rolled sideways, wing over 180 degrees, and we were abruptly dangling upside-down in our safety straps, our heads pointing at the ground. A moment later, the eagle's beak pushed itself sharply upward: up and around in a buttonhook maneuver that ended with us right-way up again and now pointing toward the target.

"Cute," Tobit said with a quaver in his voice, "but it should give us warning when it's going to—"

The plane shuddered as a missile launched.

I thought the eagle had been flying at good speed. No—the eagle was virtually standing still compared to the missile. It cracked the sound barrier as it lanced out, riding a plume of smoke that pointed straight toward the target. For a second, all we could see was the smoke, not the missile itself. . . .

"Shield your eyes!" Tobit yelled, and I closed them fast, ducking behind Oar's lolling head in case that really offered some protection.

The flash was still visible through my eyelids.

Into the City

When I opened my eyes, there was a smoking hole in the mountain. Not a crater—a hole straight into the city, with glass buildings visible below. The blast site was circular, a hundred meters in diameter and remarkably well-contained. That pleased me; I preferred not to kill too much wildlife if I could help it.

"Eagle," Tobit said to the plane, "see that nice hole? That's where we're landing."

I stared at him. "You're taking the jet into a glass city?"

"The hole's big enough," he answered. "And I suspect the elevator's not working at the moment."

The elevator was not even visible—the whole mechanism was simply gone, unless it was part of the surprised cloud of smoke that drifted in shock around the site. The automatic repair systems would clock a lot of overtime in the next few weeks.

"All right," I told Tobit, "into the hole, then head for the center of the city. Just watch out for the killer whale."

"The *what*?"

"Your ride home," I answered. Then I tried to explain what was happening.

Not Dead Yet

After slipping and weaving around the skyscrapers, we touched down in the main square, not far from the whale itself. The noise of our engines should have brought Explorers flocking around; but only a handful ventured away from the whale to greet us.

One was Ullis. She stared at me for a moment, then smiled wearily. "I never believed you were dead."

"Who said I was dead? Jelca?"

Ullis nodded. "He's gone crazy. He used loudspeakers to send an announcement all over the city. You had attacked without provocation and he'd been forced to kill you." She looked at me stonily for a moment. "Why would he say that when it wasn't true?"

"To stop you sending out a search party," I replied. "I know something he wants to keep secret."

"I still tried to find you," Ullis said, "but I couldn't get outside—Jelca's locked off the elevator."

"Don't worry," Tobit assured her. "The elevator isn't locked any more." Under his breath he added, "It's hard to lock anything that's been reduced to slag. . . ."

"Where's Jelca now?" I asked.

"No one knows," Ullis replied. "And I haven't told you the worst part. He's rigged the whale. It's going to take off within the hour."

Responsibility

I gulped in surprise. "The ship is taking off?"

"It went into its launch cycle last night," Ullis said. "Things have been frantic since then."

"But surely someone can stop it."

"Jelca must have planned this a long time ago," Ullis replied. "He planted secret activation devices in almost every system on the ship. Disconnecting them safely will take more time than we have; and it would be disastrous if some systems fired while others didn't. We can always rip out wires till nothing on the whale works, but it would take so long to repair things afterward . . ." She shrugged. "Besides, half the Explorers don't want to stop the countdown. They say we're ready to go; they're glad Jelca stopped any further delays."

"So," I said, "you intended to fly off without worrying what Jelca was up to?"

"Some people have waited thirty years for this day, Festina. This is their only chance to get home. Besides," Ullis lowered her eyes, "I volunteered to stay behind. To find you and to deal with Jelca." She took a deep breath. "He *is* my partner."

"*Was* your partner," I told her. "And I'm the one who has to stay behind. I can't leave this planet, Ullis. It's too complicated to explain, but believe me, I can't go. I'll take care of things."

"You may need help—" Ullis began.

"No," I interrupted. "I don't want you. And don't you have useful things to do on the ship?"

She blinked. And blinked. "Some of the communication software is in rough shape." Her voice was a mumble, filled with guilt.

"You have to go." I laid my hand gently on her arm.
"And I have to stay."

"Jelca's my responsibility. . . ."

"He's mine now," I said. "You have duties on the ship.
Go. Please."

She blinked again, twice, then kissed me and walked off
slowly. The other Explorers followed on her heels.

First Things First

"That was fucking maudlin," Tobit announced in a loud
voice.

"What are you still doing here, Phylar?"

"Keeping you company, Ramos. When you're all by
yourself, you brood."

"Go with the others," I told him. "There's space for
you on the ship—you can have the cabin I equipped for
myself. Or take Jelca's cabin . . . he won't need it."

"First things first," Tobit replied. "They won't launch
for a while, and there's no way I can contribute. On the
other hand, I *can* help you carry this little lady to get recharged with her ancestors. That's what you want to do,
isn't it?"

I patted his hairy shoulder. "Thank you, Phylar. You're
a tribute to the Corps."

He belched deliberately. "A fucking humanitarian—
that's me."

We found a cot in a nearby blockhouse and carried Oar
up the central boulevard. The city surely had more than one
tower where ancestors could rest their tired brains; but I
aimed for the tower containing the Sperm generator. The
odds were good Jelca was holed up there, waiting for the
whale to take off. Once it was gone . . .

I couldn't guess whether he would activate the generator
as soon as the Explorers left, or put it on a delay circuit so
he had time to take shelter elsewhere. Was he suicidal or
not? If he turned on the generator immediately, he would

die—either sucked directly into space or pulped by the windstorm that would result when air started spewing into the vacuum. But maybe Jelca didn't mind dying, as long as he got his "revenge"; and the sooner he put his plan into effect, the less time I had to stop him. He knew I was alive. Considering the monstrous explosion when Tobit and I blasted our way in, he might guess I'd gotten past the unworking elevator.

Then again, the walls of the tower were opaque; and for all the explosion's destructive power, it hadn't made much noise. . . .

Maybe he didn't know I was coming. Maybe. But I couldn't take that chance. I had to assume he might activate the generator as soon as the ship was clear of the roof doors. That gave me less than an hour to stop him.

Sateen

I told Tobit to wait with Oar outside the tower. "Afraid of booby traps?" he asked.

"Yes." I stepped inside the building. Nothing went boom. On the other hand, Jelca's radiation suit wasn't in its hiding place. He had to be wearing it, and watching over his doomsday machine on the top floor.

"All clear," I told Tobit as I came back out. "We'll run Oar inside, then you hightail it back to the ship."

"What are you going to do?"

"Jelca's on the top floor. I'm going to pay him a visit."

"Dressed like that?" He snorted in disbelief. "You know how many rads these damned towers produce? It's one thing to duck in for a second then duck out again— that's no worse than having a few X-rays taken. But if you mosey in, ride the elevator, and spend a few minutes handing Jelca his ass . . . you won't have a working blood cell left in your body, Ramos. Hell, by the time you get to Jelca, you may not be able to stay on your feet. The only consolation is that the radiation burns will keep your mind off the radiation sickness.''

"Wait here," I told him; and I ran into Jelca's home next door. Moments later I ran out again, my arms full of the shimmering shirts and pants I'd seen tossed around Jelca's room. "Radiation gear," I announced, throwing a bundle at him. "Suit up."

Shirt, pants, socks, and gloves. It would have been nice to find a balaclava for head covering, but there was nothing like that. As a substitute, I started wrapping a shirt around my face; but Tobit pulled it away and handed me his helmet. "Happy birthday," he said.

"This is the second birthday present you've given me."

"And I'm keeping count," he replied. "You're going to owe me big, Ramos." He tossed a wad of cloth haphazardly over his own face, proclaimed, "I can't see shit," then stumped back to where Oar lay.

He looked ridiculous—dressed in silver tinsel, the shirt so tight over his belly I could see the indentation of his navel as his gut strained against the fabric. When I put on his helmet, it smelled of rotgut and vomit, almost strong enough to turn my stomach . . . yet I said to him, "You're a gentleman and Explorer, Phylar."

"Don't turn mushy on me, Ramos." He picked up his end of Oar's cot. "Let's move."

Obstacles

We placed Oar in the center of the first room—right where she'd get the most light. Her body relaxed as the radiation began pouring into her . . . as if the warmth had already started to ease her pain. Still, she showed no signs of consciousness, and I could hear the ugly crackling in her lungs each time she took a breath. Gently I arranged her body, flat on her back with arms outspread, like a flower open to the sun; then I laid her axe beside her, just as ancient warriors would lie in their tombs with weapons close at hand.

"It's not a fucking burial!" Tobit groaned. "Stop wasting time."

"If you're in a hurry to get back to the ship, feel free to go."

"I'm in a hurry to make sure you can do what you have to," he replied. "In case it hasn't crossed your mind, getting to the top of this tower might not be easy."

"What do you mean?"

"Let's go to the elevator."

He marched toward the center of the building, with me close on his heels. When we reached the elevator, he pressed the call button.

Nothing happened.

"Oops," I said.

"The bastard already proved he can sabotage these things," Tobit pointed out, "although this time, he's likely just locked it off at the top."

"Maybe there are stairs," I suggested.

"Ramps," Tobit replied. "There were ramps in the tower at Morlock-town. The whole building has to be serviceable by robots . . . and that means the bots need a way to the top in case the elevator itself breaks down." Tobit's cloth-covered head swiveled around; I could imagine him peering through the cloth, straining to see. "That door," he said pointing. "That should go to the ramps. All these towers are likely built on the same design."

I went to the door. The latch moved when I pressed it, but the door wouldn't open.

"Stuck?" Tobit asked.

I stepped back and drove a side kick into the door—not hard enough to endanger my foot, but with plenty of strength to loosen any stickiness from a poorly fitted doorframe.

The metal door boomed from the impact, but did not budge.

"That Jelca boy thinks ahead," Tobit muttered. "He's starting to piss me off."

The Muse of Fire

Tobit and I spent a futile thirty seconds bruising our shoulders as we attempted to break down the door; but it was metal, solid and unyielding—far too strong for us to make more than an ineffectual dent. As we stepped back panting, I said, "Perhaps we should break into the elevator instead."

"And what if we did?" Tobit asked. "You think you can climb eighty storeys, hand-over-hand on the cables?"

"Maybe."

I couldn't see his face under the silvery fabric, but I could feel skepticism radiating toward me.

"All right," I said, "why don't I smash down this door with Oar's axe?"

"You'd break your wrists," he replied. "And there's an easier approach to try first."

He walked into the next room, planted his feet firmly in the midst of the motionless ancestors, and cleared his throat. The next sounds to emerge from his mouth were a mishmash of syllables, some falsetto, others bass, some so liquid they dripped with saliva, others harsh like a man choking. The tone was strong but not forced—commanding and confident. When he finally paused, I could hear rustling from every corner of the room. Closed eyes blinked. Fingers twitched.

"You speak their language?" I whispered in amazement.

"I've been Grand Poobah to the Morlocks for eight years, Ramos. You think I let the glass glow under my feet?" He turned back to the ancestors and spoke again, his arms spread wide, his diction clear.

In one corner of the room, a glass arm moved. Closer to hand, a glass head lifted, blinked and stared. Someone sighed. Someone else took a deep purposeful breath.

"I thought their brains were mush," I whispered.

"Just bored," Tobit replied. "You can catch their attention if you give them something they've never heard before."

"So what are you saying?"

"What I remember from *Henry V*—some asshole of an admiral forced every academy instructor to teach a Shakespeare course. Now I'm telling the glassies, 'Once more unto the breach,' and all that crap. Stiffen the sinews, summon up the blood, break down the door." He paused. "I don't know how the fuck I'm going to translate 'Saint Crispin's day.' "

But he rose to the challenge. Tobit orated, and his audience answered. I can't imagine the ancestors understood much of what he said—even if Tobit spoke their language, these people wouldn't know what to make of a "muse of fire" or "Harry, England and Saint George!" Nor did I think Tobit could stir their souls with Shakespearean poetry . . . not translating off the cuff and from memory. More than anything, he was getting through to them on the strength of sheer novelty; they had never heard a man in silver lamé harangue them to attack France, and it was bringing them to their feet.

Mouths twisted into smiles. After centuries of dormancy, something had changed—changed for all of them. Even those who had been slow to rouse themselves were sitting up with interest, their eyes glittering.

Hands clenched into fists. Spines straightened proudly. Tobit pointed at the locked door.

Ten seconds later, the door was no longer an obstacle.

My Present

"I can take it from here!" I shouted to Tobit. My ears still rang from the thunder of glass shoulders, strong as rhinos, smashing the metal door down.

"You're sure?" Tobit asked.

"Get back to the ship before it blasts off."

"What if you need more help?"

"Don't be stubborn, Phylar. I'm giving you a ticket home . . . as a birthday present."

"Ooo—look who thinks she's learned to manipulate people." He snapped me a backward parody of a salute. "Get going yourself, Ramos. Do something non-sentient to Jelca before he does it to you."

He turned and lumbered away. I watched for a moment, then saluted his back. Call it another birthday present.

In the Stairwell

I had eighty storeys of ramps ahead of me. No matter how pressed for time I might be, running was out of the question; I settled for a light jog and wondered how long I'd be able to keep it up.

Far above, the tower ramps clattered with the clack of glass footfalls. Tobit's speech had inspired the ancestors so much, they hadn't stopped after breaking down the door— they were still charging ahead, howling to spill French blood at Agincourt or whatever they thought they were do- ing. I didn't try to keep up with them; not only were they stronger and faster than my mere flesh, they were less wor- ried about running out of wind. The stairwell burned with the same radiation as the main tower rooms. Even as they raced along the ramps, the ancestors were recharging, keep- ing themselves powered.

There was another reason I didn't try to catch up with the ancestors: I needed time to decide how to handle Jelca. First, grab his stunner—that was obvious. And I had one strong advantage over him: I could see clearly through the tinted visor of Tobit's helmet. Jelca, on the other hand, would be half-blind with the radiation suit covering his eyes . . . like looking through glittery cotton cloth. In a straight fistfight, the odds were stacked in my favor.

As long as he didn't shoot me first. One sonic blast, and

I'd be unconscious for six hours . . . or until Jelca killed me, whichever came first.

How could I avoid getting shot? Stealth if possible. If I could sneak up and take him down fast, I had nothing to worry about; but if he saw me first. . . .

"Idiot," I said aloud. "Why didn't you pick up your own stunner?" Yet the prospect of using the same weapon as Jelca filled me with revulsion. I knew I was being irresponsible—considering the stakes, I should have been ruthlessly willing to shoot Jelca in the back if that's what it took. But some subconscious inhibition had stopped me from thinking about my own stunner until now—and I had no time left to go back for the gun.

Was there anything else I could use as a weapon? I took a mental inventory of my belt pouches, now tucked under the radiation shirt and pants. What was I carrying? Things for taking soil samples, a small disk camera, my first aid kit . . .

. . . which contained the scalpel. . . .

I laughed out loud. There in the stairwell, I leaned against the wall and laughed. Unable to stop giggling, I untucked my lamé shirt tail, opened a pouch, and pulled out the knife.

The scalpel.

"Fair's fair," I said to the walls. "Fair's fair."

I didn't know what I meant by that.

To give the blade some weight, I taped some mineral sample tubes to its handle. The tubes were only the size of my fingers, but they were lead-lined in case they had to hold radioactive materials. When I was finished, the knife was well-balanced and heavy, suitable for stabbing or throwing. I found myself tempted to hold it up and say, "Yarrun, I owe you this." But I didn't do it. There comes a time when we outgrow dramatic gestures.

At the Top of the Ramp

Halfway up the tower, I passed the first glass body: an ancestor with no sign of injury. There were two more another floor up. I stopped briefly to examine them. They muttered something and turned their backs on me.

"Tired of going up ramps?" I asked. "You and me both."

Their initial enthusiasm had eroded. Who wouldn't get bored, racing up storey after storey, with no change of scenery? The closer I got to the top, the more bodies I found . . . until on the eightieth floor, I came to the last ancestor, lying in the open doorway that led out of the stairwell. He must have disciplined himself to stay with the task, all the way hoping to find some stirring amusement at the end of the trip. When he reached the finish, only to find a room exactly like the ones downstairs, he had sunk to his knees in disappointment.

Welcome to the Explorer Corps, I thought.

I didn't charge out onto the floor. Jelca might have heard the door open; even now he might be lying in ambush, ready to blast me into unconsciousness. I waited, listening. I listened for five whole minutes by my watch, and might have waited longer if I hadn't heard something.

A rumble.

A roar.

A vibration under my feet.

The whale was taking off.

The Launch

It would have been a sight to see: the roof doors opening and the glass orca soaring out on plumes of smoke and flame. With luck, Tobit had made it back in time. I breathed a prayer for those aboard, then moved cautiously out of the stairwell. There would never be a better time to sneak up on Jelca, with the sound of blast-off loud enough to cover my approach.

Scalpel in hand, I stole forward.

The building's glass rattled as the launch continued. The ancestor lying in the stairwell lifted his head with one last show of interest . . . then pouted and lay down again.

Three rooms between me and Jelca.

Room 1: the roar outside increased, moving upward. I could swear the ship was sliding straight past the building, scorching the tower's exterior with belches of fire.

Room 2: with a roar, the sound of engines swept past the building, up, high up, heading for the roof, as echoes banged off every building in the city.

Room 3: the noise suddenly eased, and I knew the ship had cleared the roof doors, out into open sky where its sound could spread through the mountains. The echoes were still loud enough to cover my soft approach to the last room, if only Jelca was looking in some other direction.

But he was looking straight at the door. His pistol pointed straight at the door too.

"Don't move a hair," he said with theatrical calm. "I can pull the trigger faster than you can move out of the way."

I knew he was right.

The Laying of Blame

"So who are you?" he asked conversationally. "Ullis? Callisto?"

His question confused me. Then I realized my helmet had opaqued itself enough that Jelca couldn't see my face.

"It's me," I said. "Festina."

He inhaled sharply under his radiation mask. "Festina? Of course." He gestured with the pistol toward my hand. "I should have recognized you by the scalpel. Still your weapon of choice?"

Ouch. "You really are a shit, aren't you?"

"Thanks to you," he answered. "You backed me into a corner. If you hadn't left me with no other options. . . ."

"Spare me the excuses."

"But you're the one to blame," he insisted. "You forced me to shoot Oar when you knew it would kill her. You

made it impossible for me to be an Explorer. . . . So now
I'm something else."

"A dangerous non-sentient," I said.

"Exactly. And if I'm going to be damned forever, the
least I can do is live up to the title."

I sighed. "You're quoting some bubble, aren't you? And
a bad one at that. Since you can't impress me as a human
being, you try it as a villain. That's pathetic."

"I'm not trying to impress—"

"You are!" I shouted . . . not because my words could
affect him but because I'd heard a sound behind me. "If
you weren't trying to impress me, you would have shot the
second you saw me. But you want to gloat. You want to
justify yourself. Or you want to act out some bubble you've
seen where the villain acts menacing to pretend he's more
than a pissy little schoolboy. Honestly, Jelca . . . destroying
a world because nobody likes you!"

"You liked me once," he retorted. "You *adored* me.
And you weren't the only one. Eel adored me. Oar adored
me . . ."

"I did not!" shouted a voice behind me. The next moment, an axe whizzed past my head.

Battle Rejoined

The axe was not balanced for throwing. It flew fast
enough to take Jelca by surprise, but only struck his arm
with its handle as it passed by. It glanced off the wall behind him and clattered to the floor.

Jelca raised his pistol.

Unlike the axe, my carefully prepared scalpel flew with
perfect precision. I threw it with a simple flick of the wrist,
in the instant before I dove out of the doorway. It slashed
into Jelca's fingers where they wrapped around the butt of
his stunner. He screamed. The stunner fell.

"Hah!" The laugh rang through the room. Oar leapt past
me, heading for Jelca. "You killed my sister, fucking Ex-

plorer! You tried to kill me. Now we will see who is such a thing as can die.''

She moved sluggishly, and there were smears of dried fluid tracked down her chin. Even so, she had been strong enough to wake from her coma, clearheaded enough to figure out what had happened, and stubborn enough to climb eighty storeys in search of vengeance.

Now she plunged toward Jelca, her hands reaching for his throat. The attack was awkward, off-balance; her dizziness showed. Jelca dodged, deflecting her rush to one side. He took one quick glance in the direction of his stunner, but it was too far away. Instead, he turned the other direction: toward the Sperm generator.

"No!" I cried. The maniac intended to turn it on. If it activated now, a Sperm-tail thousands of klicks long would establish itself in a single second—a tail waving out of control, lashing up out of the atmosphere and into space. The generator itself was bolted down securely, but those of us in the room weren't. All three of us would make a very short cold trip into hard vacuum.

With nothing else close to hand, I whipped off my helmet and heaved it across the room, catching him hard in the back of the head. The blow struck with a resounding crack. He pitched forward, sprawling onto the black coffin of the generator . . . but his hand was still moving, searching for the activation switch.

"Stop him!" I yelled. "That machine will kill everyone!"

Oar lashed out a foot and kicked Jelca in the side—not a skilled kick, but strong enough to lift him and flip him back half a meter. He dropped onto the coffin again, this time spreadeagled on his back. I couldn't tell if he'd fallen closer or farther from the generator's switch; but he was still conscious, still moving, still reaching out to turn on the machine.

With no time to get to my feet, I slithered across the floor, straight toward the stunner. My eyes were on Jelca;

his hand fumbled with something on the far side of the generator . . . probably the switch.

I grabbed the gun and fired fast without aiming—even if I didn't hit him full on, the edge of the sonic cone might stagger him. But I hadn't appreciated the power of the amplified pistol. Hypersonics smashed against the glass wall over Jelca's head and shattered it to crystal rain, exploding it outward in a shower that left a gaping hole in the tower.

Air whistled outside as glass shards pattered onto Jelca's radiation suit. He could ignore the shards; what he couldn't ignore was the clumsily wielded axe coming at him.

Oar tried to chop Jelca like she would chop a tree—a hard blow straight down toward his chest. If she had been at full strength, he never would have blocked the blow; but she was weak now and bleary. He caught the axe and stopped it, both arms extended as he seized the axe handle at the base of its head.

For a moment, they both were frozen there: Jelca fending off the axe, Oar trying to force it down onto his sternum. Then Oar whispered, ''Fucking Explorer. This is what expendable means.''

She let go of the axe, grabbed his arms, and jumped with him, straight out the hole in the wall.

Part XVIII
EGGS HATCHING

Cleaning Up, Sweeping Away

I walked halfway across the room, intending to look out the window. Then I stopped. There was nothing outside I wanted to see.

Before my eyes took too much damage from the radiation, I picked up the helmet and put it back on. The smell of it sickened me. A lot of things sickened me.

With a few sharp jerks, I yanked out the wires between the Sperm generator and its battery. I wanted to damage the machines more permanently, but didn't know what would be safe. There were people in this tower; if the generator contained nuclear materials or antimatter, smashing it might set off an explosion.

I didn't want to hurt anybody, did I?

It was easy to unlock the elevator—Jelca had simply attached an override chip to the control panel. Once I disengaged the chip, I rode to the bottom floor and carefully moved back all the ancestors Jelca had disarranged. It allowed me more time to put off going outside.

I still had to go out eventually.

Jelca was dead, of course—no mere human could survive such a fall.

It didn't help that he'd been holding Oar's axe.

I sometimes think Oar might have lived if she hadn't

been so broken already. But she was half-dead before she fell, and now she'd finished the job. She did not breathe; her heart was silent.

Oar was such a thing as could die. According to her beliefs, that made her holy . . . sacred.

Sure. Why not.

I carried her into the tower and laid out her body again, axe by her side. Maybe the light could bring her back, even from this; but I didn't wait to see.

Jelca I left in the street.

Barren

The central square was empty, except for the eagle-plane off to one side. I shouted, "Phylar!" several times, but the only answers I got were echoes. He must have made it to the ship in time.

The city was silent. Barren. I couldn't face it. Suddenly I found myself in the eagle, shouting, "Take off, now, up!" . . . a fierce panic to get out. The plane rose in a whine of engines, through roof doors that were still open from the whale's launch. With no one in the city to close them, the doors might stay open forever.

The sky outside brooded in gray melancholy, but the open air was not as oppressive as the abandoned city below. My panic ebbed; and I realized it was foolish to leave so hastily. There was still a wealth of Explorer equipment down in the city—things I would need if I was going to live on this planet the rest of my life.

And I was.

But I didn't need to go back down right away. I could stay outside . . . watch the birds . . . see if I could find any eggs to start a new collection. . . .

I told the eagle to land beside the remains of the lark; it seemed like appropriate symbolism. For a while after touching down, I just sat inside the plane, listening to the engines cool and watching the overcast clouds wisp around the distant peaks. Getting out of the cockpit required more energy than I possessed. Eventually though, I forced myself to move: down to the ground where I took off Tobit's helmet and breathed the still air.

Behind me, a bootstep scraped across stone.

I turned slowly, too burnt out to bother with defensive reflexes. If there was someone here, it could only be another Explorer . . . perhaps one of the old ones, stranded on Melaquin for decades and turned coward at the last moment, too fearful to return to an outside world that had surely changed.

The newcomer was a woman, wearing the gray uniform of an admiral. "Festina Ramos?" she blurted in surprise.

I saluted. "Admiral Seele," I said. "Welcome back to Melaquin."

Chee's Partner

Seele didn't answer. For a moment, I thought she was staring at my cheek; then I wondered if she was seeing anything at all, even though her gaze was on my face.

"You left me your egg collection," she said at last.

"Yes."

"It was my first hint you'd been sent to Melaquin."

"And that's why you're here?"

"I suppose so," she nodded. "I got to thinking. . . ." Her voice trailed off.

"You remembered you were once an Explorer," I said. "That you once looked like me and were marooned here too. So you came to rescue me?"

"I don't know what I came to do," she answered. "I came . . . I came to see. The city. I didn't know anyone was here. Our sensors picked up the starship launch; I thought everyone would be gone." She paused. "The High Council would have a collective attack of apoplexy if they knew I was here."

"And you wouldn't dare risk their displeasure," I said,

"or they'd send you back here. Like they sent Chee. Did you know about that?"

"I heard what happened to Chee after the fact. Exiling you here with Chee . . . possibly the council thought that would send me a message."

"That's all we were? A message for you?"

She shook her head. "Chee was always a thorn in their side. That spy network of his—rubbing their nose in the incompetence of the bureaucracy. The smart councillors knew they needed him, but the ones who just liked wielding power. . . . Some people hate interference, even when it saves their asses. Eventually, they caught Chee with his guard down, and away he went."

"Away he went," I repeated. "I watched him die."

Admiral Seele bowed her head.

Understanding

After a while, Seele murmured, "We should get out of here."

"Don't hurry," I told her.

"Festina," she said, "ever since Chee and I escaped, the High Council has stationed two picket ships in this system, to make sure no one leaves again. Do you think this is the first time I've tried to land on Melaquin? I'm an admiral; I have a ship at my disposal. Every now and then, I try to come, but the pickets always turn me away. When I received your egg collection, I came once more, wondering if this would be the time I'd defy the pickets. I lurked in this system's Oort cloud for more than a day, trying to make up my mind. Then, suddenly, you Explorers launched a ship; a ship with Sperm capability." She smiled. "That sure as hell caught the pickets napping. The two of them bolted after the Explorer ship and must be in deep space by now."

Seele grabbed me by the arm. "I saw my chance and I took it, Festina. The first time in forty years I've been able to land on Melaquin. I came to see my old city. I came to see some glass friends . . ." She shook her head. "Never mind. I've found you instead. Our sensors picked you up while your plane was flying. And now you have a chance to escape! The others won't succeed—the pickets will snare them with tractor beams and drag them back to this planet. But while the pickets are gone, you and I can get clear. Let's go, Festina. This chance may never come again."

"So I should save myself and leave the others in the lurch? That's what you and Chee did all those years ago."

Seele looked stricken. "We don't have time to discuss this. . . ."

"I have all the time in the world," I told her. "The way I see it, you found a working spaceship in the city below. . . ."

"Yes, but—"

"And you took off without worrying about other Explorers banished on the planet. . . ."

"It was a small ship, and we had no way to locate the other—"

"Then," I kept going, "you got back to Technocracy space and cut a deal with the High Council to save your hides. You'd keep your mouths shut, and in exchange, the council would make you admirals. Isn't that it? So you and Chee got cushy positions while other Explorers kept disappearing."

"Festina, you have to understand—"

"No, Admiral," I interrupted, "you've picked the wrong day for me to be understanding." I turned away from her in disgust. "And you've picked the wrong woman to save," I shouted over my shoulder as I stomped back to the eagle. "Just because I remind you of your damaged young self—"

"Festina," Seele said.

Something in her tone made me turn around. She was aiming a stunner at me.

"I'm like a magnet for those guns," I told her.

Then she shot me.

My New Quarters

I woke up in bed. The bed was in a standard officer's cabin on board a starship. My head throbbed with all the leaden pain that comes from a stun-blast. In a way, that was a blessing—I couldn't focus my mind on other ugly thoughts that threatened to devil my conscience.

Much as I wanted just to lie there, wincing each time my pulse bludgeoned my frontal lobes, I faced a physical imperative—after hours of unconsciousness, I urgently needed to empty my bladder. Groaning, I made myself vertical and sat on the edge of the bed until purple things stopped exploding behind my eyes. Then I staggered to the toilet, did my business, and continued to sit on the seat, staring dully at the wall.

My head throbbed. I counted sixty blunt pulses of pain, then stumbled back toward the bed. As I passed the desk, I noticed a plain white pill sitting on top of a card that read, THIS MIGHT HELP. I swallowed the pill immediately, on the theory it couldn't possibly make things worse.

In a few minutes, the pain did ease a little: enough to let me take stock of my surroundings. Yes, I was in officer's quarters, almost exactly like my cabin on the *Jacaranda* but a mirror image—on the port side instead of starboard. The room had no decorations, but standing near the door were three packing crates, lined against the bulkhead. I opened the lid of the closest one and saw many small objects wrapped in wads of cotton.

My eggs.

My eggs.

Tears came to my eyes. I was too scared to touch a single egg; I just looked at the cotton-wrapped bundles, counting them over and over again . . . only the ones I could see at the top of the open box.

My eggs.

"This is stupid," I said aloud. "I lost Yarrun and Chee and Oar, and I'm overjoyed over some eggs?"

But I was. I had not quite lost everything. Not quite.

The Stars

The door chittered and Admiral Seele walked in. Doors open for admirals, even if you don't give permission to enter.

"You're awake," she said. "Sorry for being abrupt, but we were wasting time."

"So you shot me. Just what I'd expect from an admiral."

"No," she replied. "A true admiral would have ordered someone else to shoot you. I'm still an Explorer at heart."

I had to smile in spite of myself. Then a sobering thought hit me. "You don't really intend to take me back to the Technocracy?"

"If you prefer," Seele said, "I can drop you off at a Fringe World. Admirals can order course changes on a whim."

"You can't drop me anywhere but Melaquin. The League will kill me if I try to enter interstellar space. I'm a murderer."

She lifted her eyebrows.

"I am," I insisted. "I killed my partner. And I would have killed Jelca if Oar hadn't beat me to it."

"Festina, I can't believe—"

"Believe it," I snapped. "I'm a dangerous non-sentient. And now that I've told you, your life is on the line too. If you let this ship leave the Melaquin system, we'll both be snuffed out."

"Then we'd better go to the bridge," Seele said quietly.

She led me out the door and down the hall, up a companionway and through the hatch leading to the bridge corridor. There, we passed a man wearing Social Science green and he saluted . . . first the admiral, then me, although I only wore the skirt and top built from my tightsuit. He must have thought I was a civilian, and civilians on Fleet vessels were almost always dignitaries of some kind.

"Admiral on the bridge!" someone barked as we entered the bridge proper. A few people snapped to attention; most remained at their posts. Protocol is one thing, but duty is something else—even vacuum personnel knew that.

"Captain Ling," Seele said to the man occupying the captain's chair, "could you please activate the view screens?"

"Yes, ma'am." He twirled a dial and the main screen brightened to reveal a starscape. It was no different from any other starscape you might see. That's why view screens are almost always turned off, except to impress visitors. No FTL ship navigates by sight. Running with the screen active would simply distract the crew from watching more important things: the gauges and readouts that gave solid information instead of useless scenery.

"Now, Explorer Ramos," Seele pointed to the screen, "what do you see?"

"Stars," I answered.

"Captain Ling," Seele said, "what is our current distance from Melaquin?"

Ling gestured toward the navigator. The navigator said, "9.27 light-years, ma'am."

"Are we in interstellar space?"

The navigator's eyes widened slightly. "Yes, ma'am."

"Out of any star's local gravity well?"

"Yes, ma'am."

"Thank you," Seele said. "As you were."

She turned and stepped back into the corridor. A moment later, she took me by the dumbstruck arm and pulled me after her.

"You see?" Seele said in a gentle voice. "Whatever you did, you aren't non-sentient. The League is never wrong about these things. We're alive and we've reached interstellar space; therefore, Festina, you are *not* a murderer." She gave the ghost of a smile. "It's almost as if God has personally declared you innocent."

The Admiral's Story

Back in the cabin, I told Seele everything. This time was different from when I confessed to Jelca. Then, I was trying to connect with him, partly to reach his sanity and partly to reach mine. Now, I was trying to connect the facts: to see the chains of cause and effect, to understand why the League had incomprehensibly given me a reprieve.

Seele said nothing as I talked—no attempt to make me admit that Yarrun's death was an accident, no easy comments on what I should or shouldn't have done. She simply listened and let me tell the story. When I was finished, she asked, "What do you want to do now?"

"Apart from pushing the High Council out an airlock?"

She didn't smile. "Is that what you need to do, Festina?"

"Someone should." I gave her a look. "Why didn't you?"

"You think Chee and I could actually sway the council?" She shook her head. "We gave it a shot: all the silly things you see in entertainment bubbles. Letters marked TO BE DELIVERED TO THE PRESS IF SOMETHING HAPPENS TO US. Sworn affidavits, with accompanying lie-detector certificates. A plan for confronting the council in public forum . . . naïve nonsense. At worst, we could have made ourselves an inconvenience—forced the council to sacrifice a scapegoat low down the chain of command. But before we could do even that, we were outmaneuvered. We'd taken too long to set things up. The council was ready for us."

"What happened?"

"We were shown trumped-up documents proving we were mentally unstable . . . histories of our inventing complaints to get back at superiors who were only doing their jobs. The frameup was quite thorough. Maybe we could defeat it in court, if we had enough resources to expose the lies; but we didn't." She spread her hands wide, then let them fall. "What could we do? And the alternative they offered looked better than getting locked up as liars or paranoids."

"The alternative was becoming one of them!" I protested. "How could you stomach that?"

"I may have become an admiral," Seele said, "but I was never one of *them*. That's an important distinction. The

Outward Fleet has many admirals: seven different ranks of them. Only the top rank sits on the High Council. Most other admirals do reasonably honest work—pushing papers, organizing this project or that, keeping the wheels turning. The council are the ones who make policy. Chee and I weren't even traditional admirals. We were officers without portfolio, so to speak. Or perhaps, officers without politics—without obligations to people who had paid us favors and without the ambition to seize more power. The shrewd half of the council realized they needed people like us to be troubleshooters and muckrakers . . . just as they needed Explorers for the same work. They need people to do the job, Festina. To stand apart from the mentality that says, 'It's someone else's problem,' and to do the thing that needs doing.

"Chee set up his spy network to keep an eye on planetary bureaucracies," Seele went on. "I did the same within the Admiralty itself. We did good work, Festina. We saved lives that would have been lost through greed and negligence. I'm proud of what I've done, even if I had to put on an admiral's uniform to do it."

"But you still let them send Explorers to Melaquin," I said.

"How could I stop it?" she asked. "The High Council *likes* using Melaquin to solve their problems. It's convenient. And the League of Peoples doesn't object. That's what makes the council happiest; the League doesn't give a damn. If the League ever intervened—if there was even a suggestion the League *might* intervene—the council would cower and back off. They're terrified of being labeled a non-sentient governing body."

"Like the Greenstriders," I said.

"Precisely. But for forty years, I've tried to think of a way to involve the League in Melaquin, and haven't made a millimeter of headway. Sending humans to an Earthlike world doesn't put them in lethal danger . . . not when you compare Melaquin to almost every other planet in the galaxy."

"No . . ." I said slowly.

"I promise you," Seele went on, "I've tried to rescue Explorers from time to time, but I've always been stopped by the picket ships. You're the first person I've got out, and that was only because the ship with the other Explorers distracted the sentries. I've tried to help as much as I could. Most of the time, I hear advance rumors about missions to Melaquin, and I tip off the Explorers involved. Unfortunately, the council moved on Chee while I was distracted with other business. I only found out when I received your eggs. . . ."

Her voice trailed off, but I was only half paying attention. "Admiral," I said, "I know what I want to do with my future."

"What?"

"First, we head for the High Council chambers on New Earth. . . ."

The Chamber of the High Council

Guards saluted crisply as we marched into Admiralty headquarters—saluted Admiral Seele, of course, not me. I wore nondescript black coveralls, without insignia. It was one of the five recognized uniforms for Explorers, but it was also the sort of drab attire any civilian worker might wear. Since I had no apparent blemishes or flaws, the guards likely took me for nothing more than a repair-worker.

Gaining admittance to the High Council chamber took more work: mostly bluster on Seele's part. She repeated the word "urgent" to more than a dozen obstructionist deputies before we were grudgingly passed through. Anyone else might never have bullied the gatekeepers into surrender; but as semiofficial troublespotter for the Outward Fleet, Seele could demand immediate attention in a crisis. When the last bureaucrat buckled under to Seele's insistence, we only had to wait in the council's anteroom for five minutes: just long enough to be scanned for hidden weapons and for Seele's identity to be verified.

They can't have bothered to identify me. If they had, they might not have blithely admitted an Explorer who was supposed to be on Melaquin.

The doors in front of us opened. Admiral Seele strode forward, with me matching step two paces behind.

The president of the council, Admiral Vincence, smiled politely as Seele reached the foot of the Round Table. He did not invite her to take a chair. "Admiral Seele," Vincence said, "you have an urgent need to address us?"

"There is a pressing matter for the council to consider," Seele replied. "But I will not be the one to address you." She gestured for me to come forward. "Proceed, Explorer."

Several admirals whispered at the word "Explorer." Apart from Chee and Seele, I may have been the only Explorer who'd ever entered the chamber. I saluted with perfect crispness. "Admirals," I said, "my name is Explorer First Class Festina Ramos, and I bring important news from Melaquin."

The whispers swelled into hostile murmurs. I kept my eyes aimed straight ahead, on Vincence. He stared back, unruffled; when the mumbling receded he said, "I've heard of you, Ramos. Were you not assigned to explore Melaquin under the command of Admiral Chee?"

"Yes, sir." For a moment, I was surprised he had bothered to learn which Explorers were sent with Chee. Then I remembered I had probably been handpicked for the Landing because Admiral Seele had shown interest in me.

"I suppose," Vincence said, "that this pressing matter concerns Admiral Chee? Or is it the Explorers who recently attempted to leave Melaquin? You must be aware that they failed. Their ship has been confiscated and they themselves returned to the planet's surface. Do you and Admiral Seele think you can blackmail this council into changing that?"

"No, sir," I replied.

"Then what do you wish to tell us?" He spoke with an air of languid condescension.

"I wish to inform the council that it transported a dangerous non-sentient creature to Melaquin."

The sharp intakes of breath around the table were the most satisfying sounds I have ever heard in my life.

"The creature was Explorer First Class Laminir Jelca," I went on. "To my certain knowledge, he murdered two sentient beings on Melaquin, and attempted genocide on an entire sentient species. Jelca could only have traveled to Melaquin under the express orders of this council. Therefore, the council must be held responsible."

"How do we know this is true?" a nearby admiral asked.

"Because I say it's true," Seele answered from my side. "Have I ever lied to the council? And do you think I'd lie about something as serious as this? Jelca nearly destroyed Melaquin's entire biosphere."

"But that has nothing to do with us!" blurted a man on my right. "He couldn't have been a murderer at the time we sent him."

"You're right," I agreed. "In fact, it was the action of this council that drove Jelca to non-sentience. His rage at being marooned turned him into a killer."

Admiral Vincence wasn't looking nearly as languid now.

"Furthermore," I continued, "I must inform this council that the introduction of Explorers to Melaquin has severely disrupted the native society. There have been incidents of rape, property destruction, and ruinous cultural pollution. Even if such acts are not explicit violations of League statutes, they demonstrate a pattern of jeopardy this council cannot ignore."

"Explorer!" Vincence snapped. "This council will decide what it can and can't ignore."

"No, Admiral," I replied, "the League of Peoples will."

Seele stepped up beside me and placed a document on the table. "Admirals," she announced, "I am officially presenting you with the Explorer's report of all that she witnessed on Melaquin. In light of the report's contents, I recommend that the council immediately terminate all missions to Melaquin, for the safety of the sentient race living on that planet. The council cannot keep sending potential murderers into a peaceful and defenseless society. I might point out, the case of Laminir Jelca demonstrates that previous good behavior is no guarantee a person will remain sentient under such conditions. If you continue to banish Explorers to Melaquin, the League will surely conclude you do not care if one of those Explorers becomes infuriated to the point of murder."

"But we didn't realize this was happening!" the admiral on my right protested.

"You do now," I said. "And if you don't do anything to correct it, the League will know."

Silence fell around the table. At last, Vincence collected himself. "Our thanks for your report, Explorer. May I ask you and Admiral Seele to withdraw into the anteroom? The council must discuss these matters."

Seele and I snapped perfect salutes and did an about-face. In perfect silence, we left the chamber.

Slow to Catch On

Ten minutes later, Vincence came out to see us. As he entered, I heard raised voices inside the chamber; but Vincence closed the door too quickly for me to tell what they were saying.

"A few are slow to catch on," Vincence told us with an apologetic shrug. "They think if you two disappear, we can continue with business as usual. They don't understand the League . . . not as well as you obviously do. Now that we know there's a risk, we *have* to take action. Anything else would be gross indifference to threats against sentient life. The High Council would be branded non-sentient, and the whole Fleet grounded until we were removed."

"So what are you going to do?" I asked.

"Under other circumstances, we might force a few councillors to resign and blame it all on them; but we won't fool the League with token gestures. Whatever we do has to be *real*. I should think we'll appoint a commission to review all Exploration practices and make sure we aren't subjecting other sentient races to unnecessary risk.''

"There have been similar commissions before," I said.

"True." Vincence gave me a thin smile. "But we'll have to follow the recommendations of this one: the League will be watching. They're always watching." He turned to Seele. "We'll need your input, Admiral, when we decide who's appointed to the inquiry. No toadies—people who will honestly ask the necessary questions.''

"I'll tell you one name right away," Seele replied. "Festina Ramos.''

I tensed but Vincence only nodded. "Ramos is at the top of the list," he agreed. "It will show our contrition. We'll also include some other Explorers from Melaquin—we can't sweep them under the table. Full disclosure, full acknowledgement of blame . . . at least behind closed doors. If we do everything else right, we won't have to wash our dirty linen in public." He chuckled without humor. "Thank God the League has plenty of caste species where the leaders never explain decisions to underlings.''

"Sir," I said, "if you think I'll keep quiet —''

He held up his hand to stop me. "Here's the offer, Ramos. I've skimmed your report enough to see details which are . . . politically delicate. Do you really want the public to know that an Explorer tried to rip away the atmosphere of an inhabited planet? The outcry would hurt the Explorer Corps as much as the High Council. And there's no point in revealing it now. You've won—period. The Council *must* stop sending Explorers to Melaquin. We have to review every aspect of Exploration missions. We have to admit our mistakes and do everything we can to rectify them. We also have to make reparations—to the other banished Explorers and to you. In the spirit of which . . . do you want to become an admiral?''

"Not especially," I said.

"That doesn't surprise me," Vincence shrugged. "But I think you'll do it anyway. Chee's position is vacant . . . and before you break into cursing, yes, he was victim of a great injustice too. We'll schedule an inquiry to decide whose head should roll. In the meantime, however, Admiral Chee needs a successor. Since most of his spies are retired Explorers, we think they'll be more cooperative if their new leader comes from the Corps."

"I don't want to be an admiral," I told him. "The thought turns my stomach."

"Festina," Seele said quietly, "the job is important. I know what you must be feeling—I felt the same forty years ago. But someone has to do Chee's job. Someone has to take the responsibility."

"I'm an Explorer First Class," I objected. "A dozen ranks away from admiral."

"Chee's people will teach you the job," Vincence said. "He has a top notch staff. You'll have their respect and the respect of government leaders too. You're smart, you're committed, and best of all, you're an Explorer who doesn't look like an Explorer anymore. Perfect admiral material."

I caught my breath. I forced myself to remain calm. "All right," I said, "I'll take over Chee's work."

"Good," Vincence smiled.

"And for the good of the Corps, I won't tell the public what Jelca did on Melaquin."

"Also good," Vincence nodded.

"And you can make me an admiral," I said.

"Done," Vincence replied.

"But . . ." I reached up to my cheek, dug in my fingernails, and pulled down hard. The artificial skin came off like an adhesive bandage, ripping away from my cheek with a good fierce sting. "I'm afraid," I said, "I'm going to be an admiral who looks like an Explorer."

My Second Graduation

And so. . . .

This afternoon, the Explorer Academy held its annual graduation ceremony. As always, a number of admirals sat on the podium. As always, one of those admirals gave the commencement address.

This year, that admiral was me.

Me with my purple birthmark. My disfigurement. My pride.

The lecturer who introduced me claimed I was the Explorer who made good. The Explorer who had earned respect. The Explorer who sat on the review commission and made a difference.

Let's hope that's true.

I stood in front of the graduating class, ready to tell them their world was changing. "Greetings," I said, "I am a sentient citizen of the League of Peoples and I beg your Hospitality. My name is Festina Ramos and I take great pride. . . ."

The rest of my words were drowned out by applause.

JAMES ALAN GARDNER lives in Waterloo, Ontario, Canada, with his wife, Linda Carson, and two cantankerous rabbits. He has published numerous pieces of short fiction in such places as *Amazing, The Magazine of Fantasy and Science Fiction, Asimov's Science Fiction Magazine, OnSpec*, and the *Tesseracts* anthologies. In 1989, he was the Grand Prize winner in the Writers of the Future contest. He has also won an Aurora award for Best Short SF Story in English (1990).

In his spare time, he plays piano, practices kung fu, and recovers from bruises. Half the time he writes computer documentation and the other half he writes SF. Guess which half he likes better.

AVON
EOS

PRESENTS AWARD-WINNING NOVELS
FROM MASTERS OF SCIENCE FICTION

PRISONER OF CONSCIENCE
by Susan R. Matthews   78914-0/$3.99 US/$3.99 Can

HALFWAY HUMAN
by Carolyn Ives Gilman   79799-2/$5.99 US/$7.99 Can

MOONRISE
by Ben Bova   78697-4/$6.99 US/$8.99 Can

DARK WATER'S EMBRACE
by Stephen Leigh   79478-0/$3.99 US/$3.99 Can

Coming Soon

COMMITMENT HOUR
by James Alan Gardner   70827-1/$5.99 US/$7.99 Can

THE WHITE ABACUS
by Damien Broderick   79615-5/$5.99 US/$7.99 Can